D0735670

CO
RUNA
FIND
COW

You're not going to kiss her. Get that idea out of your head right now. You don't need the hassle.

But the more Brady tried not to think about kissing her, the more her lips beckoned.

"You got a name?" he asked.

"Do you?"

"Brady. Brady Talmadge." He put out a hand.

She looked at his palm as if shaking hands was an alien concept, then finally took it for a brief second, smirked like someone enjoying a private joke, and said, "Annie."

"No last name?"

She paused. "Coste."

"Well, Annie Coste, you can join me inside for a meal, my treat, or you can find yourself another ride and be on your way. It's up to you." Damn, he hoped she chose the latter option. She had trouble scribbled all over her. Yeah, so why had he broken his own rules? Because he was a sucker for doe-eyed damsels.

Sucker.

By Lori Wilde

THE COWBOY AND THE PRINCESS
THE COWBOY TAKES A BRIDE
THE WELCOME HOME GARDEN CLUB
THE FIRST LOVE COOKIE CLUB
THE TRUE LOVE QUILTING CLUB
THE SWEETHEARTS' KNITTING CLUB

Forthcoming
A COWBOY FOR CHRISTMAS

Available from Avon Impulse
THE CHRISTMAS COOKIE CHRONICLES
Carrie
Raylene
Christine

LORI WILDE

The
COWBOY
and the
PRINCESS

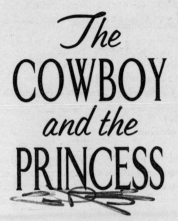

AVON

An Imprint of HarperCollinsPublishers

This is a work of fiction. Names, characters, places, and incidents are products of the author's imagination or are used fictitiously and are not to be construed as real. Any resemblance to actual events, locales, organizations, or persons, living or dead, is entirely coincidental.

AVON BOOKS
An Imprint of HarperCollins*Publishers*
10 East 53rd Street
New York, New York 10022-5299

Copyright © 2012 by Laurie Vanzura
Excerpt from *A Cowboy for Christmas* copyright © 2012 by Laurie Vanzura
ISBN 978-0-06-204777-9
www.avonromance.com

First Avon Books mass market printing: August 2012

Avon Trademark Reg. U.S. Pat. Off. and in Other Countries, Marca Registrada, Hecho en U.S.A.
HarperCollins® is a registered trademark of HarperCollins Publishers.

Printed in the U.S.A.

10 9 8 7 6 5 4 3 2 1

CHAPTER ONE

You might be a princess if . . . you have to ditch your bodyguards to get some "me" time.

Brady Talmadge had five unbreakable rules for leading an uncomplicated life.

One stormy June night in Texas, he broke them all. Starting with rule number five.

Never pick up a hitchhiker.

He'd honed the rules through twenty-nine years of trial and error, most of them compiled while towing his vagabond horse trailer from town to town, and as long as he stuck to his edicts, life flowed as smooth and simple as the Brazos River ambling to the Gulf.

In regard to the hitchhiker rule, he learned it the hard way. He had a permanent whup-notch on the back of his skull from a pistol-whipping meted out by a wiry, goat-faced thief who'd taken him for thirteen hundred dollars, his favorite belt buckle, and a pair of ostrich skin cowboy boots. Never mind the four-day hospital stay that drained his savings account to zero because he'd had no health insurance.

On the satellite radio, the weatherman warned of the fierce line of unrelenting storms moving up from Hurricane Betsy. "It's gonna be a wet night, folks. Find someplace warm and dry to hole up with someone you love."

Brady took the exit ramp off Interstate 30, heading for the parking lot of Toad's Big Rig Truck Stop on the outskirts of Dallas. His headlights caught a lone figure huddled on the road shoulder, thumb outstretched. Automatically, his hand went to his occipital bone.

No dice.

Lightning flashed. Thunder crashed. Rain slashed. The hitchhiker shivered violently.

Sorry about your luck, fella.

The eighteen-wheeler in front of Brady splashed a deluge of water over the skinny stranger. Small, vulnerable. Been there. Done that. Lived through it. The fella raised his face and in a flash of fresh lightning, from underneath the hooded sweatshirt, he saw it wasn't a guy at all, but a woman.

No, a girl actually. Most likely a runaway.

Don't do it.

Trampas, his Heinz 57 mutt—who, come to think of it, was a hitchhiker of sorts as well—peered out the window at the dark night and whimpered from the backseat. A year ago, Brady had found the starving puppy, flea-bitten and tick-ridden, on a long stretch of empty road in the Sonoran desert.

He was already driving past her. He'd almost

made it. Then hell if he didn't glance back and meet the girl's eyes.

Please, she mouthed.

Aw, shit.

He didn't mean to do it. Hadn't planned on doing it, but the next thing he knew he was slowing down and pulling over. And that's when he broke rule number four.

Avoid damsels in distress.

That rule came to him courtesy of a short-skirted cowgirl broke down off Route 66 in Flagstaff. She thanked him for changing her flat by inviting him back to her place for a home-cooked fried chicken dinner and rocking hot sex, except she neglected to tell him she had a grizzly bear–sized husband with a high temper and a hammy fist.

Brady rubbed his jaw. He wasn't going to give the runaway a ride. Just get her inside the building and out of the storm. Maybe buy her a meal if she was hungry. He would toss her a few bucks for one of the cheap bunk-and-bath motels attached to the truck stop and advise her against hitchhiking.

Meddling. That's meddling in someone else's business.

Yeah, and where would he be if Dutch Callahan hadn't meddled in his life fourteen years ago?

Prison most likely. Or the bone orchard.

He hit the unlock button, knowing it was a bad idea, but doing it anyway. The hitchhiker ran for his truck. She was short enough so that he couldn't see anything but the top of her head from his perch behind the wheel without peeping into the side view mirror, but he heard her fumble the door handle on the passenger side.

The howling wind snatched at the door, ripping it from her pale, trembling hand and throwing it wide open.

Brady glanced down.

The hitchhiker looked up.

Her eyes were a dusty gray, too large for her small, narrow face, and she stared right into him as if she knew every thought that passed through his head, yet didn't hold it against him.

He tried to take a deep breath, but to his alarm, discovered that he couldn't.

For one brief moment, they dangled in suspended animation. Their gazes meshed, their futures strangely entwined.

Drive off!

Of course he didn't, couldn't. Not with her standing there looking like a soaking wet fawn who just lost her mother to a hunter's gun. But the impulse to run, Brady's instinct to avoid complications at all costs, fisted around his spine and wouldn't let go.

"Thank you for stopping," she said in a voice as soft as lamb's wool. Looped around her shoulder she carried an oversized satchel. "Your kindness is much appreciated."

The breath he'd tried to draw finally filled his lungs with a swift whoosh of damp night air. He nodded.

Somehow, she managed to plant her feet on the running board, grab the door in her right hand, and then swing up into the seat in one long, smooth, ladylike movement. Her satchel rustled as she tugged the heavy door closed behind her, and with a solid click they were cocooned inside.

Alone.

Her scent, an intriguing combination of rain and talcum powder and honey, filled the cab, vanquishing his own leather, horse, and beef jerky smell. The sweatshirt hoodie was tied down tight under her chin so that he couldn't see her hair, but her eyebrows were starkly black in startling contrast to skin the color and texture of fresh cream. She possessed the cheekbones of a Swedish supermodel, as high and sharp and cool as the summit of Mount Everest, but in spite of that barrier of heartbreaking beauty, there was something about her that had him yearning to toss an arm around her shoulders and tell her everything was going to be okay. Maybe it was because she was so ethereal—pale and slender and wide-eyed.

She wore dark blue jeans with a sharp crease running down the front of the legs. Plain, brown, round-toed cowboy boots shod her petite feet. In spite of being drenched, both the jeans and boots looked brand-new.

Trampas leaned over the seat, ran his nose along the back of her neck.

"Oh." She startled, laughed. "Hello." She reached out a hand to scratch the mutt behind his ear. He whimpered joyously. *Attention hound.*

"Down, Trampas," Brady commanded.

The dog snorted but reluctantly settled, his tail thumping against the backseat.

The hitchhiker turned to snap her seat belt into place, the satchel now clutched in her lap.

"I'm not going anywhere," Brady said. His words hung like a curtain in the air between them, not making a lick of sense coming from a traveling man who dragged his home behind him.

She raised her head and met his gaze again. "I beg your pardon, sir?"

Speech eloped. Just ran right off with his brain. On closer inspection, her eyes weren't simply gray, but loaded with tiny starbursts of sapphire blue. He motioned toward the gas pumps. "I was just . . ."

She canted her head and studied him as if every word that spilled from his mouth was golden. "Yes?"

"Gonna get some gas."

"That is acceptable." She folded her hands over the satchel.

Huh? As if she were giving her permission? "And supper. I was gonna have supper."

"Here?"

"Yes."

"Then why did you stop to pick me up?"

Beats the hell out of me. "You looked cold. And wet. You looked cold and wet."

"I am," she confirmed. "Wet and cold."

He reached over to turn on the heater, angling the air vents toward her. He had never turned on the heater in June in Texas. First time for everything. "Why didn't you go inside the truck stop?"

She shrugged as if the gesture said it all.

"No money?"

Her slight smile plucked at him.

"You hungry?"

The shrug again, accompanied by a shy head tilt. She licked lips the color of red honeysuckle, and for no good reason at all, he thought of caramel—sweet, thick, chewy. If he kissed her, she would taste like caramel. He just knew it.

You're not going to kiss her. Get that idea out of your head right now. You don't need the hassle.

But the more Brady tried not to think about kissing her, the more her lips beckoned.

"You got a name?" he asked.

"Do you?"

"Brady. Brady Talmadge." He put out a hand.

She looked at his palm as if shaking hands was an alien concept, then finally took it for a brief second, smirked like someone enjoying a private joke, and said, "Annie."

"No last name?"

She paused. "Coste."

"Well, Annie Coste, you can join me inside for a meal, my treat, or you can find yourself another ride and be on your way. It's up to you." Damn, he hoped she chose the latter option. She had trouble scribbled all over her. Yeah, so why had he broken his own rules? Because he was a sucker for doe-eyed damsels.

Sucker.

That was the operative word.

"I am hungry," she admitted.

"Great," he said.

Great as a busted axle. Why had he picked her up? Stupid. Glutton for punishment. Misguided sense of chivalry. Dumbass. What a total dumbass. What was wrong with him? But come on, how could he have left Bambi shivering by the roadside when some unscrupulous son of a bitch could have given her a ride instead? Things had been humming along just dandy and now he was stuck with her. If he'd kept driving—which he couldn't have because he was almost out of gas—he would be in Jubilee within ninety minutes. Jubilee. The closest thing he'd ever had to a real home. He didn't want to take her there.

She's not your problem. You can't save everyone, Talmadge. It's not like you're a paragon yourself.

The thoughts loped through his head as he fueled his truck underneath the protective awning and put Trampas into the trailer. The dog curled up on his bed in the air-conditioned living area and gave him a look that said, *I like her.*

"Only because she scratched your itch," Brady grumbled, and shut the door.

He climbed back inside, pulled the truck around the rear of the building with the semis, and looked over at Annie. Raindrops still clung to her long eyelashes and the hoodie of her sweatshirt. Was it weird that her eyebrows were dark, but her eyelashes were light?

As they walked into the restaurant, the big red digital clock on the wall over the door flashed 9:15. The place was rowdy busy. A port in the storm. Truckers in baseball caps and cowboy hats lined the red and chrome swivel stools at the counter up front.

Several men craned their necks for a better look at Annie. Brady took a step closer toward her, rigging himself up in that she's-with-me strut that came naturally to a cowboy in the company of a good-looking woman. The hum of voices and clang of silverware drifted to the vaulted rafters. The air smelled of diesel exhaust, chicken-fried steak, and yeast rolls.

Brady stood back to let Annie go in front of him.

She hesitated, resistance in her eyes as if uncertain how to proceed. C'mon. Surely she'd been in a truck stop before.

"This way." He held out his arm as a guide and ushered her past the front counter on their left and the clear glass refrigeration units chock-full of homemade pies, spread high with meringue, sitting on rotating shelves. She stopped to stare at the pies, as awestruck as a five-year-old.

"We'll get some for dessert," he said.

Her beaming smile heated him up like an electric blanket on a cold winter night. "Really?"

"You can have two slices if you like." Brady escorted her past the "Seat Yourself" sign to an empty booth in the back of the room situated underneath the head of a mule deer buck.

Eyeing the taxidermied animal, she slid across the red vinyl seat, untying the string of her hoodie as she went, and then she slipped the satchel from her shoulder. She cleaved to the thing like she had gold bars in it.

Brady secured the seat across from her.

She tugged off the hood, revealing black hair chopped short and spiky. It looked as if she'd taken a pair of jagged-teethed pruning shears and hacked it off herself, but he supposed it was probably some hip salon cut that cost a hundred bucks or more. The harsh hairstyle, paired with her wide gray-blue eyes and pale skin, gave her the appearance of an anime cartoon heroine—waifish and innocent—accentuating the whole damsel-in-distress thing.

Next, she wrestled out of the sweatshirt, revealing a simple white blouse with cap sleeves, showing off toned arms that knew their way around a biceps curl. She was not the typical truck stop hitchhiker. No piercings (not even her ears), no tats (at least none he could see), no skimpy, too-tight clothing flaunting too-big breasts. She was like a daisy sprung fresh in the garden. No, that was too common. Not a garden daisy, but a rare buttercup growing on a mountaintop. Sunny, sweet, lustrous. Unexpected. Special.

Special?

What the hell? Where was that coming from?

If he were smart, he'd pass her twenty bucks, get up, and walk out. Clearly, he was not smart because instead of doing that, he took off his straw Stetson, settled it on the bench seat beside him, and ran a hand through his hair.

The right side of the booth butted up against a thick, rain-painted plate-glass window. Outside, the vapor lamps glowed ghostly in the rumbling storm. Inside, someone with a sense of humor set the jukebox playing "Let it Rain" by David Nail.

Annie harvested a napkin from the red and chrome dispenser on the table and started polishing the Formica surface, whisking away crumbs left behind from a slapdash busboy's one-swipe attempt at cleaning the tabletop.

A waitress, dressed in a retro pink dress with a white bib apron and battered sneakers, bopped over with two menus tucked under one arm and two glasses of water in her hands. "Here y'all go," she said. "I'm Heather and I'll be back in a minute to take your order." Then off she went.

Brady shifted his attention back to Annie. Her head was bowed over the menu. One dainty finger slid down the list of offerings.

"What is chili?" she asked, raising her head to meet his gaze.

He startled again, just as he had when she climbed into his truck. Something about those eyes unraveled him in a way he'd never been unraveled and Brady was no stranger to peering into the eyes of gorgeous women. "You've never eaten chili?"

She shook her head.

"You're not from Texas."

"How do you know?"

"Texans cut their baby teeth on chili."

"I am not from Texas," she admitted.

"Where you from?"

She rested one hand on the satchel beside her. "What is chili exactly?"

"It's ground or shredded beef cooked in a tomato-based sauce."

"And served cold?"

"No. It's hot. Both temperature and spice wise."

She looked puzzled. "If it is hot, then why do they call it chili?"

Something was decidedly off about this one. "Dunno. Sarcasm maybe?"

"Sarcasm?"

"They don't have sarcasm where you're from?"

"May we get some?" she asked.

"Get what?" Brady asked, his mind rambling

to all possible meanings of the phrase "get some."

"Sarcasm?"

"Chili."

"Okay," he said, just like that. So much for rule number three.

Never order chili at a truck stop.

That rule was self-evident. No unsavory details needed, but when the waitress came back, Brady handed her the menus. "Two bowls of chili. I'll have a Coors and the lady wants . . ."

"Might I have a cup of tea?" Annie asked.

"You mean hot tea?" The waitress gave her a strange look. Probably not too many truckers ordered hot tea.

"Yes, please. Thank you." Annie sat like she had a ruler implanted in her spine. Straight. Proper. "Earl Grey if it is available."

"I'll see what we got." The waitress pivoted and scooted off.

Annie hugged herself, grinned. "This is so enjoyable."

Brady cocked his head, trying to detect some kind of accent, but her speech was as plain as a Midwest newscaster. Sometimes her word choice was a little formal, a little stiff, which didn't quite jibe. Who was she? Her inscrutable gray-blue eyes revealed no secrets. "What is?"

"Ordering chili in a truck stop with a real-life cowboy."

"Are you from another country?"

"Are you?"

"No," he said.

She spread her hands, delicate and smooth, against

the Formica tabletop in a prim gesture. She wore no rings, no bracelets. No jewelry at all. Her nails were short and painted with clear polish. Simple. Understated. Elegant. No adornments needed. "And there you have it."

What was she talking about? He felt as if he'd missed a step or two in the conversation. She looked so young. Not a single wrinkle on her face. No blemishes either. Flawless complexion.

"How old are you?" he asked. What if she was underage? This could be the beginning of a major snafu.

"How old are you?"

"Twenty-nine."

"I'm twenty-four."

"Naw." He shook his head. "You can't be twenty-four. I'd say twenty at most."

She raised both palms out from her head, shrugged. "It is true."

"You have some great genetics."

She glanced around the room at the other diners. "This place is quite interesting."

Interesting? Furrowing his brow, Brady followed her gaze. Nothing special as far as he could see. Asking her where she was from wasn't getting him anywhere. Clearly she didn't want to talk about her past or why she was on the run. He understood that impulse. He tried a different track. "Where are you going?"

"Where are *you* going?"

"Jubilee."

"Where is Jubilee?"

Dammit, here she was doing it again, running the

conversation in circles. "About eighty miles south-west of here."

"Is that where you live?"

"No."

"Why are you going there?"

"A job."

"What kind of job?"

"I work with horses."

"You are an equine veterinarian?"

"Not exactly."

"What exactly?"

"You could be a reporter, you know, with all those questions. Are you a reporter?"

"No, I am just naturally curious about people," she said quickly. "What exactly?"

"I work with horses who've been emotionally traumatized."

"Oh!" She broke into a big smile. "Like the Horse Whisperer in that dramatic novel by Nicholas Evans."

"It's not as glamorous as Robert Redford made it out to be in the movie, but yes, I do rehabilitate horses who've been injured or harmed or developed phobias."

"How did you get started in that line of employment?"

"I just sort of fell into it."

"Is it a difficult job?"

"Not from my point of view. But horses are sensitive, highly intuitive animals. You have to know how to handle them."

"How is that?"

"With a gentle hand and a loving heart."

"I like that." She leaned forward. "What an exciting profession."

"It's just what I do." He paused. "But I do love it."

"Where do you live when you are not healing horses?"

"In my trailer."

Dejection flickered across her face. "You do not have a home? You are a homeless person? I have never met a homeless person. Is it truly terrible? Being without a home?"

Beam me up, Scotty. I don't know what planet I've landed on, but the hitchhikers in these parts are freaking nuts. "I live in my trailer. That's my home."

"Traveling from town to town?"

"Living on the road is the ultimate freedom. Footloose and fancy-free. I can go anywhere I want, any time I want to go. No limitations. No expectations."

"I cannot imagine such circumstances."

"No roots, nothing holding me back."

Annie pressed the fingertips of both hands against her lips. "It sounds so sad."

Brady blinked. Something dark and uncomfortable slithered across the back of his mind. Something he couldn't capture or name, but it slithered all the same. Swift and heavy, scraping his brain. "What's so horrible about freedom?"

"It is lonely."

"No, no. Not lonely at all. I have my dog, Trampas, and friends all over the country, and there's the horses and . . ." He trailed off, trying to think of all the wonderful things about his life.

"No one special," she finished for him.

Brady snorted. "Hey, if you're so happy and your life is choked with special people, what are you doing hitchhiking in the rain on a Friday night?"

She pulled herself up on the edge of her seat and looked down her nose in a stately expression of the highborn. "I am out for an adventure."

"Yeah? Got away from the zookeeper, did you?" Now, that was tacky. He shouldn't have said it, but his gut poked at him.

"Pardon me?" The regal expression vanished and the vulnerable girlishness was back—hurt, disappointed.

Brady shook his head. "Never mind."

Thankfully, the waitress showed up, interrupting the weird conversation. "Toad's chili twice." She sat two blue bowls of steaming cinnamon-colored chili, swimming in the glistening grease of too much cheddar cheese, in front of them. She plunked down Brady's beer with barely any foam, and then she slid a small metal pitcher of hot water in front of Annie, along with a tea bag. "No Earl Grey. All we got is orange pekoe."

"Thank you." Annie graced the waitress with a smile as if bestowing a title upon her. "May I have an additional spoon, please?"

"Sure thing." The waitress grabbed an extra spoon for her.

Brady peered into his bowl and accepted his fate. That's what you got when you broke rules. He dug into the chili. Just as he feared, it was deceptively delicious.

He tried to blank his mind and focus on eating, but then the satchel on the seat beside Annie moved.

Huh? Was he seeing things? He narrowed his eyes and noticed the sides of the satchel were made of braided mesh.

The satchel moved again.

"Whoa!" Brady jumped. Which wasn't like him. Usually he was laid back, not the least bit jumpy, but things just kept getting weirder.

Annie looked up. "What is it?"

He pointed. "Your bag moved. Twice."

"Oh." She put a dab of chili on the end of her spoon and reached for the satchel.

A little brown head popped from the side corner of the bag, and a tiny black button nose twitched.

"What the hell is . . . *that?*"

Annie laid a finger to her lips. "Shh, this is Lady Astor. My best friend in the whole world."

Shiny black eyes fixed on him.

"Seriously? That's a dog?"

"Lady Astor is a Yorkshire terrier. She is one year old and she weighs six pounds." The Yorkie lapped chili from Annie's spoon.

"You brought her with you on Annie's Big Adventure?"

"Of course. I could not, in all good conscience, leave her at the pal . . ." She trailed off, got a strange look on her face, and finished with "leave her home alone."

"Ever heard of a kennel?" Did they have those in whatever la-la land she was from?

Annie glared as if he had suggested she run the dog through a blender.

"Hey, you're the one who carries her around in a satchel."

A distraught furrow creased her brow. "She is comfortable in it. The mesh sides let air get in. It keeps her dry in the rain and I bought the most expensive one they had and—"

He raised a palm. "You don't have to justify it to me."

"Do you really think it is a bad thing that I keep her in a satchel?" She worried a paper napkin between her fingers.

"Why do you care what I think?"

"I am not—" She shut her mouth.

"You're not what?"

She tilted her head back and gave him that condescending glare again. "Disregard that."

"C'mon, you can tell me." Brady hated secrets. Had since he was a kid and he'd learned—well, there was no point going *there*—but whenever he was around someone who was obviously hiding something, he couldn't resist nudging for full disclosure. He'd discovered a lot of unexpected things about people that way. "It's not like you're ever going to see me again. Your secret is safe with me."

"I have no secret," she insisted, but her earlobes pinked and she did not meet his gaze.

"None? Nothing? Not even a tiny white lie you want to confess?"

Her eyes widened and she seemed even paler than before. Did the woman ever go out in the sun? "No."

Brady's lie-o-meter went off. Big time. He did not know who or what Annie Coste was, but she spelled complication in capital letters.

Lady Astor finished licking the spoon, and then burrowed back into the satchel. She did seem to like it in there.

Annie picked up the second spoon that the waitress had brought her and daintily dipped it into the chili. Brady couldn't help watching her bring the curved stainless steel up to her full pink lips. When they finished their meal, they ordered banana cream pie and Annie attacked it with gusto.

"I am not allowed to eat like this at home." She moaned a soft sound of pleasure and put a hand to her stomach.

"Allowed to?"

She ignored that, flicked her tongue out to lick a spot of frothy meringue from her upper lip, laughed. It was an airy sound that had real joy behind it, a gleeful laugh that embraced life in a hard hug. If he never saw her again, he would always remember the sound of her laughter, because it sounded like freedom.

For some reason, just hearing her laugh made him laugh and they both sat there underneath the mule deer, the smell of grease in the air, the taste of banana cream pie on their tongues, laughing and looking at each other and having a high old time together. It was the most fun he'd ever had at a truck stop, bar none.

Slowly, her laughter drained away.

So did his.

They were left with just the looking.

Mesmerized, he pulled a palm down over his mouth. He couldn't figure out what compelled him more, his attraction to her or his curiosity about her.

The healthy, masculine part of him was already toying with the idea of seducing her. She was sexy in an unusual way and it had been months since he'd taken pleasure in the company of a willing woman. But his gut was saying back off. Something wasn't right. All was not as it seemed.

To distract himself, he turned and peered out the window. The rain was still washing down in angry torrents. Through the dark night, a long black limousine emerged and pulled up to the gas pumps.

"Now there's a sight you don't see every day at a truck stop in this neck of the woods unless it's prom night," Brady said. "But prom was two weeks ago. Unless it's a school with a late prom."

"What is that?" Annie asked in her slightly prissy, nondescript tone.

It drove him nuts that she had no birthplace-identifying accent. Who was she? Where was she from?

"Limo."

The chauffeur got out to fuel the vehicle. The rear door opened and two other men emerged. They were dressed in expensive suits tailored to perfectly fit their bodies. One man was tall, the other squat, and they both wore sunglasses at night and jaunty fedoras pulled down low over their foreheads.

Who were these guys? Mobsters? Secret Service? The Blues Brothers?

Then he remembered that former president Franklin Glover's daughter, Echo, was getting married this weekend and the president's ranch, where the nuptials were being held, weren't far from here. It had been all over the radio for days.

Most likely they were Secret Service. But in a limo? He would have expected a black Cadillac Escalade with bulletproof glass.

Brady felt movement beside him, turned his head to see Annie had gotten up to come peer over his shoulder. He swung his gaze back to the window. Her warm breath tickled the hairs on the nape of his neck.

A fierce craving hammered down his spine and drove to his groin. He swallowed hard, fighting off the reaction. Yes, okay, she got a rise out of him, but he did not have to do anything about it. In fact, a smart guy would get the hell out of here as fast as possible. Unfortunately, Brady had never been particularly smart when it came to women. He always seemed to go for the troublesome ones.

The two guys from the limo broke into a trot, rushing to get out of the rain, and headed for the front door of the restaurant.

Annie made a noise of distress.

Brady jerked his head back in her direction.

She stood clutching his cowboy hat in her hands, her head raised expectantly. "May I sit here?"

"Um . . . sure."

She set his straw Stetson on the table and sank down beside him, her gaze coddling his. She did not look out the window. Did not glance around the room. Her eyes were on him and him alone.

Unnerved, he scooted as far across the seat as he could, his shoulder bumping up against the cool glass window.

At that moment, the Blues Brothers came into the seat-yourself dining area, scanning the room as if searching for someone.

Annie leaned in closer.

There was nowhere else for Brady to go. This

development took him completely by surprise. He didn't know if he liked it or not.

"You are very handsome," she said.

"Um . . . okay."

"I want to kiss you."

Stunned, he blinked. "Huh?"

"Kiss me."

"What?" Had he heard her correctly?

"Kiss me."

The Blues Brothers were talking to Heather, the waitress.

Do not kiss her. Something is not right. Warning! Whatever you do, do not kiss her!

"Kiss me now!" she demanded, and puckered those honeysuckle lips.

He held up a palm like a stop sign. "I don't think so."

"Why not?"

"I don't like being bossed around."

"Please," she wheedled.

"Well, when you put it like that," he drawled. "No."

"You do not find me desirable." She reached out to stroke his chin with an index finger. He caught a whiff of her talcum powder scent.

"Quite the contrary."

"So why not?"

Brady peered into those big gray-blue eyes and he was a goner. Ah shit. What the hell? Why not? Illogically, he pulled her into his arms and proceeded to dismantle rule number two.

Always trust your gut.

Her lips were heated satin, melting Brady's self-control like cotton candy dunked in hot soda pop.

She tangled her slender arms around his neck, tugging him closer, but she did not loosen her jaw.

Mystified, he lightly rested the tip of his tongue against her bottom lip. Was she going to let him in?

"Hmm, mmm." Annie increased the pressure of the kiss, but she did not part her teeth.

Okay, this was the first time he'd ever had a woman beg him to kiss her and then not let him fully do the job. Brady didn't like to brag, but he knew he was a good kisser. Many a woman had told him so.

Kissing was his second favorite part of lovemaking. He loved to taste things. Explore. Savor. Push limits. And he'd been right. Annie did taste like caramel. He wanted more.

She loosened her arms around his neck, broke the lip-lock, rested her forehead on his. "Are they still there?" she whispered.

"Who?"

"The men in the suits and fedoras."

Once more, Brady shifted his gaze to the dining room. The Blues Brothers were gone. He glanced back at Annie. Took in her glistening lips. Inhaled her innocent fragrance. Heard her soft intake of breath.

Right then and there, he trifled with his number one rule for leading an uncomplicated life. The rule that had kept him safe, satisfied, and single for twenty-nine years. The rule he was about to shatter into a million little pieces.

Never tell a lie.

"They're still here," he said. "You better keep kissing me."

CHAPTER TWO

You might be a princess if . . . your nickname is Buttercup.

Princess Annabella Madeleine Irene Osbourne Farrington of Monesta, the smallest country in Europe, was running away from a very complicated life.

No, that wasn't quite true. She was running *to* a life of simple, unrestrained pleasure. At least, that is, for the next six weeks.

After that, she must return to Monesta and wed forty-two-year-old Prince Theodore George Jameson Forsythe of Dubinstein, the second smallest country in Europe. In a prearranged marriage that was protocol for royalty in her country, she'd been promised to Teddy since she was twelve years old, and while she'd managed to put off the wedding by getting her PhD in comparative literature (with a specialization in works of the American Southwest), in less than two months she would be twenty-five.

The age at which her father, King Phillip, decreed she *would* marry.

Although she and Teddy weren't officially, officially engaged (no engagement ring or party yet), the last wedding details had already been planned. The date was set. Her fate forever sealed.

But until then, she was in America, living her dream of having a wild romantic adventure before she settled into the staid role as Princess of Dubinstein and started producing heirs.

She could barely believe it. No one who knew her would believe it either—shy, obedient Princess Annabella kissing a wild, handsome Texas cowboy a mere two hours after she'd run away from former president Glover's compound with a little help from her cohort, bride-to-be Echo Glover.

It felt thrilling, exhilarating, and exotic.

Erotic.

Add to it the fact that she'd never kissed anyone besides Teddy, and those had been nothing more than restrained, chaperoned pecks. Kissing Brady Talmadge was, well, mind expanding to say the least, and she wished it would never stop.

This was exactly what she needed. *He* was exactly what she needed—a man with more sex appeal than morals. A footloose man who preferred no strings attached. He was perfect for what she had in mind.

"Annie," he whispered against her mouth, the sound vibrating an exuberant tickle through her.

Annie.

Her heart tripped, skipped.

She was glad she had thought of the nickname. No

one in Monesta ever dared call her anything so informal. The name had a cowgirl ring to it. Like Annie Oakley. She approved of the idea of being an Annie. Annie was spunky, levelheaded, the girl next door.

Annie was a lot like Princess Ann from *Roman Holiday*, her favorite movie in the entire world. In fact, that movie was what had given her the courage to spread her wings and fly the coop. She had also learned from Princess Ann's mistakes, and she even made a list of pitfalls to avoid when going AWOL from a royal life.

She was Annie Coste now.

She'd taken her old nursemaid's last name, and that felt right too. Annabella had been closer to Rosalind Coste than she had ever been to her own mother.

Immediately, that thought made her feel disloyal. It was unfair to gauge her mother against Rosalind. Queen Evangeline had died at age fifty-two of a heart attack at *her* mother's funeral. In the course of one short week, eight-year-old Annabella had lost both her mother and her only surviving grandparent. If she was being truthful, she scarcely missed them. Rosalind was the one who had really raised her.

But Brady's mouth was doing crazy things to her, making her stomach pitch and her knees wobble, and she forgot about all that ancient history.

His tongue strummed lightly over her lips, his breath came in hot, electric waves against her skin. The intimate taste of him flooded her with intense, unexpected desire. She melted against his chest, shaken to the core, aroused and hoarding every sensation lighting up her body, tucking it into her memory for those long, tedious years ahead with Teddy.

She forgot they were in the dining room of a truck stop. She forgot that she had asked him to kiss her in the first place because her bodyguards, Chandler and Strawn, had somehow traced her here in spite of the disguise she donned and she was desperate to hide her face. She forgot about everything except Brady Talmadge and the fact she had a very narrow window of time in which to live out her dreams.

Knowing this experience was short made it that much sweeter. At any moment, Chandler could clamp his hand on one shoulder, Strawn on the other, and they would drag her back to the limo, back to the president's compound to collect her things, and then back to the private plane that would whisk her back to Monesta. Adventure over before it ever really began.

She was making the most out of every second. She had her eyes wide open. She knew precisely what she was doing.

Annie curled her fingers through Brady's unruly cocoa-colored hair. His masculine scent—leather, spice, and cotton—filled her nostrils. He was sheer rugged poetry. His dark eyes drew her in, the romance of the West. She'd been fascinated with cowboys since childhood when Rosalind had read her bedtime stories from the novels of Louis L'Amour and Zane Grey.

It felt like the wickedest kind of freedom, stolen and sweet. What she was doing was wrong. She knew it, and yet, for the first time in her life, she felt as if she'd found her true self. She was so tired of rules and protocol and performing her duties. She always worked hard to be a good girl, a good daughter, and a good princess. She accepted her fate of marrying wealthy Prince Theodore without complaint because it was good politics for her country. She'd been born into privilege and luxury. She knew how lucky she was. She felt guilty for wanting more, for longing to be ordinary.

But Audrey Hepburn in *Roman Holiday* had wanted the same thing. Just one sweet taste of an ordinary life. One brief period of time when the heavy yoke of noble responsibility was off her shoulders. Audrey gave her hope for a short-term reprieve.

While other young girls dreamed of being royalty, Annie had dreamed of going to school like a normal child instead of having tutors come to her. She longed for friends she picked herself rather than having confidantes selected for her. She ached to go out alone without an entourage of bodyguards and yes-people tagging along.

In childhood, she used to lie in bed at night and imagine that Gypsies had kidnapped her from her cradle in the middle of the night. Stolen her from her real family. Jack and Jane Jones, who lived in a cottage by the sea and ate bacon and scrambled egg sandwiches for supper.

She pretended she had lots of brothers and sisters and she had to wear hand-me-downs and walk to school because her family had only one car. Of course, she couldn't come up with a reasonable explanation for how she had ended up in the household of King Phillip and Queen Evangeline, or why the Gypsies would steal such an ordinary girl.

But it was a fantasy she could not conquer. Annabella had always felt like a fish out of water. She once thought that other children of royalty might feel this way as well, so on one of the courtship dates, she asked Teddy if this was what it had been like for him growing up, if he too felt as if he didn't belong on the throne. Did his heart long for an ordinary life among ordinary people?

He had looked at her as if she had completely lost her mind. "Annabella," he said, placing his palm on her forehead, "do you have a fever?"

No, she did not have a fever, just a heartfelt longing for normalcy. But considering Teddy's reaction, she was way off base about how other royals felt about their lot in life. But of course he would not question his path; how silly of her to have considered it. This was a man who would be king. A man who loved playing polo, his silver Bugatti, skiing the Swiss Alps, flying his Gulfstream on weekend jaunts to Monte Carlo. A man who had christened his yacht *The Teddy Too*. A man with an irrational fear of mice, mentholated medications, tetherballs, and therapeutic massage. Why would he long for a regular Joe life?

Brought up to be a perfect princess by never rocking the boat, Annie had smiled at Teddy, forced a laugh. "I was simply making a joke."

"Well," he said, "don't bring that up with anyone else. People would not understand."

No, she supposed they wouldn't. Most people would give their eyeteeth to be members of a royal family. What they didn't understand was that royalty carried such a tremendous burden. She didn't feel up for the job. But no one wanted to hear the rich and privileged whine about their problems. So Annabella shut up and tucked her secret away, but she never stopped longing for the experience of just once in her life being like everyone else.

And now here she was, kissing a cowboy in a truck stop restaurant. A dream come true.

Maybe she could make this last just a wee bit longer. She knew it had to end, even if Chandler and Strawn had left for now. They'd be back. And if they couldn't find her, once they accepted defeat, they'd gird their loins and grit their teeth and call her father and admit they'd lost her. Then the media hoopla would begin. Would her thin disguise be enough to save her at that point?

Briefly, she felt sorry for her bodyguards. They didn't deserve to lose their jobs because she'd given them the slip. When this was over, she'd talk to her father and make sure they kept their positions. It wasn't their fault. She and Echo had been plotting this caper for months. Echo was the only one who even semi-understood Annie's motives.

In the meantime, Annie was fully enjoying this kiss. She might never get another kiss from anyone except Teddy, and that depressed her more than she could say.

It was not that Teddy was such a bad guy. He was okay enough for a balding, short man with a banty rooster strut. It wasn't as if there were many options. For the most part, royalty still married royalty. Yes, Prince William had married Kate Middleton, but Monesta wasn't as forward thinking as England. Potential suitors for her hand arose from a very small pool of candidates. Teddy had been the best of the limited lot.

Then Brady slipped his hot tongue between her lips and all other thoughts flew from her head. Unbelievable, this sensation. Sheer heaven.

At last she let go of her fears, loosened her jaw, let him in, and succumbed fully and completely.

He cradled her in his arms, at once bold, yet gentle, exploring her with his lips. She closed her eyes, savoring everything—the taste of his warm mouth, the feel of his arms tightening around her waist, the sound of patrons chuckling. They were on display, but she didn't care. That in itself was something. She'd been groomed, schooled, educated on the proper etiquette in every social situation. She'd been taught never to show her true emotions. Never do anything in public that would embarrass her or the House of Farrington.

For over twenty-four years, she had kowtowed. Obeyed the rules. Done as she'd been told.

Now, she was flaunting her freedom.

It would not last. Could not last. She knew that. She had a responsibility to the people of Monesta, even though her father had remarried a much younger woman and her stepmother Birgit had given birth to Annabella's half brother Prince Henry, which meant she would never sit on the throne. She had been indoctrinated into service of her country from birth. It was as much a part of her as the color of her hair. Which for now was dyed jet black. She had chopped it off short with a pair of scissors in Echo Glover's bathroom and colored it with hair dye Echo had smuggled in for her.

For the first time it occurred to her that she could be big trouble for anyone who came to her assistance. People like Echo, who'd helped her elude her bodyguards, and Brady, who'd been so kind to pick her up on the roadside and buy her a meal.

Guilt hobbled her and she put a hand to his chest, pushed him away, broke the kiss.

The dining room erupted in applause.

Annie's cheeks heated. She ducked her head. This was bad. Calling attention to herself. If she wanted her six-week-long adventure, she definitely had to maintain a low profile, especially if Chandler and Strawn were still in the vicinity. She darted a glance out the window and saw to her relief that the limo had departed. They were gone.

She drew in a shaky breath. Reached up to finger her lips still tingling from Brady's kiss.

He possessed a strong chin stubbled with dark beard. The rough scruff had scratched her skin during the kiss, but in a wholly attractive way. Teddy never had beard stubble, his cheeks baby-butt smooth. Then again, he never kissed like that. Full of raw, hungry passion that made her toes curl inside her cowboy boots.

Brady's eyes were the color of strong coffee—black and hot. His nose was straight and just a bit too big for his face, but it lent him a noble air, a king by nature, if not by birth. But while his face declared power, his manner suggested easygoing fun. He walked with a slow, loose-limbed gait as if nothing alarmed or excited him. He had a bad-boy glimmer in his eyes, and Annie suspected women stood in line to capture his attention.

"Well," he said, "well."

That's when she knew their kiss had left him as speechless as it had her. What did you say after a kiss like that? *My world has been upended, never to be righted again?* Of course she couldn't say that, but she felt it. Her stomach rose, fell, lurched. Jubilance buoyed her. It was crazy, getting swept away by the first man she met on her adventure.

But that's the way it had happened for Princess Ann. Joe Bradley all the way. Honestly, if she squinted, Brady did have a bit of Gregory Peck in him. The height. The lankiness. The steady, easy speech.

Brady fished out his wallet. Laid money on the table, picked up his cowboy hat, and settled it on his head. "As pleasurable as that was, Buttercup, I've got to hit the road."

Buttercup.

He'd called her Buttercup. Another movie princess. Princess Buttercup from *The Princess Bride.*

Had he somehow guessed who she was? Her pulse somersaulted. Was her game over?

But no, he was smiling without suspicion in his eyes. Guileless.

That was when she realized the jukebox was playing "Build Me Up Buttercup." He had stolen the nickname from a 1960s-era song about a fickle girlfriend, but she did not mind. Annie smiled back. No matter where he'd gotten it, Buttercup was a term of endearment. Flattered, she pressed a hand to her chest. No one besides Rosalind had ever used a term of endearment for her and Rosalind called her Noodle. Buttercup was a step up. Perhaps it was the cowboy way. Giving out nicknames that made a woman feel special. She embraced the word.

Buttercup.

"I will be right with you," she said, picking up her satchel. Lady Astor moved inside the carrier. She could feel the little dog against her rib cage. "I must first visit the . . ." She paused, unaccustomed to speaking about bodily functions in public.

"Oh, I'm not taking you with me," he said.

"What?" She tried not to sound alarmed, but she heard it in her voice. "You are going to leave me here alone?"

"This is where I found you."

"But you were going to give me a ride to Jubilee."

"I never said that."

"What am I going to do? Where am I going to go?" She was disappointed, but now she sounded needy. She did not wish to sound needy. Needy was unattractive. So was fear. But the shine was swiftly wearing off her adventure.

Not yet. Not so soon. She was just getting started.

"I'll give you some money so you can get a room for the night," he said.

"What have I done to displease you?" It was something she asked her father quite frequently. He was the kind of man who withheld his affection when she displeased him. Now she was sounding desperate to go along with the neediness. Unbecoming.

Stop whining. You are a princess. You do not need to beg or cling.

"You pleased me too much," he said gruffly.

She frowned. "I do not understand."

"That kiss . . ." He shook his head. "Well, it could get a man into a lot of trouble."

"What does that mean?"

"You're a fine-looking woman, probably real nice too. In fact, you're too nice."

"You are abandoning me because I am nice?" Perplexed, she stared at him.

"You're a big complication and I'm an uncomplicated guy. With me what you see is what you get."

She raised her chin. "I see a chicken."

A grin crawled across his handsome face. "You're going for the insults, huh? Does that normally work for you?"

"I just want a ride."

"Somehow, I don't believe that."

"Sir, obviously you have mistaken me for a woman of loose moral character," she said.

His grin widened. "Those are your words, not mine."

Why was she holding on to him so tightly? She didn't need Brady Talmadge to have an adventure. True, he was the most magnificent kisser she had ever come across.

He's only the second man you've ever kissed. How would you know? Let him go.

But it was raining outside and he made her feel safe and . . . and . . . She wanted to go with him. To see this town called Jubilee, to watch him whisper to horses. It might not make much sense to anyone else, it did not really make much sense to her, but the impulse punched against her hard.

"All right," she said, pulling the strap of the

satchel up higher on her shoulder and flapping her hand dismissively. "Away with you."

She didn't need him.

Hmm, just as Audrey Hepburn had not needed Gregory Peck?

That was a movie. This was different. She learned from Audrey. She had Lady Astor for company, five hundred dollars in a secret compartment in the satchel. It had been all the money she could get her hands on. Her trust fun paid a monthly stipend to her bank account, but she wasn't allowed to carry her own cash. Or as her mother had been fond of saying, filthy lucre should never sully royal hands. Cash was crass.

Chandler and Strawn provided her with money when she needed it and she had credit cards. But if she used the credit cards, she could be traced. She planned on getting a job to tide her over through the next six weeks. She wanted a job. Longed to have the pleasure of making her own money. Yearned to feel that surge of independence one presumably got from providing for oneself.

And she would have it. She was determined. She didn't need Brady to make her dreams come true. There would be other cowboys. She would meet other people. There was nothing special about this man.

"Thank you for the meal," she said. "It was a pleasure to have made your acquaintance. You have my permission to depart."

The skin around his eyes crinkled as if he found her amusing. "I wasn't aware that I needed your permission."

"You do not." She had to be careful. She could give

herself away with comments like that. She was not in Monesta where everyone was at her beck and call.

"Please have a safe journey to your destination." Annie held out her hand.

The minute their hands touched, she felt it again, that powerful surge of electricity that stole the air from her lungs.

He looked startled and quickly snatched his hand back, his eyes coded. "You have a safe journey too," he mumbled, and ambled away.

Annie watched him go, a lump of sadness blocking her throat. She would have enjoyed kissing him again, but never mind. She had other problems. Like where to spend the night?

She found the ladies' room, but when she stepped inside and caught her reflection in the mirror, she startled and for the briefest second wondered: *Who is that?*

A foreigner looked back.

Inky black hair, which had once been the color of twenty-four-karat gold, curled in short, spiky wisps with impish bangs. Just a few short hours ago her tresses had trailed to the middle of her back. She wore the brand-new cowgirl clothes that she had borrowed from Echo—a white, Western-cut blouse that caused the blue in her gray eyes to pop, a big silver belt buckle with a Texas Star on it, stiff, sharply creased dark blue jeans, brown, round-toed cowboy boots with a slanted riding heel. Just looking at her, no one would believe she was a runaway princess. All she lacked to complete her attire was a cowboy hat.

A thrill pulsed through her. She had done it. She had actually run away.

She filled one of the sinks with water and let Lady Astor out of the satchel to have a drink. When she walked out past the row of truckers at the counter, insecurity gripped her anew. She kept her head held high. She certainly knew how to do that. She stared straight ahead and imagined she was walking the hallways of Farrington Palace where men bowed and women curtsied in her presence.

The bravado did not work. She could feel heads turn as she went by. Anxiety slid under her skin. She was calling attention to herself again. This was not good.

"Hey baby," one guy said.

She sailed past as if she hadn't heard him.

"Will you look at that critter?" another one snickered. "Prettiest lot lizard I've seen in a long time."

Was he speaking about her? And what did this term "lot lizard" mean? Annie's heart thumped faster.

After she had sneaked out of President Glover's compound while everyone was distracted by the rehearsal dinner, she simply started walking, the sense of adventure stirring her blood. She had Lady Astor. She had been safe. She never once felt in any danger.

She had been naive, she realized now, feeling the heat of masculine gazes upon her body. She did not dare look around. Just keep walking, running the gauntlet, apprehensive to get to the door. Get out of here. She pushed open the door and stepped out into the rain.

Not exactly the salvation she was searching for.

Water flowed like a river from the sky. Lightning filled the darkness in periodic flashes. Thunder made her jump. She huddled underneath the awning, eyeing the big, rumbling diesel trucks pulling in and out of the parking lot. The heavy hiss of air brakes chuffed a perilous lullaby.

She hunched her shoulders and another unsettling thought occurred to her. What if Chandler and Strawn were still in the vicinity and saw her out here?

The spirit of adventure that had gotten her this far eroded in the face of reality. She was in a predominantly masculine environment and she was unprepared for it. In Monesta she was accustomed to having servants do her bidding. Whenever she wanted to go somewhere, a chauffeur drove her. Whatever she wanted to eat, someone cooked it. Whatever she wanted to purchase, someone bought it. She was never alone and now here she was without anyone to rely on, save for Lady Astor.

Annie swallowed, shivering in the shadows. A side door opened and a man came out. He wore a brown cowboy hat, stiff black jeans, and a blue short-sleeved shirt. He fished a cigarette from his pocket, dipped his head to light it, stuck the lighter back into his pocket, and ambled over, blowing smoke from his nose like a dragon. "Hey, baby," he said.

It was the same man who had called to her inside the restaurant.

She turned away from him.

"Oh, it's like that, is it, sister?" He shuffled closer. "Too good to talk to me, huh? Only going for those clients with a big wad in their pockets?"

She wasn't sure what this vile man was talking about, but he was quite unsavory and smelled both dank and astringent. "Take your leave, sir," she said. "I am simply awaiting a ride."

"I got something you can ride." He gave a crude laugh and grabbed himself inappropriately.

No one had ever spoken to her in such a manner. Annie was taken aback but tried not to show it. "I do not want trouble."

"Now that don't sound like any fun."

From inside the satchel, Lady Astor growled. The Yorkie was very attuned to Annie's emotions.

"Fun is not my goal," she said.

Which was a lie. Fun was precisely her goal when she embarked on this adventure, but this was decidedly not fun. She was going to go back inside. At least there were people around. She turned for the door, but the man moved quickly to block her escape.

"Don't be like that." He reached out a finger to stroke her arm.

Annie struggled to suppress a shudder. She didn't want him to know how scared she was.

"We were just getting to know each other. C'mon, I'll give you a lift. Where you headed?" He grabbed for the satchel.

Lady Astor poked her head from the bag and sank her sharp little teeth into his index finger.

"Son of a whore!" he exploded. "That hairy rat bit me!"

Annie cringed, drooped against the wall, praying hard that someone would come out of the restaurant or pull into the parking lot. She opened her mouth to scream, but before she could get a sound out, he clamped a palm over her mouth, yanked her up tight against him.

"C'mon girlie, no lot lizard is turning her nose up at me. I got cash and I'm taking what I want."

Relief rippled the tension from Brady's muscles. Tonight, he might have broken his five unbreakable rules for leading an uncomplicated life, but it wasn't too late to undo his mistakes.

Well, except for the chili. It was too late to uneat the chili, but so far his stomach hadn't kicked up a protest. Maybe that rule could be safely bent.

The other rules he'd cobbled back together. He ditched the hitchhiker, simultaneously turning his back on a dangerous damsel in distress. He trusted his gut when it urged him to flee and he had told Annie the truth.

He was free and clear.

The road lay open. The simple path beckoned. After letting Trampas out to do his business, he put the dog back into the trailer, climbed into the cab of his one-ton dually pickup truck, shook the rain off his clothes and pulled around to the front of Toad's. He had a straight shot onto the highway. No oncoming vehicles. All he had to do was drive.

But then he made the mistake of glancing into his rearview mirror.

There was Annie, satchel clutched close to her chest, shivering underneath the awning outside the restaurant.

And she wasn't alone. A mangy-looking cowboy had hold of her elbow and was dragging her away from the entrance and toward the shadows.

Annie struggled, fighting to get away from the guy. Even in the darkness, Brady could see alarm in her eyes.

She's not your problem.

Maybe not, but he couldn't sit here and watch some guy accost her.

How do you know he's accosting her? He could be her old man, dragging her back home. You know better than to get involved in a domestic dispute. You'll be the one losing your teeth over it.

Annie opened her mouth to holler, but her outcry was lost in the noise of the storm. She dropped her satchel. Lady Astor was in there. Brady's gut lurched and it wasn't from the chili.

The cowboy had his arm around Annie's waist now. He had lifted her up off the ground and was dragging her toward a dilapidated old truck with Bondo doors. She was fighting him hard, kicking with the fury of a wild mustang, slapping at his head, knocking off his hat, but she was no match for the much larger man.

Anger bulleted Brady from the cab and he hit the ground running.

"Hey!" he shouted, but the wind snatched his voice up and threw it toward the stormy sky.

The mangy cowboy almost had her to his truck. Brady ran full throttle. Good thing he took a three-mile jog every morning. Otherwise he might not have made it to them before the guy got her inside his pickup.

As it was, Brady reached the truck just as Cowboy Mange got the passenger side door open. He'd been so busy struggling with Annie that he apparently hadn't heard Brady's boots slapping against the wet pavement. Brady seized the seedy cowpoke by the shoulder and spun him around.

Letting go of Annie, the cowboy doubled up his fists.

In the momentum shift, Annie lost her balance and stumbled to the ground. The man let out a growl and started swinging. He'd been drinking. Brady could smell whiskey on his breath.

Brady was a lover, not a fighter. It wasn't that he didn't know how to fight or that he backed down from one. He'd been raised in a nest of brothers. Of course he knew how to fight. It was just that he preferred nonviolent solutions, favored turning away anger with a joke and a smile, sidestepping the bullies with some dazzling comment that sailed over their heads.

But in this situation, he had no choice. The dormant warrior in him came charging to the forefront. Chivalry, the thing that had gotten him into trouble time and time again, roared to life. He met the cowboy's assault, punch for punch, his blows landing solid and strong.

"Don't pick on defenseless women."

"Ha! She was soliciting. I was taking her up on the offer when she got cold feet."

"I very much doubt that." Brady belted the man hard in the face. Anger—that volatile fire starter—pushed hot against his fist, surprising him, but he hated hearing ugly things said about Annie.

The man swore, swung at Brady.

He ducked. The punch sailed over his head, and Brady hit him again for good measure.

Then he heard a sound that chilled his blood, the hard slinking noise of cold steel. Saw the flash of silver in the light from the parking lot lamps.

A switchblade. The son of a bitch had a switch-blade.

Fear pooled in his belly, liquid, quicksilver. His gut was saying, *Get the hell out of here, champ. Live to fight another day.*

"C'mon," taunted the drunken cowboy, swinging the knife through the air. "Let's see what the white knight is really made of."

Brady raised his palms. "Now, now, no need for bloodshed."

"Oh, I think there's plenty of need. Guys like you think you're so tough and strong, but you're nothing but a pretty boy who likes to play hero. Try spending ten years in Huntsville. That'll make a real man of you."

Huntsville was the biggest prison in Texas. It housed the worst offenders and it was where the state carried out the death penalty.

"Put the knife down, mister, get in your truck, and drive away. That'll be the end of this."

"You think I'm going to let a pretty boy like you tell me what to do?" the man sneered. "I'll say when it's over." He lunged, knife outthrust.

Brady jumped clear. "Annie," he commanded. He couldn't see her. She was behind him some-where, but he could hear her breath coming in hard, startled gasps. He thought about the Yorkie in the satchel, hoped Lady Astor was okay. "Go back into the truck stop. Get help."

"Oh no, you don't," the knife-wielding ex-con snarled and moved to grab for Annie.

"Sorry, scumbag," Brady said. "I can't let you do that." He brought his leg up and kicked the man in the kneecap.

The ex-con yelped like a cowardly coyote and let loose with a string of vile cusswords.

Annie got away and was running across the parking lot, headed for the entrance to the restaurant, the satchel looped over her head, clutched it tightly against her. Relief rolled over him. At least she and Lady Astor were out of immediate harm's way.

Brady, however, was not.

Grunting, the ex-con raised the knife and brought it down.

Brady dodged just in the nick of time.

No, not quite.

He felt the stinging burn as the tip of the knife blade grazed the right side of his face cutting him from his ear to his jaw. He grunted, manacled the man's hand. They tussled. The stench of whiskey and cigarette smoke blew over him.

As the fight roiled on in the slog of rain, a pain-in-the-ass voice at the back of his brain kept up a running commentary.

Great. Just great. Here you go and get your face all sliced up over a girl you don't even know. Yes, you had to defend her. Of course you had to defend her. You had no choice on that score. You're not about to let a helpless woman get dragged off by some Neanderthal ex-con rapist. That's not what's at issue here. The issue is you stuck your nose in where it didn't belong. You had to play hero. You just had to break your own rules. Pick up a hitch-hiker. Go for the damsel in distress. It's not like you haven't been warned. For godsakes how many times have you been in a fix like this over a woman? A smart man would have learned his lesson by now. But you? Oh no. Not the cowboy in the white hat. And for what? You don't know this Annie charac-ter. She could be a pickpocket, a thief. She could be a lot lizard. She's hiding something. You know she's hiding something. That is the one thing that is clear about her. She's harboring secrets. She's a liar. And now you've gone and gotten yourself cut up over a liar. Smart, Talmadge. Real smart.

In spite of the lack of cooperation from his own conscience, he managed to wrest the knife from the drunken man's hand. In the distance he heard sirens. Saw people pouring out of the restaurant to watch the fight. He thought of having to stick around to fill out a police report. He had somewhere to be and he had a feeling that Annie, with her secret, didn't want to get involved with the police any more than he did.

Drawing every bit of strength he had left, Brady cocked back his hand and delivered a mighty blow to the man's chin.

The guy's head flopped back. He was out cold.

Brady shoved the ex-con off him and staggered to his feet. He looked up at the cluster of people watch-ing slack-jawed. "Don't let this guy leave. When the police get here tell them he attacked a lady in the parking lot."

The group gave a collective nod.

He pulled a bandana from his back pocket, wiped at the hot, sticky ooze tracking down his face, and staggered toward his truck and gooseneck trailer. His vision was hazy. He couldn't see through the rain soaking his eyelashes.

An arm went around his waist. Soft and feminine. *Annie.* Immediately, his spirits soared and he felt better.

The sirens screamed closer.

"Let's get out of here," he said.

She didn't argue. Brady opened the passenger side door and she climbed in.

"Are you okay?" Briefly, he put a hand on her shoulder.

She nodded, wide-eyed, steely-jawed. Her dichotomy plucked at his curiosity. Her vulnerability tugged at his heartstrings.

"He didn't hurt you?"

"No."

"How about Lady Astor?"

Annie stuck her hand inside the satchel, petted the dog's head. "She is fine."

Relief filled his mouth. He shut the door and walked around to the driver's seat and swung into the cab. He took a minute to draw in a deep breath and then started the engine and drove away.

"You're bleeding," Annie gasped as he pulled onto the highway entrance ramp.

"Flesh wound. It's nothing." He kept the bandana pressed to his right jaw.

"That man cut you because you were helping me."

"That about sums it up."

"You are in pain because of me."

"It's not the first time a pretty woman caused me pain."

"This is terrible."

He shrugged. "I've suffered worse."

"I am so sorry."

"It's not your fault. I shouldn't have gone off and left you. I should have given you a ride. Leaving you alone back there was like ignoring a toddler on the freeway. I'm culpable."

"Pardon me?" Irritation tinged her voice.

"What?" He winced against the pain. "You're pissed off at me now?"

She folded her arms over her chest. "You compared me to a toddler."

"I don't know where you're from, lady, but you're out of your league here. It might be nice if instead of giving me the stink eye, you might acknowledge that."

"What is this stink eye?"

"The dirty looks you're sending me."

"I am allowed to express my displeasure at your comparison."

"I did save your fanny." He slipped a glance over at her.

"You did," she relented. "Thank you for protecting me. I am very grateful. I should have said that before."

"Don't mention it."

"But I am not a toddler on the freeway. I have—" She broke off abruptly.

"You have what?" he prodded, his curiosity whetted.

"Never mind."

"You really like your secrets, don't you?"

"That is none of your business."

"It is if your secrets keep getting me in trouble."

She said nothing for a long moment. "You are safe."

"You're not going to tell me, huh?"

"No."

Okay, he'd just been put in his place. She seemed to have a queenly skill for slam-dunking him. He couldn't get over the paradox of her. She was at once supremely self-possessed, yet on the other hand she came across as innocent as a newborn foal. He'd never met anyone quite like her.

"What is this term 'lot lizard'?" she asked.

"Truck stop term for a lady of the evening."

"A lady of the evening?"

Brady shot her a look. Was she for real? "A professional."

"What kind of professional?"

"A woman who exchanges sex for money."

"Oh," she said. "You mean soiled doves."

"Huh?"

"Is that not what Texas cowboys call fallen women?"

"Maybe in 1875. Where did you get your information about Texas? Louis L'Amour novels?"

She raised her chin. "Actually, yes, and Zane Grey and Elmer Kelton and Larry McMurtry. I think the term 'soiled dove' is much more forgiving than 'lot lizard.' One should have compassion for a woman reduced to such desperate straits."

"Biscuits and gravy! You're one in a million, you know that?"

"Is that a compliment or a complaint?" she asked.

"Take it either way you want."

"I am going to assume you are benevolent since you befriended me."

"I wouldn't say befriended exactly."

"You came to my aid in my hour of need. That is the definition of a friend in my book."

"Is this the same book where prostitutes are called soiled doves?"

"Yes." She primly folded her hands in her lap. "You are making fun of me."

"Just a little bit," he admitted.

"I could make fun of you if I chose."

"Yeah?" He couldn't resist rising to the bait.

"Goll dern hell yeah," she said in her comical version of a Texas accent.

It was the funniest damn thing he'd ever heard, such archaic cowboy language coming from such a proper young lady. Brady burst out laughing. "You're priceless, Buttercup. You made my night in spite of the assault and battery you just got me involved in."

"I never asked for your help."

"Don't turn all high and mighty on me. I like you."

"I like you too," she said grudgingly.

"So where are you headed?" Brady asked, giving in to the inevitable. He'd picked her up. He was stuck with her, at least for tonight.

"I will go wherever you are going."

"You have no destination?"

"I am looking for a new way of life."

"And anyplace will do?"

"Yes. Take me to Jubilee with you." In that moment, with the tilt of her head, she looked like an ebony-haired Charlize Theron, cool, patrician, smoldering, and totally smoking hot.

When Brady didn't argue, that's when he knew he was seriously screwed.

CHAPTER THREE

You might be a princess if . . . you identify with
Audrey Hepburn in *Roman Holiday.*

The blurry lights of Dallas slipped away as
they headed west toward the town of Jubilee.
The radio played softly. A song Annie did not
know sung by a man with a gravelly voice. "On the
Road Again" flashed green on the digital readout of
the satellite radio. Willie Nelson. The song seemed
apropos. Fated almost.

The truck's engine panted. The tires strummed.
The windshield wipers swished, rhythmically
wiping away the continuously falling rain.

Both of Brady's hands gripped the steering wheel,
his eyes fixed on traffic. His hair was mussed; his
straw Stetson sat on the console between them. The
long cut from his ear to his jaw curved like a paren-
thesis.

The blood on his face had dried. He was right.
It was a superficial wound. Still, she had an over-
powering urge to trace her finger along the wound,

coo words of comfort to him the way Rosalind had cooed to her whenever she fell ill. A tender touch and soft language could soothe an ache. Why was she feeling that way? Was it because he had swooped in and saved her from the unsavory character in the parking lot?

He had been hurt protecting her, this cowboy hero who could have stepped from an old Western movie. Her stomach reeled, listed.

She caused his pain. Yes. This was her fault. She admitted it. She acted rashly out of character. Her world was byzantine, but out here, in the unknown, well, she was stumbling around wreaking havoc on Brady's simple life. He was a good man. He should not have to clean up her messes.

She thought of Princess Ann from *Roman Holiday* and how enchanted the character had been with the way the Romans lived. How her innocence had gotten her into trouble and Joe Bradley had rescued her.

Brady was her Joe Bradley, and Annie was making the same mistakes. She felt the same enchantment for Texans, and in that enchantment, loneliness tugged at her. She wanted so badly to belong here: to be part of this world she had vividly imagined for years, but no matter how much she wished it, she did not belong. She would never belong anywhere ordinary. She was royalty. A birthright she could never leave.

Annie had been six years old when she first realized how truly different she was from everyone else and it had all happened because her mother would not allow her to visit the carnival.

Vividly, she remembered watching the carnival crew set up the rides and displays. They had unloaded animals from train cars—elephants hooked together trunks to tails, tigers in cages, prancing horses. She recalled the posters plastered all over town, featuring fire eaters, contortionists, chainsaw jugglers, and sword swallowers. Rosalind regaled her with tales of sideshows and thrill rides and delicious food. The servants' children whispered in the hallways about the amazing experiences to be found at the carnival.

From her bedroom window, Annabella could see the lighted Ferris wheel circling high into the sky, and before she fell asleep on those long summer nights, she would rest her hands on the windowsill, nestle her chin on her stacked hands, and stare wistfully out at the boardwalk.

Excited voices filled the air along with tempting scents of portable food—cotton candy and funnel cakes, turkey legs and caramel apples, corn dogs and French fries. Foods that Annabella was never, ever allowed to taste, much less eat, but it made her mouth water. The delighted shrieks of children on roller coasters reached her ears, the colored lights on the rides dazzled her eyes.

Then the queen would come into the room, close the window, draw the curtains. "Nasty things. Nasty people. You have everything you could possibly want. Why are you so fascinated by the lowest common denominator, Annabella?"

Why couldn't Mamman understand how bright lights beguiled? Annabella was expected to stay behind the iron gates, the stone walls of Farrington

Palace, and gaze longingly at the world that went on without her. She wanted to ride the Tilt-A-Whirl with the village children. She longed to walk into the House of Mirrors and see her body distorted first tall, then short, fat then thin. She yearned to play games of chance—toss rings over the necks of bottles, throw a ball through a hoop, blow up balloons with a water gun until they popped.

Night after night, she gazed through the window at all that she was missing, a prisoner in her luxury. How disappointing to play checkers with Rosalind when she wanted to have her palm read by a Gypsy fortune teller with rings on all fingers and cheap jangly bracelets at her wrists. How frustrating to eat fresh strawberries dipped in sugar when she wanted to gorge on strawberry ice cream and buttery popcorn. How unsatisfactory to fall asleep on a goose down pillow when she wanted to win a giant teddy bear at the midway and go to bed with it clutched in her arms.

By the last day of the carnival, Annabella was sick with longing. After tonight the carnival would vanish for an entire whole year. But it just so happened this night was Rosalind's one night off a week and she was spending it at the carnival with a friend.

Her nursemaid tucked her into bed, kissed her head, and whispered, "Good night, Noodle, I will see you tomorrow."

The second the door closed behind Rosalind, Annabella sprang from the bed in her pajamas. She ran to the window, threw it open, and shimmied down the big oak tree growing beside the wall. She reached Rosalind's little blue Peugeot in the car park before her nursemaid did. Heart thumping, Anna-bella climbed into the backseat and lay down on the gray carpet. It smelled of licorice and she stayed curled up quiet as a cat. If Rosalind caught her, she would scold her and make her get out of the car.

Even so, she could not contain her excitement. It was the first time she had ever run away. The first time she ever dared anything rebellious. Without the allure of the carnival, she would never have done anything so defiant.

After Rosalind stopped the car and the door closed behind her, Annabella lay for a long moment, holding her breath. Then tentatively, she sneaked out of the backseat and found herself in wonder-land. The sights were as gripping as she imagined—the lights, the sounds, the scents, the textures, the crowd. She'd never been alone in the midst of so many people.

She felt at once very big and incredibly small.

Finally, finally all her dreams were coming true.

For a long time, she stood just staring at the wonder of it all. Her hands curled into fists, her nose twitching, not knowing what to do first. She ran up to a booth to buy some cotton candy, but then the man asked her for money. He was short with greasy black hair and a mustache as big and thick as a push broom. He smelled sweaty and there was dirt underneath his long fingernails. He wore a tight shirt with no sleeves and there were pictures of naked ladies drawn on his fleshy upper arms.

Ashamed, Annabella dropped her gaze; she did not want to look at the man with naked ladies on his arms, but she wanted that cotton candy.

"Money," he insisted, rubbing his thumb against two fingers in a circular motion.

She had no money and he would not give her the candy.

Stubbornness set in. She was a princess and unaccustomed to being refused anything by a servant. "Give me the cotton candy," she demanded haughtily.

"You pay, you get."

She snatched the cotton candy from his hand.

"Thief," he accused and lunged for her.

Annabella danced from his grip. She was not a thief. She was hungry. Starving for the ordinary experiences of ordinary children. Defiantly, she bit into the sweet, pink fluff. It dissolved against her tongue and she laughed out loud at the joy of it.

The man raised a hand as if to smack her, but there was her bodyguard, Reynaldo, grabbing the man's hand. "Strike the princess and it will be the last mistake you ever make."

The cotton candy man's eyes grew wide. "Pri-Pri-Princess Annabella." He fell to his knees in front of her and began kissing her feet. "Please forgive me. Take the cotton candy, it is yours."

But Annabella didn't want the cotton candy any longer. It had been ruined. Everything had been ruined. Her bodyguard snatched her up, tossed her over his shoulder, and carried her back to the palace. All she saw of the carnival was upside down from behind Reynaldo's back.

The bodyguard delivered Annabella to her mother in the upstairs parlor. It was the coldest room in the house and her mother's favorite. Even in the summer, Annabella often shivered in the draft slipping from the stained-glass window. A heavy tapestry of dark colors and hues hung on the wall, it made the room feel colder still. The carpet was equally dark. In the corner stood a stately grandfather clock with a large pendulum. It swung back and forth, ticking loudly.

Snowflakes. Whenever she was in this room Annabella thought of snowflakes. She shivered, knowing she was in trouble.

"You were right, Your Highness." Reynaldo bowed low before the queen. "I found the princess at the carnival eating cotton candy."

"Look at your face!" Her mother gasped, horrified. She dismissed Reynaldo with a wave. "You may go."

Annabella raised a hand to her face. It was sticky. Pink goo stuck to her fingers, evidence of her sin.

Her mother grabbed her by the shoulders, marched her to the mirrored wall at the back of the room. "Just look at yourself. You look like a guttersnipe. Ordinary. Common. Cheap."

The queen snapped her fingers and the servant who had been standing silently beside the velvet curtains at the window sprang forward.

"Bring me a wet cloth," she commanded.

The servant nodded, slipped away.

Queen Evangeline shook her shoulders. "What is wrong with you? What were you thinking? Going out into the streets alone? You could have been kidnapped! Shame on you for scaring your mother half to death."

Annabella hadn't thought about any of that. All she wanted was to go to the carnival. She burst into tears.

"Stop that crying. You stop it right now." Her mother shook her again, more forcefully this time. "A princess does not cry. Tears are for weak, ordinary people."

The door opened and Rosalind came in with a wet washcloth. "I am so sorry, Your Highness." She did not meet Queen Evangeline's eyes, but kept her head bowed. "The child hid in the backseat of my car. I did not know she was there."

Her mother snatched the cloth from Rosalind, shot daggers at the nursemaid with her eyes. She squatted before Annabella and scrubbed at her face. "Filthy carnival. Nasty people. You could have gotten a disease, Annabella. You are a princess. You are a . . . *Farrington*. You are above such shenanigans. You have a duty and an image to uphold. Do not ever do anything like this again or you will be severely punished."

"Mamman, I just wanted to have fun."

"Well, you cannot have fun. Not that kind of fun. You are special. You are chosen." The queen shifted her glare to Rosalind. "This is all your fault."

"I am dreadfully sorry." Rosalind worried her hands.

"You are too indulgent with her. You read her those silly, romantic fairy tales. I want it to stop. No more stories about cowboys and knights in shining armor."

"It is not her fault, Mamman," Annabella protested. "I sneaked into her car when she was not looking. Rosalind did not know."

"And how did you get out of your room?" Her mother glowered.

Annabella ducked her head, as sheepish as Rosalind. "I climbed down the oak tree."

"Reynaldo," Queen Evangeline called sharply.

The bodyguard appeared in the doorway. "Yes, Your Highness."

"Cut down the tree outside Annabella's bedroom window."

"Your Highness, the tree is two hundred years old."

"Cut it down."

"It will be done." Reynaldo bowed and then vanished as quietly as he had shown up.

The queen turned her attention back to Rosalind. "We had an agreement."

"Yes, mum," Rosalind mumbled. Standing beside the tall, dark-haired queen, the blond nursemaid looked young, fair, and fragile.

"You violated our agreement."

"I beg your forgiveness."

"You know what I can do to you."

"Yes, Your Highness." Rosalind raised her head and in that moment, boldly met the queen's stare.

Something dark and silent passed between them, a look that Annabella did not understand. Her mother squeezed Annabella's shoulder tight, drew her up against her body. Her hands trembled. The queen was trembling. She was afraid of Rosalind?

The stare-down lasted a long minute more, then the queen cleared her throat, tossed her majestic head, and glanced down her nose at the nursemaid. "You are dismissed."

Rosalind notched her own head up, stuck her chin in the air. "For tonight?" She clenched a fist. "Or forever?"

Queen Evangeline licked her lips, hesitated, and then said firmly, "For tonight. But in future we will have no more of these incidents. Is that understood?"

"Yes, Your Highness."

"You will make it perfectly clear to *my* daughter that she is above the common people. She is a ruler. It is in her bloodline."

"In her bloodline," Rosalind echoed, and without dropping a curtsy, she turned and stalked from the room.

"Annie?" Brady's voice tugged her from the past and put her back in the pickup truck beside him.

She blinked, glanced over. She still couldn't believe she was here. Free for the first time since she was six years old and running off to the carnival for cotton candy. But now she fully understood the hidden threats her mother had been trying to protect her from. It was dangerous enough out here without anyone knowing she was a princess. What had she done?

Momentarily, she considered the consequences of her actions. Her father would be upset. Teddy would be confused. Rosalind would be alarmed. She regretted causing them any upset, but this was something she had to experience. Before she committed herself to Teddy for a lifetime, she had to see the world through different eyes. She couldn't fully explain her longing to anyone else, but it had dogged her from infanthood—the feeling that there was a simpler path for her to follow.

She spoke of it to Rosalind. Carefully of course,

testing the waters. Her nursemaid had assured Annie that her emotions were nothing more than prewedding jitters. She had been born into the complex life of royalty. There was no long-term escape. It was her duty, and should be her honor, to rule over Dubinstein with her husband.

Husband.

That was the sticking point. In less than two months she'd be forever shackled to a man she did not love. If only for a little while, she desperately wanted to know what it felt like to be desired by a man that *she* was attracted to.

A man like Brady Talmadge?

Just looking at him made her body grow warm in soft places. He wore faded jeans with a rip in one knee, probably caught it on barbwire once and never bothered mending it. His hair, as dark as the color she'd dyed her tresses, was neither clipped short nor long, but a medium length just on the right side of shaggy. She lowered her eyelids, looked at him through the fringe of her lashes, not wanting him to see that she was inspecting him.

Why not be honest? No point fooling herself. She was admiring him. All manly muscles and angular bones.

"Annie," Brady repeated. "You awake?"

She had trouble hearing him over the masculine rumblings of the big diesel engine. "Yes."

"Who were those guys?" he asked.

"What guys?" She stared at the dashboard of his truck. There were all kind of knobs and dials lit by a faint green light. A laser radar detector, GPS tracking device, and the satellite radio were mounted there. It reminded her that she had tossed her cell phone in the lake on her way from the presidential compound so that she couldn't be tracked through the GPS inside it.

"You know what guys. The men at the restaurant. One tall. One short. Sunglasses at night. Fedoras. Not your typical truck stop patrons. The ones you were so anxious to hide from that you asked me to kiss you."

"Oh, them. They were just some people I did not want to see," she said.

"How come you didn't want to see them? Were they old boyfriends?"

"That is a very impertinent question."

"Impertinent, huh?"

"Examine this topic from my position if you will," she said.

"What position is that?"

"You told me you do not like liars. Do not make me lie to you."

"I don't like people who keep secrets either. Secrets aren't good for anyone. C'mon, let the truth out. You'll feel better."

"You cannot expect full disclosure from someone you just met."

"Why not?"

"By nature, humans are reluctant to trust. Unscrupulous individuals could use their secrets against them. People need to protect themselves from getting hurt. Life never taught you that?"

"Life taught me secrets are the things that hurt people the most."

"What secrets hurt you?" Annie murmured.

"We're not talking about me. I gotta know one thing," he said. "This thing you're running from, is it a husband or a possessive boyfriend?"

In a way, it was, but she knew that was not how he meant it. "No."

"That's good to know."

"What are *you* running from?" she asked.

"Who says I'm running from anything?"

"You are pulling your home behind you."

"Roots," he said. "I'm running from roots."

"Roots?"

"You know. Like tree roots."

"And why are you afraid of tree roots?"

"I don't like being tied down."

"You have been married before?"

"No. That's the point."

"Have you ever come close to getting married?"

"No, but hey, how come I always end up answering the questions and you keep sidestepping them?"

"Because people like to talk about themselves more than they enjoy listening to others talk about themselves."

"You saying I'm self-centered?"

She shrugged. "I am saying you are normal. You like to talk about yourself. You run away from commitment . . ."

"You're hardly in a position to judge."

"I did not say that I was."

"Darn straight."

She canted her head. He was handsome enough to be an outlaw. Especially when he flashed that grin. She did not have much experience with men, outlaws or otherwise. "May I ask you a personal question?"

"How personal?"

"You do not have to answer."

"What do you want to know?"

"What do you want most in life, Mr. Talmadge?"

"Brady," he said. "You can call me Brady. After all I did save you from that guy back there."

"You did. I said thank you. Now answer the question."

"You have a way of ordering people around. It's polite and all, but it's still ordering. Bossy. You're bossy."

"So you do not know what you want most in life?"

"I want for nothing. I'm living the dream."

"How does one get to be that happy?" she mused.

"By keeping things simple. Not getting involved. Light. That's the way to get through life. Light and easy."

"You got involved with me tonight."

"You caught me at a weak moment. Atypical."

Wind buffeted the truck. A fresh round of upset rain pounded the windshield. Brady slowed.

"Does it always rain like this in Texas?" Annie asked.

"This time of year? Hardly ever. But an unseasonably early hurricane hit Brownsville this morning at dawn, and we're reaping the fallout. You don't like rain?"

"It is very sunny where I am from."

"And where is that?"

"Shh." Annie brought an index finger to her lips. "That's another secret."

"You know that's driving me nuts. I think it's why you keep hinting at secrets. You enjoy seeing me squirm."

"Curiosity killed the cat."

"You know," he said. "I never understood that saying. Just how *did* curiosity kill the cat? I want specifics."

"I think it means he stuck his nose in where it did not belong and someone cut if off."

"His nose or his curiosity?"

"Maybe it was something else altogether."

"Are you threatening me, Annie Coste?" he teased.

"Now why on earth would you think that?"

"You're a sharp one. How did you learn to be so slick? Lots of younger brothers and sisters keep you on your toes?"

"Why younger?"

"You're too highhanded to be anything but the oldest child."

"I am an only child." Sort of. It was the way she saw herself. There was Henry of course, but he was so much younger, he was more like a nephew than a brother.

"So where did you learn the saucy give-and-take?"

"My nur—" She almost said "nursemaid," but stopped just in time. Regular people didn't have nursemaids growing up. Rosalind was only sixteen years older than she. They'd had a sisterly relationship when other people were not around to discourage it. "My neighbor," she finished. "We were close. Do you have brothers or sisters?"

"Four brothers."

"Gracious, your poor mother. Five boys."

"We did give her hell," he admitted ruefully.

"What is your birth order?"

"Middle child."

"Hmm, that offers a bit of explanation."

"What do you mean?"

"Perhaps that is the reason why you are a nomad. Growing up, you felt displaced."

"Who says I felt displaced?"

"It is the fate of the middle child. Is it not? To be displaced. What do your brothers do?"

"Cody, my oldest brother, is thirty-five. He's a chemical engineer. Works in oil and gas. He's married and got two boys. Big house, big mortgage, all those things that trap a man."

"You are afraid of being trapped."

"I'm afraid of talkative hitchhikers."

"What about the other brothers?"

"Colton is second oldest. He's thirty-three. He's a rancher, lives in Montana. Leif is twenty-seven, he's getting married next year. He's a musician in Austin. My youngest brother, J.D., is twenty-three and a bull rider."

"You are all cowboys?"

"We are."

"Did your parents move around a lot when you were children?"

"Nope. They've lived in the same house for thirty-six years."

"Where is that?"

"Llano."

"Is that far from here?"

"About a three-hour drive. You done with the interview?"

"For now." She stretched, raised her arms over her head, felt her blouse slip from her waistband and expose a stretch of bare abdomen. She noticed that Brady noticed. "Do you like navel rings?" she asked.

He coughed, blinked. "What?"

"Navel rings. I understand they are quite popular. Do you like them?"

"Um, I dunno. Yeah, I guess. Sure. Why?"

She placed a hand to her belly. "I think a navel ring would be quite seductive. A small gold hoop, winking in the light. A navel ring says, *I am a daring woman.*"

"Are you?" Brady asked. "A daring woman?"

She tilted her head and gave a coy smile. "I think I'll get a navel ring. What else do you think I should have pierced?"

"Uh . . . uh . . ." A disconcerted expression crossed his face. He was so busy staring at her belly that when oncoming headlights rounded the bend ahead, Annie realized he'd had his eyes off the road long enough to drift into the wrong lane.

She reached over, took hold of the wheel, and guided the truck back to where it belonged. Immediately, he clamped his hands over hers. "I've got it."

Heart thumping, Annie let go, eased back against her seat. The heat from his palms lingered, seeping through the backs of her hands, drifting into her bloodstream. An indolent flash of something erotic yawned, shook its sleepy head, smacked its lips. "Next time, you should consider keeping your eyes on the road."

"Next time, you shouldn't talk about piercing parts of that awesome body with a man pulling a forty-foot horse trailer behind him. I've got a vivid imagination about those places you're considering piercing."

She reached to finger her earlobes. "I was talking about my ears. What were *you* thinking?"

He swiped a palm across his forehead. "That a woman like you shouldn't poke unnecessary holes in herself."

"Then I am fortunate that it is not your decision." She didn't even know for sure if she was going to get her ears and navel pierced. She just wanted to do something to remind her of her wild Texas adventures in the years ahead. "I suppose I could get a tattoo instead."

"No!"

She startled, splayed a hand to her chest.

"Absolutely no tattoos," he said.

"You have a tattoo," she pointed out, peering at the galloping horse on his right biceps partially hidden by the short sleeve of his shirt."

"That's how I know you don't want one. You can't take it back once you do it."

"It is a very lovely tattoo. Why do you regret it?"

"I didn't say I regretted it. I said you can't take it back."

"If you do not regret it, why would you want to take it back?"

He scrunched up his face. "Why do you ask so many questions?"

"There's so much to learn!"

"Learn?"

She pressed a hand to her mouth. Tightrope walking. She had to be careful. She felt a strange urge to tell him all her secrets. That was a fatal impulse. "I can share one secret."

"What's that?"

"I'm only in Texas for a few weeks and then I must depart."

"Back to where you came from?"

"Back to where I came from," she echoed.

"So this is a sabbatical of sorts."

"Exactly."

"The hitchhiking, piercings, tattoos are all your attempt to cram the most living into the least amount of time." Outside the rain went from splattered to patter. A sliver of moon swam in a sea of black clouds.

"You understand."

"What precisely are you taking a sabbatical from?"

"Other people's rules," she replied honestly.

"I've never been a fan of other people's rules myself."

"I have observed that."

"You've already got me figured out."

"Yes, I have dove-holed you."

"Dove-holed?" Brady hooted. Making fun.

"Is that not right?" She worried her collar with her fingers.

"What? Oh, you mean pigeonholed."

"Yes, that is it. Wrong bird."

Brady's warm, rich laugh rolled right over her. "You're something else, you know that?"

"What else?"

"It's an expression. Meaning you're different. Special."

Yes, she knew that. Being different and special was what she was running away from. "What is it like?" she asked.

"What?" He turned on his blinker, changed lanes to pass a slow-moving truck transporting ice cream. A picture of a cow was plastered on the side of the truck along with a slogan proclaiming: "Simple Pleasures." The cow wore a red bell around her neck and was smiling like a human.

"This place called Jubilee."

He shrugged. "It's a horse town."

"Does that mean that it is a very small town?"

"You're thinking of a one-horse town."

"So may idioms. What is the difference?"

"Jubilee literally is the cutting horse capital of the world."

"What is a cutting horse?"

"Usually it's a quarter horse, but it can be other breeds. Once upon a time cutting horses were used to work livestock on a ranch. Now, mostly it's a sport."

"A sport?"

"Like rodeo events. Bull riding or steer wrestling."

"Cutting horses are not in the rodeo?"

"No, they have a venue all their own."

"I see."

"It's clear why you came here to learn."

"I can assure you that my education is quite comprehensive," she said, mildly offended. "I speak six languages."

"No kidding?"

"*Je parle français.*"

"French."

"*Ich spreche Deutsches.*"

"German?"

She had to speak German. It was the national language of Dubinstein. "Excellent guess. *Eu falo o português.*"

"Portuguese."

"*Parlo Italiano.*"

"Simple and to the point, those Italians."

"*Hablo español.*"

"*Poco.*"

"Oh, you speak Spanish as well?" That surprised and delighted her.

"Buttercup, you're in Texas. We all speak a little Spanish. Almost half my customer base speaks Spanish."

"May I see it sometime?"

"What's that? My customer base."

"These horses being cut."

"No, no, the horses aren't cut. They're the ones doing the cutting."

"What do they cut?"

"Cattle from the herd."

Annie had no idea what he was talking about, but it sounded fascinating. In Monesta they didn't have cattle. Not enough land. They raised sheep and goats instead.

"But you should really see a rodeo before you go back home."

She knew what rodeos were. She had seen them on television. "Will you take me to a rodeo?"

"We'll have to see about that. I don't make promises I can't keep."

That was a good thing. He was a man of his word.

"So tell me more about Jubilee. What are the people like?"

"It's about as perfect as a town can get. The people are friendly, they help each other, but they're very focused on their horses."

"That is good for your business."

"It is," he said. "We're almost to Jubilee. Tomorrow you can find out about it for yourself. We should be there a little after midnight. The rain has slowed down our time."

"This will be fine."

"You got arrangements? A place to stay? Friends you can call?"

"No," she admitted, feeling stupid. She should have made better plans. But she was so afraid that too much planning would lead to her immediate capture.

"Where are you going after this?" he asked.

"I do not know."

That answer didn't seem to bother him, as if he understood not having plans. "You can spend the night in my trailer."

"Thank you for your generous offer, but I do not know if that is a wise idea."

"Where else are you going to stay?" he asked.

She didn't answer because she didn't have one.

"I know the trailer is small and there's only one bed, but you're welcome to share it."

Annie swallowed the gasp that rose to her throat. "You are asking me to sleep with you?"

Although she felt scandalized, she had to admit that she held a secret desire to make love to a cowboy before she was bound to Teddy forever. She was supposed to stay a virgin until her wedding day. It was the way things were done. She had always done what was expected of her, but part of her yearned for just one out-of-the-box experience before she committed to a lifetime of a loveless marriage.

Just once she wanted to feel something real. She wanted great sex like the kind she saw in movies and read about in books. She wanted to spread her wings and fly just a little bit. She wanted to know what great sex felt like, and instinctively, she understood that Brady could provide such an experience for her. She wanted her own version of *Roman Holiday*.

But she barely knew him. Had not expected to find the opportunity for sex with a good-looking cowboy so soon in her adventure. And as much as she might want it, she wasn't ready for it.

"I'm saying you can sleep in my bed and I promise I won't touch you. No hanky-panky. Just sleep."

"What if—" She stopped, cleared her throat.

"What if?"

"I wanted to do more than sleep?"

"I don't think that would be a good idea for either of us."

"I thought men always wanted sex."

"I might want sex, Buttercup, but I don't have

to have it. Especially with a woman who's keeping some mighty tall secrets."

"Not even if *I* want to?" She reached over and touched his thigh, shocking herself.

"You're playing with fire," he said. "Watch out or you just might get burned."

CHAPTER FOUR

You might be a princess if . . . you can't sleep when there's something hard in your bed.

Brady took Highway 51 to Tin Top Road and traveled ten more miles to Green Ridge Ranch. At this hour of the morning, the ranch lay in darkness. He bumped over the cattle guard, the trailer rattling as they went. He parked in the graveled driveway a quarter of a mile from the ranch house.

Joe Daniels, the owner of Green Ridge, was a good friend. Recently, Joe had married Dutch Callahan's daughter, Mariah, and they had a baby boy named Jonah. The same Dutch Callahan who'd picked Brady up on the side of the road when he was fifteen, running away from his childhood as fast as he could. Dutch had brought him here to Jubilee. Given him a job and a place to live. Back then Joe's father had owned Green Ridge, before he'd retired, sold the ranch to Joe, and moved to the neighboring town of Twilight. That was fourteen years ago.

Every time Brady came to Green Ridge, he thought of Dutch, who'd worked there as a trainer. Everywhere he looked he saw his mentor. In the buildings, the fences, the vast stretch of land.

Annie had fallen asleep, her head lolled on the headrest, Lady Astor curled up in her lap. He cut the engine and glanced over at her. Her flawless skin glowed pale and ethereal in the darkness. Her breathing was deep, untroubled. She looked so damn naive.

As quietly as he could, Brady opened the door and got out. He chalked the tires, but left the trailer hooked to the truck. He'd leave the unhitching details for tomorrow. He let Trampas out of the trailer to go to the bathroom, stretched, yawned, and stared up at the stars.

For the most part, the rain had passed. Sprinkles dampened his skin and water stood in puddles. Bullfrogs shrieked. The wind whipped his shirt and a lock of hair fluttered across his forehead. He ran a hand over his jaw, rough with beard. He was one of those guys who started sprouting a five o'clock shadow fifteen minutes after he shaved. His fingers gingerly explored the fresh cut clotted with dried blood. Not deep. He would live and the scar would enhance his cachet with the ladies.

He felt peaceful here, more than in most places, although Brady adapted quickly to new environments. He knew how to make himself at home wherever he went. But Jubilee was special and even though he knew he would never really settle down, if he ever did, this would be the place.

But right now, an uneasy feeling rippled the surface of his peace. The woman sleeping inside his pickup truck spooked him. He wanted her with a hard, insistent craving, and that was dodgy stuff. She was a hundred and ten pounds of trouble and he'd gone and offered to let her sleep in his bed.

Biscuits and gravy, Talmadge. What the hell were you thinking? You haven't been thinking straight since you picked her up.

Guilty.

He was guilty as charged. Addled. Empty-headed. No excuse for it.

The moon had come out, glowing ghostly against the black shadows. In the distance, he heard a horse nicker. Trampas's ears pricked up. The dog loved horses almost as much as Brady did. Unfortunately, horses weren't always fond of the dog. And Brady always did what was best for the horses. Unlike many cowboys, he never wore spurs, or used a crop. He believed slow and gentle was the best way to approach a horse. No exceptions.

Brady remembered his first glimpse of this ranch. It had been from the bed of Dutch's pickup truck. How he immediately felt at home here and everyone had made him feel welcome. He wasn't new to the ins and outs of hard labor. He was a country boy after all. What was new to him were cutting horses, cutting horse cowboys, and the cutter way of life.

Dutch had led him to the barn, showed him the cutting horses in the stable. Told him to muck out stalls. Brady had been happy to do it. He loved the smell of hay and leather and horses. His only problem was that he got so caught up in grooming and riding and tending the horses that he forgot all about his other ranch hand responsibilities.

"You remind me of me when I was your age." Dutch laughed. "Except you're better-looking."

Then one day one of Mr. Daniels's pregnant mares got hung in a downed barbwire fence and cut herself up pretty badly. They called the vet, but the high-strung horse was hysterical and wouldn't let the vet anywhere near her. She reared up on her hind legs and pawed the air, lips frothing, nostrils flaring. Even Dutch, who was a wizard at taming horses, couldn't calm her. Everyone stood around scratching his head, watching blood stream down her damaged flank, afraid to approach her in case she did herself more harm or the stress caused her to go into early labor.

Brady could literally feel her pain. A visceral pummel straight to his gut. The sensation burrowed under his skin like a sickness. A candle flame of terror burned in the mare's eyes. She tossed her head, mane flailing. The pulse beat hard in her long neck nicked with barbwire wounds.

He took a deep breath, dived to the bottom of the calm, serene pool inside himself. The place he dived whenever his old man went on a rampage and beat the living shit out of him just because he was feeling ornery. It was a cool, deep, unruffled place. Every muscle in his body relaxed, while at the same time he straightened his shoulder, raised his chin, and moved slow, easy, and unflinchingly toward the mare.

"Careful boy," Mr. Daniels said, but Dutch put a

hand on the rancher's arm and drew him to the far side of the barn. The vet followed.

"There now," Brady murmured, comforting her the way he'd comforted himself those dark lonely nights cowering in bed with bullwhip welts striped across his back. "There now. You're safe. You're above the pain. It's okay. It's all right."

Immediately, the mare stopped thrashing. Her frightened eyes met his.

"Yes," he cooed, "yes, yes. You're a good, good girl."

She half lowered her eyelashes. She was still breathing heavily, her flanks heaving in and out. The coppery smell of her blood scented the air.

"That's right. You're safe. Relax. Let go." A tranquil energy flowed through him, languid and vibrant.

The mare moved restlessly, snorting in air, but she didn't bolt or rear up. Acting purely on instinct, Brady kept speaking to her, low and controlled. When he got close enough, he touched her neck, firm yet gentle. He put two fingers on her pulse point. She quieted instantly and her breathing slowed.

"Well, I'll be damned," Dutch whispered. "Will ya look at that?"

A flush of pride beat through him. He'd never had a father figure who complimented him and he was ravenous for praise. He ran a hand down the mare's back. She quivered, but then her muscles uncoiled as she soothed. After several minutes of touching, she allowed Brady to slip the halter on. He held her, cajoling and comforting as the vet came over and worked to sew up her wounds.

"You got the touch, boy," Dutch told him after it was over. "A natural talent."

Brady guessed that learning how to deal with the abuse his father had dished out to him, but spared his four brothers, had been worth something. His ability to find peace in the midst of pain had given him his career.

And now he was back where he'd begun, except this time with some unexpected baggage.

The passenger side door opened and Annie got out of the truck.

"Are we here?" she asked, blinking at him with those smart gray-blue eyes in the dusty light of the quarter moon. The wind billowed through her unzipped sweatshirt, ruffled her hair. She stood straight, graceful.

God, she had a way of looking sophisticated and genteel when anyone else under the circumstances would appear rumpled and wrung out. What made her so different? How did she manage to look so much like a high mountain buttercup, pristine and beautiful? Fascination moved through him. Tightened up in his chest.

"We are," he confirmed.

She sank her hands on her hips, assessing their surroundings. "So this is Jubilee."

"Actually we're ten miles south of Jubilee. This is Green Ridge Ranch where I'll be working."

"Oh, okay." Annie set Lady Astor on the ground. The tiny dog started sniffing around.

Trampas spied the Yorkie and, goofy doofus that he was, raced over to start the universal canine ritual of heinie sniffing. Lady Astor, however, had other plans. She spun her fanny away from him, tossed her fierce little head, and let out a sharp bark. *Back off, buster.*

"Lady Astor," Annie scolded. "Be nice."

The Yorkie growled at Trampas.

Brady's mutt lay down and then rolled over on his belly, paws pulled up close to his body in complete surrender.

"Seriously, Trampas? You're giving up alpha dog status to a hiccup with hair?" he asked.

"Excuse me," Annie protested. "That is my dog you are denigrating."

"Sorry," Brady mumbled. "But you gotta admit she barely qualifies as a dog."

Annie sank her hands on her hips, angled him a haughty stare. "She has got *your* dog on his back."

"She does at that. Trampas, have some self-respect. Get up."

Instead of obeying, Trampas wriggled in the dirt, put out a paw to Lady Astor, and made begging noises.

The Yorkie's nose went in the air and she trotted off to take care of business.

"Pathetic," Brady scolded his dog. "Done in by an arrogant little female."

Trampas didn't look the least bit ashamed. In fact, he gazed at Lady Astor with adoring, love-struck eyes.

"Is there a place where I could . . ." Annie cleared her throat, moistened her lips.

Brady's gaze hooked on her mesmerizing mouth. "Go to the bathroom?"

"Um . . . yes." She looked uncertain now. There it

was again. That paradox he found so maddeningly sexy. Prim yet brave.

"Inside the trailer." He walked over to lower the steps of the trailer. He unlocked the door, and then held out a hand to help her up.

"Will you keep an eye on Lady Astor?"

"Absolutely."

She took his hand like it was her birthright to have men wait on her. She sniffed delicately. "It's dark."

He reached around to flip on the twelve-volt light switch.

"Oh," she said, sounding surprised. "It is rather nice in here."

"You were expecting a hovel."

"You *are* a bachelor."

"That doesn't mean I'm a slob. This trailer is my home. I take pride in it."

She turned around in the entryway, scanning the space as Brady perched on the top step, holding the door open. The back end of the trailer housed three horse stalls. He used them mainly when a horse needed to be isolated. Sometimes, he rented himself out as a transport service for folks who bought and sold horses. For now, the back trailer was empty. The opposite end of the trailer housed Brady's bed, which was located up over the head of the goose-neck trailer. To one side lay a small kitchen area, a stovetop, no oven, a refrigerator, and a postage stamp–sized table with two chairs. Across from that was a small sitting area. The shower was on one side of the unit, the toilet on the other.

Brady stepped into the trailer with Annie and

opened the bathroom door. "Toilet," he announced.

She tilted her head at him. "You are going to stay in here while I . . . ?"

"Where should I go?"

"I prefer to use the facilities in private."

"There's a door between us."

"A very thin door."

He lifted an eyebrow in amusement. Prissy along with the prim. "Fine. I'll go back outside. I better make sure your dog isn't kicking the stuffing out of my dog."

Brady ventured back into the night, drawing the door closed behind him. Lady Astor was sniffing at water puddles, completely ignoring Trampas, who was crawling on his belly after her. "C'mon, show some dignity, will ya?"

Trampas looked shameless.

"Face it, buddy. She's never going to give you the time of day."

Trampas ignored him.

Brady sighed. He needed to schedule the dog for a neutering. He'd meant to do it, but kept putting it off because of his travel schedule. But the dog was over a year old. It was time.

He whistled. Reluctantly, Trampas got up and trotted over. "You are sleeping in the back tonight. You're too muddy for the bed." He pulled a leash from his pocket, clipped it to Trampas's collar, and guided the dog to the back of the trailer. Trampas whimpered in protest, glanced back at Lady Astor, and let out a mournful howl.

"She's so far out of your league it hurts. Just give it up." He put Trampas inside, fed and watered him.

"She's a high-toned purebred and you're nothing but a ragtag ruffian."

While he was doing all this, Lady Astor came over to watch the proceedings, her little ears sticking straight up. He had to admit the Yorkie was cute as all get-out with those perky little ears and sassy attitude. "Gotta hand it to you, Trampas, she might be out of your league, but you got good taste. She's pretty and got gumption to boot."

He closed the back door of the trailer, scooped up Lady Astor, and carried her inside. The Yorkie cocked her head and stared up as if passing sentencing on him.

"Well?" He looked at her. "Do I pass the test?"

Her warm little tongue flicked out to lick his thumb.

"Looks like we're gonna be good friends. Sorry I called you a hairy hiccup."

Annie was still in the bathroom. There wasn't much space to move around. Brady deposited the little dog on the half-sized sofa, and she immediately curled up into a little ball to watch him. He stripped the sheets off the bed, got out fresh ones, and proceeded to put them on the lone narrow mattress.

Ahem. Seriously, you're going to do this? You're going to sleep on this tiny little bed next to Annie and not touch her? How do you plan on accomplishing that?

The bathroom door opened and Annie emerged dressed in a long, silky underwear thing. The word "peignoir" popped into his mind. He didn't know where the word came from. Probably one of the women he dated had told him that's what it was called. Whatever it was named, Annie looked completely stunning in it—floaty and feminine, clothed in a sexy cloud of white.

Dammit.

Why couldn't she have worn cotton footie pajamas? That he could have resisted. But in this sheer gown it was all he could do to keep from reaching over and pulling her into his arms.

"Hey," he said gruffly.

"Hello." She tucked her hands behind her back. "Do you require any assistance in making the bed?"

There it was again, that overly formal speech. Where was she from? His curiosity climbed into a rocket ship, took a blast to Mars.

"Naw, I just about got it." He shifted away from the sight of her in the frothy nightie.

Brady slid his hands under the corner of the mattress, tucking in the sheet. He'd been in bedrooms with more than his share of women, but he could not recall a moment as odd and awkward as this one. He could hear her breathing, soft and quick. She was as unnerved as he. No doubt in his mind. Maybe even more so.

Annie cleared her throat.

He turned. "Yes?"

"Your face needs attention." She gestured toward her own cheek.

"What?" He reached a hand to his face. "Oh yeah." He'd forgotten about the cut, but now that he touched his jaw, he felt the sting anew.

"Sit down." She patted the seat of the straight-backed chair.

"It's okay, I'll tend to it later."

She gave him that do-as-I-say look that she was so good at and pointed at the chair. "Sit. Attending to your wounds is the least I can do after you were carved up over me."

Feeling like Trampas, he sat.

"Do you possess first aid supplies?"

"Under the bathroom sink."

She hurried into the bathroom, reappeared with the first aid kit. She stepped close to him. He tried not to look at her breasts, so perky and high, but hell, he was only human. He did his best to be covert about it, but one look at those smooth, perfect breasts and he stiffened.

Quickly, he crossed his legs, settled his hand over his lap. *Do-da-do-da. Stop with the boner, champ.*

Luckily, Annie was busy digging around in the first aid kit. She came up with a small bottle of hydrogen peroxide and a folded square of gauze. She soaked the gauze with the peroxide, then leaned over to slowly start working on the dried blood.

Brady's entire body tensed. The gauze scratched. The peroxide bubbled foamy against his skin. He closed his eyes. He needed something to distract him from her nearness, from the silky glide of her peignoir rubbing over his knuckles, from the soft sound of her breathing, from her baby powder fragrance mixed with the lemony zest of his bar soap. His mental gears ground hard, trying to make sense of this situation and how he'd gotten here with her. He fisted his hands.

"Does that hurt?"

"It's okay. Keep going."

He gulped, wanting to ask her the question he'd been dying to ask. He kept his eyes closed, so he wouldn't intimidate either one of them. He knew how intimidating direct confrontation could be. His old man had been one of those kinds of guys who crowded your space, got in your face, and spewed spittle when he yelled. When the old man was really picking on him, when his bullying was in high form, and beating Brady just wasn't taking the edge off his anger, but instead inflaming it, his four brothers would form a human shield, encircling him, screaming at their father to back off.

That's when he felt the safest. Encircled by his brothers. He was going to ask Annie the question he needed to ask, but he wasn't going to make eye contact. Wasn't going to do anything to threaten her.

"Annie," he said softly, "I really need to know something."

It took her a minute to answer. "Yes?"

"You can keep your secrets, but since I am sticking my neck out for you, then you have to tell me if you are in any danger from the Blues Brothers? Am I?"

"The Blues Brothers?"

"You really aren't from America, are you?"

"No."

"Are you from Canada?"

"Do not worry. You are in no danger from the . . . er . . . Blues Brothers."

"Not Canada, huh? I know you're not from Australia. I have a good friend from there and you don't sound anything like him. New Zealand?"

"Why does it matter where I am from?"

He shrugged and finally opened his eyes. She was standing back, examining her handiwork. They were only a couple of feet apart, but in this small space it was as far apart as they could get. "It doesn't."

Their gazes met.

"That's not your real hair color, is it?"

She reached up a hand to her choppy hair. "How did you know?"

"You dyed your eyebrows to match the hair, but your eyelashes are blond. Can't hide that. You're a natural blond. Iceland?" He reached up to finger her hair.

She drew back. "What?"

"Are you from Iceland?"

"No."

"You're on the run. Hiding out."

"If I say yes will you drop the questions?"

"Okay."

"Then yes, I am hiding out."

"Did you—" He broke off. He'd been about to ask her if she'd committed a crime, but a promise was a promise. He would drop the questions. For now. But somehow he couldn't see her as a criminal.

That's how they lure you in.

"I am going to put the butterfly closures on your wound. So hold still." She seemed in no hurry to return to violating the boundaries of his personal space.

"I'm waiting."

She cleared her throat, hardened her chin, and ripped open the package of butterfly closure strips. She didn't look at him, she looked *into* him and he stared boldly back, seeing past the wide-eyed mystery she wore like a veil.

Her eyes told him things that her fear and distrust would not let her say.

I need help. I'm in over my head. You're all I've got.

Or maybe it was just his damn ego talking. Two hours ago, he'd ditched her as trouble he didn't need. Now he realized she was as vulnerable as an orphaned newborn foal in Yellowstone's Lamar Valley, where the wolves lived.

She dropped her gaze, worked on closing the edges of his wound with the butterfly bandages. Her gentle fingers pressed against his skin. It was all he could do not to shiver.

"There," she said breathlessly, and stepped away again. "All done."

"Thank you."

"You're welcome."

A long silence stretched between them, sticky as a cobweb.

"It's after one in the morning. Time for bed." He uncrossed his legs, placed both palms on his knees.

"Time for bed," she echoed, her voice slow as maple syrup on a winter morning.

They kept watching each other. Her gaze roved over his face. He could feel her sizing him up. He was doing the same. The woman was different and he could not reconcile the fact that she was on the run from something, someone. What had he stumbled into?

"I'll get into the bunk first," he said. "That way you won't be closed in."

"Thank you." The grateful expression on her face

told him he'd nailed it. She was afraid of having her back against the wall.

He shucked off his boots. "I'm just going to brush my teeth." He jerked his thumb in the direction of the bathroom.

"I'll get Lady Astor settled."

He went his way. She went hers.

Inside the bathroom, Brady stared at himself in the mirror. His cheek was mended with the stark white skin closures. He squirted a dab of toothpaste on his hard-bristled toothbrush. Winced when he opened his mouth wide enough to get the brush in. The damn cut hurt.

"What in the hell are you doing?" he mumbled to his reflection. "You wanna get your teeth knocked out by whoever is looking for her?"

No, no, he did not. Tomorrow he would find someone else to pawn her off on, but for tonight, he couldn't really do anything except live up to his offer to give her a place to sleep. Port in the storm. That was him. More than one woman had told him so.

You're my port in the storm, Brady, his last girlfriend had said.

He'd liked that. His stupid ego. Then she'd dumped him for another man.

No one gets serious about a port in the storm, she said when she walked out carrying the Jack LaLanne juicer she bought him for Christmas, a pair of inline skates slung over her shoulder, and wearing a diamond engagement ring big enough to choke Santa Fe that he had not given her.

No one needed a safe port when the sun was shining.

* * *

Annie couldn't believe she was in bed with a cowboy. She had dreamed it for so long she could not be sure she was really awake. To prove it, she pinched the underside of her arm.

Ouch.

All right. Wide awake. This was no dream. She curled her toes against the crisp, cool sheet and thought of the way Brady had looked as she had tended to the wound he acquired while defending her honor. Her white knight. There was no ignoring him. His big body filled the tiny space, his scent filled her nose, his face filled her mind. A cowboy. An honest-to-goodness honorable cowboy.

He climbed into bed wearing nothing but a pair of boxer briefs and a cotton T-shirt. She had tried not to notice how the cotton material stretched over biceps as hard and round as Granny Smith apples. The inked artwork on his right arm of a galloping horse, mane flying, fascinated her. She had an urge to press her mouth to it, trace the outline of it with her tongue.

The rain started again, drumming against the roof.

She smiled into the darkness. She was here. Now what? How did a princess go about seducing a cowboy?

The spot behind her knees went itchy. Her entire body heated. The sensation started at the tips of her toes and rolled upward, spicy as truck stop chili—hot, heavy, urgent.

Brady wasn't asleep either. She could hear his quick, shallow breathing. Neither one of them had moved. Both lay on their backs, staring up at the ceiling.

Don't make waves. Rosalind had drilled it into her head. *Remember the three A's. A princess is always accommodating, accepting, and agreeable.* The triple A princess. That was she.

Annie had struggled so hard to live up to that diktat. She'd been an obedient daughter never questioning the plan for her life. She believed she had accepted her marriage to Teddy. Would do whatever was required of her by her country.

Or so she thought.

Then she received the invitation to Echo Glover's wedding. She and Echo had met as teenagers when Echo's father had been president of the United States and Echo and her mother had vacationed in Monesta. Her stepmother, Birgit, had invited the first lady and her daughter to stay at Farrington Palace, and for four wonderful weeks, Annie had known what it was like to have a sister.

She and Echo had kept in touch over the years, through letters, phone calls, text messaging. Neither one of them had been allowed to have a Twitter or Facebook account. It was considered improper conduct, not to mention a legal and security liability for women of their positions.

The minute Annie opened Echo's wedding invitation, so close to her own impending wedding, she had known it was her last chance to experience a normal life, if only for a few brief weeks. It had taken a heated argument to persuade her father to allow her to attend the wedding. Teddy, surprisingly enough, had been on her side.

"Let her spread her wings, King Phillip," Teddy advocated. "I'm pleased that my future queen has friends in America, and it would serve me well for my wife-to-be to gain a more sophisticated view of the world."

That had made her feel extremely disloyal. Here Teddy was trying to help her and she was planning on cheating on him.

It's not cheating. Not technically.

Although she'd been promised to him, and their wedding was planned, Teddy had not yet slipped an engagement ring on her finger, wanting to play the field as long as he could in the fading glory of his bachelor days. They had never been intimate and they both knew their relationship was not a love match.

Justifications. She knew a rationalization when she heard it.

Suddenly, she felt ashamed of herself. What was she doing here? What did she really expect to come of this? Even if she seduced Brady and they had wonderful sex, then what? What if she went back home and Teddy turned out to be a lousy lover and she spent the rest of her life longing for Brady? That would be tragic. Better to never know what she was missing.

Oh dear. She sank her top teeth into her bottom lip. Her hands were clasped over her chest. She twiddled her thumbs.

"Can't sleep?" Brady asked.

"Strange bed," she said. "Hard mattress."

"I can't sleep either and it's my bed."

"Strange bedfellow."

"There is that."

They inhaled a simultaneous breath.

"We could talk," Brady said. "If you like."

"About what?"

"Whatever comes to mind."

Hmm. That left plenty of open ground to cover. *Think of something nonsexual.* "How did you get to be a horse whisperer?"

"I was always naturally drawn to horses."

"I like horses too," she said.

"Do you know how to ride?"

"No, but I've always wanted to learn."

"I could teach you to ride. If you'd like."

"Really?"

He rolled over on his side. She stayed put on her back, but from her peripheral vision, in the glow of the nightlight, she saw him stack his hands underneath his head. He was watching her.

"Sure," he said.

"Does that mean I can stay here with you for a little while?" she ventured.

"Until you can find other arrangements."

"You're very generous."

"Not really. I'm just a sucker for a pretty face."

"You say the oddest things."

"You find compliments odd?"

"Manipulative, generally."

"You think I'm manipulative?"

"Most people are."

"You must come from money," he said flatly.

"What makes you say that?" She wasn't about to confirm it. She didn't want anyone in Jubilee connecting her to Princess Annabella, because when word finally got out that she was missing, it would be all over the media. Everything she'd ever done had ended up in the media. Which was part of the reason she never did anything that would shame or embarrass the royal family.

"I don't know." Brady paused. "I suppose it's in the way you carry yourself."

"In what manner?"

"As if the world is your oyster."

"I do not do that . . ." She bit her bottom lip. "Do I?"

"Sort of, yeah. You've got this regal tilt to your head and a way of looking down your nose that can make a guy feel put in his place."

That bothered her. She didn't want to come across as condescending or dismissive. Her mother had been like that and it bothered her to think she had absorbed those traits. "I apologize if I have done anything to cause you to feel that way."

"It's my problem. Not yours."

"What do you mean?" Intrigued, she rolled over on her side to face him and tucked her hands under her cheek just as he had done. They stared into each other's eyes.

"The thing that makes me so in tune with horses is the same thing that makes me thin-skinned with people."

"Thin-skinned? What does that mean?"

"I read too much into peoples' motivations. I have a tendency to take things personally even when they're not intended that way."

"I'm not sure what you mean."

"Well," he said, "like now for instance."

"Yes?"

"I'm picking up on the vibe that you're conflicted."

"Could you elaborate?"

"Your body is rigid, tight. You're nervous."

"Who wouldn't be? I am in bed with a stranger."

"You'd be surprised," he said. "Some people like being in bed with a stranger. They seek it out. For the thrill."

"Do you go to bed with a lot of strangers?" she asked, feeling suddenly, inexplicably jealous. She pursed her lips, crossed her arms over her chest.

"Not a lot, but a few," he admitted.

"What do you like about sleeping with strangers?"

"It's interesting."

"Do you . . ." She cleared her throat. She didn't know how to ask this next part, but she sorely needed to know if this was to end up the way she was hoping it would end up. "Practice safe sex?"

"I do," he said. "But to be honest, it's been a long while since I did anything like this."

"Like what?"

"Picking up a stranger. Offering her a place to bunk."

"But you *have* done it."

His guilty grin said it all. He was perfect as he was. Flaws and all. He was just what she needed. He'd confirmed it. She was looking for an adventure. A casual fling with a man who would not fall in love with her.

"Except not lately?" she ventured.

"There was this woman, about two years ago. I thought we might have something going."

"What happened?"

He shrugged. "We didn't have anything going."

"Did she break it off or did you?"

"She left. Took my Jack LaLanne juicer with her. For her new bodybuilder fiancé."

"She broke your heart."

"I wouldn't go that far," he drawled. "But she confirmed an old lesson."

"What was that?"

"Never trust someone with a secret."

"She really hurt you."

"No biggie. I'm not the settling-down type. And the juicer? Way too much trouble. Just buy the juice at the store and be done with it."

Annie touched his forearm. "I'm out of my element."

"So I've noticed." He reached up to ensnare her wrist with his thumb and index finger. "Please don't do that."

"Do what?"

"Touch me like that."

"Why not?"

"I'm hanging on by a thread here. You really have no idea what your touch does to me, do you?"

"Should I?"

"You're a gorgeous woman in the prime of life. You figure it out."

"I . . ." Her stomach stumbled. "Do I turn you on?"

"What do you think?"

"Do you want to make love to me?"

He took her hand and guided it under the covers. She touched something hard. "Oh my."

"Yeah, oh my."

She gulped. She had never touched a man's erection before. She had heard about it. Felt it when she had danced close with Teddy, but she never put her fingers to one, even one cloaked behind a pair of cotton underwear. It felt like hot velvet steel.

Abruptly, he let go of her wrist.

Her eyes met his. He stared at her.

Into her.

"Annie."

"Brady." She breathed.

"This isn't going to work. Lying here beside you. Not touching you. You're too much woman for that."

"What are you going to do?" She hauled in a deep breath. Her pulse hammered so hard she heard it rushing blood through her ears.

"I'm going to go sleep in the backseat of my truck." He sat up.

"No." She put a restraining hand to his bare chest, marveled at the strong, hard strata of muscles. "Don't go."

"I can't stay." He shook his head. "If I stay—"

"What?" she whispered, scarcely breathing.

"I can't be held accountable for my actions."

"What if I do not want you to be held accountable for your actions."

"Do you even know what the hell you're saying?" His voice hissed like sizzling hot coals splashed with ice-cold water.

Did she? Probably not.

All she knew was that she ached deep inside. An ache that caught fire the moment he'd picked her up on the side of the road, an ache that had built steadily from the kiss in the restaurant to culminate here in his bed.

She craved him in a wholly physical way. Hungry need bit into her. Below her waist she felt a demanding stirring. She had never experienced such a strong sexual sensation. To date, her desires had been sedate stirrings. Mild interest. Academic curiosity. Nothing like this full-bore yearning that made her heedless to everything sensible and right.

"Annie," he whispered hoarsely, and the next thing she knew he was pulling her to him.

His arms encircled her. It felt good. It felt right. She pursed her lips, waiting for his kiss.

When it came, the kiss was light, seductive. A sweet tease. She moaned softly and burrowed closer.

He threaded his fingers through her hair, slipped his mouth from hers to slide slowly to her neck. When he got to the underside of her jaw, his kisses turned to tender nibbles. Erotic sensation swamped her entire body, skipping from nerve ending to nerve ending, a joyous warning of what was in store.

She wanted this. Wanted it more than she could say. But she worried that if she made love with him, she would be forever changed. That she couldn't go back to her well-ordered, well-planned life. That once she tasted of the cowboy myth she would discover it was not myth at all, but a way of life she could no longer live without.

She made a soft noise, a high reedy sound, half protest, half plea. She wanted him to take the reins, to leave her helpless and breathless. Pleasure, unlike anything she'd ever experienced addled her brain, left her witless.

"Tell me," Brady said, his hands skimming over the silky material of her peignoir. "What do you like?"

"What do *you* like?" she said, using her fall-back technique of answering a question with a question. She had learned that answering a question with a question gave her time to gather her thoughts and formulate a plan. The delaying tactic offered her some small measure of control, and as a woman whose life was not her own, she took a great deal of comfort in it.

"I'm a pretty simple guy," he said. "The basics work for me. I don't need anything fancy, but I'm not opposed to it if that's what you're into. A little light bondage? Role-playing? Sex toys?"

"Goodness." She had not expected that.

"But I'm very satisfied with regular sex. I'm a meat and potatoes kind of guy."

"Meat and potatoes." She laughed. "What does that mean?"

"Just you and me and the equipment God gave us."

"My." She giggled. "Do you have protection?"

"I've got condoms. How about you? Are you on the pill?"

"The pill has been taken care of." The royal physician had started her on birth control pills to control irregular periods.

"So why are we still talking?" he asked gruffly. "I want you, you want me."

Yes, she did want him. Very much. But this was her first time. She didn't know how to tell him that. She knew well enough that an almost twenty-five-year-old virgin was an anomaly in this day and age. "I . . . well . . . Can we take this slowly?"

"Buttercup, slow is my modus operandi," he drawled in a sultry, dark voice that sent delighted shivers through her.

"That's good," she said, relieved.

"Now, let's stop talking and start kissing."

CHAPTER FIVE

You might be a princess if . . . you're a twenty-five-
year-old virgin.

Every sensible bone in Brady's body was telling
him that this was not a good idea. He knew
better than to get involved with a secret-keeping
woman. He had the self-control to turn her down.
Or at least he thought he did until he started kissing
the sweet underside of her jaw and heard her soft
purr of pleasure.

You've just been too long without sex.

That was true enough. He'd been busy. On
the road. And while he did have a reputation as
something of a ladies' man, he was not—tonight
exempted—much one for one-night stands. He did
like light, casual relationships with women who
were in the same frame as mind as he was, and that
certainly seemed to be Annie, but her secretiveness
gave him pause. She was in some kind of trouble and
she was using him as the fall-back guy. It wasn't the
first time a woman had used him in such a manner

and he figured it wouldn't be the last, but Annie was different somehow.

For one thing, she seemed so damn fragile while at the same time she exuded a toughness that belied her cultured air. He had to admit he was intrigued. He wanted to know more.

And he wanted more of her kisses.

His body heated up quickly. His erection tightened and surged. His dick was clear on the subject. Sex would be a nice way to take the edge off the aching wound on the right side of his face.

Normally, he wasn't a man much troubled by excess contemplation. He was a sensual guy. He liked things tactile—the feel of a horse beneath him, leather reins in his hands, boots on his feet. Most men were more visual than anything else, and while Brady enjoyed seeing a naked woman as much as the next guy, he also had a powerful need to run his hands over things, to touch and feel, textures, shapes, temperature. His palms and fingertips absorbed sensory input far more acutely than either his eyes or his ears.

As a kid, he never missed an opportunity to pocket a fascinating found object—a bumpy tortoise shell, fuzzy caterpillars, prickly pieces of twine. When they got their summer haircuts, he loved to run the flat of his palm over his brothers' buzz cuts even though it usually ended up getting him punched. When he lost a baby tooth, he couldn't resist poking his tongue through the gap, exploring the strange terrain. And he had loved nothing more than walking barefoot in the sand, curling his toes in the fine grit.

His fingers traced Annie's rose petal skin, detecting the heat of her veins. He pressed his lips to the pulse point at her throat, felt her heart flutter. She was excited.

So was he.

He tasted her. All part of the tactile experience. Beneath the sweet caramel lay a deeper, more womanly flavor, salty and satisfying. He licked lightly, familiarizing himself with her flavor, letting it roll over his taste buds.

He couldn't seem to get enough of tasting her. He took his time and she seemed to like his leisurely approach, even though she was a bit hesitant. Touching him lightly, then moving her hand away as if she was shy. He'd been with a few shy girls. On the whole, they turned out to be quite wild in bed. It was true. You had to watch out for the quiet ones. They were usually making up for lost time.

Who was she really? Where had she come from? What kind of trouble was she dragging with her?

She kissed him back, her lips yielding, but her body was still tense. She was nervous. He reached up to knead her shoulder muscles. "Relax, Annie."

"I am trying . . . I . . ."

"Uh-huh," he murmured. "What is it?"

"I . . . have not . . . I am . . ."

"A bit rusty at this?" he guessed.

"Yes—"

"Don't worry, Buttercup. You're in good hands. I've got the wheel."

"I want . . ."

His fingers went to the silk tie holding her skimpy lingerie closed at the neck and he deftly untied it. "I'm listening," he said, exposing her creamy white flesh. He pressed his lips in the center of her chest.

She wriggled beneath his touch. "That . . ."

"Yes?"

"Tickles." She giggled.

"Let's try more pressure." He kissed his way over to her left breast. Her breasts were the perfect size. Not too big, not too small. He loved the weight of them in his palm as he cupped them. The size of navel oranges.

Her nipples beaded tight and she arched her back. "Please . . ."

"You want me to suck your nipple?"

She nodded mutely.

He grinned and lowered his head, pulled that saucy nipple into his mouth, ran his tongue over the tight bud.

Annie went wild. She gasped and jammed her fingers through his hair. Her breath shot out hot and raspy. He increased the pressure and she squirmed against him.

"Ooh, ooh."

"Now for the other one." He moved to the other side, parting her nightie out of the way to find the nipple of her right breast just as eager and hungry as the other.

"I . . . I . . . I . . ."

"What is it, Buttercup?"

Her head thrashed against the pillow. "I never knew. I never knew."

"Never knew what?"

"It could feel . . . I could feel . . . Oh, Brady, I can *feel*."

He smirked against her nipple. Yeah, okay, he

was proud of himself. He knew his way around the female body. If that made him a braggart, then so be it. But pleasing her pleased him. He liked making her feel good.

Romantic. He was making this romantic. It wasn't romantic. Just scratching an itch. Fun. They were having fun. Nothing wrong with that as long as they both had their eyes wide open and their hearts closed up tight, because he did not know her. She was on the run. A smart cowboy would not be here, but Brady, well, no one had ever accused him of being Einstein.

Annie's slender fingers traced his rib cage hesitantly. "I want . . ."

"Yes?"

"More. I want more."

"I can handle that." He went to work in earnest. Taking his time, but moving things along, heating her up. Hands touched. Lips kissed. Breath intermingled.

Annie was responsive, but underneath it all she seemed inexperienced. Was she really twenty-four? That gave him pause.

"You sure you're over eighteen," he said.

"I am."

"You sure this is what you want to do?"

"Certain."

"You can back out now. Things haven't gone too far."

"I want you," she confirmed.

Brady swallowed and asked himself the same questions. Was this what he wanted to do? Did he want to back out before things had gone too far? Before he had time to fully process the repercussions, Annie raised his T-shirt and started planting kisses along his belly.

His body responded. Going harder than he thought possible. He tensed, waiting to see where her hand would travel.

She stopped short at the waistband of his underwear. In the darkness, her eyes met his. The glow of the nightlight over the sink cast faint illumination throughout the trailer.

They deadlocked there. Gazes fused. Neither moving. Simply breathing.

Her lips parted and he claimed her mouth again. He always enjoyed kissing, but he couldn't seem to get enough of those lips. Many guys he knew didn't like kissing or even foreplay very much. They got straight to the action. Poor dumb slobs. Look at all the great tension they lost out on.

You're losing out too. Going at this so soon. Where's the teasing and the banter and the flirting? He liked the buildup, the thrill of the chase; by tumbling into bed with her so quickly they were missing out on a lot of fun. *Where the hell is your self-control?*

It was shot, busted, gone. The buildup between him and Annie had been condensed into a few short hours and came on hard and strong. Stronger than any attraction he had felt in a very long time, and Brady couldn't say why. But there was something about her that he couldn't resist. Something more than the wild-eyed, vulnerable, beauty-in-distress thing she had going on. Although he had to confess, he did find that appealing. Why did he have this need to rescue women?

Maybe because no one had rescued him?

That wasn't fair. His brothers tried to rescue him. But he'd been a lost cause.

No, there was something about Annie that you didn't find in most modern women. Perhaps it was because she was a contradiction in terms—on the one hand innocent and naive, on the other, un-expected, bold, and self-confident. Maybe it was because she was secretive. But if that were the case, shouldn't her secrets turn him off? Secretive women had always been a deal breaker before, but with Annie her furtiveness only seemed to fuel his arousal and make him determined to find out what she was hiding.

She is not going to tell you. Not tonight. And then tomorrow, she'll probably be on her way, back on the road, thumbing for the next ride.

A sheaf of loneliness fell against him. Why did he suddenly feel so lonely? It wasn't loneliness. It was disappointment, regret that he would never know her full story.

Pillow talk. After they made love and were lying in each other's arms drifting off to sleep, her guard would be down and he could more easily elicit an-swers to the questions he ached to ask.

Except Annie had no notion of his plans and ap-parently, she had some plans of her own, licking his skin with her wicked little tongue. "Make love to me, Brady. Please."

What cowboy could resist a request like that from a good-looking filly?

In that moment, biology was in the driver's seat and caution lay in the rearview mirror. He pawed off the rest of her nightgown, and then stripped off his own underwear. He reached into the drawer at the head of the bed, fumbled for a condom.

Annie was nibbling his nipple now. Turning the tables. Paying him back.

He got the condom on. Barely. His hands shook with anticipation, excitement, fear.

Fear? What was he afraid of? He had nothing to be afraid of. Right?

She lay on her back. Brady posed over her. His erection pressed hard against her hipbone. He cradled her head between his forearms, positioned on the bed to bear his weight, looked deeply into her eyes, and fell all the way to a clear bottom pool.

"Annie."

She smiled up at him.

He edged her knees apart. She was barely breathing now, but her gaze never left his face. Her legs parted. Her hands went around his neck. Urging him forward, pulling him in.

The tip of his shaft pressed against her feminine doorway, and slowly, he pushed forward, muscles quivering, excitement racing along his nerve endings, anticipating the soft sink into her succulent folds.

Except that he met with tight resistance. No easy slip. No sweet glide.

What was this?

Then it hit him all at once and the realization staggered him.

Annie Coste was a virgin.

Right in the middle of everything, just when Annie was on the edge of having the experience of a lifetime, Brady stopped. He levered himself up on his arms, stared into her eyes, his face darkening with confusion.

"What is it?" she whispered.

"You . . . you're a virgin," Brady stammered.

Annie brought a palm to her chest. Oh dear, did this mean he was not going forward? She reached up, twined her arms around his neck to pull him down for a kiss, but he kept his body rigid, unmoving.

"Annie?" he chided.

"Yes," she admitted. "But that does not have to ruin the moment."

"I disagree."

Annie caught her bottom lip up between her teeth. Maybe it was a good thing he backed off. She did not know if she was really ready for this. She loosened her grip from around his neck. "You no longer want me."

"Oh, I want you very, very much, but this isn't the way. Not the right time. Not the right place. I'm not the right man."

"You are," she insisted. "I have been a virgin long enough."

"There's nothing wrong with being a virgin," he said. "It's a good thing. But man, twenty-four? Seriously, you're twenty-four and still a virgin?"

She notched her chin up. "I am almost twenty-five. So what if I am?"

"Nothing . . . it's just that . . . where are you from? In America most girls lose their virginity at a much younger age."

"I have . . ." How to explain it without giving herself away? "I have led a sheltered life."

"I'll say."

"I do not understand why being a virgin is a problem. Make love to me and I will be a virgin no more. Problem solved."

"You've waited this long for a reason and for some other reason you've decided to give your virginity to the stranger who picked you up on the roadside? That doesn't feel right to me. You're acting out and I'm not going to be the fall guy."

"You do not want my virginity?"

"No." Brady pulled a palm down his face, but he looked sorry to have to say it. "I do not."

Rejection tasted salty in the back of her throat, like tears. Her chest constricted and she couldn't catch her breath. She bit down on her bottom lip. "You do not find me sexy?"

"Yes, God yes. I find you very sexy. That's the problem. You deserve to give your virginity to someone who loves you, someone that you love. You've waited this long, why not wait for the right guy?"

She considered that. It sounded good but she didn't really have enough time to find someone to fall in love with, and besides, if she fell in love she would just have to leave him. There would be no fairy-tale happily-ever-after for Princess Annabella.

Hot sex with a good-looking cowboy was as close as she was ever going to get. "Did you give your virginity to someone you loved who also loved you?"

"It's different for guys."

"Why is that?"

"Men can separate love from sex."

That irritated her. She came from a country that put the needs and desires of men above those of women. In Monesta, a male heir usurped a female heir. Always. Just because a person was born with a penis did not give them more rights. Not in Annie's opinion.

She knew things were different in America. She read books, and Echo Glover was her best friend. Echo had taught her a lot on that score.

In fact, Echo had been the one to hatch the plot to get her out of the presidential compound during the wedding rehearsal. She wondered what was happening there now. She wished she could talk to her friend. Echo had a very matter-of-fact view of sex and love and men and marriage. Her husband-to-be, Abel Escabedo, worshipped the ground she walked on, and Echo told Annie that was the way it was supposed to be. The man should love the woman more. If the man loved her more, the woman had all the power.

Annie didn't know what to think about Echo's theory. She thought perhaps loving each other equally was the real way to go, but she had no experience with love, could not trust her own opinion on that score.

Brady rolled away, his back thumped against the wall of the trailer as he got as far away from her as he could get. "Don't feel bad about this. I'm not rejecting you, just the situation."

What a truckload of cattle manure. Of course he was rejecting her. He did not want to have to deal with the burden of her virginity. He was probably afraid that if he made love to her she would imprint on him like a baby duckling and follow him around everywhere. Utter nonsense.

She sat up in bed, leafed through the covers to find her peignoir. "You, sir," she said, "are not worthy of the gift of my virginity."

"That's exactly what I was trying to tell you." He looked at her as if searching for a truth he would not find.

Annie felt the same way. Led on. Unsatisfied. "I thought you were chivalrous and kind and understanding and yet you demean me by saying I have to live by one set of rules while you, a man, are honored to live by another."

He looked confused, his cocoa-colored eyebrows pulling into a frown. "What are you talking about?"

"I'm talking about the way men think they know everything. Contrary to masculine opinion, having a penis dangling from between your legs does not give you the key to the universe."

"Whew." Brady blew out his breath. "Clearly, I stepped in something here."

"Yes, yes you did." She found her nightgown, tugged it over her head, jammed her fingers through the flimsy armholes, and cinched the thin lacy belt tight around her waist.

Brady's eyes were glued to her breast the entire time.

"You want me," she said.

"I do," he admitted.

"But you won't take me."

"Nope." He shook his head.

"This is unfair."

"Maybe, but I hate to see you sell yourself short."

"I don't understand. What does that mean?"

"You could do so much better than me."

"Now who is selling himself short?"

"Annie." He reached out a hand but she shied away. He dropped his hand. "Having sex with me would mean something to you."

"Now who is overestimating himself?"

"I meant psychologically. It's your first time. Your first time should be special. Even if you don't mean to, you're going to have feelings for me if we make love because I would be your first lover."

She huffed out a breath, folded her arms over her chest. "My, you do think highly of yourself."

"It's not me. It's the situation. If you gave me your virginity, you'll start to think it means something."

"No I will not."

"You can't force yourself to change your feelings."

"You do not know me at all, or what I am capable of feeling."

"That's true and another reason why we shouldn't sleep together. We're strangers."

"That did not bother you before."

"I don't have long-term potential."

"I know. That is precisely the point." She crossed her arms, blocking his view of her breasts. "I do not want long-term potential."

"You don't?"

"I don't. I can tell you are a ne'er-do-well."

"I wouldn't go so far as to say ne'er-do-well.

I've done well. I do well," he protested. "I'm a well doer."

"I do not mind that you are a ne'er-do-well. That's why you're perfect."

"Stop saying that word."

"What word? Perfect?"

"Ne'er-do-well. Who says words like that?"

"I do not want long-term potential. I want the opposite of long-term. I want someone with the potential of a nanosecond. I want a man who pulls his home behind him. This is a man who does not put down roots. Roots are for stumbling over. With you, there will be no stumbles."

A variety of emotions moved across his face—surprise, disbelief, confusion, and then, finally, effrontery. "You want to use me for sex?"

She smiled. "Is that a bad thing?"

"I—" He shut his mouth, opened it again. "You . . ."

"Yes?"

" . . . are a very odd woman."

"Perhaps that is true."

"I don't know your situation or why you were hitchhiking on the side of the road in the driving rain or why you're offering up your virginity to the first guy who gives you a ride, but there's some kind of twisted psychology going on behind those gray-blue eyes and I'm not going to be a part of it."

She shrugged. "If that is how you feel. It is your loss."

"It is. I can accept that." Brady grabbed up a pillow. "Could you scootch over please? I'm going to sleep on the floor."

Annie swung her legs aside so he could climb down from the bunk, frustration and disappointment surging through her. For one brief moment she thought every wonderful dream she ever dreamed about making love to a cowboy and exploring Texas was about to come true.

Do not give up so easily. You have six weeks. There are more cowboys in the rodeo than this one.

It was true. She knew it. She was in Texas. There was bound to be a cowboy on every corner. Yet she could not help thinking that this cowboy was the one she had been waiting for.

Forget him. Just leave. Get on the road, stick out your thumb, and take off.

The shy, go-with-the-flow part of her wanted to run away, to just forget all about this one and go find a new cowboy to have an adventure with. But the stubborn princess part of her, the brave, lively part that had gotten her this far, balked.

She was tired of letting men tell her what to do. Tired of letting other people dictate the path she should take in life. She was tired of being a reactionary. It was time to become an activist, to take a role in creating her own future. At least, that is, for the next six weeks. She didn't have to leave Jubilee just because Brady was here. She wasn't going to allow herself to be chased away by some virgin-phobic horse-whispering cowboy.

This was the right place and she was staying put whether Brady Talmadge liked it or not.

CHAPTER SIX

You might be a princess if . . . you're involved in a prearranged marriage.

Annie dreamed that Teddy had come looking for her like Lord Farquaad in *Shrek* and brought the national band of Dubinstein along with him in his search. The orchestra kept playing "Bang the Drum Slowly," but she couldn't figure out how the Dubinstein band knew the Emmylou Harris song.

Then she realized the banging was coming from outside her head. She opened her eyes and stared up at the ceiling, blinking. Where was she?

The banging noise continued.

Who and what was that? She sat up, clutching the sheet to her breasts, and remembered everything that had happened—or rather had not happened—the night before. Her cheeks heated. She'd thrown herself at Brady and he'd rejected her because she was a virgin.

"Rousting you, Talmadge," came a masculine

voice from outside the trailer. "It's almost six A.M. Get your lazy ass up."

Lady Astor sprang from her spot on the small sofa and barked sharply. From the back of the trailer, Trampas joined in, letting loose with a loud *woof, woof, woof.*

Annie looked down to see Brady struggling to his feet. His hair was mussed, his eyes narrowed with sleep. He wore nothing but his underwear. His chest was gloriously muscled. Her gaze hooked on that broad expanse of skin and she could not look away, but then he turned and she got a good view of his bare back.

Annie sucked in her breath and plastered a hand over her mouth to keep from crying out. There were numerous old scars running the length of his back as if he'd been repeatedly beaten with something. What in God's name had happened to him? She fisted her hands. She wanted to assault the person who had assaulted him.

Yawning, Brady grabbed at his T-shirt from the floor and shimmied into a pair of blue jeans as the banging continued. He had not noticed she'd seen his savaged back. Lady Astor and Trampas kept up their racket.

"Talmadge!"

"Who is that man and why is he intent on waking the dead?" Annie asked.

"That's my friend Joe. Get dressed and come out to meet him," Brady said, doing up the buttons on the cowboy shirt he threw on over the tee and headed outside.

After the door slammed shut behind him, Annie

heard the sound of males greeting each other in that good-natured, insulting way they had.

"What the hell happened to you, Talmadge? You look like hammered dog crap."

"Hey, at least I've got an excuse. I got in late. Didn't get much sleep."

"What's with the slice and dice on your face?"

"This? You should see the other guy."

Annie pulled back the curtain of the tiny window and peered out into the sleepy blue-tinged dawn to see Brady playfully punching the upper arm of a man about his own size and age. The man wore a black cowboy hat and he punched back. They exchanged a flurry of feigned blows. Annie rolled her eyes. Men. Apparently, they were the same the world over, little more than overgrown boys.

She scrambled from the bed, quickly got dressed, brushed her teeth, and ran a hand through her spiky hair. The haircut felt strange, alien. She put on the cowboy boots Echo had bought for her, leashed Lady Astor, and went outside.

"Whoa!" the man exclaimed when Annie emerged from the trailer. "You didn't tell me you had company."

Brady looked chagrined, waved a hand. "Joe Daniels, Annie Coste. Annie, Joe."

"Delighted to meet you," she said.

One glance told her Joe Daniels liked Wrangler jeans, bull riding, sunshine, horses, and his friend Brady. He doffed his cowboy hat and bowed in an exaggerated gesture.

He knows I am a princess! For one brief second panic flooded her. Then she realized it was simply

Joe's teasing, gentlemanly way. He wasn't bowing to her royalty. He would have bowed to any woman popping out of Brady's trailer.

"Mornin', Annie. I'm sorry for pounding on the trailer. I had no idea there was a lady inside," Joe apologized.

"It is all right."

Lady Astor, not one to be ignored, was tugging on the leash trying to get to Joe. The bold little Yorkie loved most everyone, especially the attention they bestowed on her.

"Why, aren't you cute." Joe squatted to scratch Lady Astor behind the ears. She preened like the prima donna she was, turning in circles just to impress him. "What does Trampas think about you?"

"He's stone cold in love," Brady said, "but Lady Astor hates his shaggy self."

"Lady Astor?" Joe smiled.

"Believe me, that daring bit of fluff thinks she's royalty."

Joe straightened. "Got up this morning and saw your trailer. Mariah thought you might want a home-cooked breakfast so I'm inviting you over."

"Is Mariah doing the cooking?" Brady asked suspiciously.

"Don't worry." Joe chuckled. "Your stomach is safe. Since we had Jonah we've hired a housekeeper who does all the cooking. Mariah has enough on her plate with the baby and the weddings. She's shorthanded at the shop."

"Joe's wife, Mariah, is a wedding planner," Brady explained to Annie. "She runs her own business here in Jubilee."

"Is she seeking for someone to hire?" Annie blurted, not even knowing she was going to say it. She wanted a job. Part of the adventure of living like a normal person was having a regular job to go to, open a bank account, rent her own place, do all the things regular people did. "I need a job."

She cringed at her own words. She sounded so desperate.

You are settling too soon. You took the first ride anyone offered. You attempted to seduce the first cowboy you met. Now you are trying to claim the first job opportunity that comes along. Do not let your eagerness lead you to the wrong place with the wrong people.

But Joe looked like a nice man. He had a big, welcoming smile and a firm handshake. His arms were burdened with muscles, his jaw clean-shaven. If his wife was half as nice as he was, Annie would love working for her.

"Do you have experience in wedding planning?" Joe asked.

"No, but I am a willing learner."

Joe plastered a palm to the nape of his neck and Annie realized she'd put him on the spot. "I'll let you talk to Mariah about that. Come on up to the house. You can meet her. Have some breakfast."

"We'll be there as soon as we give the dogs their breakfast," Brady said.

Joe nodded and headed back to the big ranch-style house. Annie hadn't been able to see it in the dark last night, but in soft colors of dawn, their house was something right out of a cowboy movie. Constructed from limestone and accented with wood finishes, the sprawling hacienda had a clay tile roof, an elevated stone porch, and a wide veranda with hanging baskets filled with colorful plants.

Her blood stirred. Yes. This was it. There was nothing wrong with taking advantage of whatever opportunity came her way. Here she was, at the home of a real-life cowboy. There were a lot of small buildings scattered around—sheds and barns and a bunkhouse and a corral. Curly-haired red and white cattle grazed in a nearby pasture. The air smelled fresh and clean. The ground was still soggy from the heavy rains.

Without speaking to each other, she and Brady let Lady Astor and Trampas do their morning business, fed them, and then put them back up inside the trailer. She cast several sidelong looks Brady's way, but she said nothing. She did not want to stir up fresh conversation about her virginity,

They walked to Joe's house for breakfast. Annie wanted to tuck the Yorkie in her satchel and take her inside with her, but she didn't know how Mariah Daniels felt about animals in the house. She was trying to be more considerate of what other people thought. When you were a princess, people did what you wanted. It was easy to become self-centered like her stepmother, Queen Birgit. It was a fate Annie was determined to avoid.

After their walk through the field, mud clung to their boots. They scraped them on the boot scraper provided on the front porch for that service. Once their boots were clean of mud, Brady rang the doorbell.

A petite young blond woman, a good three inches shorter than Annie's own five-foot-four stature, met them at the door with a grinning baby cocked on her hip, a teething biscuit clutched in his hand. She wore a pair of faded blue jeans and a red scoop neck shirt and she was barefoot. Her toenails were painted a pearlescent peach.

Annie studied the woman with her blond hair pulled back into a ponytail and felt an immediate twinge of regret. She missed her own long blond hair, but knew she had no choice but to whack it off and change the color if she wanted to stay incognito. She could not run the risk of having anyone recognize her as the Princess of Monesta.

"Good morning, good morning, it's great to meet you." She shook Annie's hand, ushered them inside. "I'm Mariah."

"Annie." She smiled, feeling shy.

"And you, cowboy." Mariah went up on tiptoes to wrap her free arm around Brady's neck and tugged his head down to kiss him on the cheek. "Long time no see, stranger."

"I've been busy."

"You could have called. There's this modern invention called a telephone. Ever heard of it?"

Sheepishly, Brady ducked his head. "I know, I know."

"C'mon in. Ruby is making breakfast." Mariah guided them through the house.

They passed through the living room. The television was tuned to early morning news. Annie barely glanced at the screen, but startled and took a second glance when she realized it was her face flashed on the screen. Instantly, she stilled. Her disappearance had already made the news? She had not expected this. Would she be recognized here?

"Princess Annabella of Monesta was taken ill last night," the newscaster said, "at the home of former president Glover. She was in town for the wedding of his daughter, Echo. It's reported the princess has mononucleosis and has been advised against flying home in her delicate condition. She will recover at the president's compound. In other news . . ."

"The poor princess," Mariah said. "Can you imagine? Falling ill in a foreign country. She's got to be feeling homesick."

No, that wasn't what she was feeling. Not at all.

Chandler and Strawn were handling this exactly as Princess Ann's handlers dealt with *her* escapades in *Roman Holiday*. By denying she'd run away and blaming her absence on illness. Annie imagined her bodyguards had lied to her father as well. If they told him they'd lost the princess, they'd immediately lose their jobs.

"Annie?" Mariah touched her shoulder. "This way."

She took a breath and followed her hostess into the kitchen. Saffron light poured through the French doors casting the ginger terrazzo tile in a cheery, good morning glow. Wonderful smells coaxed them to the table—garlic, onions, bacon, and coffee. Annie's stomach rumbled. Many hours had passed since the truck stop chili and banana cream pie.

"Sit, sit," Mariah invited as she fastened the baby into his high chair and took a seat beside her son.

Joe moved behind his wife's chair and paused to drop a kiss on the top of her head. Mariah glanced up at him, a happy smile on her face.

The housekeeper brought food to the table. Platters

of meat, eggs, and pancakes. Annie's mouth watered.

"Let's say grace," Joe said.

Annie was confused for a moment until everyone bowed their heads and joined hands, Ruby included. Oh, they were offering a prayer of thanksgiving for their food.

Brady reached for Annie's hand on one side, Mariah's on the other. As Joe said the blessing an unexpected happiness curled inside her. This was what it was like to be a normal person. Friends and family sitting around the table, holding hands in thanksgiving for the food before them.

Usually, Annie took breakfast alone in her room, brought up the stairs for her by one of the servants. She ate at her desk while flipping through a book or surfing the Internet or staring out the window at the people walking along the seawall.

Her father and stepmother shared their meals in their apartment on the opposite side of the palace on the days, that is, when they were even in Monesta. They spent a lot of time in Birgit's home country of Denmark. A nanny ate with Annie's nine-year-old half brother, Prince Henry, in his wing of the palace. Annie could go days without running into her father, stepmother, or brother.

Once she got to Dubinstein her life would be much the same. She and Teddy would not be sharing a bedroom. She would have her own quarters and Teddy would visit her boudoir on nights his libido drove him there. Annie opened her eyes even though Joe wasn't finished with the blessing and looked around at the little group. Sadness pulled her shoulders into a slump and longing formed a knot of self-pity in the bottom of her stomach. She could never have something like this long-term.

Just be thankful you have it now. For this sweet moment. Savor it to remember later.

"Amen," Joe said.

"Amen," everyone else echoed, and Annie joined in.

Baby Jonah cooed and banged on the tray of his high chair with a spoon. Little yellow ducks paraded across his bib. Thin wisps of light brown hair stuck up on his head and he had big eyes like his mother.

"Scrambled eggs coming right up, little mister," his mother said, and put a small bowl of eggs in front of him.

Jonah immediately grabbed a fistful in both hands.

"Just like his daddy," Mariah said with love in her voice as she caught her husband's eye. "Grabbing for life full throttle."

Joe grinned at his wife. Mariah silently mouthed, *I love you.*

Annie felt as if she and Brady were intruding on a private moment. Then it occurred to her that she would never have this kind of intimacy with Teddy. Pushing aside the unsettling thought, she dipped her head and concentrated on the food.

"Little Bit," Joe said.

"Uh-huh," Mariah answered, spooning applesauce into their son's mouth. Jonah cooed, spewing applesauce on his bib, and then laughed as if it was the funniest thing ever.

"Annie here is looking for a job. I told her you were shorthanded at the shop." Joe poured maple syrup over his waffles.

"Really?" Mariah's head came up and her smile widened. "Do you have any experience in planning weddings, Annie?"

No. Not even her own wedding. Protocol and a royal wedding planner dictated the details of her nuptials to Teddy. Annie had not gotten much of a vote on anything. Not that she really wanted one. Whenever she tried to offer an opinion it had been vetoed, usually by Birgit, who, unasked, had assumed the role of mother of the bride.

"No," she admitted.

"What kind of job experience do you have?" Mariah asked.

This was the part of her adventure she hadn't been looking forward to. Applying for a job. While she wanted to work, she had no idea how to make the job search happen. "I have been at university."

"What's your degree in?" Mariah studied her with a discerning eye, and for one startling moment, Annie feared she would see right through her.

"I have a PhD in the comparative literature of the American Southwest."

"You have a PhD?" Brady's jaw dropped.

"I do."

"That explains the soiled dove reference," Brady muttered.

"Soiled doves? I'm confused." Joe scratched his head.

"It is unimportant to the topic at hand. My knowledge of soiled doves does not enhance my qualifications to plan weddings," Annie said.

"A PhD in comparative literature of the America Southwest," Mariah echoed, looking underwhelmed with her qualifications but trying not to show it. "Well, that's quite an accomplishment."

Yes. A degree that prepared one for no career at all beyond teaching comparative literature, and Annie had not gone for a teaching certificate. She had no need for one. She had a trust fund from her mother. She received a monthly stipend of forty thousand dollars. She didn't need to work. Which was the reason that she so badly *wanted* to do so.

On the whole, when she got to Dubinstein as Teddy's princess she would be a figurehead. Expected to do nothing more than charity work, attend political events, and produce heirs for Teddy.

"What jobs did you hold down while you were in college?" Mariah asked brightly.

"I was . . . um . . . fortunate enough not to have to work," Annie explained.

The surprise on Mariah's face said it all. "You've never held a job?"

Annie shook her head. "I feel it is long past time for me to get started."

"Hey, you've got all your life to work. Don't feel badly about getting a late start." Mariah reached across the table to pat her hand. "How long are you planning on staying in Jubilee?"

Annie was afraid that if she told her the truth Mariah would not give her the job. Who wanted an assistant who would be in town for only six weeks? But she really needed this job. She'd left herself with no out, bringing only five hundred dollars, a change of clothes, and Lady Astor. She was determined not to return home early if she could help it. "I am not sure."

Mariah considered this a moment, while at the same time tearing a waffle into bite-sized pieces with her fingers before passing it over to her son, who was busy decorating his hair with applesauce. "I could use a gofer."

"A gopher?" Annie wrinkled her brow, not understanding the idiom.

"An assistant," Mariah amended. "Someone to run errands."

"That would be grand." Annie clasped her hands together. "Brilliant. Thank you."

"I'm afraid the position doesn't pay much. Ten dollars an hour."

"I'll take it!" Immediately Annie realized she'd made a mistake. Mariah was going to ask for a social security number or a green card or some kind of proof of her identity.

"I admire your enthusiasm," Mariah said. "Can you start tomorrow at ten?"

"Mmm." Annie stalled. "Is there any way you can pay me cash?"

"You mean under the table?"

Annie nodded.

Mariah hesitated. "You don't want me to report your income to the IRS?"

"It's not that I want to avoid taxes," Annie hedged.

Mariah lowered her voice. "Are you in some kind of trouble?"

Annie glanced down at her hands. She hadn't fully thought this whole thing through. Mariah was clearly an ethical woman. She wasn't going to pay her under the table. "I can't take the job, can I?"

Mariah laid a gentle hand on Annie's forearm. "I've had some tough times myself," she said. "I tell you what. I hold off filing the paperwork, just until you've had a chance to get on your feet. After that, I'll have to have a social security number and I'll have to report your pay. If you can solve your issues by then, you've got a job."

"Thank you," Annie said. "Thank you so very much."

Mariah shifted her gaze to Brady, then back to Annie. "Will you be staying with Brady in his trailer?"

"Oh no," she said so swiftly everyone at the table whipped their heads around to glance at her. "Brady just gave me a ride. We're not . . . that is . . . um . . . he's not . . ."

"Annie needs her own space," Brady rushed to say.

He seemed awfully anxious to get rid of her. Which was good of course, she did not want to spend another night in that cramped little trailer with him. But her feelings *were* a bit hurt.

"Do you know of anyone who is renting out a room?" Annie asked.

Mariah leaned over to pick up the bits of egg that the baby had knocked onto the floor, and then she glanced over at her husband.

Joe shrugged, apparently reading her mind. "It's your cabin."

"There is a cabin at the back of our property. It's not much to brag about, but it does have a new roof and a fresh paint job. You're welcome to stay there."

"How much is the rent?" Annie asked, suddenly aware that her adventure included finding a place to live that she could afford on a salary of ten dollars an hour. She'd never had to think about money before. It was fun and scary, exhilarating and nerve-wracking all at the same time.

"The place is just sitting empty, it might as well have someone living in it. You can have it as part of your salary compensation," Mariah said.

Gratitude welled up inside her. "Really?"

Mariah looked at Annie with such kindness that she immediately felt terrible for lying to this nice woman. "Sure. Just pay the electricity bill."

"Thank you so very much."

"You're welcome. After we finish breakfast, I'll take you over to the cabin and you can get settled in. And you, mister," Mariah said, turning her attention to Brady. "You don't have to stay in your trailer unless you want to. There's a perfectly good guest bedroom going to waste upstairs."

"You know me, Mariah," Brady said. "The lone wolf."

Mariah rolled her eyes, whispered behind her hand to Annie. "He just wants you to feel sorry for him."

"I do not," Brady protested. "I simply like my privacy."

"Then why didn't you just say that?" Mariah teased.

A few minutes later, after Ruby had cleared the breakfast dishes and Mariah had cleaned up her son, they drove to the modest, one-bedroom log cabin that sat a half mile from the main house. The entire place was smaller than Annie's walk-in closet at the palace, but she loved it the minute she saw it.

Behind the cabin was a large building. Mariah told her that it used to be a horse barn but it had been converted into a reception hall for the cowboy weddings that took place in the small, white clapboard chapel that stood underneath an old oak tree several yards away. The branches were so expansive it reminded Annie of the tree that had once grown outside her bedroom window. A quarter mile beyond the chapel lay another building, a corral and a big gateway arch with a hand-etched wooden sign declaring: "The Dutch Callahan Equine Center."

"I lived in this cabin when I first came to Jubilee," Mariah said. "You should have seen it then. The place was falling in."

"It is very quaint," Annie said, admiring the antique rocker on the front porch as they climbed the steps.

"Quaint wasn't the first thought that popped into my head, but if that works for you . . ." Mariah had Jonah balanced on her hip and she pulled a key from the pocket of her blue jeans to unlock the door.

The house smelled dusty, but it was tidy. The furniture was old, the kitchen tiny.

Dark wood paneling covered one wall, a double window was seated in another.

Perfect. It was absolutely perfect. This was what she'd been searching for. Cramped, age-scarred, earthy, rustic. She could find herself here. Unfurl, blossom. She was a tight rosebud hungering for this sandy soil to open, spew fragrance, bloom. Six weeks. She had six weeks to flower, and her transformation started now. Annie could not wait.

Mariah wrinkled her nose, went over to draw

the curtains, and cracked open the window. Jonah reached up to grab a fistful of his mother's ponytail, and she didn't even flinch. A mom, accustomed to the tugging. "I didn't realize how stuffy it was in here."

Annie gazed out at the pasture beyond, saw soft green rolling hills, horses and cattle grazing. Not the sea view she had from her bedroom window in Monesta, but beautiful simply because it was not. "It is lovely, truly."

"Lovely?" Mariah chuckled. "You have a generous definition of lovely."

"What is not to love? Cowboys and ranches. Animals and pasture. Clear blue skies."

"It's really quiet here. Most people don't like this kind of quiet."

"And yet Jubilee is the cutting horse capital of the world, is it not?"

"It is. You'll find out soon enough the full extent of that."

Annie cocked her head. "Tell me."

"We're talking cutting horses, 24/7, 365."

Annie frowned. "I do not understand."

"Folks around here are ate up with horses." Mariah put a hand to her forehead. "Oh listen to me, I'm talking like them now."

"Who?"

"Texans." Mariah laughed. "I learned how to fit in so well, I've picked up their speech."

"You are not a Texan?"

"Well, I was born here, but raised in Chicago. Acclimating was a bit of an adjustment at first."

"What does the expression 'ate up' mean?"

"Consumed. The raising and showing of cutting

horses consumes this town. As I said, you'll see for yourself soon enough and then the next thing you know you'll be talking like them too."

"This is good." Annie hugged herself. "I am ate up with happiness."

Mariah laughed. "You're very easy to please."

"'Life is a grand adventure or it is nothing at all.'"

"Helen Keller, right?"

"Yes." Annie smiled. Mariah was sharp. "Yes, Helen Keller."

"Where have you been living?" Mariah untangled her son's fist from her hair. "Scratch that. It's none of my business."

"Scratch that?" Annie did not understand the expression.

"Forget I asked the question."

"Oh yes, of course."

Mariah canted her head and studied Annie so long that she started to worry she had egg on her face or that somehow Mariah had recognized her in spite of her close-cropped hair dyed black. "How long have you known Brady?"

"We met last night."

"Where at?"

"A place called Toad's Big Rigs."

"A truck stop. You met at a truck stop?"

"We did. Is that bad?"

"Nooo. It's as good a place as any to meet, I suppose."

"We had chili. It was quite good, but not cold at all."

"Brady ate truck stop chili?" Mariah sounded shocked.

"He doesn't eat truck stop chili?"

Mariah shook her head. "It's one of his unbreakable rules."

"Unbreakable rules?"

"Brady's got a code he lives by. To avoid complications."

"A code." Annie clapped her hands. "I like a man with a code."

Mariah looked at her funny.

You have to tone it down. Try a little better to fit in. You are going to start raising suspicion. You have said too much. Gone over the edge. If you want to fit in, speak less, observe more. You are good at observing and keeping quiet.

It dawned on Annie that the reason she never spoke up to her father, had never really made herself heard or her needs known was that she had always felt as if she was not royalty material. That if she upset the applecart he would send her away. Even before her mother had died, Annie had felt this way. She could not even say why. Perhaps it was the high expectations placed on her. Expectations she seemed incapable of living up to. Maybe that was why she already liked it here so much. No one expected anything from her.

Mariah led her down the short, narrow hallway, opened the door to the single bedroom. "It's only got a twin bed. I hope that'll do. I'll send Ruby over to freshen the place up for you."

"No, no. I *want* to do it."

Mariah gave her another odd look. "Okay."

"Thank you," Annie said. "Thank you so much for giving me a job and a place to stay. I am forever in your debt."

"You're welcome," Mariah said, then paused. "Word to the wise, when it comes to Brady, be careful."

Uneasy goose bumps raised on her forearms. Was Mariah going to tell her something scary about Brady? "Careful?"

"He's one of those easygoing guys and he makes you think troubles just roll off his back. He's an optimist, with an infectious laugh, quick metabolism, and a big heart even though he won't admit it. He's been hurt a lot in the past and he won't admit that either. And the reason he hates people who keep secrets is because he's got a few of his own that he's pretty ashamed of."

"Are you warning me off?"

"Nope," Mariah said cheerfully, laying a firm hand on her shoulder and giving off whiffs of baby oil, applesauce, and scrambled eggs, a smell that announced, *I'm a mom.* "This is a promise. You hurt Brady and you're going to have to answer to the whole town of Jubilee."

"I would never hurt Brady. It is not my intention to hurt him. I know he is a good man. The last thing I want is to hurt him."

"I'm sure that's true," Mariah said. "But I had to put that out there. Just in case."

Mariah rattled her, but Annie shook it off. She envied Brady that he had friends who loved him so much that they worried about his choice in women.

And in spite of the fact that Mariah had basically threatened her if she hurt Brady, she really liked the woman.

Jonah fussed and yanked at his mother's ponytail again.

"What is it, tiny cowboy? Do you have a dirty diaper?" Mariah put her nose to the backside of his elastic-waisted denim pants. "Phew! My stinky boy."

This motherhood business had an unsavory side. Then again, so did pet ownership. Messiness and love seemed to go hand in hand.

"Tell you what," Mariah said, "let me get this little guy cleaned up and turned over to Ruby, then I'll take you with me into Jubilee. My crew and I have got a wedding here on the ranch at six this evening and there's the usual last-minute rush, but if you want to hang out in the background, you're more than welcome to see what my Saturdays are like."

"I would love that," Annie said. "I just need to check on my dog first. She is locked up in Brady's trailer."

"Hey, leave her in the house with Ruby. She loves dogs as much as she loves kids."

"Are you sure?"

"Absolutely. The more the merrier."

Annie smiled. Even though she did not have any definitive plans, everything seemed to be unfolding organically. In just over twelve hours from the time she had given her handlers the slip, she had hitched a ride with a handsome cowboy, almost lost her virginity, landed a job, and acquired a place to live. It seemed too easy. And that was sort of taking the fun out of it.

If Rosalind were here, she'd say, *Never trust what comes too easily. There is always a catch.*

Rosalind.

Oh goodness. She had forgotten to call Rosalind.

CHAPTER SEVEN

You might be a princess if . . . you're from a land far, far away.

S o," Joe said as he and Brady walked to the horse barn after Mariah took Annie to the cabin. "Annie Coste."

"Gorgeous morning." Brady took a deep breath of fresh air, inhaled his favorite scent—horses.

"Who is she?"

"It's good to be back in Jubilee. Didn't realize how much I missed it."

"You've never brought a woman around to meet us. What's special about this one?"

"Did I mention how darn good it was to see you again?"

"You're bordering on keeping a secret, Talmadge."

Joe knew how to get to him. Apparently, his buddy wasn't going to let him off the hook. "I gave her a ride last night. End of story."

"No, oh no. Please don't tell me that you picked up a hitchhiker."

Brady shrugged. "Tell me about Miracle. What happened to your prizewinning horse?"

"After what happened to you four years ago, I can't believe you picked up a hitchhiker."

"I'm here to help Miracle, not talk about my stupidity."

"You broke two of your own rules. Never pick up a hitchhiker and avoid damsels in distress. How did this happen?"

"You don't know the half of it," Brady mumbled, thinking of all the rules he'd broken. Dammit, why had he told Joe about his unbreakable rules?

Um, because you were sharing whiskey shots during Dutch Callahan's wake. Drunken grief. Common mistake.

"Excuse me?" Joe cupped a hand around his ear.

"I said I'm sorry to hear about Miracle."

That got Joe away from the topic of Brady's foolish rule breaking. "Yeah." His voice cracked and his eyes clouded with pain and remorse. "All my hopes are pinned on you. I'm at the end of my rope. The vets threw up their hands. They'd doctored his wounds. He healed physically, but mentally? Nothing's worked. If Dutch were alive . . ." He paused, and then went on to tell Brady in specific detail all the techniques they had tried on the horse.

"I'll do the best I can. Miracle is a special horse. He's got the spirit to pull through."

Joe opened the barn door. They walked inside and Joe escorted him to a dark stall at the back. "I keep him out of the light. It calms him."

The minute Brady touched the stall door, he felt the prizewinning quarter horse's pain. Miracle was backed in hard against the far wall, trembling like a newborn foal.

"It breaks . . . my heart." Joe's words came out cobbled, clotted.

"Tell me again what happened," Brady murmured, studying the once beautiful animal through the slates in the stall. Miracle's eyes were wide, fearful. His neck was nicked with scars. Brady's own heart ached for what the stallion had gone through. He could see trauma in his eyes.

"It's been almost four months now," Joe said. "I thought he would get better with time, but he's more isolated than ever."

"Tell me about that night." Brady knew this was tough for his buddy to talk about, but if he was going to help Miracle, he had to know everything.

"We were coming back from a futurity. Cordy and I," Joe said, referring to his ranch foreman. Joe hauled in an audible breath, rested his arms on the bar of the stall, rested his chin on his arms, and gazed regretfully at Miracle.

The cutting horse had once belonged to their mentor, Dutch Callahan. Before Dutch died, he traded Joe the stallion for the small section of Green Ridge Ranch where the old ranch hand cabin stood. Mariah had inherited Dutch's land, and that's how she and Joe had met. That same year Miracle had gone on to win a four-hundred-thousand-dollar purse in the Triple Crown Futurity in Fort Worth.

"This was in February?"

"Valentine's Day. I was driving too fast, hurrying home to Mariah. I had a special evening all planned—" Joe broke off.

"Best-laid plans." Brady shook his head.

"It had started to sleet. I hit a patch of black ice and it was all over. The truck skidded and the trailer jackknifed. The next thing I knew we were on our side in the ditch. Cordy and I were trapped. We couldn't get out of the truck, but we could hear Miracle in the back screaming in pain. It was the most awful, gut-wrenching sound I've ever heard." Joe shuddered.

Brady made sympathetic noises. He knew what a tormented horse sounded like.

"I had a concussion and I kept blacking out. Cordy had a broken arm. Nobody came by on the road. Damn weather had kept everyone indoors. We couldn't find our cell phones. We were there for hours." He gritted his teeth. "Finally an old farmer came by. He called 911. The rescue squad showed up pretty quickly after that, but the firemen insisted on getting us out first. By the time we were freed and ran back to the trailer, we couldn't get the doors open. Miracle was wild, kicking, thrashing, and crying out in pain. It was the most horrible thing I ever witnessed save for when Lee Turpin burned down my barn and Clover died saving the horses."

That had been a dark day for Jubilee. Brady hadn't been in town when it had happened, but he'd admired and respected Clover Dempsey, and her loss had been almost as acute as Dutch Callahan's. Clover had been like a second mother to him.

"The firemen went to work on the trailer but it still took them another half hour to free Miracle."

"What happened to him physically?" Brady asked, his gaze never leaving the horse, who was pressed as close to the far wall as he could get, keeping his face turned away from them.

"No broken bones, thank God. He had torn ligaments in two knees and he was cut up pretty badly, but he's been skittish as hell ever since. Whenever we try to saddle him, he goes crazy, bucking and biting, eyes rolling wild. I can't do anything to reassure him or make him better. I feel like I failed him on the most basic level. I didn't keep him safe. It—" Joe broke off.

Brady reached over and clasped Joe's shoulder. "It's okay. We're going to get your horse back for you."

"I don't care if he ever competes again. I just want him to be his old self. Miracle was a thing of beauty. I never met a horse with such spirit."

"I won't stop until he's healed."

"I'll pay whatever it costs."

"It's not about the money," Brady said. "I just want to see Miracle reborn."

"Thank God you're here. I've missed the hell out of you, you ol' reprobate." Joe gave him a quick hug, patted him on the back.

"Who me?" Brady teased, happy to shift the tone of the conversation.

"So, Annie."

"Yep."

"You broke your unbreakable rules."

"Back to that, are we?" Except he didn't mind so much this time. If razzing him would take Joe's mind off Miracle's plight for a few minutes, Brady would happily put up with it.

"Hey, for what it's worth, I think Annie's really nice and she's pretty darn easy on the eyes."

"I don't recall asking your opinion."

"You know, I wouldn't hate it if you finally decided to settle down. Make Jubilee your permanent home. You know you can always come work for me."

"Thanks for the offer, but it's never going to happen, my friend. Footloose and fancy-free. That's me."

"Never say never," Joe said. "You should add that to your list of unbreakable rules."

"Yeah, well . . ." Brady tipped his Stetson back on his head. "Why don't we start work on Miracle?"

"Today?"

"You got more important things to do?"

Joe swallowed, toed the dirt with the tip of his boot. "I'm scared, Brady."

"I know."

"What if you can't fix him?"

"My cure rate is ninety percent."

"What if he's in the ten percent you can't help?"

"Stop borrowing trouble, and get me a rope. I'm cocky enough to know I'm good. He's going to be healed."

Joe straightened and nodded. "I'll be right back."

He went to the tack room, and Brady turned his attention back to the horse. "Your name's not Miracle for nothing, right? We're gonna get you through this, buddy."

Brady jiggered the metal clasp up and pushed the stall door open.

Miracle chuffed in a heavy breath. The hair along his spine rose. His nostrils twitched. His forelock quivered.

Brady stepped back and waited. From his peripheral vision, he saw Joe standing off to one side, a coiled lariat in his hand. Oftentimes owners acted like idiots, running up, getting in his way, not listening to Brady's advice, but his friend knew horses. And he knew Brady, so Joe didn't interfere. Didn't even speak.

A moment of atypical self-doubt took hold of him. What if he couldn't fix Miracle? His talent with horses was natural. God-given. He didn't plan it. He didn't advertise his skills. All his business came through word of mouth and that's how he liked to operate. Nothing formal. Nothing set in stone. Just free and easy. He'd done nothing to earn his good fortune, although he learned as much as he could about horses. Brady ran strictly on pure instinct. It was the way he lived his life. Spontaneous. Organic. And everything had always worked out.

But now, with Joe looking on, it occurred to him he had a helluva big ego, claiming he could heal a horse ninety percent of the time. It was true, but maybe he was just the luckiest son of a bitch on earth.

Miracle flattened his ears against his head, and his mouth pulled back to show his teeth in a horsey version of a snarl. The morning sun sloped through the open barn door, casting shadows over the animal.

"Let's ease off." Brady took a few steps back and accepted the rope from Joe. "We'll give him a straight shot toward the corral, then you close the barn door when he's clear of it."

Joe nodded and they moved aside, closing the other doors so that only the one leading directly into the corral remained open. Then they stepped outside the barn and waited.

Within seconds Miracle burst from the barn into the corral at a full charge, head tossed high, snorting like a steam engine. Joe ran to shut the door behind the stallion, leaving Brady alone in the ring with him. The sky was fresh and filled with cotton-puff clouds after yesterday's rain.

Brady stood loose-limbed and relaxed, the rope resting lightly against the fingers of his right hand. He controlled his breathing, keeping it slow and even. Miracle ran nervously around the ring, tossing his head, kicking up mud. Brady stayed stationary in the middle of the corral, calm, passive, waiting.

Miracle kept running, gaining speed, going faster and faster around until Brady felt dizzy just watching him. That was good. Let the horse play himself out. Expend that nervous energy. Joe was sitting on the fence beside the barn, a tense expression on his face. Brady understood how anxious his friend was, but Joe had unwittingly been transferring *his* disquiet onto Miracle.

A vehicle drove up into the yard, tires crunching on gravel. Car doors shut and he heard murmured voices, but Brady did not turn to look to see who had arrived; every bit of his attention was focused on the task at hand.

After a long while, Miracle finally slowed, his flanks heaving. The stallion stopped a few feet away, nervously eyeing Brady and the rope in his hand. He nickered and started backing up.

"It's okay, boy. We're not doing anything today except getting to know each other. You run all you want and I'll just stand here with this rope. Not going to touch you. Not going to rush you."

As if he understood what Brady had said, Miracle started a fresh round of sprints, while Brady stood like a touchstone in the middle of the ring, releasing all tension from his body, keeping his mind empty of any thoughts except those of quiet healing.

When the horse slowed again, Brady signaled to Joe. "That's enough for one day."

Joe opened the door.

Brady eased toward Miracle.

The horse skittered away from him, skirting around Joe, and rushed back to the safety of the barn. Brady trailed after him, following Miracle until he returned to his stall. Once the stall door closed tight after the stallion, he handed the rope back to Joe. "It's going to take a few days, but your horse is going to be fine. Nothing to worry about."

"Really?" Joe expelled a long-held breath. "How do you know?"

"That horse knows he's loved. He's just lost his way. All we have to do is show him how to get back home."

They left the barn and as they walked outside, Brady saw that it was Mariah, Jonah, and Annie who had driven up, and they'd been standing outside the corral the whole time, watching him with Miracle.

Mariah looked concerned and she went straight to Joe, but it was Annie who captured Brady's attention.

She was standing beside the wooden fence, her gaze fixed on his, her face alight with quiet reverence and a soft, encouraging smile.

And Brady had a powerful, perplexing urge to turn tail and run.

It was just after nine in the morning as Mariah and Annie drove into Jubilee. Past all the cowboy/cutting horse–related businesses. The feed store, the farrier, the farm and ranch supply, the First Horseman's Bank of Jubilee, Western Wear Palooza, the Mesquite Spit barbecue restaurant. All foreign—and therefore mesmerizing—establishments to Annie.

Mariah parked Joe's extended cab King Ranch Ford pickup in a circular lot of one of the four parking areas that formed a cloverleaf pattern around the limestone building of the county courthouse. They got out and made their way to Mariah's shop on the corner of Main Street and John Wayne Boulevard.

"There is a street in this town named for a cowboy actor?" Annie asked.

"Oh yeah. There's John Wayne Boulevard and Slim Pickens Parkway and Tom Mix Lane and Rory Calhoun Circle."

Annie laughed. "I love it!"

"Quaint R Us."

"Excuse me?"

Mariah waved a hand. "Never mind. That's me being silly. Don't worry. You'll pick up on the lingo around here soon enough. You *are* staying awhile?"

"For a while," she echoed.

Annie absorbed her surroundings. The town square had been constructed in the late 1800s (which compared to the buildings and landmarks in Monesta were quite young and new) and the town had preserved the old Western façade. The buildings were all limestone and completely square. The flat roofs had wooden awnings stretched out over the sidewalks to shade pedestrians. Crepe myrtle bushes were everywhere—white, lavender, pink, red. There were no parking meters on the square and most of the parking spaces were taken by pickup trucks or SUVs. She was not accustomed to seeing such large vehicles. Most people in Annie's home country got around on bicycles or motor scooters or in fuel-efficient minicars.

Everything in Texas seemed oversized. It made her feel tiny, insignificant, unimportant, and to Annie's surprise, she enjoyed the sensation.

"Howdy," they were greeted repeatedly, most people calling Mariah by name. Gentlemen tipped their hats. Ladies wriggled their fingers in a wave.

"This is a very friendly place," Annie observed.

"Very. Much different from where I grew up." Mariah chuckled.

"Big city versus small town."

"You'll see the difference soon enough. Where are you from?"

Annie hesitated. She didn't want to lie, but she couldn't come out and tell Mariah the truth, so she hedged. "A small place." That was true enough. The entire country of Monesta was about the same size as the city of Dallas.

"So you should feel right at home here," Mariah said. "There's just something about cowboys that makes a woman feel welcome."

"I love cowboys," Annie admitted.

"Cowboys *are* something else." Mariah sighed dreamily. "But they have their challenges as well."

"Which are?"

"For the most part, they tend to be the strong, silent types."

"This is bad?"

"Only if you're in a relationship with one and you have the normal feminine urge to discuss your feelings."

"I see."

"That sounds bad, doesn't it? I didn't mean it as a bad thing. In fact, speaking in generalities of course, a cowboy doesn't have to tell you what he's feeling. He shows it by his actions. You can count on a cowboy. They'll be there for you through thick and thin. And although they might not talk much, when they do talk, you know it's because they truly have something to say."

"This is how it is between you and Joe?"

"Yes."

"How long have you been married?"

"It'll be two years in December. I can't believe it's been that long because it feels like two minutes."

"You have a happy life."

"Very. I've been blessed."

"You have a beautiful family."

"Thank you. We've been talking about having another baby, but this thing with Miracle—"

"Miracle?"

"The horse Brady is working with. Miracle is Joe's prizewinning cutting horse. He was injured in an accident on Valentine's Day and he hasn't been the same since. Joe is grieving that horse something fierce."

Across the street, on the corner in front of the

UPS shipping store, was an old-style pay phone. Not that she had ever used a pay phone herself, but she'd seen them on television. What luck! Whenever she got a chance, she could slip away and call Rosalind from the pay phone. It would be difficult to trace her through a pay phone.

They reached Mariah's shop with the whimsical name, The Bride Wore Cowboy Boots.

"That is an unusual name for a wedding planning business," Annie said.

"I specialize in cowboy-style weddings. Business is thriving. We've got people driving out from Fort Worth and Dallas and beyond for real cowboy-style weddings."

"I am intrigued."

"I'll show you inside. Introduce you to the crew. It's going to be kind of crazy in here, but it's a good chaos. You'll get used to it," Mariah assured her.

Mariah was right. The minute they entered the building, a pert red-haired woman, wearing her hair in braided pigtails, the way Annie had worn her hair when she was six years old, came running up. She had on a crinkly purple skirt—broomstick skirts, Annie believed they were called from her readings on cowboy culture—a bright orange, puffy sleeved blouse with wooden buttons in the shape of cow horns, and a pair of hunter green cowboy boots. She had cinnamon-colored freckles sprinkled over the bridge of her pug nose.

"Howdy," she said to Annie, and then immediately turned to Mariah. "The bride has changed her mind. She's decided she wants tussy-mussies instead of arm sheath bouquets for the bridesmaids. Where are we going to get five tussy-mussies at this late date? What are we gonna do?"

"Prissy," Mariah said in a calm voice. "Take a deep breath."

Prissy obeyed.

"This is Annie, she's going to be working with us starting Monday. Today, she's just going to hang out and observe."

"I am delighted to make your acquaintance, Prissy," Annie held out her hands as she had been trained in a proper princess handshake designed to show deference, respect, and caring.

Prissy ignored the handshake and instead enveloped Annie in a big hug. "Pleased ta meet ya."

Annie was caught off guard by Prissy's enthusiasm, but luckily Prissy had already swung her attention back to Mariah. "The tussy-mussies?"

"What do we specialize in?" Mariah asked.

"Cowboy weddings."

"So think about it a minute. We've got the long-stemmed flowers for a sheath spray. Tussy-mussies are nothing more than cone-shaped vases with ring chains for easy carrying. Given those two parameters, what could we use to quickly make inexpensive tussy-mussies?"

Prissy's eyes lit up as she followed Mariah's line of reasoning. "Horse training cones. The small ones."

"Clever woman," Mariah praised. "What could we use for the ring chains?"

"Loose ring snaffle bits!" Prissy crowed.

"And how do we make the cones look elegant?"

"Gold foil?"

"Absolutely, and perhaps some white lace streamer ribbons."

"I'm on it." Prissy beamed and took off.

Mariah's aplomb and quick thinking impressed Annie. Plus, she admired how she'd guided Prissy to the answer and made her feel good about herself.

The office was small. Just the front desk where Prissy had been sitting, a small bistro table and chairs with sample books, and a computer for Internet searches. The walls were decorated with photographs of simple yet elegant cowboy-themed weddings.

This was the kind of wedding Annie wanted. Uncomplicated white dress made of a natural silk. Instead, her dress was a rococo monstrosity made of satin organza with heavy beading, an excess of hand-tatted lace, and a thousand-mile train. She wished she could hold her wedding in a simple white chapel instead of an ornate cathedral. Dreamed of riding away on a horse instead of in a Bugatti.

A set of double doors led to backroom storage. That's where they found another employee.

"Morning, Lissette," Mariah greeted the woman who was crouched searching through a box on a bottom shelf. "Need help?"

Lissette raised her head. Her dark brown hair was pulled up in a bun, but numerous corkscrew tendrils escaped to frame her face. She wore a yellow and white sundress and matching yellow sandals. She sported a French pedicure and a gold ankle bracelet. "Coffee and lots of it."

"I'll make a run to the Java Hut. What's up?"

"I dropped the cake topper last night and broke it," Lissette said. "I was hoping we had a similar replacement to save me a trip into Fort Worth."

"We should have something."

"I thought so too, but I can't seem to find it. Then again, I'm so sleep deprived it could be right in front of me and I'm just not seeing it. Kyle's not sleeping on a regular schedule and I ended up having to finish the cake at three in this morning, hence the fumble fingers and brain drain."

"After this wedding is over," Mariah said, "we are all going out. Joe's got VIP seating for the Fort Worth Chisholm Trail Rodeo tomorrow night. You need a break and some fun with Jake before he ships out again. Ruby will be happy to watch Kyle. I pay her triple time after hours. The woman is pure gold."

"That sounds wonderful." Lissette sighed wistfully. "Thank you so much for the offer."

"Kyle is Lissette's two-year-old son," Mariah explained to Annie. "And her husband, Jake, is going back for his third tour in the Middle East. Afghanistan this time."

Lissette pressed her lips into a straight line and Annie could see unshed tears glistening in her eyes. She did not want her husband to return to war.

"Lissette, this is Annie. I hired her to help out around here."

"Hello," Lissette said, as reserved as Prissy had been exuberant. "Welcome aboard."

"Thank you. I am delighted to meet you." Annie didn't miss the quick look Lissette darted Mariah's way. A look that said, *Where did you find this character?*

"Annie is a friend of Brady's," Mariah said in explanation of Lissette's unasked question.

Annie was fully aware she did not fit in. She was doing her best. Her mother had started her on elocution lessons when she was six so that her speech would sound neutral and as sophisticated as possible. Her father had kept up the tutoring after Queen Evangeline had passed away.

"You are a princess," King Phillip had said on more than one occasion. "You must sound like one as well."

Sometimes, Annie felt that with all the lessons and the tutoring and the coaching and the rules to follow, her essential self had been buried deep and she had no idea who she really was anymore. Honestly, had she ever known? She was merely an image of what other people wanted her to be.

Loneliness pushed at her. "I can retrieve coffee from the Java Hut for you, if it is near enough to walk," Annie offered. Not only would it give her time to clear her head, but going for coffee would allow her the opportunity to use the pay phone across the street and call Rosalind.

"That would be great." Mariah pulled a ten-dollar bill from her purse. "I'd like a small soy latte. Lissette?"

"Straight up large black coffee," Lissette said. "House blend is fine."

"Prissy," Mariah called out. "Annie's making a coffee run. Do you want something?"

"Blended iced mocha," Prissy called back.

"Where is the Java Hut located?" Annie asked.

"The block behind this one." Mariah pointed. "Get yourself something as well."

Annie did not drink coffee, but perhaps they would have hot tea. "I will return shortly."

"You're a life saver," Lissette said, and went back to searching for a replacement cake topper.

Feeling like a furtive sneak thief, even though she had no reason to feel that way, Annie left the shop and went straight to the pay phone. She dug the coins from her satchel, deposited them into the pay phone, and punched in Rosalind's phone number. The connection was spotty. The phone line crackled and hissed.

"Annabella, it is so good to hear from you," Rosalind said. "How is the bride-to-be? Is she nervous? What time is it there? How long before the ceremony?"

So much had happened since she'd run away from the presidential compound yesterday evening during the wedding rehearsal dinner that she'd forgotten Echo's wedding was still several hours away.

Apparently, Chandler and Strawn had not yet told her father the mononucleosis story, so Annie didn't say anything about it either. "Echo looks beautiful," she said. That was true. Then she went into details about the former president's ranch and the elaborate wedding preparations.

"I wish I could be there with you. You know how much I love cowboys."

"You would love it here," Annie said, looking

around at the myriad of men in cowboy hats strolling the street. "You must come to Texas one day."

"Why would I ever leave Monesta?"

"There is a whole big world out here to explore," Annie said. "You're still young enough. Just barely past forty."

"When would I have a chance?" Rosalind paused. "Unless you have decided not to take me with you to Dubinstein to care for the children you will have with Prince Theodore."

"Of course I am taking you with me." That is if Teddy still wanted her when she came back home. The thought that he might reject her because of her adventuresome exploration made her smile.

For the first time, Annie considered that maybe she had an ulterior motive by embarking on this adventure, a motive hidden even to herself. She had convinced herself she wanted nothing more than to live life like a normal person. Have a real job. Earn her own money. Make her own friends. Take care of herself. This was about independence and self-esteem.

But what if it was more than that? What if, because of her striking out on her own, Teddy deemed her unworthy of being his wife? They'd never spoken of her virginity. It had been a given. The royal physician had confirmed it.

Was this what she had secretly been shooting for all along? Was that why she really wanted to go off on her own? As a way to get out of the arranged marriage?

That is quite passive/aggressive, Annabella.

She recalled the previous night. Thought of what passed between her and Brady. If Teddy knew about that, he would be appalled. It was a deal breaker. Grounds to call off the wedding. Would he?

Annie smiled and her heart lifted. Yes. That was what she wanted. Only she hadn't been able to tell her father this to his face. He was a strong, domineering man, and in all honesty, she was a little afraid of him. He'd never hit her or spoken cruelly to her, but neither had he shown her a great deal of affection, and when Henry had arrived, it was as if she was nothing more than a means to unite Monesta with Dubinstein. She had spent her life under her father's thumb, in his shadow, and she could not deny him anything. But if she were to "ruin" herself and Teddy broke things off, then it was out of her hands.

No, this had not been a calculated plan, but if the outcome got her out of her impending marriage, it would make her a very happy woman.

"Annabella?"

"I am still here. Just know . . . just know . . ."

"Yes?"

"I love you," she said breathlessly. "I love you more than . . ." How could she say she loved Rosalind more than she had ever loved her own parents? It was a betrayal. It was disloyal. And it was the truth.

"Please deposit two more dollars," came an automated voice over the pay phone.

Annie dug into her satchel. She did not have two more dollars in change. "I have to go, Rosalind. Just know that I am safe. Nothing untoward has happened to me."

"Something is wrong. You sound odd. What is it, child?"

But she never got to answer. The connection snapped off and she was left holding the receiver and feeling like something monumental had changed inside her. Like a ship breaking from its mooring and set adrift on the sea. No structure, no guide, just wide-open space around her. She could go anywhere. Be anyone. Do anything.

Starting over fresh with a clean slate was enormously appealing. The idea tempted. What if she could stay Annie Coste forever? It was a silly fantasy, but she did not want to let go of it.

She thought of Princess Ann's reasons for her hiatus in *Roman Holiday*. The screenwriters had glossed over her deeper motivations. And she'd run away for only a day. A twenty-four-hour fling had sated Annie's role model. But one day was not nearly enough for Annie. In fact, she hadn't been gone for even a full twenty-four hours and her eyes had already been opened to so many new things. How wretched to have her eyes opened, and then never to be able to hold on to the wonders that she saw.

Misery slumped her shoulders. Would her departure from the straight and narrow path make going back to her old life that much more difficult?

And Brady? Where and how did he figure into all this?

Not knowing what was going to happen, but realizing she had already put something in motion that could not be undone, Annie hung up the receiver. Her heart was alternately both heavy and light as she meandered down the street in search of the Java Hut.

She found the coffee shop a few minutes later, stood in line for her order. *Look at me. Here I am, queuing up for coffee like a regular person.* A small thrill ran through her. She ducked her head and grinned.

Feeling very proud of herself, she carried the drinks in a cardboard container toward the exit. A cowboy held the door open for her, tipped his hat, smiled. "Howdy."

"Thank you." She smiled. A giddy sense of adventure boosted her sagging spirits. She had to live in the moment. It was the only way she could truly enjoy her time in Jubilee.

Back out on the street, she headed for the corner, the morning sun warm on her face. The air smelled of yeast bread from the bakery at the end of the block. Snatches of conversation from passersby filled her ears. Talk of horses mostly. Happiness tasted like honey on the tip of her tongue.

That is, until she rounded the corner.

There, at the intersection between John Wayne Boulevard and Bridle Lane, a long black limo sat at the traffic light.

Her heart catapulted into her throat. She stopped in her tracks. Somehow, Chandler and Strawn had tracked her to Jubilee. All they had to do was turn their heads and see her. Panic slipped hot through her veins. She glanced right, and then left. Spied a hiding place in a thin alley running behind a Western furniture store.

The rational part of her brain said: *You don't look*

like yourself. Short, black hair. Cowgirl clothes. Fetching coffee. They probably wouldn't recognize you. Not at this distance.

But she didn't want to take that chance. Not when she'd just begun to unfurl her wings.

She dived for the safety of the alley.

Great, run. Call attention to yourself.

The tip of her cowboy boot hung on an irregular edge of a paver stone sticking up from the edge of the sidewalk. The cardboard carton of coffee and tea flew from her arms. She stuck out her hands to brace herself as hot liquid splashed her. Her knees hit the paver stones. Thank heavens for the thick denim of her jeans.

She lay on the ground, palms stinging and feeling like a fool. Mariah had given her a simple assignment and she had made a big mistake.

"Miss? Are you all right?" It was Chandler's voice. "We saw you take a tumble."

She didn't dare look back, but she heard the limo engine purring at the curb directly behind her, felt the heat of her bodyguard's gaze on her spine. Without answering, she leaped to her feet and raced down the alley as fast as her legs would carry her. Thrilled to escape, but terrified that it was only a short-lived reprieve.

Her handlers had already tracked her to Jubilee. It was only a matter of time before they figured out what she was pretending to be.

CHAPTER EIGHT

You might be a princess if . . . you're embarrassed
by public displays of affection.

While Annie spent Saturday observing the
staff of The Bride Wore Cowboy Boots
put on a stylish Western wedding, Brady
helped Joe out around the ranch. To his relief, Joe
did not bring up Annie's name again. Unfortunately,
Brady's brain refused him the same courtesy.

When he was exercising the horses, instead of
thinking of ways to rehabilitate Miracle, as he
should have been, Brady's mind conjured pictures
of Annie. How she'd looked last night in his bed.
How soft her skin felt beneath his skin. How sweet
her lips had tasted. The image of her supple, naked
body had been branded on the backs of his eyelids.
All he had to do was close his eyes and *poof*, there
she was.

When the work was done, Brady and Joe sat on
the front porch sharing a beer and watching the cars
go by on the road to the wedding chapel. Ruby had

gone home for the evening and Jonah was curled up in his father's lap, sleepy-eyed and sucking on his thumb. Trampas was lying on the floor between their rocking chairs. Lady Astor rooted around in Mariah's flowerbed, looking muddy and happy.

"What happened to your face?" Joe asked, motioning to Brady's cut.

Brady told him about the fight in the truck stop parking lot.

"Ever the white knight, huh?"

"As if you have any room to talk." Brady snorted. He nodded in the direction of Mariah's wedding chapel.

"Point taken," Joe conceded, tipping his porch chair back on two legs and resting his booted feet on the porch railing.

"I guess protecting women is just the cowboy way."

The cottonwood trees rustled their leaves overhead and sunlight trickled through a dappled pattern over the flagstone walkway. A long, companionable moment passed.

"Ever thought about staying a little longer?" Joe asked.

"And do what?"

"Work for me. I need someone to run the equine center we built in Dutch's honor for disadvantaged youths. You're as good with kids as you are with horses."

"Me?" Brady hooted. "Good with kids? Where did you get that idea?"

Joe pointed at Jonah, who was staring at Brady as if hypnotized. "You've got that low, deep, soothing voice."

"I don't know a damn thing about kids."

"But you know about horses. Give it some thought."

Yeah, work for Joe while Annie was working for Mariah? Right. That was too close for comfort. "You couldn't begin to pay me what I'm worth," Brady quipped.

"That's true, but there's nothing that says you can't have people bring their injured horses to you. No reason you always have to go to them."

"You know it's easier on the horses for me to go to them than for them to come to me."

Joe shrugged. "It was just a thought. I'd like to see more of you. I miss you."

"Aw, now, don't go getting all girly touchy-feely on me. Next thing you know you'll be asking if I got a spare tampon you can borrow."

Joe reached over and punched him on the arm.

Brady grinned, took another sip of beer, noticed the parade of vehicles that kept motoring past the house. "Mariah sure has made a go of her wedding planning business."

"I'm damn proud of her."

"I'm happy you and Mariah found each other. After you lost Becca, you were a train wreck. You worried the hell out of me."

"Now who needs a tampon?"

"To good women." Brady held out his beer and they toasted, clinking the necks of their bottles together.

"A bunch of us are going to the rodeo tomorrow. It's the last day. Why don't you come along?" Joe asked. "Mariah's inviting Annie."

Annie. "Look, there's nothing going on between us? I just gave her a ride and place to sleep last night. That's it."

"So you won't mind then if she comes along? She's new in town and Mariah doesn't want to leave her on her own."

"When did you and Mariah have an in-depth conversation about Annie's well-being?"

"It's called a cell phone, buddy. Text messaging."

"You guys aren't trying to play matchmaker, are you? Because you know how I feel about settling down."

Joe shifted Jonah in his lap. The baby had fallen asleep. "You say that now, but things can change in a blink of an eye."

"Yeah, well, not everyone is cut out for marriage and fatherhood. Some of us had pretty bad examples."

"So, the rodeo. Last performance is tomorrow afternoon at five. You and Annie can ride with Mariah and me."

Annie and those honeysuckle lips. Annie, the vulnerable virgin with secrets.

For some unfathomable reason, Brady shrugged and said, "Okay."

By the following afternoon Annie had started to relax a bit after almost being caught by her body-guards for the second time since she ran away, even though she tensed every time she heard an unexpected noise. Mariah had given Annie an odd look when she'd returned to the office, splashed head to toe in coffee.

She had apologized profusely for dropping their

order, but Mariah had waved away her protests with
a smile and took her over to Western Wear Palooza
for a new outfit. Annie bought a pair of black jeans
and a blue poplin blouse with a fitted waist.

Now, here they were at Will Rogers Coliseum,
Annie wearing her new outfit, getting her first taste
of a rodeo. For years, she dreamed of seeing a rodeo
in person. Everywhere she looked she saw cowboy
hats and cowboy boots and big shiny belt buckles
and Wrangler blue jeans.

Annie shivered happily, feeling completely at
home. How was it she felt more at home in Jubilee, Texas, than she did at Farrington Palace? She
vowed to savor every second because she knew at
any moment Chandler and Strawn could appear
again, and this time, she might not be so lucky in
evading them.

Because Joe was a former bull riding rodeo champion, he had scored a VIP box for the rodeo. Annie,
of course, was accustomed to grand treatment, and
in all honesty, she would have preferred to sit with
the hoi polloi. She already knew what the view
looked like from the top and she took advantageous
event seating for granted, but Prissy and her husband, Paul, could talk of nothing but the front row
seating as they walked into Will Rogers Coliseum.

Prissy was dressed just as eclectically today as
she'd been dressed the day before, and she chattered
nonstop. Paul was as quiet as his colorful wife was
exuberant. Annie learned that he had recently returned from a second tour in Afghanistan and was
on medical leave, having lost the hearing in one ear
from being too near a bomb blast.

Once they were inside, Prissy was immediately drawn to a kiosk selling souvenirs, and Paul trailed after her.

"I'm just going to pop into the ladies' room," Mariah told Joe. "Annie, you want to come?"

Annie nodded, followed Mariah into the ladies' room.

"Paul's the sweetest guy you'll ever meet," Mariah filled her in. "Loyal as a border collie but with the energy level of a basset hound."

"Good combination." Annie chuckled.

"I'm happy Paul's stateside again. He's hoping to get stationed at Fort Hood. Of course, that would mean I'd lose Prissy if they moved to Killeen, but who I'm really worried about is Lissette."

"What is bothering Lissette?" Annie asked, washing her hands at the sink while Mariah ran a brush through her hair at the mirror. Lissette and her husband, Jake, were meeting up with them a little later.

"Jake keeps signing up to go back to the Middle East. His time was up. He'd served his country, done his due. Lissette thought he was going to get out of the army and then he reupped without telling her."

"Why?"

"Jake lost his best friend in the Towers on 9/11. He can't seem to let it go. He ships out again next week."

"How is it that they don't live near an army base?"

"Killeen is only a couple of hours away and Lissette preferred to live in Jake's hometown while he's gone. Jubilee is halfway between her folks' place in Dallas and the army base, and Jake's mom lives here too. But I worry about Lissette's son, Kyle."

"What is the matter with Kyle?"

Mariah lowered her voice, glanced over her shoulder to see who might be in the ladies' room with them, but they were alone. "I think the child might be autistic, but Lissette is having trouble facing that possibility. My heart just aches for her. She's such a talented baker. She used to be a pastry chef before she married Jake. She's changed so much over the last few months and not in a good way."

"I am sorry to hear of this." Annie could not think of anything else to say, she did not really know any of these people, but she understood that it was often easier to talk to a stranger about personal concerns. Even though she felt odd hearing about Lissette's difficulties, it made her feel good that Mariah trusted her enough to share this information.

They left the ladies' room to find Brady, Joe, Prissy, and Paul waiting outside the door talking to a couple Annie hadn't yet met.

Prissy had a brand-new purple cowboy hat perched on her head. "Look what Paul bought me." She grinned.

Rosalind would have said Prissy's taste was all in her mouth, but Annie liked Prissy's unabashed individuality. She didn't seem to care what anyone thought. It was a frame of mind Annie envied.

Beside Prissy stood a black-haired woman as tall as Joe and Brady. She was wire thin but muscular, and she patrolled her gaze over Annie like she was frisking her. The man she was with was closer to Annie's height than the Amazon's.

He wore a big smile and a bigger Stetson. His eyes crinkled up into joyous slits the minute he saw her.

When he smiled, he looked a bit like a younger version of the country-and-western singer Clint Black.

"Hi," he said. "I'm Cordy Whiteside, Joe's ranch foreman. I missed meeting you yesterday and this is . . ." He paused to sling his arm around the tall woman's waist. "My fiancée, Ila Brackeen." Cordy puffed his chest out proudly. "She's a deputy for the Parker County Sheriff's Department."

Annie could picture that. She pitied the criminal who ran up against the formidable Ila.

The crowd was growing. As more people came streaming through the door, the group shifted toward the back wall to get out of the main flow of foot traffic.

Ila nodded at Annie. "Nice to meet you. I do advise against hitchhiking."

Annie looked at Brady. "You were quite serious about the no-secrets thing, were you not?"

Brady shrugged. "I warned you."

"His brutal honesty is both his greatest strength and his biggest flaw," Ila said to Annie, then to Brady, she said, "I also advised against picking up hitchhikers. But I guess it's a good thing neither one of you followed that advice or you wouldn't be here together."

"Here we are. Sorry we're late." Lissette came rushing up, tugging on the arm of an arrestingly handsome man striding behind her. He had a military buzz cut, broad shoulders, and piercing blue eyes.

"I just realized, we've got half of the Jubilee Cutters Co-op right here. Who's watching the horses?" Cordy teased.

"The other half," Joe said.

"Cutters Co-op?" Annie repeated, feeling dumb and out of the loop. "What's that?"

"We all belong to a group that takes care of each other's ranches and horses when we're out of town," Ila explained.

"Along the line of house sitting?" Annie asked.

"Except more work."

"Why do you do it?"

Ila gave her a weird look. "Because we're like family. Families look out for each other."

"Oh." Annie felt like a girl alone in a hot air balloon with a spent pilot light, frantically cutting sandbags to keep her dream afloat. No matter how much she might wish it were so, she wasn't a part of their warm community, and it made her exquisitely sad.

"Well, everyone's here now," Mariah said. "Let's go find our seats. The rodeo is about to start."

Joe led the way and everyone paired off to follow him. Brady came up behind Annie and put a hand to the small of her back. It felt startlingly sweet, the familiarity of his touch.

He guided her up the steep steps of Will Rogers Coliseum. Below, the arena stretched out with clean, fresh dirt. The smell of beer and popcorn filled her nose.

"Can we get popcorn?" she asked Brady.

"Once we find our seats I'll go back for it."

She smiled at the joy skipping through her, but Queen Evangeline's voice drowned it out. "Filthy concession food. Filthy commoners." Ruthlessly, she shoved her dead mother's voice aside. She was old enough to make up her own mind about people. She could like whatever she wanted to like, and she liked being here with people from the cutters co-op, smelling concession stand food and horses and leather and Brady's tangy aftershave.

"Here are our seats," Mariah called from her place on the steps ahead of them. She moved into the aisle, scooting down to make room for everyone.

Once they were settled, the men went after refreshments, leaving Annie sandwiched between Ila and Mariah, with Lissette and Prissy on the other side of Mariah.

"I am so delighted to be here," Annie exclaimed. "This is just as I imagined."

"You've never been to a rodeo?" Ila sounded shocked.

Annie shook her head. Ila intimidated her a bit. She wondered what the deputy sheriff would think if she knew who Annie really was.

"Where you from?" Ila leaned in close. Her fingernails were clipped short and she had ragged cuticles and wore no nail polish. Annie knew what her mother would have had to say about a woman sheriff and it would not have been complimentary.

"You have such pretty eyes," Annie said. It was true. Ila's eyes were a mesmerizing shade of brown—the color of expensive aged Scotch.

Ila's cheeks pinked. "What?"

"Your eyes are very pretty."

"Thanks." Self-consciously, Ila reached up to brush the fringe of bangs from her eyes. "You cut your hair yourself, didn't you?"

Alarmed, Annie touched her spiky locks. How had the deputy known? Her dread fear was that the sheriff's office had received some kind of all-points bulletin to be on the lookout for a runaway princess and Ila knew all along who she was and was just waiting to trap her. But that was silly. Wasn't it? "I am experimenting with a new look."

To her surprise, Ila nodded. "Been there."

"But your hair is so pretty. Naturally black and straight."

"Comes from my Cherokee heritage," Ila said. "I used to wear it to the middle of my back."

Me too. She had not expected to have anything in common with Ila.

Annie didn't know what else to say, so she focused on watching the helpers rake the dirt smooth in the ring.

"So," Prissy asked. "What's going on with you and Brady?"

This was one thing she had not expected. How inquisitive everyone would be. When you were royalty, people did not go around asking you a lot of questions unless you had granted an interview. Maybe that was the key to dealing with their curiosity. Pretend she was granting an interview. She sat up straighter, rested her hands in her lap. "Nothing is going on."

"C'mon," Lissette said, "we've got eyes. We see the way he looks at you."

Annie's heart fluttered. "What way is that?"

"Like he could eat you up with a long-handled spoon." Prissy readjusted her purple hat.

"What!"

"Prissy, you scared her. Annie isn't from here."

"Where you from?" Prissy asked.

"England," Annie lied just to get them to shut up about it.

"You don't sound like a Brit," Lissette commented. "I spent two years in London when I was in college."

Annie panicked. What was she going to say? Before she could think of a reply, Ila said, "You're the first woman Brady has ever brought around for us to meet."

"He has a lot of women?" Jealousy jabbed at her.

"Depends on what you mean by a lot," Ila said.

Mariah frowned at Ila.

Ila slapped a hand over her mouth. "Forget I said that."

Annie turned to Mariah. "He's had a lot of girl-friends?"

"Brady's really good-looking and he's got the horse whisperer thing going on. He's had his share of girlfriends," Mariah said.

"They don't last," Ila rushed to say.

"Do not concern yourselves. I am not upset by the fact he has been with a lot of women," Annie said.

"You're not?" Mariah canted her head.

"I cannot last either."

"What does that mean?" Lissette asked.

"We are just having fun." Annie rubbed her hands down over her thighs, enjoyed the feel of the stiff denim. She'd never worn blue jeans before coming to Texas, and while she found the material heavy, there was nonetheless something very comfortable about them. She understood why everyone in town wore them. "We are on an adventure."

"Well then, more power to you," Ila said.

"Hey," Mariah said, "here they are."

The guys were back. The women scooted and re-arranged to sit beside their men, each couple pairing off, parceling out beers, colas, hot dogs, cheesy nachos loaded with jalapeños, and roasted peanuts.

"I got you a souvenir program." Jake smiled at Lissette. A look passed between the couple and Annie couldn't help wondering if Jake was giving it to her to commemorate the memory, just in case he didn't come back from Afghanistan. The thought brought a lump to her throat.

Brady handed Annie a bucket of buttery popcorn. The delicious aroma made her nose twitch. "I didn't know if you wanted a beer or not, so I bought a large if you want to share."

She had never drunk beer before either. "You mean drink from the same cup?"

"Is that a problem? I can go back and get you something else."

"No, no, sharing is fine." Sharing was a concept she needed to learn. As an only child—she was already grown by the time Henry came along—she had never had to share anything. She took a sip of the beer. It had a bitter taste she found unexpectedly likable and took another drink, felt foam stick to her upper lip. She patted it off with a napkin.

"Here." Brady took the oversized cup from her and settled it in the cup holder in the arm of the seat and nestled the bucket of popcorn in her lap.

The seats were packed in tightly together and Brady's thigh was pressed against hers. His legs were long and lean and tightly muscled. Annie was acutely aware of him. So aware that she scarcely noticed that the rodeo had begun with the singing of the United States national anthem by country-and-western legend Tanya Tucker.

Then the singing was done and the first bareback bronco rider came shooting from the gate and Annie was transfixed.

This! Oh, this was what she had been hoping to see. What an adventure!

She smiled and reached for a handful of popcorn, and her fingers brushed against Brady's as he reached for popcorn at the same time. This must be exactly what Princess Ann had felt when she'd taken off on that Vespa with Joe Bradley hanging on behind her.

Sheer, unequivocal joy.

He moved his leg, pressing his knee against hers. No accident, that. She tilted her head, cast him a sideways gaze. She wanted this man. She wanted the fantasy, she wanted to experience great sex, she wanted . . .

To be normal.

Annie moistened her lips with a flick of her tongue, heard a small, frustrated noise break from Brady on a long exhale. She darted another glance his way, saw amusement jostle with the hunger in his eyes, and she had a strong feeling that it wasn't popcorn he craved.

Brady had been to the rodeo more times than he could count. As a teen he'd even ridden on the back of an ornery bull a time or two himself. He'd been raised on the lifestyle, and for him, attending a rodeo was as routine as getting a haircut.

Another thrashing horse shot kicking and bouncing from the chute. The crowd cheered, pulling for the rider. Brady wasn't thinking about the cowboy clinging on with all his might, but about the stallion and what the animal was experiencing. How angry and/or scared the horse must be.

He studied Annie, gauging her reaction to the event.

She was captivating. Her breathing grew shallow and she leaned forward, hands curled around the railing in front of them, absorbed everything going on in the arena.

Her hair had been styled, the spiky waves softened into looser curls, and excitement flushed those incredible cheekbones a high pink, almost as if she had a high fever. She wore a form-fitting blue blouse the color of the sky at twilight. The hue accentuated the flecks of blue in her gray eyes and drew his attention to her well-shaped breasts. She had on black denim jeans, and they molded snugly across the curve of her thighs.

His gaze bounced like a super ball from her eyes to her breasts to those honeysuckle lips, then back to the boobs again. He was within inches of actual drooling.

She turned her head and caught him staring.

"Nice top," he said so it wouldn't seem like he was doing exactly what he was doing—staring at her tits.

Buttercup. Bright, saucy, sunny flower.

What had she done to his mind? He couldn't seem to think of anything else. He was a muddled mess and worst of all . . . worst of all . . . he did not care.

He liked being ravenous for her. It made him feel powerful, alive.

Not good. The wheels were coming off his life. He couldn't have been more stalled if the wheels had come off his travel trailer.

He couldn't have been more surprised. This feeling was new to him. Normally, if he felt particularly attracted to a woman, he immediately started getting itchy feet. He was a roamer who liked his space, and anything that smacked of intimacy, he avoided.

His feet remained strangely calm. No familiar restlessness, and that worried him.

I know why you're not itching to run away. She's only passing through, same as you. She's not a threat. That's why you like her more than usual.

Was it? The explanation soothed him and he blew out a relieved breath.

She slanted her head, cocking him a coy smile that made him want to shimmy right out of his pants, fall to his knees, and beg her for sex.

Nope. Can't. Never mind dignity. This one's a virgin. You are not going to have that on your conscience.

The bareback bronco–riding event transitioned into the saddle bronc riding. Wide-eyed as a kid, Annie watched the action as if she'd never seen anything so enthralling.

"Ouch!" She cringed and drew her legs up as if scrambling out of the way of the high-stepping steed when the cowboy was thrown three seconds in.

Prissy laughed and leaned across the seats to touch Annie on the arm. "Don't worry, the horse isn't coming up into the stands."

"I know." Annie wrung her hands. "It just feels too real. That cowboy's got to be hurting in more ways than one."

"You've got too much empathy," Ila said. "You're just like Brady with horses. But while you're feeling sorry for the cowboy, Brady's rooting for the horse."

Annie shot him a look.

Brady shrugged. "What can I say? She's right. I love the rides where the cowboys get thrown before the eight-second buzzer."

"Really?" Annie whispered. "I was rooting for the horse too."

They stared at each other. Annie chewed her bottom lip.

"Don't be nervous," Brady said.

"I'm not nervous," Annie denied, and reached for the beer. The hell she wasn't. He was nervous too.

She looked so sexy, her full pink lips pursed so sweetly. Her hair stuck up in the cutest damn spikes. Funny, he'd never found short hair particularly sexy before, but on Annie, hell, he found everything sexy.

Down at the end of the aisle, Lissette let out a squeal of delight. "Jake!"

Everyone turned to see what was going on. Lissette fanned out three tickets and waved them for the group to see. "For Disney World next summer, and we'll be staying at the Grand Floridian. It's the nicest place at the resort! He hid them in the souvenir program."

"When my final deployment is over," Jake said. "I *am* coming home, darling, and I know how much you've wanted to take Kyle to Disney World. Just hang on one more year. We'll get it done."

Annie put a hand to her mouth and her eyes glistened with tears. Brady leaned over and rested his hand on her knee, felt his own eyes grow a little misty. They smiled at each other, and then both simultaneously looked away.

"Yes, we will," Lissette said, and slid into her husband's lap. She wrapped her arms around his neck, kissed him hard. "And you *will* come home to me, Jacob Ray Moncrief, or I will never, ever forgive you."

"Let's pray like hell he does," Brady murmured to Joe, who was sitting on his right.

"He's making a lot of sacrifices for us all. We have to keep an eye on Lissette and Kyle for him."

"Sure, sure," he said, but that was kind of hard to do when he'd be off on the road again as soon as Miracle was recovered. Guilt chewed on Brady. He admired the hell out of Jake. When his ego got the best of him, he'd do well to remember that as much good as he did healing horses, it was nothing like what Jake did for his country.

Lissette stayed in her husband's lap as the bronco riding ended and team roping took its place. Brady explained the rules of team roping to Annie. She listened, taking it all in. The woman was a sponge. Nothing got by her. She asked sharp, insightful questions.

"So what do you think of Mariah's wedding planning business?" Brady asked during an intermission segment when chuck wagon races kept the audience entertained while the behind-the-scenes activities got ready for the upcoming events. "Are you going to like that kind of work?"

"Mariah is phenomenal," Annie said. "She is a

multitasker of the highest order. I will learn so much from her."

"I'm glad," he said, his gaze hanging on her mouth. Why couldn't he look away?

Why? Because he wanted her. Wanted her bad. Even now the smell of her talcum scent was driving him wild. What he wouldn't give to be a Neanderthal, to be able to sling her over his shoulder and carry her back to his cave.

Dust flew up from the chuck wagon races and the announcer was joking with the drivers. Neither one of them was watching the halftime show. Annie sat with the posture of a Buckingham Palace guard. She reached up to brush aside a tendril of dark hair that had fallen over her forehead. He wished he could see how she looked with her natural hair color.

"So you plan on staying in Jubilee for a while?" he asked.

"A while. How about you?"

"I'll be leaving as soon as Miracle is on the mend."

"How long will that take?"

He shrugged. "Depends."

"You should stay longer."

Tension coiled his muscles. "Why's that?"

"All your friends really like you. I think they miss you when you're not around."

Did they? Brady shrugged. "I have friends in other towns too."

"But none like these."

She was right and that's what made him itchy. He got antsy when people started depending on him long-term—too much pressure, too many expectations. He was scared to death of being tied down.

Or maybe he just didn't want to face his own mortality.

Coward, a voice in the back of his head mocked. Brady knocked the voice down, booted it aside. *Shut up.*

"Tell me something," Annie said.

Brady tightened his jaw. What was she going to ask? "Yeah?"

"Can you really read horses' emotions?"

It wasn't what he expected. "Yes."

"What's on that horse's mind?" she asked, inclining her head toward a muscular paint waiting in the wings for the next event. His ears were up, eyes alert.

"He's a competitor ready to go."

"What about the bucking broncos?"

"Those are wild ponies. Some are frightened, but most are pissed off about being contained and ridden."

"Do you believe in reincarnation?" she asked.

"Do you?"

"I do not know," she said. "But if there was such a thing, I think perhaps you might have been a horse in another life."

He liked the idea of that. "I might have been at that."

"Now for the barrel racing," the announcer came over the loudspeaker. "Our first contestant is Jodi Burnam from Clyde, Texas, riding Dewdrop."

From the far gate, a young woman on a rocket-swift quarter horse burst into the arena. The mare flew around the barrels. Brady slid a glance over at Joe. His first wife, Becca, had died in a riding accident while barrel racing. Joe looked calm, expressionless, but Mariah reached over and slid her hand over his.

"Sweetheart kiss cam!" the announcer cried out.

Brady shifted his gaze to the big screen. A cutout of a heart was superimposed over an elderly couple in the audience. Someone nudged them. They looked up and saw they were on camera.

"Come on, kiss her," the announcer called out.

The elderly gentleman gave a sly grin, took off his hat, covered his and his wife's faces as they kissed behind the hat. That got a cheer from the crowd and a chorus of "awwws."

"What is this?" Annie asked.

"They don't have kiss cam where you're from?" Brady asked.

"No."

"If you're featured on the kiss cam, you're supposed to kiss."

"What is the point?"

"It's fun."

"It seems embarrassing. Kissing in public."

"Um . . . is this the same woman who kissed me in a truck stop restaurant night before last?"

Annie's cheeks flushed. "That was different."

"That was desperation. You were hiding."

"Yes," she admitted.

Brady still had a nosy urge to get to the bottom of what was going on with her. Find out who she was hiding from. He fretted it was an ex-husband or boyfriend bent on doing her harm, but she didn't seem like a woman who'd been abused. Sheltered, yes. Dominated, no. Just who in the hell was she?

While they'd been talking, more barrel racing

competitors had come galloping into the ring. With each new rider was a fresh call of "Kiss cam."

At one point, the camera zoomed in on Jake and Lissette and they gave such a heartfelt, passionate kiss for the camera that the audience broke into applause.

"Kiss cam!" the announcer called out after the final barrel racing competitor while the computer tabulated the scores.

"Brady." Prissy tapped him on the shoulder. "It's you and Annie."

Startled, Brady looked up, saw himself and Annie on the big screen. Annie slunk down in her seat, raised her hands to shield her face.

"Kiss, kiss!" hollered the crowd.

"It's better just to do it and get it over with," Brady told Annie. "The more you resist, the more they insist."

"C'mon," the announcer egged him on. "That's a pretty young lady. Give her a kiss."

Brady shook his head, shrugged.

"Awww." The announcer sounded disappointed.

Then to Brady's shock, Annie straightened, leaned over, and kissed him.

The crowd went wild, hooting and hollering their delight at that turnabout. Brady, however, was too busy enjoying the kiss to care. He'd barely slept a wink last night, lying alone in his trailer recalling what it had been like to lie with Annie beside him.

The kiss brought it all back.

He pulled her across the seat and into his lap. She did not resist and Brady kept right on kissing Annie long after the kiss cam went away.

CHAPTER NINE

You might be a princess if . . . you own a tiara.

Kiss cam. What a delightful concept.

The rest of the rodeo blurred past as Annie sat beside Brady fingering her lips and trying not to smile. She had engaged in behavior unbecoming a princess and she loved it.

Still, it had been dumb. Her face had appeared on the big screen for all to see. What if someone in the audience recognized her as Princess Annabella? One well-placed phone call would end her adventure.

The rodeo concluded at seven-thirty and their group ended up going out of an exit on the opposite side of the coliseum from where they'd entered, and this side of the building bordered fairgrounds.

Annie caught her breath.

Strings of light bulbs decorated the midway—red, yellow, white—burning beacons hanging in the night air. The clatter of the roller coaster cars clacked on the wooden track in an upward chug. Seconds later, the cars plummeted downward, passengers screaming bumptiously. Other rides dipped and swirled and flashed. The Ferris wheel and merry-go-round, Kamikaze and Crazy Wave.

"A carnival!" Annie exclaimed. "You didn't tell me there was a carnival. Oh my, it's a carnival!"

"Comes along with the rodeo every year. You like carnivals? I wouldn't have pegged you for a carnival girl," Brady said.

"Why? Because they're generally dirty and they take your money?"

"Well, yeah. That's exactly what I thought you would think."

"But is that not the appeal?"

"It's always been the appeal for me. Give me dirty and costly and I'm there." He chortled.

"You tease." She poked him in the ribs, surprising herself.

Brady slung an arm over her shoulder. "You make it easy to tease, Buttercup. What do you like best about carnivals?"

"The cotton candy," she said, because honestly, it was the only thing she really knew about carnivals firsthand.

"You don't have to go to a carnival to get cotton candy."

"But we can go, right?"

"Hey, y'all," Brady called over his shoulder to his friends. "Annie wants to go to the carnival. Anyone else up for it?"

"Hell, yeah!" Prissy hooted. "I thought no one would ever ask." She held up a hand to Annie. "Give me some skin, girlfriend."

Annie was not sure what to do.

Prissy kept her palm upraised.

Brady leaned down to whisper in her ear. "She wants you to slap her palm. You know, high five."

Oh yes, that thing ball players did to demonstrate team unity. Tentatively, Annie reached up to slap Prissy's palm.

"That's what I'm talkin' 'bout," Prissy said.

Annie had no idea what the woman was saying fifty percent of the time, but Prissy seemed pleased, so she just smiled. Smiling, she had been groomed, was a princess's preferred default option in situations of ambiguous protocol.

"We really need to be getting home. Kyle can be a handful for a babysitter," Lissette said.

"Come on, honey," Jake coaxed. "It's our last big night out before . . ." He let his words trail off.

Nobody said anything. Jake slung his arm around his wife's shoulder and she tensed visibly. "C'mon . . ."

A muscle in Lissette's jaw twitched, but she nodded. "Okay, we can stay for a little while."

The ten of them entered the fairgrounds, walking two by two, stopping at the admission kiosk to purchase ride tickets.

Antsy to get started, Annie shifted from foot to foot, then heard Queen Evangeline's voice in her head. *A princess does not wriggle and jiggle, Annabella. A princess moves with grace and aplomb. Always.*

No. Not always. Not at a carnival with normal people who were rapidly becoming her friends.

While her mother was alive, whenever Annabella behaved in an unladylike manner, the queen made her stand in the corner on tiptoes with her nose pressed in a circle drawn on the wall. She was not allowed to move her nose outside the circle for ten minutes. If she did, the clock started over.

"I'm going to make you a princess if it's the death of me," her mother would say.

Later, when she suffered leg cramps from the tiptoe standing, Rosalind would massage her calves and sing to her. When charley horses caused Annabella to cry out, Rosalind would say, "It's important to do as the queen says. It's your duty and honor to behave like a princess."

Just thinking about it made Annie stop shuffling.

"Bumper cars. We gotta do this," Cordy enthused.

Ila rolled her eyes. "What is it with guys and bumper cars? The slams? The sparks? The whiplash?"

"Hey," Cordy said, and measured off an inch with his thumb and index finger. "I came this close to winning the state bumper championship at Bumper Cars-o-Rama my junior year in high school. I swear to God, I would have won it if Jeanna Riddle hadn't come strutting by in a micro-mini."

"Old story." Ila sighed.

"I found out later, Max Jeffers hired her to distract me, because he knew I was going to beat his butt."

"We've all heard it." Ila bumped him with her hip.

Cordy took the bump like a boat rolling with the ocean. "I had superior reflexes and Max knew it. Hell, I could rope and brand a calf in under five minutes. Let's see Jeffers do that."

"How many people here have heard this story more than once?" Ila quizzed.

Everyone except Annie raised his hand.

"So," Cordy said, singling out Annie, "Jeanna goes by and I'm a guy, of course I'm looking. You could practically see to London if you get my drift, and wham!"

"Hey look, Cordy, there goes Jeanna right now," Ila said, pointing in the direction of the crowd. "Her skirt's even shorter. This time you can see the Panama Canal."

But Cordy wasn't falling for it. "Max slams into me so hard I go flying over the top of the bumper car."

"Were you hurt?" Annie asked.

"Nooo," Ila pretended to wail, clasped her hands to her face in imitation of Edvard Munch's *The Scream*. "You encouraged him. Never encourage the bumper car story."

Cordy made a face. "I'm just saying—"

"You coulda been a contender," the entire group finished.

"I suppose I have told this story a time or two too many," Cordy conceded. "But Annie's never heard it."

"And now she has." Ila linked her arm through his. "Rather than just talking about your bumper car prowess, why not show us?"

The group moved to line up for the bumper cars.

"You sure you want to do this?" Brady asked Annie.

"Yes, please."

"My friends are a little weird," he said. "I'm sorry that they're weird."

"Do not apologize. I like them very much."

"You fit right in with this bunch, you know." Brady smiled.

That pleased her even more. "Because I am a little weird too?"

"Just like the rest of us."

Annie fell in love with bumper cars as quickly as she lost her heart to kiss cam.

The fun of slamming one's car with a heavy rubber bumper into one's friend's vehicle revved her blood. Sparks skittered along the ceiling as electricity traveled down the flexible poles to power the cars. She battled the steering wheel and squealed each time someone smacked into her.

"What next!" She rubbed her hands together gleefully when the bumper cars ride was over. She glanced around at the rides. There was a big sombrero going around in circles at the same time it swayed up and down. Down the midway lay games of chance and barkers hollering at carnivalgoers, trying to get them to come over and win a giant stuffed animal.

She spied the entrance to a shambled mansion with distorted dimensions. Too big doors, roof pitches high as a witch's hat. "Fright House. What is that?"

"You've never been on a haunted house ride?"

"No."

Brady clucked his tongue. "Such a deprived childhood."

"My parents were very strict."

"No rebellion on your part? No sneaking off?"

"Not until now."

"You never dated a bad boy?"

Annie grinned. "Not until now."

"C'mon. Everyone has to ride through the Fright

House at least once in their lives." Brady took her hand and guided her toward the line where Mariah and Joe, Ila and Cordy, Lissette and Jake were already queuing up.

Prissy and Paul announced that they were going on the Kamikaze.

"I'm not in the mood to throw up," Mariah said, and waved good-bye to them as they strolled off arm in arm.

"We love you," Prissy called to the group over her shoulder. "Just in case you're never seen or heard from again."

"Is it really that scary?" Annie asked as the ride operator directed them to a moving walkway, where they had to hurry to catch one of the two-seated cars with a high, scalloped-shell back.

The minute they sat down, music started playing through speakers piped in through the plush padding. "Werewolves of London."

Chills ran up Annie's arms. Brady pulled her into the crook of his arm as the car jerked forward and entered the dark tunnel.

"If you get scared," Brady said, "just grab on to me."

"That is a pretty corny line."

"So you're not all that innocent, huh?"

"Just because I have been sheltered does not mean I do not know when I am being played."

"Gotcha, but if you do get scared . . ."

Annie laughed. "I know where to grab."

The tunnel was deeply dark. Warren Zevon sang about a werewolf ripping out lungs. Then, suddenly, the undead were popping out at them right and left, up and down. Skeletons fell from closets. Zombies reached out to grab them. Banshees wailed. Vampires lunged. Frankenstein lurched. A headless horseman galloped beside their car. A Gypsy woman's head in a crystal ball swung cackling from the ceiling.

Their car twirled, spun, moved backward. A million giant radioactive green spiders scurried down all sides of the sweaty Fright House walls.

Annie pressed her cheek against Brady's chest and covered her eyes. She could feel the vibration of his chuckle underneath the steady *lub-dub* of his heart. She thought of the scene in *Roman Holiday* where Gregory Peck pretended the Mouth of Truth had bitten off his hand and scared poor Audrey.

What was it with men scaring princesses?

He does not know you are a princess. Remember, this experience is as temporary as a movie. Inhale it. Swallow and it is gone.

A sharp ache of sadness momentarily pushed out the thrill of Fright House, but Annie shrugged it off. She knew when she began this whole adventure that it could not last.

Brady's hand closed over hers. He lowered his head and in the darkness, amid the mechanical screeching of artificial otherworldly creatures and the jaunty strains of "Monster Mash" from the headboard speakers, he kissed her again.

The twirling and swirling was normal. Right? It was a swiveling car in a twisty haunted house. That was why she felt so topsy-turvy. No other reason. It had absolutely nothing to do with Brady's quick, wicked tongue and the long, slow way he wielded it.

His fingertips hooked under her chin. Annie

parted her teeth. He took full advantage. A conqueror invading a new country. She surrendered. Running up the white flag without one sliver of resistance.

Pathetic. She was completely pathetic.

Then the monsters stopped mashing, light vanquished darkness, ghouls ceased screaming, spiders curled up and died.

The car settled. The ride finished. They emerged whole and safe. Sort of.

"Goodness," she said. "That made my blood race."

"Mine too."

"Buy a photo of your Fright House adventure!" commanded a stubby-legged, thirtysomething attendant at the end of the line. He had short, Brillo pad hair that sprang from his head as startling as if he showered with a Tesla coil. "Right over there." He pointed to the photograph kiosk. "Go get it."

Annie started to walk past the man and join the rest of their group waiting for them over at the concession stand, but Brady took her hand and tugged her toward the kiosk. "Don't you want to see our picture?"

"Picture?"

"In the midst of Fright House they snapped our picture."

"Why would they do that?"

"To make money selling souvenir photographs."

"Oh."

"You meant it when you said you'd never been to a carnival or an amusement park."

"Yes."

"I thought you were exaggerating."

"No."

"Let's just see what we looked like in the middle of being terrified. We don't have to buy it if you don't like it."

"All right."

He led her over to the kiosk and they searched through the photographs slowly scrolling over the screen.

"Oh, oh, there we are." She pointed and giggled.

"Dude," said the kid behind the counter. "I'll print you up a copy. Only fifteen bucks."

"Fifteen dollars," Annie said. She wasn't good figuring out American currency and did not know if that was expensive or not, but before she could ask Brady about it, the attendant had already hit the button on the printer.

Brady handed him fifteen dollars.

"I am not even sure I want it," she said.

"Hey, it's a memory. Might be the only picture you'll ever have of us together," he tossed it off casually, but something about his tone punctured her lungs, instantly deflating them like a pinprick to a balloon.

The attendant passed Brady the picture encased in a cheap but cute paper frame of the Fright House background. He handed it to Annie.

In the photograph, she had her eyes clenched closed, her hands gripping the restraining bar as if it were a life preserver, her spiky hair wildly tousled, her mouth open in an ecstatic shriek.

But it was Brady's image that mesmerized her. He was in profile, his gaze clipped to her face; the expression carving his features said, *I want to take this woman to bed*. The heat from his stare blistered her skin. Both now and in the photograph.

Annie raised a hand to her heated cheeks. "You were staring at me."

"Is that a bad thing?"

"You did not even see the ride."

"I saw what I wanted to see."

"You missed out on the experience."

"No, I didn't. The experience was watching you experience Fright House for the first time. Thank you for taking the ride with me."

She beamed at him. "It was fun, was it not?"

"Hollywood could make a movie of it—the thrills, the chills, the kissing. Who should play us?"

She wanted to say Gregory Peck should play him, but the reference was too old and besides he didn't look that much like Peck. She squinted at him, trying to decide which young actor he looked the most like. "Colin Farrell, minus the Irish accent. The dark hair, those soulful eyes."

Brady cocked his head. "You look like someone familiar. I've thought so all along. Audrey Hepburnish."

Annie's breath came out in a hot *whoosh*. Was he going to finally recognize her? Her pulse quickened. No, no. He could not recognize her. Not yet. She wanted—needed more time.

He snapped his fingers. "I know. You look a bit like Carey Mulligan."

Tension leaked from her limbs. "Oh yes. Maybe so. I never thought of it."

"Wispy with a winning smile. Coy but sensible. Smart eyes."

"I am not wispy."

"You're thin as a barbwire fence." He raked a gaze over her body. "You need to eat more banana cream pie."

"You are given to hyperbole. I have hips." She slapped both palms against her derriere.

His smile turned sly. "Yes, yes, you do. Very nice hips, I might add."

She wanted him to stop looking at her. She was afraid he would finally see Princess Annabella beneath the short, black hair. "May we go through the Fright House a second time?"

"I thought you'd never ask."

"And this time you can grab on to me if *you* get scared."

Brady chuckled. "You, Annie Coste, are awesome. The more I hang out with you, the more I want to hang out with you."

"I agree. About hanging out with you I mean."

"This could be seriously habit-forming." He leaned closer.

Annie did not pull away. "Addictive."

"One thing leads to another."

"The next thing you know your friends will be staging an intervention. No more Fright House for Brady and Annie."

"Then come the withdrawal symptoms."

"Ouch. Painful."

"Ah, but the yearning."

"Tragically melancholic. You, sir, are a romantic."

"So we should stop it right now. Let's not take a second turn through the Fright House."

"Or we could just say to hell with it and take the gamble."

"You said hell." Brady looked shocked. "I've never heard you curse."

"You are rubbing off on me. Those bad habits again."

Laughing, they got back in line.

After the second ride through Fright House—this time neither one of them saw the ride, they were too busy kissing—they came out to find their friends had dispersed. Brady got out his cell phone and called Joe. They agreed to meet at the entrance in an hour.

"It's just you and me." He winked.

Annie's mouth went dry. Alone with a cowboy at a carnival. Queen Evangeline would highly disapprove.

"Wanna get some junk food?" He inclined his head toward the concession stand.

"I would love some."

"Name your poison?"

"You sound like a Wild West barkeep."

"Louis L'Amour again?"

"John Wayne Western."

"Turkey leg? Nachos? Fajitas?"

"How about something sweet?"

His eyes lit up. "I'll go for that." It was their turn at the counter. "What'll you have?"

"Cotton candy."

"Really?" He scratched his cheek. "You're full of surprises."

"What's wrong with cotton candy?"

"You seem more like a cherry cheesecake kind of girl to me. Rich and off limits," he said.

"You are on a fishing expedition. Trying to figure out where I am from."

"You," he said, "are too smart for my own good. We'll have one cotton candy, a package of moist wipes, and a large water."

"You expect me to get messy?"

"No, I expect me to get messy. Here. You take the water." He paid for the purchases, and Brady unwrapped the plastic from the cotton candy as they walked away. He plucked a chunk of cotton candy from the pile of pink fluff on the stick. "Open up."

"What?"

"Open up."

"You are going to feed me."

"Please don't tell me that you've never done that either."

"I have told you. I have been seriously deprived. What is the custom?"

"When teens start dating they do dopily romantic stuff like feed each other."

"So this is an accepted courtship ritual?"

"Only when you're into acting like a kid at a carnival. Or . . ." He lowered his voice. "Sex play with food."

Annie shivered. "My, I am getting quite an education."

He dangled the cotton candy in front of her. "Open up."

Annie opened her mouth, felt the spun sugar dissolve instantly on her tongue. It tasted as delicious as she remembered.

"More?"

She opened her mouth.

Brady fed her another mouthful.

"Now," she said, plucking the cotton candy from his hand. "My turn to feed you."

They walked around the fairgrounds feeding each other cotton candy and talking.

"So what else have you never done?" Brady asked.

"It would be easier to ask what I have done."

"What have you done?"

"Acquired my PhD."

"Yeah, let's not talk about that. It makes me feel dumb." He tossed all that was left of the cotton candy—a cardboard tube—into a nearby trash can and opened up one of the premoistened towelettes.

"Where did you go to college?"

"Didn't."

"Oh?"

"And before you ask, I didn't finish high school either. Got my GED though."

"That counts."

"Not really."

"Why did you drop out of high school?"

"I wasn't the studying kind."

"The bad boy we were talking about earlier."

"Not really bad," he said. "I just didn't fit in at home."

Annie knew that feeling. They might be miles apart education-wise, but they had things in common.

Not that it matters. In fact, the less you have in common, the better. This is just going to be a lovely affair. A good time. That adventure you are craving.

"I'm guessing you never played a carnival midway game."

"You would be correct."

Brady stopped in front of a basketball toss. The barker was urging him to come over. Three balls for two dollars. Try his luck. Win a prize.

"Which game would you like to try?"

"Let us select one in which we can compete with each other."

"Like the shooting gallery? Or the water guns and the balloons."

"Yes."

"This way." He ushered her over to the water gun game. People were sitting at stools waiting, while the barker tried to round up more people to get the game going.

"Ooh, I want the red one." Annie plunked down on the stool with a red water gun.

Brady took the stool beside her. "I've got to warn you, when I was a kid, I was wickedly accurate with a water gun."

"I feel led on."

"I'll go easy on you."

"I want to win one of those," Annie said, pointing at a large plastic dog bone chew toy. "For Lady Astor."

"That thing is bigger than your Yorkie."

"So? She's a determined little dog."

"I've noticed."

"Ready?" called out the barker. "On your mark . . ."

Annie readied her gun, closed one eye, sighted the scope. Her target was a red balloon.

"Get set."

She waved a hand at Brady. "You better get into position."

He grinned. Curled his finger around the trigger.

A bell rang and immediately everyone on the stools around them started pumping the squirt gun as hard and fast as they could. Annie shot a quick glance over at Brady; they were neck and neck. "I am going to beat you," she crowed. "I am going to claim that bone."

"Ha! No first timer is going to beat me."

In a syncopated rhythm, they pumped the triggers of their squirt guns, sending cool streams of water jetting through the air into the holes of the round balloons. They were laughing and squirting and Annie couldn't remember when she had ever had this much fun.

Bam!

A balloon popped but it was neither Annie's nor Brady's.

A kid jumped up, did a little victory dance. "I won it, I won it, uh-huh, uh-huh."

"He is a gloaty winner," Annie said, getting up from the stool. "Apparently I am a failure at this."

"Don't blame yourself," Brady teased. "The kid is younger and quicker. Better reflexes. Face it, we're over the hill."

"Speak for yourself." Annie pushed a fallen strand of hair from her eyes, spied a panda bear the size of Bolivia dangling from a hook over at the ring toss game. "Oh look, look." She tugged on Brady's sleeve. "Win that for me."

"You obviously have more confidence in my ring tossing skills than I do."

"Cowboys play horseshoes, do they not?"

"Maybe in your Louis L'Amour Westerns. Not in real life."

"Come on." She reached up to squeeze his biceps. "You've got muscles. You're a natural."

"Tossing a hoop around the neck of a bottle has nothing to do with muscular strength."

"All right. I admit it. I was just trying to butter you up so you would win that panda bear for me."

"What's the attachment to the panda?"

"When I was a girl, the ambass—" Annie broke off. She had just been about to tell him a story of the Chinese ambassador visiting Farrington Palace and bringing with him the present of a stuffed panda bear for her.

"The what?"

"Nothing, never mind."

"You were about to tell me something. I want to hear it."

"Win me the panda bear and I'll consider telling you."

"Okay," he said. "I'll give it a shot."

He spent ten dollars on rings. The barker showed him where he had to land the rings in order to win the panda bear. They were in the dead center of a lot of bottles and they had the widest necks.

"That does not seem fair," Annie said. "It is rigged against winning the big prize."

"Of course it is. That's how a carnival midway works."

"Like casino gambling."

"On a very inexpensive scale. You've been to a casino?"

"With my father."

"Vegas?"

"No."

"Atlantic City?"

"Win me the bear and I will tell you."

"Get ready to part with your secrets, Annie Coste." Brady aimed, let go of the first ring. It bounced off one of the bottles that would have garnered him the panda if it had landed. Annie held her breath. What if he won? Was she really prepared to tell him who she was?

She imagined the expression on his face when he found out. She knew that everything between them would change immediately. No more rodeos. No more carnivals. No more banana cream pie at a truck stop or feeding each other cotton candy. No chance of having sex with him.

He took a second throw.

She crossed her fingers, prayed that he missed.

The ring fell over the neck of a bottle but it was not a prize-winning bottle.

The next ring went wide and the next.

Yes. He only had one ring left. The odds of him winning were very slight indeed. Annie let out her breath.

"This is it, Buttercup. I'm gonna win that panda and you're gonna have to start talking."

He poised, eyeing the bottle. Annie's muscles tensed. He flicked his wrist, released.

The ring flew into the air, flipped once, and landed around the neck of one of the bottles. It had a yellow tag on it.

"We have a winner!" the barker enthused.

"Yes!" Brady pumped his fist. "Hand over the panda."

Perspiration broke out on Annie's forehead. She wasn't ready to tell Brady who she was and ruin everything. She had been having so much fun. Why had she made this stupid bet? Maybe she could lie. Except she was a terrible liar. He would see right through her.

"You owe me some secrets," Brady murmured, his mouth near her ear.

A shiver—part sexual anticipation, part fear—ran through her.

"You didn't win the panda, sir," the barker said.

"What do you mean? The ring landed over the bottle fair and square."

"Your bottle had a yellow tag. Not a cream tag. A cream-colored tag is for the panda."

Brady blew out his breath. "Well, what *did* I win?"

"This, sir." The barker reached under the counter and pulled out a cheap plastic rhinestone-encrusted tiara.

Brady started laughing, leaned over, and settled the tiara on her head. "It's no panda bear, Buttercup, but hell if this doesn't make you a princess in my book."

He slung his arm around her and guided her toward the front gate.

Annie glanced up. Brady looked down. His eyes locked on to hers, dark and intense. His fingers tickled the back of her neck, teasing, stroking. She burrowed against his side, breathed in his scent, and grinned to herself. She was utterly aware of this masculine man. How his full lips tipped up at the corners, how the faint lines at his eyes crinkled, how his warm laugh heated her up inside. For one glorious moment she was completely happy.

And then she spied the men in sunglasses and fedoras.

CHAPTER TEN

You might be a princess if . . . you've never had to work for a living.

Annie tensed beside him, faltered in her step.

"Buttercup?" Brady asked.

She did not answer. Brady followed her gaze. The Blues Brothers.

They'd tracked her here. He didn't know how or why or who. He only knew Annie was trembling.

Instinctively, he tucked her closer to his side. Brady did not understand his impulse. She could have been on the lam from the law. In their suits and Ray-Bans, these guys could surely be FBI. But right or wrong didn't even factor into it. She was threatened and he was going to take up for her.

End of story.

"Easy, Annie," he murmured. "I've got your back. They'll have to go through me to get to you."

"It is not . . . I am not . . ." She wrapped an arm around his waist and said no more.

The Blues Brothers were combing the edges of the

crowd. Smoothly, Brady put a hand to Annie's back and guided her toward a side exit away from the two men. He could feel the snaps of her bra through the thin cotton of her shirt, felt her lungs expand and contract in quick, shallow breaths. He used his body to camouflage her from view in case the men in the fedoras happened to glance his way.

"We gave 'em the slip," he said, stopping a moment to watch the Blues Brothers move in the opposite direction until they were swallowed up in the crowd.

Annie shifted nervously. "Let us depart before they return."

"We have to find Joe and Mariah."

She hitched in a deep breath. Brady peered at her in the light from the Ferris wheel circling on the other side of the chain-link fence. Damn, but she was so beautiful. Just looking at her made it hard for him to think. Her long eyelashes fluttered like a delicate butterfly flitting over a vibrant trumpet vine. He pictured himself holding her in the crook of his arm, depositing kisses on her eyelids, feeling those lashes flicker against his lips. She stirred every lustful impulse in his body and drove him crazy with desire.

"C'mon," he said, escorting her over the asphalt, away from the festivities and toward the other end of the coliseum where they'd parked.

His cell phone rang. He answered it one-handedly, knowing it was Joe. "We're already in the parking lot."

"We'll be right there," Joe said, then hung up.

Brady pocketed his cell.

"I feel so lawless." Annie planted a palm on her

chest and Brady couldn't help checking the place-
ment. Right over one magnificent breast.

"Why's that? Does the law want you? Are those
guys G-men?"

"G-men?"

"FBI."

"No, oh no."

Damn him, he wanted so much to believe her.
"So why the lawlessness?"

"Because being with you makes me feel . . ." Her
cheeks pinked. "As if I'm breaking all the rules."

"What rules?" He laughed, feeling uncertain.

Annie shrugged, sliced a stunningly sexy look his
way. "There is just something about you, Brady Talmadge, that makes my blood sing."

That should have scared him. Any other time,
with anyone else, it would have him backpedaling.
But instead, he thought, *I ache to make you wail
opera all night long. In my bed.*

Her eyes widened and for a second he thought he
said it out loud, but when she slapped her hand over
her mouth, he realized she'd simply shocked herself.
Their gazes locked and he remembered every single
thing about her supple, smooth body. His fingers
tingled, itched to undress her. His mouth hungered
to taste her. His erection surged against the zipper
of his jeans. "I've got a cure for that."

She caught her bottom lip up between her teeth.
"Is it terribly naughty? Your cure?"

Oh yeah.

"Hey, I thought we were supposed to meet up at
the gate," Joe said, ambling up with his arm thrown
over his wife's shoulder.

"Sorry for the miscommunication." Brady shrugged.

"Thank you," Annie whispered, and tightened her grip around his waist. Brady had to admit that the half hug felt pretty darn good.

As Joe unlocked the doors of his pickup truck, Brady leaned over to whisper. "One of these days you're going to have to tell me what's going on."

"One of these days," she promised with a nod.

Jolted, Brady—the guy who preferred to keep his relationships light, easy, and unattached—realized he'd just made future plans with a mysterious woman he barely knew, but couldn't seem to keep his hands off of.

Annie lay in bed in the out-of-the-way cabin listening to the wind whip through the willow trees outside her bedroom window. Lady Astor snuggled beside her. If it weren't for the little dog, she would feel so alone out here, especially after the wonderful evening she had just spent with Brady and his friends. But she had been having so much fun that she had allowed herself to be lured in by a false sense of security. Chandler and Strawn were still after her.

She understood now why Brady had stopped making love to her when he discovered she was a virgin. He was right. It would have meant something. He already meant something to her.

Curling on her side around Lady Astor, Annie whispered, "It's okay. We've got each other. Through thick and thin. It's me and you."

Lady Astor roused, blinked, licked Annie's cheek.

"It's just a sweet dream. I know. Soon enough it will be over. But there's no need for regret. We will remember this time for the rest of our lives."

The Yorkie stretched, shook her head, put a paw on Annie's shoulder.

"Do you need to go outside?"

Lady Astor gave a short bark.

"All right." Annie threw back the covers and Lady Astor dived off the bed. She slipped her feet into slippers and, yawning, shambled for the door. The digital clock on the bedside stand glowed yellow. Two A.M. Tomorrow was her first day on her new job. She was not going to be at her best if she didn't get some sleep soon.

She opened the door and stepped out on the veranda, hugging herself against the tepid breeze. Lady Astor ran down the steps, barking fiercely, and disappeared into the dark. Goose bumps raised on Annie's arms. She'd read stories of Texas. Knew there were rattlesnakes and coyotes and bobcats and other dangers lurking in the brush.

"Lady Astor," she called sharply, her heart racing. "Come back here now."

As usual, the headstrong dog did not obey, she ran like Toto going after a flying monkey. Suddenly, her barking ceased.

Annie's stomach pitched and she scurried after the Yorkie heedless of her own safety. "Lady Astor!" she cried, imagining horrible things. What if an owl had swooped down and snatched the little dog in its talons? "Lady Astor!"

The clouds shifted and the moon came out. A man stepped from the shadows.

Annie halted.

It felt as if those glow-in-the-dark spiders from the Fright House were scrambling over her skin. Was it one of her bodyguards? Had they tracked her from the carnival?

Then she saw that the man had Lady Astor in his arms and the dog was joyfully licking his face with puppy kisses. All her limbs went weak. "Brady," she whispered.

"Did I scare you? I didn't mean to scare you."

"Wh-what are you doing here?"

He set Lady Astor on the ground and she ran circles around him as he ambled closer to Annie. "I couldn't sleep. Thought I'd take a walk."

"I couldn't sleep either."

He kept coming, encroaching on her personal space until the tips of his boots almost touched her house slippers.

"I've been doing a lot of thinking," he said.

She shifted, feeling invaded, but she did not back up. She held her ground. Raised her chin. Summoned every ounce of royal blood she possessed. "Yes?"

"The other night, in my trailer, I made a mistake."

"Oh?" The wind snapped her nightgown, blowing the flimsy material against her breasts, but Brady's eyes did not leave her face. She felt dizzy, giddy.

"If you're still interested in losing your virginity, I'd be honored to . . . Ah crap, this isn't coming out right." He jammed fingers through his hair.

"No, no, you were absolutely right. I understand now what you meant, why you refused me," she said. "It was the right decision."

At the same moment, he said, "What I mean to say is, I want it to be me. I want to be the guy who, you know . . . ushers you to womanhood."

She put two fingers to her mouth to suppress a giggle. "Ushers me to womanhood?"

"See, there's no good way to say this that doesn't sound cheesy or creepy. It's why I've been pacing up and down in the dark trying to get up enough courage to knock on your door."

"But what about my secrets? You told me you don't like secretive people."

"I don't. Normally. But you . . . well, I just want to be with you. Make love to you. I don't care why you've held on to your virginity for so long. I don't care if you're a nun running away from the nunnery. I don't care if you've just escaped from Siberia. I don't care if you got a fatal diagnosis and you've decided to live life to the fullest before you die . . ." He cringed. Brought both hands to the side of his head. "No, no, I don't mean that. I do care. I care very much. I'm mangling this. Let me just leave now and forget this conversation ever happened."

He turned to leave, but she put a restraining hand to his arm. "Wait."

Brady turned back. Hope glimmered in his eyes. "Yes?"

"I want you too."

He inhaled audibly. "Okay, wow, that's great."

"But," she said, "you have to realize that this can't mean anything long-term."

"Because of your secret?"

"Yes. I can only stay in America for six weeks. Are you still interested?"

He looked as if he simultaneously wanted to dance a jig and throw up. "I'm not ready for anything long-term either. But I don't want to sound like a jerk. I don't want to be a jerk. I just can't get you out of my mind."

"I cannot stop thinking about you either."

He took her hand, laced his fingers through hers. "I don't want to do anything to hurt you."

"I feel the same way," she said. "About hurting you, I mean."

"So."

"So."

"Can we do this? Can we make love and not hurt each other?" she whispered.

He nodded. "I think so. If we go into this with our eyes open."

"I am willing to give it a try if you are."

"If we're going to do this, we're going to do it right," Brady said. "We need to make your first time special. Even if this relationship is temporary, I want you to know you're still special to me."

Annie felt her cheeks heat. "You are special to me too."

"We need to date. Take this slow. Play it out. Savor this experience," he said.

"Brady." She breathed. "You have no idea how much this means to me."

He traced her jaw with his left thumb, his right hand still holding hers. The way he stroked her felt so incredibly intimate. He leaned in.

The night sighed.

Annie sighed.

His mouth brushed hers, light as a whisper. His hand cupped the back of her head, her lips parted.

She was flying, floating free.

One sweet kiss, but no more. Brady pulled back. He was tormenting her. "That's enough for now," he murmured on a whisper so heavy it cracked the silent night. "If we keep kissing I won't be able to control myself."

Then with that he turned and stalked away into the darkness, leaving Annie feeling as if she had just found a pot of gold at the end of the rainbow.

For the next two days, Prissy and Lissette showed Annie the ropes at The Bride Wore Cowboy Boots. She was busy enough, learning her new position as receptionist/gofer, but she couldn't stop wondering when Brady would call or show up. So far, all she'd seen of him was when she passed him in the corral on her walk from the cabin to catch a ride into town with Mariah.

He grinned and teased and sent an appreciative gaze over her body, but he never said one word about a date. It was driving her to distraction. To keep from thinking about him, she threw herself into her work.

On Wednesday, the sister of the bride who was getting married that Saturday showed up with her young four-year-old daughter in tow. "We came to get her ears pierced," the woman announced.

"Come on into the back," Prissy said, "and I'll get you all fixed up."

They disappeared into the back room and emerged

a few minutes later, the little girl sporting a pair of flower-shaped studs. "I'm gonna be the flower girl," she announced to Annie.

"What a pretty flower girl you will make."

"I have a white basket and it's gonna be filled with rose petals. I hafta drop 'em as I walk down the aisle."

"I know you are going to do an excellent job." Annie smiled.

The little girl took her mother's hand and skipped happily as they left the shop.

"We offer ear piercing service?" Annie asked.

"I do," Prissy said. "You want me to pierce your ears?"

"I would love that."

"Let me get my box and you can pick out a pair." Prissy disappeared into the back of the store and returned with a small briefcase. "You have to start with studs, until your ears heal."

She opened up the case and set it on the desk for Annie to select a pair. There were diamond studs, plain gold studs, longhorn cow studs, opal studs, and two silver cobweb circles with a silver feather caught in each web.

"What is this?" Annie asked, pointing at the silver circle studs.

"It's a dream catcher."

"Oh, so that's what a dream catcher looks like." Annie had read about dream catchers. "A dream catcher is perfect." When she was in Dubinstein she could put on those earrings and remember that for one brief moment in time she had captured her dreams. "These are the ones I want."

"Great. Let me just get the gun."

Prissy disappeared.

"Prissy's got a steamroller personality," Mariah said. "Don't let her talk you into getting your ears pierced if you don't want to get them pierced."

"I want to get them pierced. I have always wanted to get them pierced."

"How come you haven't done it before now?"

"My mother said—" Annie broke off, Queen Evangeline's voice in her head. *Common people poke holes in their ears. Royalty doesn't disfigure their bodies, Annabella.* "My mother had a phobia of germs. She was scared I would get an infection."

"You're long past the age where you have to do what your mother says."

"I know." Annie tugged on her earlobe. "That is why I am in Texas."

"Okay, here we go." Prissy came back into the room. "You ready?"

"Yes." She cringed.

"Push your hair back from your ears."

Annie complied.

Prissy marked Annie's ears with a fine-tip Sharpie, and then had Annie look into a hand mirror. "Is this where you want them pierced?"

"That looks right."

Prissy cleaned Annie's ears with an alcohol wipe, and then went to the sink to wash her hands. Without touching the earrings, she loaded the piercing gun with the silver dream catcher starter studs.

"Is this going to hurt?" *For shame, Annabella, that sounded whiny.* Maybe, but it was difficult sitting here waiting for pain. Anticipation could scramble your thinking.

"It'll sting for just a second." Prissy waved a hand. "It'll be over before you know it."

Annie took a deep breath.

Prissy eyed Annie's earlobe, stepped forward.

Annie held up a hand. "Wait, wait."

"What is it?"

"I just need a minute."

"You're allowed to back out," Mariah said.

"No, I do not want to back out. I simply want to be prepared."

"Tell me when." Prissy stepped aside.

Annie steeled herself, gripped the arms of the chair. "All right. I am prepared."

The gun made a quick, soft popping sound. First one ear, then the next. Prissy was finished before the mild sting set in.

Annie blinked. "Why, that was nothing."

"Told you. Look." Prissy held the hand mirror up.

Annie admired her reflection in the mirror. Her lobes turned light pink, but the silver dream catcher studs looked so pretty nestled there. "Hmm. I like it."

"Just wait until you can wear regular earrings. You'll go nuts. You have a lot of time to make up for," Prissy said, and then told her how to care for her newly pierced ears.

"How much do I owe you?" She fingered her ears. Felt truly wanton.

"The earrings are $39.99 plus tax."

"And the piercing?"

"That's on the house."

"Thank you, thank you very much."

"Hey, that grin on your face is thanks enough."

Annie pulled money from her satchel and paid Prissy.

"I bet Brady will love them." Prissy gave her a thumbs-up.

Right. If he ever saw her in them. She was starting to worry that he had changed his mind about her completely.

On the drive home that afternoon, Mariah said, "I've noticed you've got some mad diplomatic skills, Annie."

"Mad?" She frowned, not understanding the reference. "Did I do something wrong?"

"Not at all. It means you're really good at handling people."

"Thank you," Annie said. "I have always believed you should treat people the way you would like to be treated."

"I've got to go to Fort Worth on Friday to meet with clients, but I also have a mother of the bride who wants to come check out the facilities here at the ranch that same morning, and I was wondering if I could count on you to show her around."

"Why me?" Annie asked, feeling flattered.

"You have the grace and finesse that Prissy lacks. I love Prissy dearly, but the woman who is coming to the ranch is from Dallas. She's wealthy, old money, politically connected, and she expects to be kowtowed to. I know she'll fall in love with Lissette's cakes and baking skills, but we need for Melinda Messing to fall in love with the venue as well. I'm confident that you can sell her on it."

"I appreciate your vote of confidence."

"Since you don't have a lot of clothes, I thought you might want to borrow one of my business suits."

"That's very kind of you."

"We'll stop by the house before I take you to the cabin."

Once they were at Green Ridge, Annie couldn't keep from searching for Brady, but his truck was gone from the driveway. Disappointed, she started to wonder if perhaps she had dreamed the whole late night conversation they'd had outside her cabin in the wee hours of Monday morning. If his plan had been to make her yearn and ache and crave, it was certainly working.

On Friday, exactly one week after Annie had run away from Echo Glover's wedding rehearsal dinner, Melinda Messing arrived at Green Ridge Ranch looking like the Highland Park socialite that she was—put together like a porcelain doll in Dolce & Gabbana from head to toe.

Annie herself wore a navy blue Ellen Tracy suit with a peach-colored blouse and designer pumps that Mariah had loaned her. She felt more like her regal self and it was a stiff, unnatural sensation. Until that moment, she did not realize how a regimented life showed up in her posture, stance, and mental outlook. She had quickly grown to love the relaxed ease of cowboy boots and blue jeans. And since she had not seen either Chandler or Strawn since that night at the carnival, she had stopped jumping at shadows and slowly began to think she would get her full six weeks of freedom.

After introducing herself to the woman, Annie showed her around the grounds.

"You look very familiar to me." Melinda Messing cocked her head. Studied Annie. "Have we met?"

"I am new to Texas."

She tapped her chin. "I've seen you somewhere before. Do you know former President Glover?"

Annie froze. Was it possible the woman had been a guest at the presidential compound and by some awful quirk of fate could have remembered her? "The guests will park here." Annie evaded the question, gesturing to a wide-open area where the grass was mown short and cordoned off by a short limestone wall. "And they'll walk this way to the chapel."

Luckily, that sidetracked her. "My daughter, Peyton, is marrying a cutting horse cowboy." Mrs. Messing sniffed. "I wanted her to get married at Christ Church in Highland Park, but oh no, she insists on getting married in a field in Jubilee."

"The wedding can be as simple or as elegant as you wish. Mariah Daniels has extensive experience in wedding planning," Annie said, then went on to share Mariah's résumé with her just the way her new boss had coached her. "I have photographs I can show you of some of the weddings her company has orchestrated."

"Peyton's father and I wanted her to marry the obstetrician she'd been dating, but out of nowhere she falls in love with a cutting horse *cowboy*." Mrs. Messing said it like it was a dirty word. "And so here we are."

"Planning a wedding," Annie said cheerfully.

"Peyton has only known him a couple of months. It's too fast."

"When something is right, what is the meaning of time?"

"Exactly, so why not take your time?" Melinda Messing pursed her lips. "What's the rush? If it's real, it will wait."

"Does your daughter truly love this man?"

"I suppose." The woman sighed. "But she's just twenty-five. What does she know about love?"

"How old were you when you married your husband?"

Mrs. Messing looked startled. "Twenty-two."

"This is the chapel." Annie opened the door.

They stepped inside the building. To Annie's eyes the church was beautiful in its simplicity. Four walls. An altar. A tall steeple. Both the interior and the exterior painted pure white. The pews were pine. The floors polished maple. At the back of the altar was a single stained-glass window depicting a cowboy on one knee, hat doffed in one hand, the other hand holding the reins of his horse, his head bowed in prayer. It was both pious and touching.

"I admit," Mrs. Messing said begrudgingly, "it holds a certain rustic charm."

"This might not be your vision of your daughter's wedding, but try to see it through her eyes," Annie said.

"I'm trying. Let me ask you something."

"Yes?"

"Let's say you were the one getting married."

I am. "All right."

"What would be five essential things you would want at your wedding?"

"My father, my friends—"

"Not people," she corrected. "Things. What would you consider wedding must-haves?"

Was this a trick question? Annie feared she was not going to pass the test.

"For example, my wedding day must-haves were my Phi Theta Kappa pin, a pale blue petticoat, four-inch stilettos, Chanel No. 5, and my grandmother's gold Longines wristwatch."

"Um . . ."

"Do you know what Peyton wants for her five things? Do you have any idea?"

"No, ma'am."

"Scarlet Old Gringo cowboy boots, a red and white checkered neckerchief, a daisy chain headband, thong underwear, and a nose ring. Can you believe that?"

"Every generation has their conventions." Personally, she admired Peyton's spirit.

Melinda Messing sighed. "I suppose."

Annie's five things weren't even *her* must-haves. They'd been preselected per royal protocol. The Farrington family diamond tiara; a floor-length, hand-tatted mantilla veil; white silk elbow gloves; gold shoes encrusted with diamonds; and a sapphire necklace.

"Please allow me to show you the reception hall," Annie said diplomatically, and escorted her over the walkway.

Mrs. Messing curled up her lip. "This looks like a horse barn."

"Very perceptive. It once was a horse barn," Annie said. "But wait until you see inside."

The reception hall had been gutted of horse stalls and renovated with all the modern touches, but still stayed true to its cowboy roots. There were hooks for hanging cowboy hats and boot scrapers in the entryway. But the floors, as in the chapel, were hardwood maple. The kitchen area for the caterers held commercial-grade appliances and boasted granite countertops. The dance floor was huge. Granted, the bandstand was a bit kitschy, decorated with hay bales and horse tack, but it was in perfect keeping with the theme.

"It's not as bad as I imagined," Mrs. Messing admitted, "but I'm still hoping to talk my daughter into a Highland Park wedding."

"We would love to have your business and we will do everything in our power to make this wedding fit your standards, while still appeasing your daughter's desire for a cowboy-style ceremony," Annie said.

Mrs. Messing eyed her again. "You remind me so much of someone, but I just can't put my finger on it."

Annie bit her lip. "I am certain that we have never met."

She snapped her fingers. "I've got it! You're the spitting image of Princess Annabella Farrington of Monesta, without the long blond hair of course. I met her last Friday before Echo Glover's wedding. I was an invited guest. But the poor dear came down with mono and couldn't attend the ceremony."

Fear stirred a stew in Annie's stomach. This was

it. She was about to be caught in her lie. "Yes, I have been compared to the princess before," she said, surprised to hear how cool and smooth she sounded.

"I bet." Mrs. Messing shook her head. "You look enough like Annabella to be her sister."

They stepped back outside to see a cowboy riding up on a horse and leading a second horse behind him. It was Brady with Trampas trotting beside him. Annie's heart did a somersault. She'd never been so grateful to see anyone in her life.

Brady tipped his hat, smiled. "Mornin', ladies."

"My goodness," Mrs. Messing said, a gleam in her eye. She put a hand over her heart. "Is he part of the backdrop? If so, I'm beginning to see the appeal of the cowboy mystique."

CHAPTER ELEVEN

You might be a princess if . . . you've never seen a jackrabbit.

"Hi," Brady said to Annie after Mrs. Messing had departed.

"Hello yourself." Annie stood shading her eyes from the dappled sunlight with the flat of her hand and glanced up at him. She felt a bit peevish that he hadn't called her and she wanted to ask him where he had been, but she did not want to sound anxious or clingy. This was supposed to be a casual relationship, after all. Clinging was the exact opposite of what she should be doing.

"Mariah told me you'd be home today."

"Great timing. You impressed Mrs. Messing and she's not a fan of cowboys by and large."

"I thought today might be a good one for your riding lesson."

"Riding lesson?"

"Sure. You said you loved horses, but you didn't know how to ride. You're in cutting horse country.

It would be a shame if you left without learning how to ride."

She gestured toward the cabin. "I need to change clothes."

"Trampas and I will be waiting right here." He swung down off his horse.

Annie hurried into the house, happy to shed the dress suit and high heels for boots and jeans. "You ready for another adventure?" she asked Lady Astor.

The Yorkie danced.

She stepped back outside, Lady Astor raced ahead of her to run past Trampas. The mutt gave chase, barking playfully.

Annie turned her attention to Brady. In that moment, seeing him backlit by the sun, his face cloaked in the shadow of his Stetson, every millimeter of air in her lungs escaped. He wore a red, short-sleeved Western-style shirt with a yoke and snaps instead of buttons. The color accentuated his tan and when he smiled, his teeth seemed impossibly white. She met his eyes and discovered he'd been studying her as closely as she'd been scrutinizing him.

A mockingbird trilled from the peach tree in the front yard, stretching its vocal range from chickadee to flycatcher to blue jay. Brady sauntered over and gazed down at Annie with those languid chocolate eyes. His fingers wrapped around her wrists. "This way, Buttercup."

He led her over to an older mare, already saddled and ready to ride. "C'mon over here and let me show you how to get on your mount."

Tentatively, Annie edged closer to the horse.

"This here is Pickles. She used to be a barrel

racing champion, but she's getting on up there in years and she's not as spry as she used to be, but she prefers female riders."

Annie petted the horse's long neck. Pickles swung her head around to sniff at Annie's skin, her lips dry and tickly. "Oh, she is lovely."

"Here," Brady said. "Hold the reins in your left hand." He draped the slack over the mare's right side. "You want to be self-assured when you get on, because a good mount immediately lets Pickles know that you know what you're doing and it will create a bond between you."

"Except that I do not know what I'm doing."

"But I do, so listen to me. While you take hold of the reins, grab hold of the base of her mane as well." He paused to demonstrate. "Now, using your right hand, take hold of the stirrup iron and put your left foot in the stirrup."

Feeling nervous, but anxious to prove her mettle, Annie took hold of the reins and managed to slip her left boot into the stirrup. She had one leg on the ground, the other suspended in the air.

Pickles shifted, moved.

Panic washed over Annie. "Whoa, whoa."

"I've got her," Brady said.

Annie slid a glance over and saw that Brady did indeed have a solid grip on the bridle.

"Just be calm and you'll be fine. Take a big deep breath if you need to."

"I am all right. Just knowing you have a hold on her makes all the difference."

"Now, grab the cantle with your right hand."

"Cantle?"

"The back of the saddle."

"Done."

"Now, bounce on the ball of your right foot." He placed a hand to her back. Instantly, she felt more secure and in control. "Push off with your right foot as you put your weight on your stirrup foot, simultaneously pulling on the saddle and the horse's mane."

"Oh dear, I fear I am not coordinated enough for this."

"Sure you are." His deep, reassuring voice rushed over her eardrum. "Ups-a-Buttercup," he said instead of ups-a-daisy as one might say when hefting a child.

That made her laugh, and with his guidance, the next thing she knew, Annie was in the saddle. Brady took the reins and showed her how to hold them with her thumbs up to give her more control.

"Ready to give it a shot?"

Annie nodded.

"Now pull on the reins lightly to turn her just like I showed you."

Annie tugged to the right. Pickles didn't move.

"Firmer."

She increased the pressure. Pickles moved.

"Oh, oh," she exclaimed. "Will you look at that? It worked."

"Of course it worked. Understand that horses are very sensitive creatures and they pick up on your moods. They're prone to nervousness, so be gentle, but they can also be stubborn, so sometimes you have to show them who's boss."

Pickles loped forward.

Brady whistled for Trampas and Lady Astor to follow them and they started off across the pasture, riding side by side, the dogs frolicking behind. Annie clung nervously to the reins. If Brady hadn't been with her, she wouldn't have had enough courage to do this.

An animal leaped from the high grass.

"Look." She pointed. "A rabbit. It is quite large."

Trampas and Lady Astor spotted it simultaneously and took off after it.

"That's a jackrabbit, Annie," Brady said as the oversized bunny outran the dogs.

"Really? I have read about jackrabbits, but I have never seen one. This is so exciting."

Brady chuckled. "You're really easy to impress."

"I just do not want to take anything for granted. I might never again see another jackrabbit in my life."

"Live in the now, huh?"

"Exactly."

"That's a philosophy I can get behind," he said.

"We are a good match on that score. Live in the moment, because at any moment it can all change."

"That's right." He cocked his head, glanced over at her.

Her skin itched from the heat of his stare and she shifted nervously in the saddle.

"Who are you really, Annie Coste?" he murmured.

The question took her breath. It had been brewing under the surface since she had met him but she kept hoping he would never come right out and ask.

She shrugged, struggled to appear casual. "Just a girl."

He shook his head. "Oh no. You're not *just* anything. I've never met anyone quite like you."

"I feel the same about you," she said.

An awkward pause strung between them like beads on a chain. A honeybee winged past them, headed for a patch of sweet-smelling red flowers carpeting the ground.

"What are those flowers called?" Annie asked, eager to fill the anxious gap in conversation.

"Indian paintbrush," he said. "Or that's what they called them when I was growing up. These days it's more politically correct to call them prairie-fire."

"I have read about them. They are even prettier in person than in description."

Trampas and Lady Astor came trotting back to them, tongues lolling, on the lookout for more jackrabbits to chase. Their horses were walking side by side and Annie could feel Brady watching her. The heat of his gaze made her tingle and blush.

She looked at the reins in her hands, smelled dark leather. Who was this man? She did not know him any more than he knew her. What was she doing here?

Before she could reiterate her motivations, Brady trotted ahead of her and glanced back over his shoulder. He wore a short-sleeved green plaid snap-down shirt and faded button-fly Wranglers, his straw Stetson cocked back on his head. "You're doing a darn good job of riding that horse."

"I am?" Pride lifted her chin.

"Yep." He offered a mischievous smile.

"Where shall we go now?" she asked.

"Let's find a nice picnic spot."

"A picnic? We are going on a picnic?" She hadn't been on a picnic since she was a child. Rosalind would take her into the woods on the grounds of Farrington Palace where they would salt hard-boiled eggs and eat potato salad and little cucumber sandwiches with the crusts cut off, made by the palace chef. "You have prepared a picnic lunch for us?"

"I cheated. I bought submarine sandwiches in Jubilee."

"What are submarine sandwiches?"

"Same as hoagies."

"I have never heard of them."

"Grinders?"

"No."

"Heroes?"

"Not in relationship to sandwiches."

"Po'-boys?"

Annie shook her head. She could not imagine any sandwich with those names being served at the palace. "What whimsical language."

"You've never eaten any of those either?"

"No, I do not think so. If I did, no one called them by those names."

"Buttercup, you have been so sheltered. My theory that you escaped from a nunnery is taking lead supposition."

Annie pressed her lips together. She wanted so badly to tell him the truth, but she knew it would ruin everything. He would be shocked, then disbelieving, and then finally surprised, impressed, and intimidated. And that would be the end of rodeos and riding lessons and picnics.

"You're not going to confirm or deny?"

He was persistent, but she was equally determined. "I thought we agreed I could keep my secrets."

"You're right, but you can't blame me for trying. The mystery just makes you that much more intriguing."

"What better reason to stay an enigma," she said. "If you learned everything there was to know about me, you'd lose interest."

He raked a sultry gaze over her body. "I very much doubt that."

He had a way of making her feel naked. "Let us just enjoy the day."

"How about here." Brady pointed to a small creek running through the property. "Underneath that old chinaberry tree. Looks like a good spot for a picnic."

They tied the horses to an elm sapling while the dogs romped in the creek. Brady took a light blanket from his saddlebag and spread it on the ground. Then he removed the sandwiches, wrapped in wax paper, from the bag along with two bottles of water. He hung his cowboy hat over a tree limb and they sat down on the blanket. Trampas and Lady Astor came running up.

"I can see we're going to have to split these sandwiches four ways." He laughed, broke off a chunk of bread from each sandwich, and gave one bite to Trampas, one to Lady Astor.

It moved Annie to see how affectionate he was with the dogs. He would make a great father someday. Too bad she would not be around to see Brady fully come into his own. He was good-looking, yes, and his muscular body was quite impressive, but sexiness alone wasn't what made a man appealing to her. Intelligence was what drew her attention; common sense caught her notice. But the number one quality that touched her heart was compassion. A man who was gentle with animals and kind to people, well, that was a man you wanted to hold on to.

Annie saw that in Brady—compassion, kindness, thoughtfulness. Was it a natural trait born into him? Or had it come through trial and error? From living a hard life and learning how to bounce back up when you got knocked down?

The way he lowered his lashes over dark brown eyes made her long to let go and tell him everything. Confess all. Ask for his lips to give her penance.

She took a nibble of the sandwich. It was quite good. Lots of flavor and ingredients—salami, ham, turkey, lettuce, tomatoes, green peppers, cucumbers, black olives, oil and vinegar on hearty whole wheat bread.

"Oops," Brady said. "Almost forgot the 'tater chips." He rummaged in the saddlebag again and tossed her a bag of potato chips.

"We call them crisps where I am from."

"Isn't that what they call them in England?"

"I believe so."

"So you're from England?"

"Do I sound British?"

"No."

"That is your evidence."

"You enjoy being cryptic," he observed, his eyelids sensual at half mast.

Lady Astor sat up to beg for a chip. Annie gave her a chiding look and the Yorkie slunk down and covered her eyes with her paws.

Brady laughed. "How do you get her to do that?"

"She knows better than to beg for food. It is behavior unbecoming a lady."

"Unbecoming, huh?"

"She's been taught the correct way to act."

"I can barely get Trampas to come when I call. How do you do it?"

"You have to be smarter than the dog," she teased. He was smart. She already knew that.

"What can I say? You've got the Lady and I've got the Tramp."

"I love that movie," she said. "So romantic. Even if it is a cartoon."

Their gazes smacked together.

Latched.

And she felt a zigzag of red-hot electricity. Everything stopped. The mockingbird in the tree went silent; the gurgling creek gone suddenly mute. Drifting dust motes vanished. The peppery taste of salami slipped from her tongue. She couldn't feel her fingers digging into the soft loaf. What sway did this handsome cowboy hold over nature, that he could make everything cease with one glance?

She was acutely aware that they were lying on a blanket. A blanket that had once been on his bed. A bed she had once been in. A bed she could be in again. Instant heat bubbled low in her abdomen. She'd never felt anything quite like this richly wicked sensation.

They finished off their sandwiches in companionable silence, washing them down with water. Annie pushed a strand of hair behind her ear, then leaned back, propping herself up with her palms flat against the blanket.

"Hey," Brady said. "You got your ears pierced."

"You noticed." She cupped a hand around her right ear.

"It's a dream catcher."

"Yes."

"Hoping to catch yourself a few dreams?" he asked.

"I am looking at one right now."

"So am I." His gaze hung on her lips.

She reached up to run a finger over her bottom lip, sizzling from the intensity of his stare. She wanted him to kiss her again, but she did not know how to do it short of asking him.

"Just let it unfold, darlin'," he drawled.

"Am I that obvious?"

"Only because I want it as much as you do."

"You could not have wanted it all *that* much," she said, more petulant than she intended. "It took you five days to ask me out again."

"All part of my evil plan to get you hot and bothered." He scooted closer, closing the gap between them.

"I am bothered all right." She pretended to be mad. "You have wasted precious time."

"No you're not. I've whet your interest."

"And you have a big ego."

"It's one of the things you like best about me."

"It is not. What I like best about you is your . . ."

"What?"

Her cheeks heated. She was no good at this flirting stuff.

"What," he persisted.

"Your backside," she blurted, when what she really wanted to say was *Your kindness, your compassion, your spirit for life*, but saying that would make her too vulnerable.

"You can say 'butt.' It won't kill you." He leaned over to run two fingers up her arm, and then he kissed her on the neck right below her earlobe.

Annie shivered and her breath grew shallow. She was warm all over. Warm enough to rip off her clothes and jump in the creek to cool down. "Um . . . are we going to . . . um . . ."

"What?" he murmured.

"Make love out here?" she whispered.

"There's no one around but you and me and nature."

"And the dogs."

Brady waved a hand in the direction of Trampas and Lady Astor. They were lying side by side, sound asleep. "Jackrabbit chasing tuckered them all out."

"What about the horses?"

"Buttercup, they ain't gonna talk, I promise." The heat in his eyes dissolved her.

"It feels so . . ." She lowered her voice even further. "Decadent."

"Just trust me." His hands went to the snap of her blue jeans at the same time his mouth came down on hers.

His kiss felt like the whole world. Big and full and complex. He cradled one arm behind her and leaned her back, while his other hand lowered her zipper.

Annie reached up to run her fingers through his unruly dark hair. He tasted salty and warm. The spot behind her knees went mushy and she was very glad she was not standing up. Her stomach fluttered, rippled.

His hot fingers slipped beneath her waistband and she stopped breathing.

"Wh-what are you doing," she whispered around his lips.

"Trust me," he crooned.

Sunlight wobbled through the leaves of the elm tree. She breathed in the earthy scent of the creek. Felt the crush of crinkly grass poking underneath the blanket.

His entire palm was flat against her lower belly, sliding down underneath the elastic of her panties. The material of her jeans tugged against her hips at the addition of his hand. He looked down into her eyes and she looked up into his. A soft, welcoming smile curled his lips.

"I've been thinking about you all week," he said.

"I have as well. Thinking of you, that is. Not me. Well, I have been thinking of me, but in the context of being with you. I mean . . . It is just that . . ."

"You chatter when you get nervous," he observed.

"I do?"

"You do."

"Well, you do have your hand down my pants."

"Uh-huh."

Annie gulped.

"You've got a full head of hair down there."

"Doesn't everyone?"

"Not everyone. Not these days. Many ladies like to keep a trim lawn."

"Oh dear. Is that bad? Should I have . . . um . . . shaved or waxed or something?"

"No ma'am. I like you just the way you are."

That distressed her instead of soothing as she was sure he meant it to do. He didn't know who she truly was and she couldn't tell him. The minute he found out that she was the Princess of Monesta, the game would be over.

"Do you have any idea how impossibly beautiful you are?" he asked, his hand slipping lower.

Annie tensed, never once taking her eyes off his. Her breath was coming and going like a light switch. On one minute. Off the next.

Then his index finger touched a spot that had rivers of pleasure running in ribbons up and down her nerve endings. Meanwhile, his mouth burned hot kisses down her throat.

"Brady," she whimpered.

He smelled so good—all sunshine and horsey. His fingers were doing things to her. Unbelievable things that had her writhing and gasping.

"I want you so bad," he said. "But I'm going to keep waiting."

"Wh-wh . . ." She couldn't even form a word.

"You, on the other hand . . ."

Then he did something so incredible she could not even begin to describe it. Something that sent a hot gush of moist warmth bathing her feminine center. All she knew was that she was trembling and tears were sliding down her cheeks and she experienced the most bone-shaking, physical inner release.

She clung to him. Shaking and sobbing. "What"—she swallowed, chest heaving—"was that?"

"Why, Buttercup," Brady said, his voice puffed with pride, "I believe you just had your first orgasm."

CHAPTER TWELVE

You might be a princess if . . . a lonesome cowboy
changes his life for you.

For the next three weeks, Brady had the time of
his life. Being with Annie made him feel stimulated in a way he'd never felt stimulated before.
Sexually, sure. You betcha. Of course. No doubt.
But basically he could get that with any pretty girl
who caught his attention.

But Annie? Well, she brought so much more to
the table that he ever imagined any woman could
or would. Around her, he felt dazzled, hypnotized,
charmed. She had a way of walking—all high and
mighty—that stirred his blood. And whenever she
looked at him with those wide gray-blue eyes, hell,
he instantly got hard.

By day, he worked with Miracle, coaxing the
horse back to himself. He did his job well. Maybe
too well. The quicker the stallion healed, the sooner
he'd be on the road again, but for the first time ever,
the allure of the road did not call to him. The old

wanderlust that usually got under his skin after a few weeks in one place, and itched like a chigger bite, never even made a welt.

While he worked with Joe's prize cutting horse, Annie quickly picked up on the ins and outs of the wedding planning business. When she talked of her work, her face lit up like a movie marquee— animated, excited. He loved to hear her speak of tulle and jacquard and pomander. He had no idea what any of it meant and he didn't care. He lay in bed and listened to her voice and planted kisses over her bare belly. She wouldn't tell him her secrets, so he would take whatever conversation he could get.

By night, they did everything *but* fully consum-mate their attraction. They kissed and cuddled. They fondled and snuggled. They watched romantic movies and indulged in some window-fogging pet-ting sessions. They canoodled and nuzzled. They did very daring things with food. They made each other come with their clothes on.

Brady created a playlist representing their time to-gether. Everything from "Build Me Up Buttercup" to "Wrangler Butts" to "Werewolves of London." She laughed out loud when she heard "Wrangler Butts" for the first time. He picked a bouquet of Indian paintbrushes for her and she graced him with a beatific smile that lit a fire inside him. She spoke to him in all the foreign languages she knew and read cowboy poetry aloud.

He took her boot scooting, and on the dance floor, she was a peacock plume on his arms, light, graceful, dazzling. The woman possessed serious dance moves. They went on couples dates. Bowling with Prissy and Paul. Shooting pool at the Silver Spur with Ila and Cordy. Playing cards with Mariah and Joe at their house.

For their intimate dates, Annie lit scented candles—vanilla, pineapple, mocha—and poured champagne and they took long baths together in the claw-footed tub in her little cabin. He rubbed her feet; she rubbed his back. They took Trampas and Lady Astor for long moonlight walks and held hands while the warm wind whispered through the willows.

By very late night, he lay in his bed in his trailer, touching himself to relieve the tension, and dreamed of Annie's sweet, hot body. He held off from going all the way because he wanted her first time to be special. But it was more than that. He was enjoying this too, and prolonging their complete joining heightened the brilliant agony. When they finally came together, it would be the ultimate.

But toward the end of the third week of dating, it was clear something had to give. His mind was fogged, his brain clogged. He spent every waking minute thinking about Annie and every wild, erotic thing he wanted to do to her. He was hanging on by a thread. Ninety percent of the time when he was around her, he was so hard it hurt. And when he wasn't with her, he couldn't sleep. Insomnia nibbled at him, insistent and relentless. He'd never been so horny in his life.

On Thursday, the same morning Brady took Trampas to the vet for neutering, he got a phone call. A cutter in Wyoming had rescued some abused and neglected horses and needed his help. A typical call, one that would usually have him hitching up the trailer and putting gas in his tank. Miracle was almost back to his old self. Joe could continue the rehabilitation on his own. It was time to leave Jubilee.

Except Brady did not want to go.

Tomorrow it was four weeks to the day that he had picked up Annie hitchhiking on the side of the road. How could things have changed so much in four short weeks?

Tonight, he was cooking dinner for her in her cabin. His specialty, spaghetti and meatballs.

He'd been thinking that maybe tonight was the night. The culmination of four weeks of priming and prepping, yet there was a part of him that was afraid to take that last step. Afraid that if he did, it might mean something more to her than it should. He didn't want her getting emotional over him. He had to make it clear to her that it was nothing more than lust and hormones driving this attraction. He wasn't a forever kind of guy, and even though she claimed she wasn't looking for promises, he was scared of hurting her.

Liar. You're scared of hurting yourself.

Okay, that was true. He'd spent his whole life avoiding entanglements and he was damn afraid that if he crossed that last line with her, he'd become too entangled to get out.

But his damn dick wanted her so badly he could barely think.

Maybe he would wait until Sunday. Tomorrow was the start of the Fourth of July weekend and for once Mariah did not have a wedding scheduled. Instead, she and Joe were hosting a barbecue cookout and fireworks display on Sunday. Sunday might be a better night for seduction.

He turned the dilemma over in his mind as he picked up Trampas and installed the groggy dog in a pet carrier in the backseat of his pickup. On the way home, he passed by the post office and it occurred to him that he hadn't checked his post office box since he'd been back in town. He used the post office box in Jubilee as his permanent address. He did most of his banking and bill paying online so there wasn't much of a need for the P.O. box, and in all honesty, he'd forgotten about it until now.

He pulled into the post office parking lot, left the engine chugging so Trampas could have air conditioning while he ran in and grabbed his mail. He hurried back out, tossed the mass of correspondence in the front seat beside the groceries he'd picked up before swinging by the vet's office.

Once back at the ranch, he let Lady Astor out of the house. Whenever Annie was working in town, he'd started routinely checking up on the Yorkie, letting the dog out two or three times a day. He carried Trampas, carrier and all, into the cabin, and then went back for the groceries and mail.

He tossed the mail and grocery sacks on the bar, let Lady Astor back inside, opened the door to Trampas's crate in case the dog wanted to come out. He turned the small television set in the living room on for noise. A celebrity entertainment show was on and he barely paid any attention to the current topic, speculation on the health of the Princess Annabella of Monesta, who hadn't been seen in public since taking ill at Echo Glover's wedding a month earlier. It was assumed she was still recovering at the presidential compound and there was much speculation whether she would be well enough for her own wedding to the Prince of Dubinstein in three weeks' time. Then the topic shifted to Charlie Sheen's latest antics.

After washing up at the kitchen sink, he set about making the spaghetti sauce. While he formed meatballs, Lady Astor danced around his feet. Trampas came moping over and lay down on the cool kitchen tile, staring at the Yorkie with moony eyes.

"You're stone cold in love aren't you, buddy?" Brady asked him.

Trampas sighed.

"It's got to be hard. Loving a girl who is so out of your league."

Lady Astor sat on her haunches, put her paws up in begging mode. Brady cast a glance down at her. "Yes, you are a beauty, but I've been giving you too many treats. You're starting to get a little pudgy."

The Yorkie barked.

"What's that? You don't care about a little extra weight? Trampas is madly in love with you just the way you are?"

Lady Astor cocked her head as if trying to figure out what he was talking about.

"Heartbreaker." He slipped her a small chunk of meatball.

Trampas thumped his tail, but didn't bother getting up.

"Sorry, buddy, vet said nothing but water for you until the morning."

At that moment, Annie walked through the door. "What smells so completely heavenly?"

"Spaghetti and meatballs."

"Mmm, sounds yummy."

Brady couldn't help noticing how her silky top hugged breasts twice as mouthwatering as any spaghetti and meatballs on the planet. And the way those dark wash blue jeans cupped her sweet ass in a denim sling, well *damn*. No matter how many times he stared at her delectable ass, he couldn't get enough of seeing it. "How was your day?"

"Great. Busy, but fun." She reached down to pet Lady Astor, who ran over for attention, and then she went over to scratch poor Trampas's ears. "How are you feeling, buddy?"

The dog gave a halfhearted wriggle.

Brady turned down the heat on the meatballs, wiped his hands on a cup towel, and went across the room to scoop her into his arms.

The second her soft breasts touched his chest, he felt like a powder keg with a short fuse—quick, hot, and ready to go off. Her hair smelled of flowers and he pulled the scent down deep into his lungs. He hugged her tighter, caging her in his embrace, and nuzzled her neck. She twined her arms around his neck, pulled his head down to hers.

Annie pressed her forehead flat against his, their noses touching. "Tonight is the night." She said it as a statement, not a question.

He saw the heat in her eyes, knew she was as hungry for sex as he was. Her desire lit fire to his short, powder keg fuse, and it was all he could do to keep from scooping her up into his arms and carrying her into the bedroom. "Tonight," he confirmed.

She quivered in his arms. The rapid hammering of her heart vibrating from her body into his. The edge of his erection pressed hard against her belly. He threaded his fingers through her hair, tilted her head back, devoured her. These possessive urges were new to him, but he did not fight against the dominating need to claim her as his own.

"Something is sizzling on the stove," Annie said, finally breaking through his fog of sexual starvation.

"Buttercup, that's me sizzling for you."

Annie laughed. "I am not making light, Brady, you are burning your meatballs."

"Tell me about it," he said, reluctantly pulling away.

"Go on, investigate the food." She waved him off. "I am going to take a shower."

His gaze hugged her butt as she walked away, tracking the elegant sway of her hips, the way those Wranglers clung to her thighs. The thought of her naked body underneath the shower spray had him closing his eyes, clenching his fists, and breathing hard through his mouth.

Soon enough. Just hang on a while longer. Get through dinner and then you've got the entire night.

She bent to pick something off up the floor and he just about came undone. God, but she was sizzling hot and she seemed completely clueless to the power of her appeal. Her guilelessness only made her hotter.

He had the spaghetti put together and he was tossing the salad when Annie came back in the room smelling of soap, her face scrubbed clean of makeup.

She was wrapped in a bathrobe. He immediately wondered if she had anything on underneath it.

His gaze hooked on hers as his fingers shredded Bibb lettuce into a bowl. She meandered to the bar. Her feet were bare. Her toenails were painted a pretty pearlescent pink. Completely lickable, those toes.

"I bought a bottle of wine. It's chilling in the refrigerator. But maybe that's wrong. Can you have white wine with spaghetti? Is it supposed to be red wine instead?" He crinkled his nose. "I don't really like red wine."

"Whatever wine you purchased is fine," she reassured him and it wasn't until she smiled that he realized just how nervous he was. He wanted this dinner to be perfect. Wanted this night to be the best either one of them had ever had. She padded to the fridge, Brady tracked her every step. She moved with such grace and style. By just walking she made him feel like a clumsy dullard.

She took out the wine. "Chardonnay is always appropriate, no matter what the dish."

"You're just saying that to make me feel better."

"You sell yourself short, Brady Talmadge and I have to wonder why."

"Hey, you're holding on to your secrets, I'm hanging on to mine." Surprise washed over him. He didn't like keeping secrets and yet here he was taunting her with his because she wouldn't tell him hers.

Real mature, Talmadge.

And yet, he wasn't ready to tell her why he'd made his five unbreakable rules for living an uncomplicated life, because, well . . . she *was* the complication that broke them all. If he told her everything and she told him nothing, she would have the upper hand.

Oh, who are you kidding. She's had the upper hand from the first minute you laid eyes on her.

She opened the wine and then searched the cupboard. "No wineglasses in here," she said, pulling out two mismatched juice tumblers. "These will do."

Her delicate fingers hoisted the bottle, tippled a few ounces of Chardonnay into each glass; she leaned her back against the counter, passed him the glass. Brady grappled blindly for the wine, his gaze hung on the fold of her robe where he could see the creamy swell of the tops of her breasts. She did not have anything on underneath that robe.

He licked his lips. She looked as sexually harried as he felt. And he was more turned on than he'd ever been in his life.

So was she.

Okay, that sounded too chuffed, but her nipples were so hard he could see them poking against the thick terry cloth.

"Tonight," she said. "We are going all the way."

"All the way," he echoed, his knees fluid as water, and touched the rim of his tumbler to hers.

Her gaze held his for the longest moment, then she tilted back her head and took a sip. She swallowed the wine down with the softest of movements, all refinement and poise.

To steady himself—aw hell, who was he kidding—to keep from dragging her off to the bedroom this instant, he shifted his concentration back to the stove.

"Mmm." She stretched over his shoulder, lithe as a cat, to peek at the spaghetti and meatballs warming on the electric burner turned low. Her chin rested against the side of his neck.

Sweat rolled down his spine and he had a death grip on the serving ladle.

"That looks delicious," she purred. "I would give anything if I could cook."

"You can learn. It's not that hard. If I can do it, you can do it."

"Mariah cannot cook." She laughed.

"Correction, Mariah doesn't want to cook, and that's okay. Life's too short to do things you don't want to do, but if you want to cook, you can. I can teach you what little I know." He turned to look at her.

"Learning how to cook takes time and practice."

"That's right."

A sad expression came over her face, but then she quickly shook it off and a bright smile lit up her face. "I am very hungry," she whispered in his ear.

A stone cold shiver passed straight from his brain to his groin and turned him to solid cement below the waist. He wanted to say to hell with the food and take her right there on the kitchen floor, but Annie was humming and setting the table.

She leaned over the table to touch his arm and he almost dropped the plates of spaghetti he was carrying.

At this rate, he wouldn't last five minutes in the sack. He chuffed in a deep breath, set down the plates, and went back for the salad.

"Does this belong to you?" she asked, picking up

the mail he'd dropped on the table when he'd come in. The mail he hadn't even glanced at because he'd been busy with Trampas and fixing dinner.

"Here, I'll take that." He reached for the mail, leafing through it quickly while Annie sat down and daintily spread a paper napkin in her lap.

Circulars. Trash. Offers for credit cards. Trash. Solicitations for credit debt reduction. Trash. A thank-you card from a lady in Albuquerque whose horse he'd rehabilitated a month ago. The woman had included a picture of the horse looking healthy and happy. Brady smiled and tucked the card in his back pocket. Another success story.

And then there was a plain white envelope looking innocuous enough until he flipped it over and saw the return address with a red, white, and blue logo declaring: Texas Department of Family and Protective Services. It was postmarked a month earlier.

For one icy, heart-stopping second he thought, *At last, someone's going to stop the abuse*. And then he laughed at the silly thought. He was twenty-nine years old. He'd stopped the abuse all on his own when he'd stumbled onto the highway and thumbed a ride to Jubilee with Dutch when he was fifteen.

"Brady?" Annie asked. "What is it?"

"It's nothing," he said, more for his benefit than for hers. Why the hell was family protective services writing to him now?

They probably just want a donation.

He almost tossed the letter into the garbage unopened along with the circulars and credit card come-ons, but his curiosity got the better of him and he slipped his finger underneath the sealed flap of the envelope, trying hard to tamp down the nervousness kicking around in his stomach.

Forget it. Tonight's the night. You're having dinner with a beautiful woman. Forget the mail.

Hesitating, he bit down on the inside of his cheek. He had nothing to worry about. Why was he worrying? Because the letter made him think of his family. That's why.

When was the last time you spoke to any of them? You saw Cody and Carol and the kids at Christmas, but it's been, what . . . three years since you've spoken to Mom?

He loved his mother, but the secret she'd kept from him was a lot to forgive. He didn't want to think about this. He wanted to eat spaghetti and make love to Annie.

But if something had happened to his mother, he was certain one of his brothers would have called. He might be the black sheep of the family, but hell, his brothers still spoke to him from time to time. And the old man? Well, he could rot in hell as far as Brady was concerned.

What if it *was* the old man? That brought a new mix of feeling surging through him—regret, hatred, disgust, sadness, and shame.

Always shame.

Only way to know what's going on is to tear open that letter and read it. No doubt it's just a dun for money and you're letting the past get you worked up over nothing.

Probably so, but this letter had the stench of complication all over it.

"Brady?" Annie asked, putting aside her napkin and rising to her feet. "Are you all right?"

"I'm okay," he said, but his voice sounded tinny, faraway.

"Something upset you."

He showed her the logo on the envelope.

"What does that mean?"

"I don't know, but I'm not going to let it spoil our evening. Let's eat." But even as he said it, he knew the evening was already spoiled. He reached across the table, touched her hand. "Maybe it would help if I start by telling you exactly what I intend on doing to you after we're finished eating."

She slipped her hand out from under his. "Open the letter, Brady," she murmured.

"Annie . . . what's in here . . ." He paused. "It's got nothing to do with you and me."

"Whatever is inside has you frowning and looking sad." She traced her finger lightly over his wrist. "Just open it and either face bad news head-on or put your mind at ease."

She was right. He gulped, tore open the envelope, and pulled out the letter with the official state of Texas emblem embossed on the paper.

Dear Mr. Talmadge,

> *My name is Mary Jameson and I'm a caseworker with the Texas Department of Family and Protective Services. I am writing to you because there exists the possibility that you are the biological father of an infant female in our care. The child's mother was one Kelly*

Deavers, who is no longer living. I would like
the opportunity to speak with you about this
matter. You may reach me at 817–555–9876. Or
feel free to visit our offices in Tarrant County.
I'm hoping to hear from you soon.

Sincerely,
Mrs. Mary Jameson

Stunned, Brady sat reading the letter over and over as if by reading it again and again it would say something different from what it said.

"Brady?" Annie touched his shoulder.

The look on his face must have scared her, and she withdrew her hand and took a step back. "Brady?"

"I told you I didn't want to open it." His voice sounded hollow. Empty. Like someone else's voice. Someone who'd had the wind kicked out of him by a wild stallion.

She pressed two fingers against her mouth. "What is it?"

His head spun. His chest hurt. He couldn't take it all in. It was like someone had shot him straight through the heart with a .45 Magnum slug and he had not died. As if he was bleeding from a hundred bulletholes and yet he could not fall down. In fact, he felt that if he tried he could walk on water and not drown.

A child.

He had a child?

Gooseflesh danced across his nerve endings, as odd and magical as St. Elmo's fire. A child. A daughter. *His.*

He sucked in great lungfuls of air. Gently, Annie pried the letter from his hands. She read it, but she did not make a sound.

He wondered what she thought of him now. Was she angry? Disgusted? Disappointed? Resentful? He had fathered a child that he had not known about. But he had known Kelly Deavers in an intimate way just a little over a year ago. Now Kelly was dead and he had a daughter. Brady didn't doubt for a second the child was his. Guilt and shame and remorse speared through him.

But when he looked in Annie's eyes he did not see anger, disgust, disappointment, or resentment. Instead, he saw only calm acceptance shining in her gray-blue eyes.

"This is wonderful," she said. "You have been given a most precious gift."

"I—" He stared into her eyes, completely lost.

"Yes?"

"The baby. She deserves better than me."

"What are you talking about?"

He waved a hand. If he had been dumped on a deserted island and told he'd have to stay there ten years all by himself before he could be rescued, he couldn't have felt more desolate. "Look at the way I live. Itinerant cowboy. On the road. No ties. Caring only about myself and having a good time. I'm not worthy of her."

"That is not true," Annie scolded. "I have seen you with horses and your friends. You are kind and loving and generous and—"

"Terrified of commitment."

"Everyone is scared. Bravery is being scared and

doing what you have to do anyway. You are brave. I believe in you."

"That would be some mighty misplaced trust."

She crouched in front of him. "Look at me, Brady."

Reluctantly, he met her eyes. Normally he wasn't so self-deprecating, but right now he could kick his own ass. He *was* acting like a coward.

"If you are this little girl's father, she deserves to be with you. No one can love her the way you can."

"It's just . . . well, I can't wrap my head around this." He splayed a palm over his forehead.

She took his hand in hers, squeezed hard, held his gaze, and whispered, "Everything is going to be all right, Brady Talmadge. Just you wait and see."

That night he lay in Annie's bed. They did not make love. They did not speak. Tonight was not the night for that. She simply held him in her arms and he lay cradled with his head against her chest listening to the steady beating of her reassuring heart.

Long after her breathing grew slow and deep, Brady lay thinking of all the implications of the letter. Kelly Deavers, a woman he had barely known, had kept the most hurtful kind of secret from him. He met her in a nightclub in the Fort Worth Stockyards where she worked as a cocktail waitress.

Kelly had been quick-witted, quick-tempered, and quick to slide into his bed. They'd partied together only three or four times over the course of a week before he'd taken to the road again on a new assignment. They'd both wanted to keep things casual. It hadn't been a big deal. Yes, they'd both bonded over the fact they'd had crappy childhoods. Kelly had grown up in foster homes, while Brady had run away at fifteen to get away from his father's abuse. They'd had a good time together. Nothing serious.

Nothing serious? She had your baby. It doesn't get more serious than that.

All the tenets he lived by had been upended. All those unbreakable rules shattered. What was he going to do?

"Brady." Annie stroked her fingers through his hair.

"I thought you were asleep."

"No, I've been thinking about your situation and . . ."

This was it, this was where she told him she wanted out. She had only signed up for fun and games, and finding out that he had a secret love child was certainly not a game. He steeled himself to hear it. He couldn't blame her. He thought it was for the best, all in all. In fact, he should be the one to suggest it.

"Do you want me to go with you?"

"Go with me where?"

"When you go to see this Mrs. Jameson."

It was so kind of her to offer. She was one helluva woman. "No," he said. "This isn't your problem. This is something I have to do on my own."

"I don't mind." She pressed her lips to his chin.

He wanted to make love to her so badly that he could almost taste it, but he couldn't. He wouldn't. Not now. Not until he knew for sure if the baby was his. He was now the complication that *she* didn't need.

Ironic, how the tables had turned.

"Thank you for offering. It means a lot." Brady wrapped his arms around her waist, hugged her tight. He might not have deserved it, but he couldn't help feeling like one of those people on the stories of true survival shows, who got into serious trouble because of bad life choices. Those poor slobs, on the brink of certain death, always looked supremely fatigued with desperate relief.

That was exactly how Annie's offer made him feel.

As if he'd scaled Mount Everest in a blizzard and managed to make it back down again with all his fingers and toes intact.

After Brady finally fell asleep, Annie crept from the bed, jammed her feet into her slippers, and went to let the dogs out. Trampas—still moving stiffly from his surgery—stayed by her side. Lady Astor, high-spirited as ever, went running off into the dark, queen of all she surveyed.

She'd grown complacent over the past month, enjoying her new life. Savoring the fact that apparently she had given her bodyguards the slip for good. She'd called Rosalind again and her nursemaid had commiserated over her mononucleosis. That let her know that her bodyguards were still searching and still had not told King Phillip of her disappearance. Someone in the Glover camp had helped them keep the secret. She dared to hope her handlers had given up on Jubilee and moved on to another location. She should have two wonderful weeks left and a chance to fulfill all her lusty dreams.

But now, everything had changed.

Brady had a child.

And it was none of her business.

She did not expect either the raddled glee or the divine melancholia chewing at her heart. She had nothing invested in this. Brady was nothing more than a special landscape in her temporary adventure. He was a memory she was making, a mental patchwork quilt to keep her vital in the upcoming cocoon of her eternal monarchy. She did not care either way.

Methinks thou doth protest too much.

He would be a perfect father. She knew he didn't see that. Probably couldn't believe it. He thought himself a vagabond, a happy loner, unstructured and unfettered. But she saw past all that. Saw to the truth of him, even if he could not see it himself. He was a man just waiting to be part of something more expansive than himself. She did not know why he shied from what he needed. Why he'd taken a circuitous route to his unknown goal. But his future was here now.

And she was not a part of it.

No matter how she wished things might be different, they were not. So she would do what she could. Support him. Be with him for the moment. Help him with the baby if he needed it. At least for the remainder of her time in Jubilee. And in the end, when it was all over and she had to tell him the truth, and walk away, Annie would have gotten what she'd come to Jubilee to find.

Herself.

CHAPTER THIRTEEN

You might be a princess if . . . you know the details
of Victorian tea ceremonies.

B rady had made so damn many mistakes. Done
all manner of things the wrong way. Failed to
do the right thing more often than not. Now
here he was facing the biggest mistake of all.

His chickens had finally come home to roost.

Mary Jameson turned out to be a plumpish
woman in her fourth decade of life with a Buster
Brown haircut and red-framed, rectangular glasses
perched on the end of a too-long nose. One glance
around her office told him she favored Gaviscon,
Galveston, bottled green chai tea, and German
shepherds.

Her face was round, her jaw soft, and her eyes
skeptical. She stood up from behind a desk constructed of a piece of plywood balanced atop gray
filing cabinets. There were two plastic chairs in
front of the desk. One piled high with papers. Files
and file boxes stacked everywhere. An aged com-

puter with a hulking old monitor monopolized the desk. On the wall behind her was a large domestic abuse poster with the picture of a sad-eyed boy clinging to the hand of a bruised, haggard woman. A spiny cactus in a small orange clay pot sat on the windowsill.

The whole thing made Brady want to turn and run, but then he thought of the child.

His daughter.

No sense getting all mushy until you know for sure. Keep it together, Talmadge. This is a fact-finding mission, nothing more. No freaking out. Not yet, not yet. You're fine. Cool. Charm her with a hundred-watt smile. You know how.

But the smile froze on his face and his tongue knotted.

The caseworker lumbered from behind her desk and moved the papers off the second chair. She waved at the chairs, pushed her glasses up on her nose, then as an afterthought, offered her hand. "I'm Mary Jameson."

"Brady Talmadge," he finally managed and shook her hand. She had a drill sergeant grip.

"Have a seat," she ordered.

Feeling like he was a kid who'd been sent to the principal's office for shooting spit-wads in class, Brady sat.

Mary Jameson glanced at her office door. "Do you have anyone with you?"

"No," he said, as alone as he'd been that long-ago night when he ran away from home. "It's just me."

The caseworker resumed her seat behind the desk. "It took you quite some time to answer my letter."

"I was on the road. My address in Jubilee is just a post office box."

She picked up a pen, clicked it, and held her hand poised over a yellow legal pad. "Where is your permanent residence, Mr. Talmadge?"

"I don't have a permanent address. I live in my horse trailer." The minute he said it, he realized how it sounded. Like he was a bum. He was just being truthful. He should have lied. Or fudged the truth. Or at least tried to put a positive spin on it. But Brady wasn't built that way. Honest to a fault.

"I see." Her tone could have frosted a four-layer cake.

"It's a nice trailer. It's got a kitchen, bedroom, bathroom. Even a small sitting area." Why was he yammering about that? *Shut up. Shut up.*

"You're itinerant." She clicked her pen again.

"My job requires constant travel."

She scribbled something on a yellow legal pad with a blue roller ball pen. He had a feeling it was less than complimentary. "And who is your employer?"

"I'm self-employed."

Her lip turned up as if she smelled stinky feet. "What do you do for a living?"

"I rehabilitate horses. With a specialization in cutting horses."

"I assume that brings you to Jubilee quite often."

"Yes."

She tapped her pen against her desk. "Well, we can discuss all that in a moment. Before we go any further we need to establish that you knew Kelly Renee Deavers."

"We had a short relationship, yes."

"A one-night stand?"

He saw judgment in Mary Jameson's eyes. "The relationship stretched over a couple of weekends I was in the area."

"So there is a distinct possibility this baby could indeed be yours."

"That's why I'm here." Brady cleared his throat. "Once, the condom broke."

"And after you left town, you never thought to call Ms. Deavers? To check on her? See what might have been the outcome of that broken condom?"

He had not. Kelly had assured him she was on the pill. "I didn't," he admitted.

"Because you assume no responsibility for your life, you go around from town to town planting your seed—" The woman broke off, pursed her lips, and knitted her brow.

"I'm sorry. That was out of line. It's just that I witness this kind of irresponsible behavior day in and day out and sometimes it just gets to me. When I see these unwanted kids, thrown away, abandoned, dumped on society to raise . . ." She blew out a deep breath. "So many of them are lost forever."

"I am here to make amends," Brady said, feeling as if he'd swallowed a volleyball. "If the child is mine, I want her."

"Do you really?"

"Yes." He fisted his hand, surprised by the vehemence in his voice and the softness in his heart. "How did you find me?"

"A bartender at the nightclub where Ms. Deavers worked said that she told him that you were the baby's father. He did admit that Ms. Deavers had had numerous lovers, so I've been trying to contact those men as well."

Brady felt like a mule was sitting on his chest. "What happened to Kelly? How did the baby end up with CPS?"

"She suffered severe postpartum depression and did not seek help." Mary Jameson's eyes were accusatory. "Miss Deavers took her own life."

Uncomprehending, he blinked. "She committed suicide?"

"Pills."

Funny, wild, warmhearted Kelly had intentionally overdosed on pills? Shock pressed in on him, weighing down his heart, lungs, belly. "I didn't know."

"Why would you? Apparently you were just her sex buddy with a faulty condom."

He hadn't been there for Kelly. She had been alone and suffering and she'd taken the only way out she could find. "I . . . I didn't know," he echoed, stupidly, uselessly.

Silence descended over the office.

The caseworker studied him and he was surprised to find a tinge of compassion in her eyes. "This must be difficult for you."

"I . . . can't really process it. Kelly's gone?"

"She is."

Brady sank his head in his hands.

"You better start trying to pull it together if you're serious about taking responsibility for your actions." Mary Jameson's brief moment of compassion had passed.

Brady straightened. "Where is the baby?"

"The child has been in foster care for the past two months."

His chest tightened. He could hardly catch his breath. He had a baby. He had to focus on that. "How old is she?"

"Three months old."

Three months. He'd missed the first three months of her life. Brady never imagined anything could hurt like this. A floodgate of emotions overwhelmed him—fear, joy, remorse, guilt. "What's her name?"

"Orchid."

"That was Kelly's favorite flower," he mumbled.

"At least you knew that much about her," the caseworker wasn't even trying to hide her disdain any longer.

He supposed he deserved it. In Mary's mind he was no different from any other deadbeat dad. "I'm just human," he said, and spread out his hands. "But I'm not the kind of man who abandons his responsibilities."

"Let's not get ahead of ourselves." Mary Jameson's voice softened. "We must establish paternity first."

"Let's do the paternity test. Bring it on."

"You can go across the street to the lab as soon as we're done here."

"How long does it take to get the results?"

"Usually three to ten days. We can ask for it to be expedited, so that you don't have to be inconvenienced any longer than necessary if the child is not yours."

"I do want her," he reiterated. "If she is mine."

"I am pleased to hear you say that, Mr. Talmadge, but I'm afraid it's not going to be that simple."

Alarmed, Brady clenched his hands. "What do you mean?"

"You're going to have to prove to me that you deserve this little girl."

"What?" He gulped, outraged, and yet at the same time, he understood exactly what Mary Jameson was saying. Who was he to be a father? He had no credentials. No experience. Nothing to deem himself worthy to handle responsibility of this magnitude.

"If you turn out to be this child's father, you are going to have to do a lot of changing before you get full custody." Mary Jameson leaned across her desk and ticked off her conditions on her fingers. "One, you're going to have to provide a permanent residence. I cannot release her to a man who travels from town to town. A horse trailer is not a proper environment for a child to grow up in."

His nomadic lifestyle, the way of life that had been his salvation, was now coming back to bite him in the ass. "Okay," he agreed without hesitating.

"Two, you're going to have to get a real job. No more of this vagabond, spotty employment stuff."

"My employment isn't spotty." No, but the payment sometimes was spotty as with anyone who ran their own business. It was okay for him to weather the dry spells subsisting on peanut butter and crackers, but kids had needs. Expensive needs. Yes, he had some savings, he didn't have expensive needs and socked away a big chunk of his salary, but it was tied up in a 401(k).

"Don't argue with me," the woman snapped. "Regular employment."

Brady raised a palm. "Okay, all right. I'll do it. I'll rent a house, get a regular job."

"That's not all." She ticked off the third condition. "You're going to have to have a support system if you want anything more than supervised visitation."

"Support system. What does that mean?"

"Do you have friends and family who can help you with child care? Who will be there to support you emotionally? Because believe me, you *will* need support. Single parenthood is the toughest thing you'll ever undertake. Do you have someone that can provide your daughter with a positive female role model? A mother? A sister? A girlfriend? A fiancée? A wife? Any kind of stable relationship? Because if the answer is no, then you better start building long-term relationships and building them quick."

Annie worried.

That morning, Brady had gone to see Mary Jameson and he hadn't called her. He'd promised to call her as soon as he found something out. He'd been gone hours. He hadn't called and Annie was worried. She couldn't imagine what he was going through, but it had to be life changing.

Why do you care? It is not as if you had a future with this man. Still, she could not help feeling melancholic.

"Where is your head today?" Mariah asked kindly, putting a hand on Annie's shoulder. "I just called your name three times. Daydreaming about that handsome cowboy of yours?"

Annie sat in front of the computer at The Bride Wore Cowboy Boots, arranging the seating chart for an upcoming wedding reception. Prissy was in the back, stocking the supply room. Seating arrangements were tricky when the bride or groom's parents were divorced and feuding. In this case, it was both the bride's and the groom's parents. Given all the hostility brewing, Annie had her doubts whether *this* marriage could go the distance.

Oh well, you won't be here to see it anyway.

"Please forgive my inattention," Annie apologized.

Mariah winked, leaned against the counter with her arms folded over her chest. "Hey, I know what it's like to be in love."

She was not in love. She liked Brady. Yes. She liked him a lot. He was a nice guy and a good friend. And he was sexy. So very sexy, but that was not love. That was like and sexual attraction and friendship and . . . All right, so she was enamored, but that wasn't the same thing as love. Right? Just because her heart skipped a beat when Brady walked into the room, it might not be anything more than her hormones calling to his and vice versa. They had chemistry. That was a given.

"I'm not in—"

The door opened, interrupting Annie in mid-denial. Melinda Messing walked over the threshold followed by a lanky man with a ponytail and a big professional digital camera hung around his neck.

Mariah spun away from the counter and hurried to meet the woman, hand outstretched. "Good to see you again, Mrs. Messing."

Annie stood, straightened. They had not heard

from Mrs. Messing since the day she had shown her around the ranch and Annie couldn't help feeling that she had somehow made a misstep with the wealthy woman.

"I'm back," Melinda Messing said.

"We're so happy." Mariah pumped her hand. "Welcome, welcome."

"Hello again." Mrs. Messing smiled at Annie.

Out of habit, Annie gave her a regal wave, rather than the local five-finger wiggle. "Good afternoon."

Melinda Messing was dressed in Ralph Lauren today. Tailored white blouse, starched dark wash jeans, Jimmy Choo kitten heels.

"Mrs. Messing," Mariah exclaimed. "It's good to see you. How may I help you?"

"Congratulations," Melinda Messing told Mariah. "The Bride Wore Cowboy Boots is on our shortlist."

"What can we do to convince you that we're the right wedding planning service for you?" Mariah asked.

Melinda Messing's eyes met Annie's, but it was to Mariah that she said, "You would become the front-runner if you could convince your assistant to pose as Princess Annabella Farrington and host a Victorian-era high tea for the wedding reception."

"What?" Mariah frowned.

Annie pulled a hard breath of air down deep into her lungs, curled her hands into soft fists. Had Melinda Messing somehow put two and two together and figured out that she actually *was* Princess Annabella? Was her whole wonderful charade about to end?

Melinda Messing broke into a wide smile. It was the first time Annie had seen a genuine smile on the woman's face. "Peyton and I have reached an agreement. I'll concede to the cowboy wedding shenanigans if she'll agree to make the reception a high tea. It was easy to convince her when she heard you have a Princess Annabella look-alike working for you."

"What?" Mariah repeated, slanting an odd look in Annie's direction.

"You're right," the photographer put in, saying something for the first time. "She could be Princess Annabella's twin sister."

"Really?" Mariah narrowed her eyes. "I don't see it."

Feeling like a bug under a microscope, Annie shifted her weight from foot to foot and forced a pleasant smile.

"Peyton adores Princess Annabella and this way we'll at least have something classy and elegant for my friends and family to enjoy."

Annie did not know how classy hiring a fake princess was, but it did not sound particularly patrician to her.

"So let me see if I understand this correctly," Mariah said. "Instead of the traditional wedding reception, you want an elaborate tea instead."

"Not just any tea, but a *high* tea." Melinda Messing raised her eyebrows when she said the word "high." "We'll have to schedule it for the official tea time. Four in the afternoon."

"Then you mean low tea." If there was one thing Annie knew, it was tea ceremony. Ten percent of her princess duties entailed going to or hosting charity teas.

"Oh, no, no." Melinda Messing looked at her as if she was an uneducated hick. "I mean high tea."

"Then you'll want tea service at six or seven P.M."

"Official tea time is at four P.M.," Melinda Messing insisted.

"For low tea, yes."

"That's incorrect."

"Low tea is traditionally held at four P.M.," Annie explained patiently. She probably should have let it go, but of tea she was certain. "In Victorian times, the upper crust took their tea at four P.M. High tea was in the evening for the workers when they came home from the factories and fields. Heartier fare is served for high tea because it combines low tea and dinner into one meal."

"You have your facts wrong," Melinda Messing argued. "High tea is for royalty. Low tea is for the lower classes."

"Nope," Prissy said cheerfully. "Just Googled it on my smart phone. Annie's right. Low tea is the elaborate tea ceremony. High tea is just a fancy way of saying early supper with tea service."

"That can't be right."

"Check it out." Prissy passed Melinda Messing her iPhone. To Annie, she leaned down to whisper, "Girl, where did you learn so much about flippin' tea?"

Mrs. Messing looked down her nose at the phone, used her fingers to make the font bigger. "Well," she said. "So it is."

Annie waited for an apology.

"Then low tea is what we want," the snobbish woman said to Mariah.

"Low tea it is," Mariah said.

Annie raised a hand. "Actually, if the tea ceremony is to be a substitute for the traditional reception, then perhaps you should consider making it
high tea served later in the day. It's at a more traditional time and you can serve heartier food."

"No." Mrs. Messing shook her head. "The wedding day is going to be plain enough. We want to go
all out with the tea."

"Because it's all about the show," Prissy put in.

"Exactly." Mrs. Messing passed the iPhone back
to Prissy. "We won't hold it in that horse barn either.
There's some lovely Victorian homes in this town,
I'm sure you can find one that could host a tea-party
wedding reception."

"That can be arranged." Mariah nodded.

Melinda Messing clasped her hands together like
a prizefighter who had just won the bout. "Excellent. Now let's talk menu. We want this as authentic
as possible. Have any of you ever been to a Victorian high . . . er . . . low tea?"

Annie and the cameraman both raised their
hands.

Everyone turned to stare at the cameraman.

"What?" He shrugged. "I like tea."

"Linen tablecloths and tea napkins are a must.
We'll need china and silver service for a hundred."
Melinda Messing paused, stroked her chin, and
rolled her eyes upward as if searching her memory
for the details of teas she'd attended.

"You'll have a hundred guests?" Mariah blinked.

"Yes, we're keeping it small."

"Small?" Prissy muttered just loud enough for Annie
to hear. "I'd hate to see her idea of a big wedding."

"A hundred guests aren't going to fit in a Victorian home," Mariah pointed out.

"Oh, we'll have it in a backyard garden."

"I've got a place in mind," Mariah said. "It's not a Victorian home, but rather a Victorian garden setting. It's called Pandora's Garden. In 1926 a British portrait painter moved with his bride, Pandora, to Jubilee—she was a fiend for cutting horses—and he built her an elaborate English garden. They're both gone now, but the gardens remain as a local treasure run by their descendants. We could host the reception tea there."

"That sounds splendid. Yes, yes, yes. Let's do that." Melinda Messing face lit up with excitement.

"What time of year are you thinking?" Mariah asked. "Texas weather is only accommodating a few months out of the year for a pleasant outdoor experience."

"Tell me about it." The woman fanned herself with a hand. "It's already like an oven outside and it's only the beginning of July. Luckily, they've set the date for next April."

"Lots of showers in April," Mariah said.

"We'll put up canopies just in case."

"Okay."

"Now, let's talk menu." Melinda Messing shifted her gaze to Annie. "What are some of your favorite tea items?"

"Water English cucumber with minted butter is traditional," Annie said.

"On white bread?"

"Sourdough might make a nice twist."

"Good idea," Melinda said. "What else?"

"Roast beef with horseradish. Stilton cheese and pear in miniature pita pockets, smoked salmon with lemon-zested butter, Black Forest ham with grainy Dijon mustard," Annie ticked off the menu of the last teas she'd hosted.

"Damn," Prissy said. "You sure know a lot about tea sandwiches."

Annie was on a roll. At last, here was something she was an expert on. "You want loose leaf tea, no tea bags. So you'll need a hundred strainers or tea balls. You'll need sugar cubes, lemon slices, milk."

Everyone was staring at her now, jaws agape.

Annie smiled, enjoying herself. "For dessert you must have scones and clotted cream. End of discussion."

"Yes, yes." Melinda Messing nodded.

"I also recommend four other dessert options. Some classics are lemon squares, ginger pecan biscuits, lavender shortbread, and the Victoria sponge cake."

"What's that?"

"It's a sponge cake elevated to celestial status by orange zest, rosewater, raspberry jam, scraped vanilla bean, iced with a delicate sugar glaze and topped with fresh raspberries," Annie rattled off.

Simultaneously, everyone—including the cameraman—breathed in a hungry sigh.

"As for teas," she went on, "I recommend having three selections. Earl Grey is the old standby, but I favor Baroness Grey. It is a blend of high-grown Ceylon black tea infused with cornflowers, lemon peels, and rose petals and flavored—as is Earl Grey—with bergamot." It felt good. This knowledge. Their admiration as they hung on her every word. She'd been hosting teas all her life and never considered it a useful skill until now.

"Wow," Prissy exclaimed. "She's the tea whisperer."

Pride puffed Annie's chest and she just kept talking, never stopping to consider she might be giving away more about herself than was prudent. "Then there is Darjeeling. It is a light golden tea from Northern India. It possesses a delicate muscatel note and it is sometimes referred to as the champagne of teas."

"She *is* the tea whisperer." Melinda Messing laughed.

Giddiness galloped over her. She did not know when to stop. "I also recommend Red Rooibos. It is an herbal decaffeinated tea with a fresh, sweet flavor."

"You are a treasure and when Peyton sees how much you look like Princess Annabella, she's going to be beside herself." The cultured woman motioned to the cameraman. "Let's get the photograph now."

"Photograph?" Annie said, but no one answered her. The next thing she knew, she was standing beside Melinda Messing while the photographer snapped their picture.

When he was finished, the older woman turned to Mariah. "I could not be happier with the arrangements we made today. I want the menu exactly as Annie described."

"Absolutely."

"And Annie *will* be available for the tea. Perhaps she could be persuaded to wear a long, blond wig so she will look exactly like Princess Annabella and preside over the reception."

"Of course she will," Mariah said.

"It goes without saying that she'll be well compensated." Melinda Messing beamed.

"I ... um ..." Annie could not do this. She could not agree to do something she knew that she would not be able to do. "I will not—"

"Mind wearing a wig," Mariah finished for her and shot her a please-do-this-for-me expression. "Right, Annie?"

"If Annie doesn't participate, it's a deal breaker," Melinda Messing said in the petulant tone of someone accustomed to getting her way.

"Right," she said with a sinking heart and promised, "I will host your daughter's wedding tea."

But it was all a lie. By next April, she would be living in Dubinstein with Teddy, most likely pregnant with their first child.

It fully hit her then. What her future would be like. What she would be leaving behind in Jubilee—the cowboy way of life, the friends she'd made, this job she loved.

Brady.

Annie's chest tightened. What had she gotten herself into? She should have kept her mouth shut, never revealed her knowledge of tea. Honestly, she hadn't thought this far ahead. Her trip was to have been a lark. She had not expected to fall in love with these people. This town.

She would not be the only one suffering for her little adventure. When the truth came out, Chandler and Strawn would lose their jobs. Mariah would probably lose the Messing wedding. Everyone who'd befriended her in Jubilee would feel shocked, bewildered, betrayed.

It was only then that Annie understood the full consequences of what she'd done and she was deeply ashamed. She was going to have to break the news to everyone, and the sooner the better.

But how?

Plagued by misgivings, Annie had almost forgotten about Brady and his problems until Mariah dropped her off at the cabin and she spied him sitting on the front porch rocking chair.

The minute their eyes met, she knew his problems were much bigger than hers.

She moved up the steps toward him.

He got to his feet, his movement setting the chair to rocking. His shoulders were slumped as if supporting the weight of the world, and half-closed lids hooded his eyes.

"You look as if you could use a hug," she said.

"I wouldn't say no to the offer."

She wrapped her arms around him, pressed her head to his chest. He smoothed her hair with his hand and they stood on the porch listening to the beating of each other's hearts and the cooing of the doves in the cottonwood trees. He smelled of horses and sunshine and hay. A smell she'd quickly grown to love.

"How did it go?" she murmured.

"It went."

"Meaning?"

"I'm awaiting the results of the paternity test."

"How do you feel?"

His body stiffened in her embrace. "I'm pretty much trying not to feel anything until there's something to feel about."

Annie nodded. "I suppose that's the best policy."

He untangled her arms from around him and stepped back to sit in the rocking chair, pulling her along with him. She ended up in his lap, his firm thigh muscles taut against her buttocks. Gently, he set the chair to rocking.

She told him about Melinda Messing and the Victorian tea. "She thinks I look like Princess Annabella," she said, carefully testing the waters. She was going to have to tell Brady the truth sometime, but she had two more beautiful weeks left before she had to return to Monesta in time for her own wedding. Did she really want to cut that short by telling too much, too soon?

The longer you let it go on, the harder it's going to be.

Yes, yes, she knew that.

"But you're not going to be here come spring, are you?" he asked.

"I can't."

"That secret of yours again."

"Yes." The impulse to confide in Brady pushed at her, but if she told him now they would never make love. Never consummate the thrill ride of their attraction.

It's too late. Far too late for that and you know it. She had to leave. There was no question of being able to stay. Yet the thought of leaving without fully knowing him in the physical sense was too much to bear.

So when he tilted her head back and started kissing her, Annie did not resist. Resisting him was useless. His life force was too strong, her need for him devastating.

She kissed him back with every bit of passion she had inside her.

If you make love to him, it is just going to be that much harder to leave.

But she knew deep down inside that no matter what she did, she was not getting out of this unscathed. She broke the kiss, pulled back. "Brady, there's something I have to tell you."

Concern darkened his eyes. "Your secret?"

"Yes."

His entire body tensed. "What is it, Buttercup?"

She moistened her lips. "I . . ."

Before she could go on, he placed an index finger over her lips. "Wait. Shh. If it's bad news, let's just let it lie for now. We've got a great weekend coming up. It's Joe and Mariah's Fourth of July party and it very well could be my last weekend as a childless man. If it can wait, Monday is soon enough to kick over that rock and dig around in each other's secrets."

"Are you certain?"

"Yeah," he said. "Let's just keep our mouths shut and enjoy each other's company for a few more days. This might be the last good time we ever have together."

"All right," she whispered, because this was exactly what she wanted too. "All right."

CHAPTER FOURTEEN

You might be a princess if . . . when you kiss Prince
Charming fireworks go off.

After their talk on the porch, Brady withdrew,
claiming he was too exhausted to be good
company and spent the night in his trailer
along with Trampas. Annie had to admit she was relieved. If he had stayed, she knew they would make
love. Suddenly, the thing she wanted most seemed
just out of reach and she was too afraid to grasp for
it, because she feared it would come up dust in her
hands.

All day on Saturday, they both helped Joe and
Mariah and the ranch hands set up for the Fourth
of July bash on Sunday.

When had she become so adept at deception?
All she'd ever wanted was a bit of an adventure. A
chance to taste life as an ordinary person. A vacation, if you will, from her royal duties.

But with dawn had come the start of a new day
and a change of attitude. Annie couldn't wait to ex-

perience this all-American event—fireworks, delicious food cooked on the grill, and time spent in or around water. Her time left was short, so she made up her mind to be happy and take things as they came. Today, she was going to enjoy herself. Monday was soon enough for problems.

The guests started arriving at Mariah and Joe's house around noon. Annie wore a dress she borrowed from Mariah, since she never got around to spending her paycheck on a new dress of her own. Not with everything else that had happened. It was nice though. Borrowing clothes. It made her feel ordinary.

The dress was pink and made her stand out with her black hair. She'd had to dye it again last week when the blond started peeping through. The dress had cap sleeves, a fitted bodice, and a soft flowy shirt that twirled around her thighs when she walked. She did not miss the hot look in Brady's eyes when she swirled into the room.

Soon the house was full and Annie met so many people she couldn't keep them straight. The party trailed out the back door to the patio and pool area. Cooling fans and open-air tents had been set up to keep the guests comfortable and shaded from the Texas heat. Country-and-western music rocked from the sound system. The grill was smoking, the smell of mesquite in the air.

Kids were already jumping into the pool, splashing and thrashing about. Cordy and Ila played lifeguards, sitting poolside, stealing kisses now and again. Lissette was in the shallow end of the pool, holding her son in her lap. Prissy and Paul lay in hammocks on the far side of the yard. Joe and Brady had gone off somewhere. Probably talking about horses.

"Did you bring a swimming suit?" Mariah asked, hoisting a tray full of cut vegetables.

"No," Annie said. She'd never swum in public. There was a pool at the palace and the family owned a secluded beach. Even though she wanted to go in and cool off, she felt shy about exposing so much bare skin in front of strangers.

"I've got a bikini you can borrow if you want to take a dip."

"You are too generous."

"Nonsense. I know what's it like to be broke and the new kid on the block."

Annie did not quite understand the idiom, but she got the gist of it. "Maybe later. Could I help you with something?"

"Grab that fruit platter from the fridge, thanks."

Annie retrieved the fruit platter and trailed after Mariah as she took the appetizers to the patio.

"I noticed you're not spending much time with Brady. Is something wrong?" Mariah bumped aside an empty patio chair with her hip and settled the vegetable tray on the table along with the other food that guests had brought.

"No, no." Annie forced a smile. She wasn't going to mention the baby. It wasn't her place. "Everything's fine."

"I am so happy you two found each other." Mariah plunked down in the chair, pulled out another one for Annie. "Sit, sit."

Annie put the fruit platter beside the vegetable

tray and sat down beside Mariah. They chatted for a while and eventually Annie relaxed.

Joe and Brady joined them in the backyard, bringing in slabs of meat like hunters and slapping it on the grill. They cooked and played with the children. From time to time, Brady would glance over and catch Annie's eye and smile. He was in the same frame of mind as she. He'd decided to make the best of their day. Enjoy the moment. He was good at that. He had taught her a lot in their short time together.

Without being asked, he brought her a glass of iced tea and leaned down to kiss the side of her neck briefly before trailing off again to jump into the pool to play with the kids. The spot on her neck tingled. The brand of his lips lingering.

Annie took a sip of tea and watched him through half-closed eyes. This was happiness. Being with friends. Cooking out. Enjoying a holiday. A languidness seeped over her. She felt dizzy with the joy of the moment. Just for today, everything was perfect.

It felt as if she'd stepped into the pages of a book or into the reel of a movie. Her version of *Roman Holiday. Annabella's Texas Holiday*. So simple and lighthearted. For now. She felt soft and the world shone sweet and pink like a peach blossom.

She rolled the happiness around on her tongue. It tasted like iced tea with lemon and sugar. Summer in Texas, Mariah told her, meant sweet iced tea. She was drinking summer, sipping Texas, ingesting holiday magic. She pushed aside the melancholia waiting in the wings like a velvet curtain ready to fall at the end of a play. For now, she was onstage.

The day wore on. They ate. They drank. Toasts were made. Finally, Mariah persuaded Annie to come into the pool. She donned Mariah's red and white polka dot bikini and she splashed with the kids, lighthearted and happy.

Brady and Joe were sitting poolside in white lawn chairs. The kids were trying to get Annie to dive from the board. She stood, dripping wet, at the end of the board, trying to decide if it was something she really wanted to do or not.

"Jump, jump, jump," chanted the kids.

"Look at her," Brady said to Joe. "Annie has the mannerisms of English royalty."

Annie's cheeks heated at the overheard conversation, and just to prove she was as ordinary as everyone else, she ran and jumped off the diving board into the circle of cheering children. She hit the water with a loud smack and came to the surface just in time to hear Joe laugh.

"Right," Joe said. "A belly-flopping English princess."

Brady dived into the pool then and they all played Marco Polo. During the game, his eyes kept straying to Annie's.

As the sun edged toward the horizon, Annie got out of the pool, slipped into one of the cabanas, and changed back into her pink dress. She wore matching sandals today, something else borrowed from Mariah, instead of her cowboy boots. When she stepped from the cabana, there stood Brady looking darkly handsome in faded Wranglers and a white short-sleeved shirt, his damp hair swept back off his forehead and smelling of Texas summer.

"Hi," he said.

"Hello," she whispered, looking into the face she had quickly come to cherish. She had no right to fall for him, but fairness didn't factor into her feelings.

Mothers were getting their kids out of the pool for watermelon, apple pie, and ice cream that Ruby was serving for dessert. Joe and Cordy and Paul had gone out into the pasture to get ready for the fireworks display. Cordy belonged to the volunteer fire department and he'd brought a water truck into the field, just to be on the safe side.

"C'mon." Brady held out his hand.

She took it.

He put an index finger to his lips. "Shh."

Annie struggled not to giggle. "What is it?"

"We're going to slip off."

"We are not going to watch the fireworks show?"

"Buttercup, where we're going you'll be able to see the whole sky without craning your neck and besides, we'll be making some fireworks of our own."

Annie's heart skipped a beat. Ever since he'd found out he might have fathered a child, Brady had not mentioned sex. But now here he was, leading her away in the gathering darkness, leaving their friends behind.

He guided her around the back of the house, crouching down, still holding on to her hand and keeping his index finger over his mouth as they dodged from car to car trying to remain out of sight of the men in the field and the women and children in the backyard.

Annie could not stop the giggle from bubbling up her throat.

"Shh," Brady said, but he was laughing too, his chest heaving from trying to hold in the sound.

The last rays of sun tipped the trees. Fireflies scooted through the gathering twilight, twinkling up there in the sky with their ghostly glow. Slinking and duckwalking as fast as they could, they made it to the barn. Inside, it was hot and stuffy and smelled strongly of horses.

"We cannot see fireworks from inside here." Annie's nose itched. She had been taught it was crass to scratch one's nose, so she wriggled it instead. Horses shifted in their stalls, munching oats. Some of the ranch hands must have just fed them. The air tasted dusty.

"C'mon." Brady guided her to the back of the barn, his palm against her hip. There was a ladder leading to the hayloft. "You first."

"You just want to look up my dress."

"I want to be here to catch you if you were to slip and fall, but yeah, the looking-up-your-dress thing is a perk."

Holding her skirt flat against her fanny with one hand, she climbed the ladder using her other.

"Spoilsport," he accused, his voice filled with smiles.

The first fireworks went off with a shriek and a boom.

The hayloft was dark and mounded with earthy, sweet-smelling straw. Annie could barely make out her hand in front of her face. Brady scaled the ladder behind her, then moved to open a set of wide double doors. Moonlight poured in just as another rocket went off, showering the sky with vivid yellow sparks. From here, it was like having nature's big-screen television set right in front of them.

Brady took a pitchfork, rearranged the loose hay in a big pile near the open doors. Once he had it to his liking, he sat cross-legged, took Annie's wrist, and tugged her down beside him. "Lean back."

She leaned back against the prickly straw, kicked off her sandals, felt the rough boards of the loft beneath her feet. Another rocket went off and then another; the smell of gunpowder drifted in on the wind. In the distance, they could hear their friends applauding and making noises of approval.

It was warm and sticky up here, but Annie did not mind. Brady cradled her in the crook of his arm and she inhaled his masculine scent. He kissed the soft indention where her ear connected to her head. She had never seen fireworks so close or been in such a private and primal place as this hayloft, Annie in her borrowed pink dress with the snug-fitting bodice, at the other edge of the world from Monesta, the other edge of an imaginary future—the edge of simplistic beauty and Brady's mouth; the rim, the summer border of holiday bliss.

She was crazy with happiness. Delirious with it. Sick. And now Brady was kissing her and holding her hand.

"It's beautiful," she whispered. "Thank you for bringing me up here."

"But not as beautiful as you." His fingertips tracked over her bare arms.

At first, she felt nothing but a slight tickling, but she trusted him. He was a man who knew how to make a woman feel good. So she waited, held her breath, readied herself for the sensation she knew he would deliver.

And then it came.

The pressure, rolling in on waves heavy as ocean swells. She closed her eyes and let the swells encompass her. She felt his mouth play over her body, nibbling and kissing, licking and swirling. The pleasure was beautiful, sublime. She wanted it to last forever, but then Brady stopped and sat up.

She opened her eyes. "What is it?"

"Everything's changed."

"I know." She sighed. They hadn't been able to keep the focus on happiness. The moment was only a moment and then there was another one and in *this* moment, the fantasy faded, dimmed.

He reached out a tender hand and brushed an errant lock of hair from her forehead. "We have to talk."

"I know."

A rapid fire of firecrackers went off in the background, but neither one of them was looking. Their gazes were hung on each other.

"You've got your secrets that you don't want to talk about," Brady said, "and I'm trying to respect that, but if we're going to be closer, if we're going to take this relationship to the next level, we really have to be honest with each other. I'm not going to push you, but it's time I told you about me."

"You don't have to do this," Annie said, fear supplanting her earlier delight. She was toeing a tightrope here, wanting to hold on to the dream, to have her proverbial cake and eat it too.

It was an impossible dream, but so sweet. How she wanted to hold on to it!

She wanted to beg him to please, please stop talking and just kiss her, but she knew Brady was going to have his say. It was time. The least she could do was listen. She owed him that. He'd given her so much. This sweet memory she could hold on to for the rest of her life.

A tumble of emotion swelled in her. She blinked, turned her head from him, looked at the sky. More fireworks exploded, a burst of red, white, blue, green. They popped, shattered, and for one brief second it was the most beautiful explosion, and then just as quickly as they had ascended, the sparks sputtered, spent, fell to earth.

Brady let out a pent-up breath, pushed fingers through his unruly hair.

"There is no need to unburden yourself to me," she said.

"If you don't want to be my sounding board, I understand," he said. "But I really do want to tell you."

"All right," she murmured, feeling both trapped and privileged to hear his story.

"I told you that I ran away from home when I was fifteen," Brady began.

She burrowed her toes into the hay, pressed the soles of her feet against the boards, brought her knees to her chest, pulled the hem of her skirt down over her knees, hugged herself. "Yes."

"I didn't even have a driver's license, much less a car, so I hitchhiked."

"That is why you picked me up on the side of the road? Because you remembered what it was like to be alone on the side of the highway."

"I knew what kind of trouble you were courting, even if you didn't."

"Why did you run away?" she asked, fully aware that she was opening herself up to the same probing questions.

He did not answer.

She rested her head on her knees, slid a sidelong glance at him. The muscles in his forearms bunched as he flexed his fingers, tension riding his nerve endings. She reached out to touch his arm. He calmed instantly, his muscles relaxing under the heat of her hand. "It's okay. You owe me nothing."

"Maybe not," he said. "But I owe it to me."

Another burst of fireworks lit the sky, but neither of them watched the colorful rockets. She moved a big toe against the rough wood of the loft floor, felt the rippling ridges. His breathing was heavy, deliberate, as if he was trying desperately to control the flow of oxygen. As if it could control the chaos of his memory. He was hurting and Annie couldn't stand it, but neither could she do anything to change the past.

"My father beat on me pretty regularly."

Annie didn't mean to cry out, but her horror was a startled, sharp gasp in the shadowy confines of the hayloft. "Those scars on your back," she whispered.

Absentmindedly, he reached a hand around to

touch his back. "The son of a bitch was fond of soaking the bullwhip in water before he used it on me."

Annie moved her hand from his arm down to find his hand and squeezed it. "Oh, Brady."

Silently, he clung to her hand. She could feel the painful memory of that long-ago time travel from his body into hers. "This was your real father?"

"There's the rub," Brady said.

"He was your stepfather?"

"In a way, but I didn't know that until I was fifteen."

A cluster of Roman candles went off in rapid succession. *Pow. Pow. Pow.*

"You told me you had four brothers. That you were the middle child. How many were half brothers?"

"All of them."

Annie frowned. "I am not following you."

"My father never whipped any of my brothers. Not once. Never touched a hair on their heads in rage. Just me. I was the only one singled out."

"That's horrible! What kind of father does that?"

"For years I thought something was wrong with me. That I deserved this kind of treatment. I was punished for the slightest infraction. If I didn't put out the garbage, I'd be whipped. If I got a C in math. If I didn't cut the lawn in a perfect pattern."

"That is child abuse! That is criminal!"

"Yeah, but I was a kid. I took his discipline to heart. I took it to mean that I was defective in some way."

"You were not defective."

"I can see that from an adult point of view, but when you're young and living it . . ." He shook his head. "I compensated by becoming the class clown.

Get everyone on my side by making them laugh. I tried to pack as much fun in a day as I could because I knew when I got home at night . . ."

"Why did your mother not intervene?"

Brady gave a harsh laugh. "I suppose she feared he'd take his anger out on her the way he took it out on me."

"He didn't beat her?" The hot barn was suddenly ice cold.

"No, just me. The whipping boy."

His pain was her pain. She felt it. Swallowed it. Her stomach burned. Her heart seared. "I can see how that would confuse and hurt a child."

"I thought it meant I wasn't worthy of the things other people got, but Dutch Callahan taught me different."

"Mariah's father?"

"Yeah. He might not have been a good dad to her, but to me, he was salvation. He took me off the road. Brought me to Jubilee. Gave me a job tending horses. He changed the direction of my life. Kept me from getting into serious trouble with the law. Kept me sane."

She admired how he raised his chin, squared his shoulders. He had been through a lot, but he had survived. She admired too how he had turned violence into tenderness. Transmuting the hatred his father had dished out into love for horses. "Dutch sounds like he was a very good man."

"He was. And after my father I desperately needed a good role model."

"Did you ever find out why your father singled you out? Why he treated you so terribly?"

Brady paused again, stared out at the night. The air smelled smoky, black. "Because of my mother's dark secret."

Overhead, more brilliant starbursts of light, a breathtaking panorama of sight and sound. Their hands stayed clenched, their backs resting against the hay.

Annie said nothing for a long time, and then finally she nudged him. He had come this far. Now, she had to know everything about the past that plagued him. "What was her secret?"

"My father lost his job after my brother Colton was born. To make ends meet, my mother took a job as a cook at a ranch near our home. Dad took to drinking to cope with unemployment."

"Job loss can be so difficult on a man's ego." Annie had read this somewhere. She had no real idea what she was talking about. In her world, the men were born into their positions. There was no taking it away. She could not really identify with Brady's situation, but she could certainly feel his pain. It was in his face, his muscles, and his tone of voice.

"My mother dealt with his drinking by taking comfort where she could find it," he said. "She had an affair with the businessman who owned the ranch. Later, he got elected to the Texas state senate."

"That man is your real father?"

"Yes."

"How did you find out?"

"He came to our house."

"Your real father came to your house?" Annie echoed. She did not know what to do or say to make things better. There was no fixing this for him.

"Yes, and as result, the man I thought was my father gave me the beating of my life."

"The beating that caused the scars on your back?"

"Yeah. After he left me bloody and unable to walk, my mother found me, tended my wounds, and finally told me the truth."

"I cannot begin to imagine how you felt."

"The emotional pain was worse than the physical pain, but at last, everything made sense. I knew I would never get along with the man who raised me and that there was no point in staying and taking his abuse."

"Why did your real father come to see you?"

"Thinking back on it, I realize he probably just wanted to see me. I don't remember the excuse he made for coming there. I only remember my old man took it out on me."

Annie stroked his head, letting him know he was safe with her. "You don't have to say any more."

"I had known all along I was different. That I did not fit in. My brothers knew it too. They tried to defend me from the old man, but once you become the scapegoat, there's no scraping that stigma off."

"So you are not really close with any of your brothers."

Brady shook his head. "They have their lives. I have mine."

"What happened after your mother told you her shameful secret?"

"I went to see the senator at his ranch. He didn't admit to being my father. He said my mother was lying, but I could see the truth in his eyes."

"How could he be so cavalier?"

"He had a family of his own and he was too cowardly to let his secret out. But he did give me some money. So I took it and I left and I told myself I would never go back. That I would never have that kind of life. I was afraid to trust. I knew how badly secrets hurt. If I'd only known why I was different, why my father did not accept it, I could have dealt with it. But my mother kept her secret and it hurt everyone involved. It's why I hate secrets. Why I keep prodding you to reveal yours. Secrets can only hurt."

She wanted to tell him. She'd have to tell him eventually. She might as well tell him now. "Brady, I—"

A deep, anguished, keening wail shattered the night.

Annie stared at Brady. "Was that fireworks?"

The second gut-ripping scream told them it was not. Fear pulsed through her. "Something awful is happening." She searched for her sandals, slipped them on her feet. Brady had already started down the steps. He waited at the bottom of the ladder for her. The minute her feet touched the ground, he took her by the hand and they ran back to the ranch house.

Fear seized Annie by the throat and would not let go.

Brady shoved open the front door, pulling Annie along with him, and they bulleted into the backyard to find their friends pale and trembling. Mariah was on the ground with Lissette cradled in her arms. Lissette clung to her, sobbing helplessly, completely broken.

The air smelled of burnt fireworks. The children stood wide-eyed. One girl sucked on her thumb. Another little boy was crying. The adults seemed frozen, unable to move. Joe stood by the patio door, his head in his hands.

"What is it?" Brady whispered to Joe. "What's happened?"

That's when Annie saw the two military men standing off to one side looking stiff and solemn in their uniforms. Her pulse leaped in her throat.

"It's Jake Moncrief," Joe said. "He's dead."

Chapter Fifteen

You might be a princess if . . . you keep your head in a crisis.

In the wake of the news of Jake Moncrieff's death, Brady couldn't believe how Annie immediately leaped into action, herding the children inside the house, taking them upstairs, calming them down, putting the younger ones down to sleep while putting a movie on the television for the older children to watch.

Brady felt lost, helpless, but Annie seemed made for a crisis. Once the children were settled, she came back downstairs, made a pot of coffee, and began cleaning the house. She stayed in the shadows, out of the way, unobtrusively doing what needed to be done so everyone else could concentrate on consoling Lissette.

Near midnight, once Lissette's parents arrived from Dallas and took her and Kyle home, and after the military casualty notification officers had departed, everyone else collected their sleepy children and somberly filtered out, until it was just Mariah and Joe and Brady and Annie left. At two o'clock in the morning, the four of them sat in the living room without talking. There was nothing to say.

"I guess we should all try to get some sleep," Joe said vaguely. "It seems so unreal. Jake was so vital."

"I keep thinking of those Disney World tickets he bought Lissette. How he promised he'd come home." Mariah sniffled into a Kleenex.

"Shh, shh." Joe took his wife in his arms, kissed the top of her head, rubbed his hand up and down her back.

"I'm going to take Annie back to the cabin," Brady said, getting up off the couch.

"There's no need. We've got a guest room."

"Thanks for the offer," Brady said, "but you all need time to grieve."

"The shop is closed tomorrow. Sleep in," Mariah told Annie.

"You do the same as well," Annie said.

"As if Jonah would let me. When you've got a baby, life goes on."

Mariah's words echoed in his head as Brady took Annie back to the cabin. *When you've got a baby, life goes on.* Very soon, that could be *his* reality.

Neither spoke on the short ride over. He pulled to a stop in the driveway.

"Are you coming in?" she asked, her hand on the passenger side door.

"Do you want me to come in?"

Silently, she got out, went around to his side of the truck, opened the door, took his hand, and led him inside the cabin. It was her turn to take charge. To be in control. Brady let himself be led.

They let the dogs out, and then let them back in again. They fell into bed with their clothes on. Exhausted and gritty, their hearts heavy. They wrapped their arms around each other and just let sleep claim them.

Hours later, the chiming of Brady's cell phone awakened them simultaneously.

"God," he muttered, fumbling for it on the bedside table. He felt as hung over as if he'd downed a quart of whiskey. "What now?"

Annie sat up, her hair mussed, eyes bleary. She looked as worn out as he felt.

"Hello?" He pressed his lips together to suppress a yawn and darted a glance at the clock. Nine-thirty.

"Is this Brady Talmadge?"

"It is." He'd been too foggy to think of checking the caller ID.

"This is Mary Jameson."

His body tensed. For one brief moment, he'd forgotten about the child he might have fathered with Kelly Deavers. "Yes?"

"The results of the paternity tests have come back. I put a rush on it. I thought you'd want to know immediately."

"Yes, yes." He gulped, clutched the phone tighter.

"Mr. Talmadge, it's been confirmed. You are indeed Orchid's father. Are you prepared to do everything I asked of you in order to claim your daughter?"

Annie watched Brady switch off his cell phone and toss it back on the bedside table.

His skin paled, his hands shook, and an unmistakable grin stole over his face. "It's official. I'm a dad."

"How do you feel about that?" A strange jittery sensation bumped along her nerve endings.

He splayed both hands to the top of his head, smoothed back his hair. "I don't know."

"Do you want her?"

His eyes met Annie's. "More than anything in the world, but I get the impression that Mary Jameson isn't going to make it easy for me to get custody."

"What does she want you to do?"

"I have to quit traveling. Find a place to live. Get a job and establish a support system."

"I can help with that," Annie blurted without weighing the consequences. *What have you done, Princess? You can't make this man promises you can't keep. There is no fairy tale here in Jubilee. No happily-ever-after for you with Brady Talmadge.*

His eyes lit up. A shift of emotions moved across his face—bewilderment, excitement, gratitude, disbelief. "How? You've told me over and over that you can't stay in Jubilee, that—"

"I can't."

Disappointment frosted his eyes. "So how in the hell could you possibly help me?"

She didn't blame him for the spurt of anger in his voice. He was overwhelmed. So she calmly and efficiently spelled out a plan that she hadn't even known she'd been planning. "You will move in here," she said. "I will help you fix the place up. Turn that big storage room into a nursery. You will go to work for Joe. Mariah told me he asked you to run their equine center."

"And where are you going to live?"

"Right here with you until it is time for me to leave."

"Does that mean . . ." He trailed off.

"That we will finally and fully become lovers?"

"Yeah."

"Is that what you want?"

"Buttercup, I've wanted you since I first laid eyes on you, but I'm a dad now and—"

She forced a smile. "This will be your last chance for a no-strings-attached relationship. Let us make the most of it."

"Annie." He reached for her, pulled her into his arms.

Helplessly, she sank against him.

"I'm afraid that if we take that last step, I'll never be able to let you go."

Tears clogged her throat, but she swallowed them back. "Sure you will. Orchid will keep you busy and you'll forget all about me." She took a fortifying breath and continued outlining her plan. "When Mary Jameson comes to inspect your living situation, I will be your support system. You can tell her I am your girlfriend or that we're engaged. Whatever you need to say to convince her."

"You mean lie?"

"Do you want custody of your daughter? Besides, I *am* your girlfriend. For now. She doesn't have to know it's temporary."

"What happens when you're gone?"

"Once you have custody of Orchid, it will not matter. You already have a support system. I have seen the way your friends look after each other.

They will look after you and Orchid too." Even as she was laying out her sensible plan, little pieces of her heart were breaking off.

He hooked a finger under her chin, tilted her face up, forcing her to look into his eyes. "Why?"

"Why what?" Her pulse quickened and her knee weakened.

"Why are you doing this for me?"

The answer to that question was an easy one, but she could not tell him the real reason. That she was in love with him. So in love with him that she would do anything in her power to make sure he was happy. But it was more than that. By helping him get Orchid, she hoped it would perhaps meliorate the lies she had told, the secret she had kept. And there was a small part of her that believed this had been her destiny all along. The role she'd been meant to play. Reuniting a father with his daughter. The thought made her feel less guilty.

"Because," she said. "That little girl needs you."

After he got the news about Orchid, Brady went up to the ranch house to speak to Joe about the job offer, and as Annie predicted, Joe was thrilled to hire him. Mariah was equally excited when Brady told her that he was moving into the cabin with Annie.

"I knew it," Mariah crowed. "I hear wedding bells in your future. Oh, this is so wonderful."

He didn't have the heart to tell her that if she was hearing bells it was nothing more than ringing in her ears. Annie had made it quite clear that her secret was too big of an obstacle to overcome.

Their relationship could never be long-term. He'd accepted that in the beginning, but now? He was confused and he didn't like feeling that way.

Then he dropped the bombshell about Orchid and his friends were all over him. Mariah hugged him. Joe pounded him on the back. "You're a dad!"

Joe started going on about how wonderful parenthood was and Mariah kept asking about Orchid and he just had to get out of their house. There was only so much enthusiasm a solitary man could take. This whole thing was new to him and he felt uncertain about the future.

Seeking refuge, he headed for the barn. It was here among the horses that he felt safest. Everything was changing. Nothing would ever be the same in his world again. Part of him was excited. A bigger part was terrified. A single dad. He was going to be a single father.

Only if you can convince Mary Jameson that you're man enough for the job.

Uncertainty pressed down on his lungs. Was he man enough for the job? The fear of not getting custody of Orchid knotted him up worse than the thought of getting her, and he hadn't even met her yet.

His daughter. He had a daughter.

He needed to ride, to clear his head, whip his fears into submission. And Miracle was the horse for the job. It was time the stallion got the remainder of his fears out of his system too. He saddled the stallion and trotted him from the barn. The horse tossed his head, chuffed out his breath. Brady could feel his own nervous energy transfer to the stallion.

With a click of his tongue, he urged Miracle to go faster. The stallion galloped full-out across the pasture, his mane streaming back, whipping against Brady's fingers. They raced together, horse and man, each one trying to outpace the demons in their heads.

For a time, as the ground sped away beneath Miracle's hooves, Brady felt rangy and freewheeling, connected to nothing but the powerful horse. A song played in his head. "Born Free." The creaking sound of the leather saddle seemed to keep time with the tune. But there was no escaping the past. History had made both him and the horse who they were now, shaped the pattern of their lives.

He had a primal impulse to keep riding and never stop. In the Old West days a man could do that. Get on a horse and ride as far and long as the horse could hold up. But now there were roads and vehicles and cities and people. The country might have been tamed, but not the cowboy spirit.

It occurred to him that he could go back, get into his trailer, and drive away. Take a modern route to liberty. He did not have to claim Orchid. He could take off and just keep going. A sense of slithering, evading, crawled across his skin.

The wistful, immature part of him toyed briefly with the idea. He'd spent a lifetime trying to escape the pain of confinement, commitment, long-term relationships, but Brady knew there was no way he could turn his back on his own child.

He saw her in his mind's eye, a round baby face, bright as a new silver dollar. Oh shit, oh shit, he was ill equipped for this. He thought of Jake Moncrief and how life could change in the blink of an eye. He thought of Annie. How good she'd been with the kids at the Fourth of July party.

And then he wished . . .

Brady wished for something he'd never wished for in his life. A wife, a real family of his very own, a place where he truly belonged.

How was that? The itinerant cowboy finally wanted a home.

Annie paced the cabin. She couldn't seem to settle down or focus her thoughts.

Brady was building a life without her in it. This was good. This was right. This was how it should be. She could help Brady get his child and walk away guilt-free. She should be happy.

She was not.

Get over this. You cannot have him. Do something productive.

Taking a deep breath, she gathered up her jumbled emotions, stuffed them down deep inside the way she'd been taught a good princess did, and started cleaning out the storeroom. If Brady got custody of Orchid, he would need a nursery.

The work did her good. Even though she had to keep shooing the dogs out from underfoot. She moved boxes out to the outside storage shed, swept the floors, knocked down spiderwebs, cleaned the lone window that looked out over a field of scarlet paintbrushes. Sweat—no, perspiration; horses sweated, princesses perspired—pearled between her nose and her upper lip and ringed the collar of her shirt. Her hair was mussed and she was feeling a bit like a happy Cinderella when a knock sounded on the door, setting the dogs to barking. From the enthusiastic tone of their barks, she could tell that her caller was Brady.

Setting her broom aside, she smoothed away the cobwebs clinging to her jeans and went to throw open the door.

Brady stood on the porch holding a pizza box in one hand, a gallon of paint in the other. "It's pink," he said as her eyes strayed to the cans. "I hope I picked the right color."

Joy zipped through her. He was moving in! "I just cleaned out the storeroom."

Their eyes met.

"Great minds," he murmured. "I thought we could have a nursery-painting pizza party."

She looked over his shoulder. A party suggested more people. "Anyone else with you?"

"Party of two," he said, stepping over the threshold only to be mobbed by the dogs. "Or maybe party of four."

"Time for you two to go outside and play," Annie said, shooing the dogs out and closing the door behind them. Her heart fluttered like a trapped parakeet in a cage and she couldn't say why. She turned back to find Brady grinning at her.

"Food first?" he asked. "I hope you like pepperoni."

"If you like pepperoni, I like pepperoni."

He frowned. "You've never had pepperoni?"

She'd never had pizza. It was not exactly a culinary staple in the palace kitchen, but she could not tell him that. She shrugged.

"One of these days, Annie Coste, you're going to have to come clean about who you are and what you're running from."

She took two plates from the cupboard and pretended she had not heard that.

She sat down opposite him, suddenly aware of how she must look with mussed hair and dirty clothes.

Brady didn't seem to mind. He slid a slice of pizza onto her plate and his smile lit her up inside. His eyes crinkled at the corners. Toasted pecans. They were the color of toasted pecans. Dumbfounded by how happy he looked, how peaceful, she shifted her attention to her plate, concentrated on discovering the joys of pepperoni, all the while listening to the sound of her pulse pounding through her eardrums.

They finished their pizza and got down to work, painting the walls the soft dusty rose of a Texas sunset. It was the perfect color for a cowboy's baby daughter. Just as she'd never eaten pizza, Annie had also never painted a wall. She was familiar with canvas—all well-bred princesses took art lessons—but not textured sheetrock. Brady showed her how to prep the wall. How to put spackle in the cracks and holes. How to prime first.

The paint smelled of hope. Of the future. A future Annie had no place in. That made her sad, so she shifted gears, working vigorously to roll on the pink, watching the shabby storage room transform before her eyes. She understood this task was special. She understood it now. One day, this would all be but a faint memory. Maybe when she saw this color again, smelled paint, she'd close her eyes and be back here.

She glanced over at Brady. He had stopped working and his hot eyes watched her. That's when she realized they had prepped, primed, and painted the walls in a little over two hours.

"Hey," he said.

"Hey." She smiled.

"Anyone ever tell you that you look absolutely beautiful with your hair spotted pink?"

"What?" Her hand went to her hair, but he moved across the floor to encircle her wrist with his fingers.

"No," he said, "leave it. I love you in pink."

Then he was kissing her as he'd never kissed her before. Full of gratitude, hope and . . . *love?*

No, no, you can't think like that. He can't love you. You can't love him. This isn't real. It's all a fantasy. A game.

Except it was not.

He picked her up. She wrapped her legs around his neck. He kissed and kissed and kissed her.

They forgot about the paint. Left the brushes to dry in the paint trays. He was unbuttoning her blouse and she grabbed the back of his T-shirt.

"Arms up." She laughed, and he raised his hands to the ceiling.

She stripped the T-shirt from his body, tossed it in the corner, and then when he clasped her again, she ran her hands down his back, feeling the raised edges of his faded scars.

He sucked her bottom lip between his teeth and carried her to the bedroom, his fingers yanking the shirt free from the waistband of her jeans. She was quite mad for him. Insane for his touch, his taste, the expression in his eyes when he looked at her.

Annie was ready to fully and completely make love to the man of her dreams, to this handsome cowboy who had captured her heart. The time was right and she wanted it for the right reasons. Not merely because she wanted an adventure, but because she cared about him deeply. Wanted to please him. Wanted him to please her.

Brady made her feel safe and cherished and ready to explore.

Serenity started deep inside her, spread out, bathing her in a calm, soothing glow of love. She loved him. Would always love him. She couldn't tell him, but she felt it through every cell in her body, through every breath she took.

He laid her out on the bed, then stepped back to stare down at her. He was trembling and his trembling made her tremble. The moonlight shining through the open curtains glinted off his smooth, muscled chest and she wanted him more than she had ever wanted anything in her life.

"Annie," he whispered, leaned over, and unsnapped her jeans.

She responded in kind, unsnapping his.

Down went her zipper.

Down came his.

He grabbed the hem of her jeans. She arched her hips to help him tug them off her. He stripped off his pants and fell onto the bed beside her. It had been more than four weeks since that first night they had almost made love in his trailer. Four weeks of waiting.

"No more waiting," she said.

"No more waiting."

She felt the shape of his love mold her and she took him in. Embraced him with everything she had in her.

The room was silent now, except for the sound of their breathing. Brady poured kisses on her face, her arms, her belly. Her bra disappeared. Then her panties. His underwear evaporated and there were no more barriers between their skin. Annie was entranced with the preciousness of it all. She breathed in his scent, her scent, the smell of the world. This world. Paint and hay and horses and home.

Her heart fluttered heavily in the still air as more and more sensations peppered her. Brady looked into her and she looked into him and she was ill with happiness. Too much pleasure. She lost her way because of it. Princess Annabella Farrington of Monesta had completely vanished, shed from the skin of Annie Coste.

She could not bear the joy any longer. It was too much. Like stolen cotton candy. Far too sweet to be acceptable. She felt elation or anticipation or something she didn't even know how to describe, but it was all through her, dominant as blood and bones. She was ready to laugh and shriek, sounds that came staggering out of her like drunken magic. A virgin intoxicated.

He took care of everything. Heating her to the right temperature, preparing the condom. He was part of her and she was a virgin no more. She burned brilliant, bright, fragile; an ordinary princess, a royal goddess of love.

She was ready to reign, but Brady held her back.

There were more sensations. Wavy spirals of pressure and heat. Crumbly prickles of textures and shapes. Crescent moons and saw-edged lace. Her body burst with unbelievable stimulation.

Annie could not bear it, Brady was so potent, and she was, in that moment, wrapped in the sweetness of unity.

All at once it was there.

A vortex of everything she had ever felt converged in a spurt of laughter that took her breath, took her heart, took all of her. Busted. Blinded. Bankrupt. And along with her, she took Brady, falling, tumbling, stumbling into the most perfect landscape of shattering release.

And that was how it happened, the unplanned seduction. The breaking of her heart as Annie surrendered both her virginity and her undying love to Brady Talmadge for now and forever.

Brady woke the following morning to find himself spooned around Annie. He buried his face in her paint-spattered hair, inhaled her talcum-powder scent, and smiled so wide it hurt his mouth. It was the first time he'd ever woken up beside a woman and not experienced at least a slight urge to run.

It's just because the sex was so damn great, he tried to tell himself. The best he'd ever had. But why was it the best he'd ever had? He'd been with far more experienced women. Done wilder, crazier things in bed. But none of it touched what had happened to him last night.

Was it because of her virginity? Could it simply

be his chuffed-up pride, because she'd chosen him for her first time?

Annie shifted beside him, opened her eyes. "Good morning," she said, and shyly lowered her lashes, stretched, yawned.

"Mornin', Buttercup."

He leaned down to kiss her, but she put a palm over her mouth to block him. "Morning breath."

"Like I give a damn about that."

She giggled.

He kissed her and the minute his lips touched her, his body heated up hot as a blowtorch.

"Will you—" she started, stopped, peered up into his eyes.

"What is it?"

"Will you make love to me again?"

"Buttercup, all you have to do is ask."

Their dawn joining was different from the heated rush of the night before. Softer. Slower. More bittersweet. Last night they'd been addled by hormones. This morning, they were fully aware of what they were doing.

An hour later they were still in bed, relaxing in the afterglow, lazily caressing each other, marveling in the sensations they stirred in each other. They might have stayed in bed longer if Brady's cell phone hadn't rung.

"You get that," Annie said. "I'll go take a shower."

"You do that." He grinned. "And I'll make us breakfast after I take this call."

Modestly, Annie wrapped the sheet around her and padded for the bathroom, but the sheet didn't quite close all the way and he got a tantalizing glimpse of her sweet fanny. He cocked his head, watching her sway away.

The phone rang for the fourth time. Sighing with pleasure, he snatched it up off the bedside table, checked the caller ID, and saw that it said the State of Texas. Instantly, the smile faded from his face and his gut tensed.

"Hello?"

"Mr. Talmadge?"

"Uh-huh." He swallowed the bowling ball–sized lump in his throat.

"Mary Jameson here."

He tightened his grip on the cell phone. "Yes?"

"I'm pleased to tell you that you passed our background check. We started running it before the paternity test, just in case."

Relief shot through him like excess adrenaline, leaving him feeling a little shaky. He had no doubt he would pass, but just knowing he was under investigation put him on edge. He sank down on the mattress. "Thanks," he said.

"Would you like to see your daughter?"

"I . . . I can see her?"

"Under supervised visitation for now."

Brady blew out his breath. "Yes, sure, when?"

"Can you make it this afternoon?"

He was supposed to go to East Texas today and pick up a horse for Joe, but he could swing by Fort Worth on his way. "Absolutely. You tell me when and where and I'll be there."

Mary Jameson gave him the details and hung up. Brady switched off the phone and he was still sitting there staring at the phone when Annie came out of the bathroom, toweling her damp hair.

"Brady?" she asked. "Are you okay?"

"Fine." Truth was, he was scared to death.

She sat beside him, placed her hand on his arm. "What is it? What's wrong?"

"I get to see my daughter this afternoon, but hell, Annie, I'm terrified."

Her smile warmed him from the inside out. "Brady, you will be fine."

"Really?" A second wave of relief washed over him. He'd never been so anxious for help in his life. "You think so?"

"I know so." She leaned over to kiss him on the forehead. "Tell the caseworker you've got support. You've got a girlfriend and she'll be here to help you when you bring Orchid home."

Yeah, he thought. *Sounds good now. But what happens once you're gone?*

"You made the paper. Good work. Free publicity for The Bride Wore Cowboy Boots," Prissy said when Annie and Mariah walked into the office later that same morning. Since Brady was going to East Texas with Trampas and he might have to stay overnight because of his detour to Fort Worth to meet his daughter, Annie had brought Lady Astor to work with her. She hated for the little dog to be cooped up in the cabin all day by herself.

"What?" Annie startled, letting Lady Astor out of the satchel.

"Yes." Mariah grinned. "They ran the story."

Prissy folded the paper to the lifestyles section, passed it across the counter to her. There was Annie with Melinda Messing. The headline read, *Local Woman Dead Ringer for Princess Annabella.*

This was news? This shouldn't be news. A sick feeling washed over her. The last thing she needed was to get her picture in the paper. She had no doubt that Chandler and Strawn had not stopped looking for her. She'd already seen them in Jubilee and at the carnival, although they hadn't been around in the last few weeks. If they got their hands on this paper, it was all over. Quickly she scanned the article.

Prominent Dallas socialite Melinda Messing has chosen Jubilee's own Mariah Daniels to host the wedding of the year as her daughter, Peyton, marries famed cutter Drew Kincaid.

"The Bride Wore Cowboy Boots was on our short list," Messing said. "But when I learned Mariah Daniels had a Princess Annabella look-alike working for her, I knew they were the wedding planning business for us. I want my daughter to have the fairy-tale wedding she deserves."

Messing is referring to Jubilee newcomer Annie Coste, who does bear a striking resemblance to Princess Annabella Farrington of Monesta. The princess, who attended Echo Glover's wedding last month, is currently recuperating from mononucleosis at the former president's compound in Dallas.

The article went on to give details of the upcoming wedding, including the tea Annie was slated to host.

"Why is this news?" Annie cried, then realized how over-the-top she must have sounded to Mariah and Prissy.

"Melinda Messing is a big cheese in Texas politics," Prissy said. "She combs her hair and it shows up in print."

"We were lucky to catch the *Jubilee Journal* on a slow news day," Mariah said. "If it had been the height of cutting season we wouldn't have stood a chance."

Annie blinked. "We?"

"Melinda's photographer e-mailed me a copy of the picture and I saw it as a great opportunity for free advertising. I wrote up the piece and sent it in. Isn't it great?" Mariah beamed.

No, no, it was not great. She had two weeks left in Jubilee and so much left to do. She had to help Brady get Orchid, and now that they'd made love, she realized just how much time they'd wasted. She had to cram as many kisses, caresses, and long, slow lovemaking sessions into the next two weeks as she could fit.

But now? If Chandler and Strawn saw this article, they would be in Jubilee before she could catch her breath, and this time, they would know exactly where to find her.

CHAPTER SIXTEEN

You might be a princess if . . . when you run away
from home they send the Secret Service after you.

B rady was meeting Mary Jameson and Orchid's
foster mother on neutral ground at Forest Park
in Fort Worth. He arrived at the designated
rendezvous area and parked his horse trailer beside
a new Prius and a battered old Jeep Wagoneer.

He took a deep, steadying breath and got out of
the pickup, spied Mary Jameson and another woman
pushing a baby carriage along the walking trail. He
felt drained suddenly and didn't know how he possessed the strength to stand. It was all too much
too soon. To hear of Kelly's suicide, learn he had
a daughter, start a sexual relationship with Annie,
lose Jake Moncrief to enemy hands, all within the
span of a few short days.

He felt both vaguely nauseated and ravenous.
Part of him wanted to walk toward them, another
part wanted to pivot on his heel and run away from
everyone, from it all. He wanted to get in his trailer

and drive away. Find a horse that needed him and heal it. That he knew how to do. This being a daddy stuff . . . this forming a relationship to last a lifetime . . . well hell, what did he know about that?

It is all right. He heard Annie's sweet voice in his head. *You can do this.*

His back itched and he could feel the old scars cut into his flesh. Scars flayed deeper than flesh. Scars that marred his soul. He wasn't good enough for them. Neither Annie nor Orchid.

"Mr. Talmadge," Mary Jameson called out, raised a hand. The two women came closer. Almost here.

He had no choice but to put one foot in front of the other and move forward. Go to meet them. No running away now.

The women stopped. The foster mom pushed back the top of the carriage and lifted up a small, wriggling bundle.

Brady's heart shifted, stumbled.

The woman turned to Brady. "Good morning, Daddy. I'm Byronny Rawlston. I've been taking good care of your girl."

Involuntarily, Brady held out his hands.

The second Byronny Rawlston put Orchid in his arms, everything transformed.

Just like that. In a whisper of a breath. Brady looked down into navy blue eyes and his world, the world he had once been so sure of, collapsed.

Here was the ultimate damsel in distress, peering up at him like he was her white knight. Her savior.

The wrecking ball hit and all at once he knew the answer to the secret of the universe. He knew why he was here. He'd been put on the face of this earth to take care of this little girl.

"Hey there, Sunshine," he murmured, surprised by the wrung-out sensation in his gut.

The old gut, which was supposed to guide him in every situation, quivered, wobbled, and had no idea what to do. He reached out a trembling finger and traced it lightly over her cheek.

This was his daughter. He was her father.

Orchid gurgled and smiled big.

Smiled at him.

Brady pooled into a puddle of pure love. Emotion choked him. He raised his head, glanced up to meet Byronny Rawlston's gaze. "I . . . I . . ." There were no words. He had no idea what to say. "I . . . I . . ."

"This is what it feels like to be a parent," the woman murmured. "Astonishing, isn't it?"

Brady looked back at Orchid. His little girl reached up to wrap her little fist around his index finger that looked big and fat in her tiny grip. "I want to take her home. Tell me what I have to do to take her home."

Mary's lips flattened into a stern line. "You must be sure. It's easy to fall in love, not so easy to make a lifetime commitment. Orchid is in a good foster home. This can't be a whim for you, Mr. Talmadge. You must provide love and care for this baby until she is eighteen years old. You must cherish her and educate her. There will be three A.M. feedings and trips to the doctor's office. This little girl will turn your world upside down in ways you've never dreamed."

Brady hardened his jaw. "I don't care."

"She's cute and cuddly now and you're feeling the rush of endorphins. You want to protect her, provide for her."

That was all true. He could not deny it.

"But how will you react when she starts walking and messes with your things? Because she will. She'll break your prized possessions. She'll—"

"Seriously, lady, you are the worst salesperson in the world," he growled.

"I'm not trying to sell you on your own daughter."

"You're trying to sour me on parenthood."

"No. No, I'm not," Mary Jameson said. "I'm trying to be honest and make you aware of what's in store. I've seen men come into my office and profess they want their children and then when they get in the thick of it, they can't fight their nature. They want a drink or they ache to gamble. They want to go out with their friends and have fun. They never expected a child to be so much work. They never expected to have the last of their carefree youth stripped away. They never—"

"Lady," he growled, "I'm not those other guys."

Orchid startled at his gruff voice. Her eyes widened and her bottom lip quivered.

"Oh, no, no, Sunshine, Daddy's not mad at you."

Orchid whimpered.

Brady felt his heart rip into two pieces at the thought he'd upset the baby. Helplessness and guilt circled his neck like a noose. It was okay. Let him be hanged. He was not going to leave this baby. He was not going to run away from her. He was going to take care of her, protect her the way a father should. He was a father now. Nothing else mattered. He lifted the baby to his shoulder. He didn't know what he was doing, but he'd seen Mariah comfort Jonah this way. He patted Orchid on the back and the baby immediately quieted. He stared triumphantly at Mary Jameson.

"I can't simply take your word for it, Mr. Talmadge. I'll need proof that you're prepared to take on the daunting task of raising a child."

"I've already got a place to live and a new job. I'm in the process of making a nursery and Annie and I . . ." He swallowed. This was the part that made him hesitate. He didn't want to lie. Technically, he supposed it wasn't a lie. Annie was his girlfriend. At least for now.

"Annie?" Mary Jameson's frown deepened.

"My . . . my girlfriend. You told me I needed a support system. I've got a support system. I have a girlfriend willing to help me."

"I'll take all this under consideration," Mary Jameson said.

"What do you mean you'll take it under consideration?" Panic pushed at him. "You said if I found a job, got a home, established a support system that I could get custody. I passed the background check. What more do you want?"

Orchid whimpered again.

He forced the tension from his body, patted her gently on the back, and lowered his voice. "She's *my* child."

"And right now, she's my responsibility."

He fought to keep his emotions reined in. Getting upset with the caseworker would not win him any brownie points, plus he didn't want to upset Orchid.

"All right," he said. "You are in charge, Mrs. Jameson. What happens now?"

"Go finish the nursery, then next week, you give me a call. I'll come check things out. If all meets with my approval, we'll see where we go from there."

"A week? I have to go a whole week without seeing her again?"

"We need to run a background check on your girlfriend, and I'll be out of the office on vacation."

"Background check. On Annie?"

"If she's going to be one of the child's caregivers, then yes, she needs to have a background check as well." She took a form from her notebook. "Get her to fill this out. We're going to need both driver's license and social security numbers. You can fax it to me."

Fear iced his veins. "So hypothetically, if the background check on Annie were to turn up something—"

"You don't know her all that well, do you? This is a relatively new relationship?"

"If the background check were to turn up something less than favorable," he continued, ignoring her questions. "What would it mean in regard to getting custody of Orchid?"

"If your girlfriend turns out to have a criminal record, Mr. Talmadge, and you chose to stay with her, then in all good conscience, I could not turn the child over to you."

Panic quickened the pulse in Brady's throat. He forgot all about East Texas and Joe's horse. All he could think about was Annie. Would she give him permission to have Mary Jameson run a background check on her? Or was her secret too dark that she simply could not do that?

Things had come to a head. He had to know her secret. He couldn't ignore it any longer. As long as they were just playing and having a good time, it had been fine. But now he had a child. He had to think of Orchid. He couldn't have Annie in his life if it jeopardized his chances of getting his little girl.

You don't have Annie in your life. Not long-term. She'll be leaving anyway.

Yes, that was true. But having a woman who was willing to help him with Orchid. A support system, as Mary Jameson called it, would assure he would get his daughter sooner rather than later.

But not if she had a criminal record.

It was a miserable situation, but Orchid had to come first. She was a baby and he was all she had.

Dammit! How had he allowed this to happen? Brady slammed the steering wheel with the palm of his hand. He'd broken all his rules for leading an uncomplicated life. That's what had happened. "Stupid. Stupid."

Trampas slunk down in the backseat, covered his eyes with his paws. Lady Astor had been teaching him her tricks.

"Not you, buddy," he told the dog. "Me. I'm the dumbass."

Brady was so busy castigating himself that it took a minute for him to see what he was seeing when he turned down John Wayne Boulevard headed for the town square. Two men in black suits, sunglasses, and fedoras getting out of a limo.

His gut took a nosedive. The Blues Brothers were back.

And this time they weren't alone. Pulling into parking spaces on the cloverleaf in front of the courthouse were half a dozen black Cadillac Escalades. More guys in black suits and sunglasses, minus the fedoras. These guys *were* Feds.

Shit, just what the hell kind of trouble was Annie in?

Brady fumbled for his phone, dialed the number to the bridal shop. Annie answered on the first ring.

"Hello?"

The men were getting out of the vehicles, converging on the shop.

Brady whipped the truck around, changed direction. The back of the trailer bounced up on the curb in his crazy turn-around. "Go out the back exit immediately. I'll meet you there. I'm pulling the horse trailer."

"What is it?" She sounded alarmed.

"The Blues Brothers are back."

She hung up the phone.

Thirty seconds later Brady was in the alley behind The Bride Wore Cowboy Boots. Annie was running, face pale, her satchel clutched to her side, Lady Astor's perky little head poking out of the side corner.

Annie charged around the truck, jumped into the seat beside him, Brady peeling off down the alley before she'd gotten the door closed tight. When they bounced from the alley out on Main Street, Brady glance in the rearview mirror just in time to see the Blues Brothers and a cadre of Secret Service agents march into Mariah's shop.

* * *

"Start talking now," Brady said. "No more bullshit. Who are those guys? Why are they after you? What have you done, Annie? Is your name even Annie?"

Annie was sick. It was here. The moment she'd feared for weeks. She gripped the dashboard as Brady rocketed down the main road out of Jubilee.

"Answer me!" he commanded.

She'd never seen him looking so angry. "Yes, no, sort of."

"Yes, no, sort of what?"

"My name *is* Annie. Sort of. It is a nickname."

"What's your real name?"

"Annabella."

"What about Coste," he said through gritted teeth. "Is that your last name?"

"No."

"What is your last name?"

She gulped. "Farrington."

"And what is so damn special about you that the Blues Brothers have called in the Feds? Did you rob a bank? Are you an international terrorist? Some super-rich man's daughter?"

"The latter. Sort of."

"Just tell me or I swear to God, I'm going to pull this truck over and kick you out on the side of the road."

"You would not do that."

"Once upon a time, I would not have, but I'm a dad now and I could lose custody of my daughter over your antics and your lies, so yeah, go ahead and try me, Annabella Farrington. Just who the hell are you?"

Annie understood his anger. She did not blame

him. She had brought this all on herself. She had led him on. She was ashamed of herself. She regretted how she had hurt him. It had been wrong, this deception. All of it. From the very beginning. Her escape from President Glover's compound, hitchhiking, coming to Jubilee, moving in with Brady. Falling in love with him. Her reckless, selfish drive for an adventure would hurt a lot of people. The citizens of Jubilee would feel duped. She had never wanted to hurt people. And the last thing she wanted was to come between Brady and his daughter.

"My full title is Princess Annabella Madeleine Irene Osbourne Farrington of Monesta."

Dead silence followed her announcement. She peeked over at Brady. He had the steering wheel in a death grip and his jaw was clenched. The wound he'd gotten defending her honor had healed to a faint pinkish scar. "Could you repeat that?"

She took a deep breath. "I am Princess Annabella Madeleine Irene Osbourne Farrington of Monesta, destined in a prearranged marriage that will merge the bloodlines of our countries to wed Prince Theodore George Jameson Forsythe of Dubinstein."

Another long silence.

"Biscuits and gravy, that's one helluva mouthful," Brady finally said, then added in a sarcastic tone, "*Princess*."

"You don't believe me?"

"It's the most farfetched thing I've ever heard and I wouldn't believe you except for two things. The Blues Brothers and their posse back there and the fact that Princess Annabella arrived in the U.S. over four weeks ago for the wedding of former president

Glover's daughter and I happened to pick you up just a few miles from the presidential compound. So, yeah, as unfathomable as it seems, I do believe you."

Annie exhaled audibly. "You're mad at me."

He grimaced. "Not so much mad as, oh, I don't know . . . *betrayed*."

"I didn't know how to tell you."

"So you suggested we move in together. Well, oops, you forgot to tell me you were engaged."

"Teddy and I weren't officially engaged. It hadn't been announced."

"But there's a prearranged wedding?"

"In three weeks," she admitted.

"You're a piece of work, you know that?"

"I never set out to hurt you," she murmured. "You told me from the beginning you were a temporary kind of guy. You liked to keep things light. That was just what I was looking for. I took you at your word and now you are mad at me because of it."

"Dammit, Annie," he yelled. "I fell in love with you!"

Trampas whimpered from the backseat. Lady Astor barked from the satchel.

Annie's breath stopped altogether. "What did you say?"

"I tried my best not to, but I fell in love with you," he repeated through gritted teeth. "But the joke's on me. I fell in love with a freaking princess. A real live princess who even if she loves me back I have absolutely no chance of ever being with. None. Zero. So yeah, excuse me if I feel angry and hurt and betrayed and forsaken and . . . *heartbroken*."

Annie laid a hand against her own heart, felt

tears rolling down her cheeks. "Oh, Brady, I am so, so sorry. I love you too."

They ended their relationship where they began it. At Toad's Big Rig Truck Stop. This time over breakfast instead of chili.

"For old times' sake," Brady said ruefully.

They'd been unable to resist one last night together. They'd spent it on the small mattress in his trailer in the parking lot of the truck stop, making love for hours as the big rigs rolled in and out. They hadn't slept at all. They'd made love and cried and made love again and cried some more.

They ate, but did not speak. What was there to say?

Annie had learned so much over the past few weeks—how to cook, how to clean a house, how to arrange flowers for a wedding bouquet, how to be useful during someone's time of grief. She'd been to a Fright House, watched a rodeo, painted a nursery, gone on a picnic, and gotten her ears pierced.

And a handsome cowboy had made love to her long, slow, hard, gentle, and everything in between.

She had achieved what she'd set out to do. For the last four and a half weeks, she'd lived the life of an ordinary person. She'd become Annie Coste inside and out. The thought of returning to Monesta brought tears to her eyes.

She did not miss her homeland. It felt alien to her now. She did not want to go back. More than anything in the world, she wanted to stay here with Brady and raise Orchid in the quaint cottage. She wanted to go to more rodeos and carnivals. She wanted to play cards with the members of the Jubilee co-op. She wanted to ride horses and play ring-around-the-rosy with Orchid as she grew. She wanted to have babies of her own with Brady. Oh! She wanted so many things. Things she knew she could not have.

She was royalty. She owed something to her country. The sense of duty that had been drilled into her since girlhood warred with her dreams. She could not win. Like Audrey Hepburn in *Roman Holiday*, she had to give up her Gregory Peck to assume her birthright.

Annie longed to kick and scream at the unfairness of it all. She'd finally found happiness, a place where she felt she truly belonged, and she must turn her back on happiness and walk away.

"Have you ever seen the movie *Roman Holiday*?" she asked him.

"No. What's it about?"

"A runaway princess. It's my favorite movie."

"Imagine that."

"It gave me some unrealistic ideas."

"So I gather."

"Brady . . . I never meant to hurt you."

"And yet you did." His eyes smoldered.

"If I could take it all back, I would."

"I wouldn't," he said.

"You would not?"

"Without meeting you I would never have been ready for Orchid."

"You would have."

"No. It wasn't until I met you that I ever considered settling down a viable option. Maybe that's why we met. So you could help me prepare to care for this child that's coming into my life."

"You taught *me* so much."

Moisture glistened in his eyes. His jaw tensed. "It's time to go."

"You cannot take me any farther," she said. "You will run into massive security, and who needs that. You may pull over here."

Brady slowed the truck, pulled over on the access road. "I hate the thought of you and Lady Astor out there walking alone."

Annie patted her satchel. "We'll be fine."

"Trampas is going to miss her something awful."

"He will have Orchid to drive him crazy as soon as she starts crawling."

"You're probably right about that."

Brady glanced down. Annie stared out the window.

"In *Roman Holliday*," Annie said, "Princess Ann makes Joe Bradley promise not to watch her walk away. She tells him to just drive away and leave her as she leaves him."

"This isn't a movie." Brady's voice cracked.

"The circumstances are hauntingly familiar."

"I'm gonna have to rent that flick."

"You'll love it," she said, paused, added, "or maybe not."

They looked at each other. He reached for her. Hugged her so tight she couldn't breathe. Didn't want to breathe ever again if it meant breathing without him. He kissed her hard. Annie clung to him. Tears filled her eyes.

"I must—"

"I know."

She reached for the door.

"Annabella?"

Back to that already. "Yes."

"You have a wonderful life, you hear?" His voice cracked.

Annie put a palm to her mouth. The pain was so acute. She had never known how badly a broken heart could hurt. She was born into royalty. She had no choice. Her life was not her own.

She stumbled from the truck, the satchel with Lady Astor in it clutched to her chest. Then just like Princess Ann, she started running, putting as much distance between herself and the man she loved as fast as she possibly could.

Dammit.

In his heart, Brady had known all along that Annie was too good to be true. His gut had tried to warn him, but his heart had not wanted to listen. She'd been everything he'd ever hoped for in a woman. Smart, sophisticated, and yet down-to-earth, hardworking. A real helpmate. She'd been so kind and loving about his daughter. So accepting of his friends. Why did she have to turn out to be a runaway princess?

He wanted to go back into the presidential compound, risk life and limb and beg her to step down from the throne. To abdicate and move to Jubilee. It was a stupid impulse and he knew it. Royalty did not give up their birthrights to be with the likes of him. She might have enjoyed playing at the cowgirl life, but soon enough the novelty would have worn off. She would miss her adoring subjects and life in a rambling palace. She would want to see her own family, her homeland, and eventually she would come to resent him because she had given up her birthright to be with him. No, he could not, would not ask her to give up her life for his. This was the way it had to be. No matter how much he loved her.

Hot tears burned at the backs of his eyelids but he bit down on his tongue to hold them at bay. Hell, he did not cry. He wasn't a crier. All those times his father had beaten him, he had not cried. He'd held in his pain, tamped it down, swallowed it away. He'd focused on what he could control in his life. His thoughts. His attitudes. He'd latched on to happy-go-lucky like a lifeline and he'd sworn off commitment and involvement. And then one little girl had changed all that.

Brady blew out a breath. He didn't need Annie. Sure, he would miss her. Miss her more than he could say. But he'd get over her. Eventually. If he really loved her, he'd let her go to her destiny and be happy for her. He'd cherish the memory of their time together and he would move on. He had to. He had Orchid now. She needed him. That was the important thing. He had a daughter who needed him. Because of Orchid, he could survive anything.

What was a little heartbreak after all?

And in the end, he'd have a great story to tell his grandchildren about how he once dated the Princess of Monesta.

Brady smiled to himself in the darkness. It was a good fairy tale. One he'd cling to with all his might.

It was the only way he could get through losing the only woman he'd ever truly loved.

Brady swiped at his eyes with the back of a hand. His chest hurt so bad. Could he be having a heart attack? He'd been driving for over an hour headed for East Texas to pick up Joe's horse and he could not stop thinking about Annie. Tormenting himself with visions of her pink honeysuckle lips and big gray-blue eyes.

The pain will ease. You have Orchid to think of. It's time to grow up. Snap out of it.

He blew out his breath. Turned on the satellite radio.

"In news at the hour," said the newscaster, "word from former president Glover's ranch in Dallas, Texas, is that Princess Annabella Farrington has recovered enough from her bout with mononucleosis to return at last to Monesta for her upcoming nuptials to the Prince of Dubinstein. Annabella fell ill four weeks ago while attending the wedding of President Glover's daughter, Echo, who is still honeymooning in Fiji. And in other news . . ."

Brady snapped off the radio. It hadn't taken the powers-that-be long to call a press conference and spin the hell out of a missing princess. He didn't envy Annie and the lofty, untouchable life she'd been born to lead.

CHAPTER SEVENTEEN

You might be a princess if . . . you have a special
destiny.

A week after she left Texas, Annabella gazed
out the window, looking across the palace
lawn to the ocean below. Between Chandler,
Strawn, the presidential spin doctors, and Rosalind,
they'd managed to keep her misadventures in Texas
a secret from King Phillip. Former president Glover
hadn't wanted anyone to know.

Her father thought she really did have mono and
had spent the last month recovering at the former
president's home. Annabella felt bad about lying
to her father, but when she'd learned he never even
bothered to call and check up on her, a bit of the
guilt faded. The nagging notion that she was little
more to her father than a means of marrying Monesta to Dubinstein grew longer roots.

Her gaze tracked the expanse of blue water. It
was so beautiful. A sight she had awakened to all
her life. Why did it make her feel so empty now? She

was home and yet she had never felt so displaced. She would be leaving soon, anyway. Heading north to Dubinstein after her wedding. Dubinstein. A place of tall, dark pine trees, mountainous terrain, and cold temperatures. A place far removed from her sunny spot beside the sea. And yet, when she thought of moving to Dubinstein, it was not Monesta she missed, but Jubilee.

Annabella's gaze shifted, moving from the scenery to the Louis XV writing desk. On it sat the picture of her and Brady at Fright House. She pulled it out every day, gazed at it longingly before hiding it again in the secret compartment. She reached for the picture, traced their faces with an index finger. Very soon she was going to have to lock the snapshot in a safe where it could never be found. Lock away Annie's wild adventure for all time.

A heavy sigh filled her lungs. She ran a hand through her hair. A little longer now and back to its original color. She told her father she cut it during her illness because she hadn't had the strength to wash long locks. The last of Annie was slowly fading away.

Her heart crimped and she curled her fingernails into her palm. By tomorrow night, it would be official. She would be Princess Annabella Madeleine Irene Osbourne Farrington Forsythe of Dubinstein. After tomorrow, there was no going back. All she would have left were memories.

She scanned the boardwalk and the old memory resurfaced. The first time she'd run away and stolen cotton candy. Then she thought of another cotton candy, eaten with Brady at the carnival. A lump formed in her throat. She would not cry. Tears solved nothing. The past was gone. So were Brady and Orchid.

Except not Trampas.

Lady Astor yawned and stretched from her spot on her pillow, showing off her round little belly. When they had returned home from Texas, she had been so listless that at first Annabella thought she was simply pining for Trampas, but when she refused to eat for two days in a row, Annabella had the royal vet come in to examine her.

"Lady Astor is pregnant," he said. "Congratulations. She's going to have puppies."

"What a naughty way to bring home a souvenir," Annabella scolded her, but she had been glad. If she couldn't have Brady and Orchid, she could at least have lots of little half Yorkies.

Behind her, the door opened.

Annie turned from the window to see Rosalind in the doorway.

"Might I come in, Your Highness?"

Annie waved her over the threshold.

Rosalind closed the door behind her. She paused, curtsied.

"Please," Annie said. "Do not do that."

"It is tradition, Princess."

"I have decided I do not much care for tradition."

A faint smile lifted Rosalind's lips, quickly to be replaced by a somber expression. "May I speak frankly?"

"You may."

"I must tell you something important. It is a secret I have been keeping for over twenty-five years. A secret that weighs heavily on my heart."

Annie moved to the bed, sat down, patted the spot beside her. "Have a seat, dear Rosalind, unburden yourself."

Rosalind wrung her hands. She did not sit. "I am not certain it is the right thing to do. You are getting married, moving away."

"You are going with me."

"You might not want me after you hear what I have to say."

"How dark can your secret be? Please, sit down."

"Not on your bed. It would not be proper."

"Sit," Annabella insisted.

Rosalind finally eased down on the edge of the bed, took a deep breath. "This is the most difficult thing I have ever done."

Annie touched her knee. "It could not be that bad."

"You might think so when you hear what I have done."

"It affects me?"

Rosalind nodded.

A sense of foreboding slid down Annie's stomach. "I am listening."

Rosalind gnawed a thumbnail. "I do not know where to begin."

"Try the beginning."

Rosalind blew out the long-held breath, did not meet Annie's gaze. "When I was sixteen I met a man and fell madly in love."

"What is so unusual about that?"

"This man was special."

"In what way?"

"He was a cowboy. We do not see many of those in Monesta."

"No," Annie agreed. "We do not."

"He was from America. On vacation with his family. He was twenty. We met when he took a tour of the palace."

"You were working here then?"

"Yes, I had just started working as Queen Evangeline's chambermaid."

"You have been working hard your whole life."

"Most of it," Rosalind agreed. "Anyway, Tate and I fell in love at first sight. One look and we were smitten. It was like in a movie or a romantic novel. We knew we were fated to be together."

Annie had a feeling she knew where this was going. Rosalind was going to give her a lecture on how it was important to let go of the things that weren't right for her. She didn't need the lecture. She'd been lecturing herself nonstop since her return from Texas, but she would not say anything. Rosalind had been her closest confidante for her entire life. The least she could do was hear her out.

"We made love. I was too young. I shouldn't have made love to him. We both knew I was too young, but we wanted each other so badly that we could not help ourselves."

That was how it had been with Brady. The compelling, magnetic pull that rendered her helpless to resist him. She understood.

"Tate vowed to find a way for us to be together. He would be graduating from college soon and he would return to Monesta once he had a job and he would ask for my hand in marriage. He promised he would be back."

"I'm guessing he never returned."

"He did not." Rosalind sighed. "The plane he and his family were flying in went down over the Atlantic Ocean just an hour after it left the airport."

Annabella touched her shoulder. "Oh, Rosalind. I am so sorry. I never knew."

"It was over twenty-five years ago. How could you know?"

"Is that why you never married? You never found anyone you loved as much as you loved Tate?"

Rosalind picked at invisible lint on her sleeve. "Partially."

"There was another reason?"

"I was pregnant."

"Oh, Rosalind." Annabella did not know what to say. She was a bit shocked. She'd never thought of her nanny as a mother. "But you don't have children."

"But I do," Rosalind said. "I have a daughter."

"You gave her up for adoption?"

She nodded.

"Have you kept up with her? Do you know where she is?"

"Yes."

"Who is she?"

Rosalind looked Annabella squarely in the eyes. "She is you."

Her old nursemaid's words did not register. Annabella blinked. "I beg your pardon."

"You," Rosalind said. "You are my biological daughter."

Annie's head spun. She furrowed her brow trying to make sense of this new knowledge. "But I can't be your daughter. I'm Princess Annabella of Monesta. How could I possibly be your daughter? You're not saying that my father, King Phillip . . ."

"No, oh no." Rosalind held up both palms. "Nothing like that. Tate was your father."

"I don't understand. How can I be a princess and your daughter at the same time?"

Rosalind's eyes met hers, full of unexpressed emotion. "Do you recall the story of Moses from the Bible?"

"Yes, Moses's mother . . ." Annie trailed off and everything was suddenly crystal clear. "You gave me to Queen Evangeline and King Phillip and became my nursemaid like Moses's mother."

Rosalind nodded.

Annie was struck mute. Emotions flooded her, a torrent of feelings she could not decipher or separate. Tears sprang to her eyes. "Y-you're my biological mother?"

Rosalind nodded.

"But . . . how?"

Rosalind got up and paced in front of the window, clasped and unclasped her hands. "Queen Evangeline and King Phillip desperately wanted a child. Secretly, they tried everything. Evangeline drank special teas. The king took vitamins and herbs. They underwent several rounds of in vitro fertilization, but back in those days, it was not as successful as it is today. Ultimately nothing worked. They managed to keep their infertility problems deeply hidden, but

the queen was desperate for a baby. When she realized I was pregnant and alone, she hit upon the idea
of taking my baby."

"Why didn't they just adopt me?"

"Don't be naive, Annie, it's just not done with
royalty. You have been raised around these people.
You understand the importance of bloodline and
proper heirs."

These people.

As if she was not part of them. She was not part
of them. What a novel concept. She tested it out like
a tongue testing out a missing tooth. It was sore and
raw, but not awful. In fact, she liked it. She was not
really royalty.

"So," Rosalind continued with her story. "The big
charade began. The queen and I flew to London to
live there together during my pregnancy. Supposedly
to be near cutting-edge medicine while she was waiting for the birth of the baby. In reality, of course, it
was to hide what we were up to. We stayed together
in an apartment, just she and I. Whenever she went
out, she would wear what is called an empathy belly
so she would look pregnant A foreign doctor came
in once a week to check me. He was bribed hand-
somely for his silence. No one else knew. When you
were born, it was announced the queen had given
birth and we flew home a month later."

"I can't begin to imagine what that was like for
you." She still could not wrap her head around the
notion. Rosalind was her real mother.

Rosalind met her eyes and all Annabella saw was
love. "I had to do it. I had no husband to help me.
My parents were elderly and infirm. By giving you

to the king and queen, I was giving you a royal life and I would get to be your nursemaid, by your side every day."

"Yes, but to be my mother and not be able to tell me . . ." Annabella's voice cracked.

"It was a pain I had to learn to deal with. A mother's love can survive anything, Annabella."

Annie tried to make sense of what she just heard. Part of her was shattered, but another part of her felt blissfully free. This explained so much. Why she often felt as if she did not belong. How the queen had been both caring and distant by turns. How King Phillip had never really been demonstrative with her. Why he seemed to have lost interest in her altogether when Henry was born, why he insisted on marrying her off to Teddy. Once he had his real heir, he wanted her out of the way. It stung, but it made sense. It also explained why she'd always felt like a fish out of water. That's exactly what she was.

"My real father was a cowboy?"

"That he was."

"Why are you telling me this now? Why didn't you tell me before?" Annabella asked.

"There were restrictions placed on me. Legal, contractual restrictions. If I ever breathed a word of this to anyone, not only would I lose my pension, but you would be cast out. You would lose your place and your name. I could not do that to you."

"And yet you're risking it all by telling me now. If this goes public, you'll lose everything. Your pension, everything you got in return for giving me up."

Rosalind nodded. "I will also be ostracized from Monesta. My citizenship will be revoked."

Annie gasped, raised a hand to her mouth. "Mama, no."

Tears spilled from Rosalind's eyes. "You called me Mama."

"But you are my mother. What else should I call you?"

"You can't call me Mama. If anyone were to ever hear it, we would both be banished forever."

"Mama," she whispered.

Rosalind opened her arms wide and Annabella ran to her embrace.

Mama. All these years her real and true mother had been right in front of her. Loving her unconditionally. Rosalind had given her up to give her a better life. Love for the woman who'd been her nursemaid welled up in Annabella's heart and she squeezed her tight. They stood a long moment embracing. Then finally, Annabella pulled back and looked into her mother's face. "Thank you so much for telling me."

"I had to let you know on the eve of your wedding day."

It hit her then. She was not royalty. She was not a Farrington. She was not the Princess of Monesta. It felt as if a magnificent burden had been lifted from her shoulders. There was no protocol she had to follow. No rules to hold her back. She was free to walk away from her union to Teddy. She had no obligation to go through with this. In fact, if Teddy discovered who she really was, that would stop everything immediately. He would not marry a commoner.

A commoner. She was a commoner.

Giddiness skipped through her.

The barrier between her and Brady, the big, insurmountable obstacle was gone. All she had to do was pick up the telephone and call him.

Except it was not that easy.

If Rosalind's secret came out, so many people would be affected. The king, for one thing. Her stepmother. Her half brother. Teddy. But most of all, it would affect Rosalind. She would lose the guaranteed pension and be banished from her homeland.

Annie could not take this lightly. If she went public nothing would ever be the same again. Yes, she could go back to Texas, try to repair her relationship with Brady, become Orchid's mother.

Her heart melted at the thought of Orchid. Once upon a time she'd been a tiny baby just like that, belonging to two mothers.

What was she to do? If she kept silent and protected Rosalind, she would have to marry Teddy and move to Dubinstein.

On the other hand, if she came clean, told the truth, held a press conference, revealed everything, she could have Brady and Texas, but that would mean exposing her mother and rocking the House of Farrington to its core.

Annie had a big decision ahead of her and she had no idea which path she was going to choose.

When Brady saw that the caller ID said Monesta, his heart stopped.

Annie.

Or rather Princess Annabella.

He told himself to be calm. To be cool. To show no emotion, but he practically vaulted over the couch to snatch the cordless receiver off the dock. Orchid, who was in her playpen gnawing on a stuffed animal, looked up at him wide-eyed. Once Mary Jameson learned Annie was out of the picture and that Mariah and Prissy and Ila and Lissette had all offered babysitting services and freely agreed to a background check, she'd given him custody of his daughter.

"Hello," he said breathlessly.

"Hello," said a crisp feminine voice on the other end of the line. "Is this Mr. Brady Talmadge?"

It was probably Annabella's appointment secretary or executive assistant or whatever royalty called the people who made their phone calls for them. Disappointment winnowed down into his gut. "Yes."

"You don't know me," the caller said. "But my name is Rosalind Coste."

"Annie's old nursemaid?"

"She told you about me?" Rosalind sounded surprised, but proud.

"She did. She said you were the one who really raised her."

"I'm more than that, Mr. Talmadge."

"Excuse me?"

"I am Annabella's biological mother."

It took a minute for that to sink in as Rosalind began telling him a tale of how she was Annie's birth mother and had given her away to Queen Evangeline and King Phillip.

"That's some story, Ms. Coste," he said, when she'd fallen silent. "But why did you call to tell me all this?"

"I broke the news to Annabella. I know she's having trouble processing it—"

"And you thought I could talk to her?"

"No, that's not it at all." Rosalind sounded irritated at his interruption. "I told her who she really was so that she would be free to step down, step away, and not marry Prince Theodore. I told her so she would end her engagement. So she could go back to you."

"But she's not doing that, is she?"

"It's not because she doesn't want to be with you. She has cried herself to sleep every night since she returned from Texas."

"It's her choice."

"That's just it, Mr. Talmadge. I don't think it is her choice. I think she feels she has to protect me. If she goes public with the information I just gave you, I will lose everything. My pension, my home, my country. She's sacrificing herself for me."

"What do you want me to do about it?"

"Do you love her, Mr. Talmadge?"

Brady did not hesitate. "More than life itself."

Rosalind let out her breath. "We cannot allow her to marry Prince Theodore. The wedding is tomorrow evening. Time is of the essence."

"What do you have in mind?"

Rosalind cleared her throat and told him her plan.

A thousand guests jammed the cathedral pews. Twenty thousand more gathered in the pavilion outside the church and spread out through the town. Reporters were everywhere. Security was at the utmost. Organ music played a wedding march written by a Dubinstein composer. The cloying smell of too many flowers filled the air. Multitudinous candles adorned the altar.

This was it. Annabella's wedding day.

It should have been a fairy tale. A dream come true.

It was not.

She looked over at the man that for twenty-five years she had believed to be her father. He smiled at her in a grandfatherly fashion. She knew she cared about her. Of that she had no doubt. He might not love her as thoroughly as her real father would have loved her, or as much as he loved his real child, but he did love her in his way. The last thing she wanted to do was hurt him. Nor did she want to hurt Rosalind or bring shame on the House of Farrington. So she would do what had to be done. She would walk down that aisle and seal herself to the Prince of Dubinstein. She would do her duty. Honor her family. Save Rosalind. Keep the secret.

Brady might not approve, but it's what she had to do.

Brady.

Her throat tightened and she fought back the tears that threatened to mist her eyes. It was as it should be. He had his life, she had hers. They had had a wonderful time together. He had taught her a lot, but he was just a memory now. It was time to let go.

"Are you ready?" her father asked.

She nodded.

King Phillip held out his hand. She gave him her arm. He tucked her close to his body.

As the music swelled, the doors swung open and they stepped into the chapel.

The massive church was packed, standing room only as more people tried to cram inside. Cameras flashed. Silence fell over the congregation. Everything felt extremely solemn.

At the end of the long aisle, Prince Theodore stood waiting. Silver sprinkled his dark hair, or what he had left of it. His round face smiled. He wasn't a bad man. She would make the best of this.

The heavy perfume of her rose and orchid bouquet overwhelmed her. Orchids. She took a deep breath, thought of a baby far away. She glanced around for Rosalind, but did not see her. She wished she had Lady Astor with her, but the royal pooch was in her bedroom, lazy with pregnancy.

The walk up the aisle seemed an eternity. Heads turned. Murmured voices followed them.

"Such a beautiful bride."

"Too bad her mother didn't live to see this day."

"I hate that she's moving to Dubinstein."

"Prince Theodore is a lucky man."

Annabella forced a smile for her subjects, even though inside she felt so out of place. She knew now why she'd never belonged. She had never been royalty. It was not in her blood. But she'd decided to go along with the pretense, because after all, what choice did she have? She could not sacrifice Rosalind's future for her own happiness.

Rosalind.

Her real mother.

Again, she glanced around the chapel. Where *was* Rosalind? The last time Annabella had seen her was over an hour ago when she'd helped Annabella get dressed. She had to be here somewhere.

Annabella and the king reached the front. He passed her hand to Prince Theodore's.

Teddy caught her gaze. His eyes were reassuring. She could do this. She would do this.

The minister raised a hand and started the blessing.

Annabella's hand trembled. She could stop this. Stop it right now. All she had to do was tell the truth. She could have Brady and Orchid and Texas, but that meant hurting so many people in pursuit of her own happiness. She and Brady had already broken up, already passed through the eye of the hurricane. No point going back. Not at the expense of so many others.

"We are gathered here today," the minister said, "to join Princess Annabella and Prince Theodore in holy matrimony."

"Stop!" A loud masculine voice shouted from the back of the room. "Stop the ceremony right now!"

Annabella spun around, heart thumping. She could not believe what she was seeing. A man in a gray Stetson, Wrangler jeans, and cowboy boots. Swaggering like John Wayne at a shootout. A complete standout among all the pomp and circumstance.

It was Brady! Stalking determinedly toward the altar. He had come for her!

But why? And how? She told him there was no chance they could be together. No hope at all.

She had no idea how he'd gotten past security, but here he was.

The minister glared at him. "And who are you, sir?"

"I'm the cowboy who loves her," Brady said. He shifted his gaze, caught Annie's eyes. "I can't allow you to make the biggest mistake of our lives."

"You cannot." She stared at him beseechingly, willing him to understand. "Rosalind—"

"Who do you think called me? She's outside right now. On the steps of the cathedral. Giving an interview to the press."

"No," Annie whispered.

"She's telling her secret. She wants the truth to come out."

Annie swung her gaze to King Phillip who was sitting in the front row pew with Birgit and Prince Henry. His real family, his real heir. His face was pale, but when his eyes met hers, he nodded. Was he giving her his permission?

"Annie." Brady held out his hand. "It's okay to tell the truth. Who do you want to be with? Where do you want to be?"

"You," she whispered. "I want to be with you and Orchid. I want to be in Texas with our friends. And Lady Astor wants to be with Trampas. She's pregnant, you know."

"Then come with me." Brady reached out for her hand.

She was on a roller coaster. A wild adventure she never dared dream could be hers. She turned to the bridegroom. "I am sorry, Teddy, but I am not the woman for you."

Teddy stood there stunned, openmouthed, not fully grasping what was happening.

Bravely, Annie tossed her bouquet to the ground,

stepped up to the microphone at the pulpit, and faced the crowd. Brady clung to her hand, squeezing tightly. Her lifeline. Infusing her with strength. She could do anything as long as he was beside her.

"I," she announced, in a wavy voice filled with a million emotions, "am not a true princess."

Then all hell broke loose.

EPILOGUE _____

You might be a princess if . . . you live happily ever after.

The media dubbed it the Royal Wedding That Wasn't. Annie's confession hit Twitter and Facebook and YouTube and in under a minute, it went viral, crashing servers around the globe, and forever cementing tiny Monesta in the top ten royal scandals of the last one hundred years.

Even though Annie and Brady wanted to immediately take off for Texas, it wasn't that easy. There were pieces to be picked up, loose ends to tie, legal issues to address, and relationships to mend.

It turned out King Phillip was actually relieved to have the secret out in the open. He confirmed Rosalind's story, adding his point of view and that of Queen Evangeline. He told Annie how much he loved her, and it filled her heart with joy to hear him say it. They talked for hours, something they had never done before.

"You are always welcome here," he said, "and I

will always consider you my daughter, but I understand that it is time for you to discover who you really are. If you have any lingering questions, you can call me anytime."

"What about Rosalind?" Annie asked. "She violated her contract. Will she be ostracized from Monesta?"

"I could never cast out your real mother," he said. "Consider the contract null and void."

They parted on the most amicable of terms, both relieved and joyful that they were able to forgive and forget.

Once Annie had received the king's blessing, it was time to smooth things over with Teddy. At first he was miffed, but that turned out to be only because he believed she'd made him out to be a fool. Dubinstein was in an uproar over the whole thing, and that put him in a petulant mood. But once he learned that Brady was a horse whisperer, his ears perked up. "Could he come to Dubinstein? I have an ailing polo horse that's dear to my heart."

So Brady went to Dubinstein with Teddy to heal his horse while Annie stayed behind in Monesta to run the gauntlet first with media interviews and then with the royal lawyers. Brady wanted to stay by her side during the ordeal, but she wanted to spare him the nitty-gritty so she asked him to act as an ambassador of sorts, smoothing over Dubinstein's hurt feelings.

Between the lawyers and King Phillip, it was agreed that she could keep her monthly stipend from Queen Evangeline, even as they officially stripped her of her title. It was all right. Annie did not feel wounded by legal machinations. She understood. She wasn't a princess and she was proud of it.

Even though she was allowed to stay in Monesta, Rosalind accepted Annie's offer to move to Texas. Annie and Rosalind would have plenty of time to get to know each other as mother and daughter.

Brady did such a swift and thorough job of rehabilitating Teddy's horse that Teddy made him the royal horse whisperer of Dubinstein. Annie and Brady were welcome in both Dubinstein and Monesta any time they chose to visit.

But neither one of them could wait to get back to Jubilee.

The minute Annie set foot on Texas soil she knew she was home. The Jubilee Cutters Co-op threw a big welcome home party that lasted far into the night.

Brady and Annie were married a month later at Mariah's cowboy chapel on Green Ridge Ranch. All the usual suspects were there. Joe and Mariah and Jonah. Ila and Cordy. Prissy and Paul. Lissette and Kyle. And Rosalind.

They tied the ring to Trampas's collar and he served as ring bearer. The bride wore cowboy boots and so did the groom. When the nuptials were over, they rode off on Pickles to the Dempsey ranch that Brady had bought. It was going to be their new home.

Rosalind looked after Orchid for a few days at the cabin while Annie and Brady honeymooned, sealing their love with lots of long, lingering kisses.

"So," Brady said, as he undressed his bride, sliding the white wedding gown off her shoulders. "Are there any lingering secrets we need to reveal?"

"None here," she said. "How about you?"

"What you see is what you get. Plain and simple."

"Cowboy," she said, leaning up to kiss him on the end of his nose. "No matter how much you like to pretend otherwise, there is nothing plain or simple about you."

He tightened his arms around her. "I can't believe how much time I spent running from this."

"What?"

"Commitment. Roots."

"I'm glad you did. Just think what would have happened if you'd settled down before you met me."

"You'd be the Princess of Dubinstein right now."

"You rescued me again, Brady Talmadge. You have a thing for damsels in distress."

"On the contrary, Mrs. Talmadge, you rescued me. Without you, without Orchid, I'd still be a lonely old cuss pulling my home behind me telling myself I was happy in my isolation. You showed me the world, Annie. You gave me a reason for being."

She wrapped her arms around his waist. "So about those five unbreakable rules . . ."

"They've all been shattered to bits."

"I was thinking we needed new unbreakable rules."

"Rules for what?"

"A long and happy marriage."

He reached for the zipper on her dress. She held her hair off her shoulders. "I'm up for it. What do you have in mind?"

"Rule number five. *Never go to bed angry.*"

"I'm in."

"You get to make up rule number four," she said. "This marriage is a democracy, not a monarchy."

"How about *No secrets.*"

"That works for me." She slipped her arms around him.

"You get to make up rule number three." He nibbled her neck.

"*Never stop dreaming.*"

"Gotcha," Brady reached up to finger the dream catcher earring nestled in her earlobe.

"Your turn." She ran a hand down his back, tracing the crisscross of scars there.

"*Let go of the past,*" he said firmly. "Forgive and forget."

"That just leaves rule number one."

They looked each other in the eyes. Brady kissed her tenderly. "What are your thoughts on rule number one?"

"That's easy. *Never, ever stop loving each other.*"

"Princess Buttercup," he said. "I never, ever will."

Then he scooped her into his arms and carried her to bed and they made love, soft, slow, and sweet until they both knew through the very marrow of their souls that this union was their true destiny.

And they lived happily ever after.

Keep reading for
a sneak peek at
Lori Wilde's next
Jubilee, Texas novel

A COWBOY FOR CHRISTMAS

Coming in Fall 2012
Only from Avon Books

When she got right down to it, Lissette Moncrief's infatuation with cowboys was what *really* started all the trouble.

There was something about those laconic alpha males that stirred her romantic soul. Their uniforms of faded Wranglers, scuffed cowboy boots, jangling spurs and proudly cocked Stetsons represented rugged strength, fierce independence and a solemn reverence for the land. Their stony determination to tame wild horses, mend broken fences and tend their families made her stomach go fluttery. Their cool way of facing problems head on, no shirking or skirting responsibilities weakened her knees.

A cowboy was stalwart, and steady, honest and honorable, stoic and down-to-earth. At least that's what the movies had taught her. From John Wayne to Clint Eastwood to Sam Elliott, she'd crushed on them all. She loved Wayne's self-confident swagger, Eastwood's steely-eyed ethics and Elliott's toe-tingling voice.

When she was sixteen, Lissette and her best friend, Audra, had snuck off to see a fortune-teller at the Scarborough Renaissance Fair in Waxahachie. Inside the canvas tent, Lady Divine, a pancake-faced woman in a wheelchair, spread spooky-looking cards across an oil-stained folding table. She wore dreadlocks tied up in a red bandana and a flowy rainbow caftan. On the end of her chin perched a fat brown mole with long black hairs sprouting from it like spider legs. The tent smelled of fried onions and the farty pit-bull terrier mix stretched out on a braided rug in front of her.

Lady Divine studied the card alignment. She tapped her lips with an index finger and grabbed hold of Lissette's tentative gaze, but she didn't say anything for a long dramatic moment.

"What is?" Lissette whispered, gripping the corner of the cheap greasy table, bracing for some horrific prestidigitation like, *you have no future.*

"Cowboy."

"What?" Lissette thrilled to the word.

"There's a cowboy in your future."

"Will he become my husband?"

"Only time can say."

Eagerly, she leaned forward. "Is he handsome? What's he like?"

"Dark." Lady Divine's voice turned ominous.

"In personality or looks?"

"This cowboy will influence you deeply. He brings great change."

"In a bad way?" She knotted a strand of fringe dangling from the sleeve of her jacket.

Lady Divine shrugged. "What is good? What is bad? Who can know? You can't avoid this cowboy. He is inevitable."

The fortune-teller continued with the reading, but Lissette absorbed none of the rest of it. She was so stunned by how the woman had zeroed in on her cowboy infatuation. Later, she and Audra had dissected the woman's uncanny prediction. They were in Texas, after all. The likelihood of running across an influential cowboy at some point in her future were far above 50/50. Not such a mystifying forecast in that context.

Most people would have blown off the reading, dismissing it as nothing more than the slick pitch of a smarmy woman who made her money telling gullible people what they wanted to hear. But for a girl besotted with cowboys the fortune-teller's prophecy had not only mesmerized Lissette but set her up for heartache.

If she hadn't been convinced that a cowboy was her future, she would never have ignored the warning signs. If she hadn't romanticized Jake into a modern-day version of John Wayne, she wouldn't have married him. If he hadn't sounded like Sam Elliott on steroids, she wouldn't have heard the lies he told her. If she hadn't duped herself into thinking that he was the second coming of Clint Eastwood, she wouldn't have had a child with him. If she hadn't swallowed the cowboy mystique hook, line and sinker, she wouldn't be here in Jubilee, Texas, the cutting horse capital of the world, dealing with this new life-shattering situation all by herself.

Then again, how could she regret anything that had given her a son?

She glanced at her two-year-old, Kyle, who was seated in the grocery cart. Unable to draw in a full breath, she ran a hand over Kyle's soft brown curls as he sat in the grocery cart eating cheddar goldfish crackers from a lidless sippy cup decorated with images of gray Eeyore. Cheesy, yellow crumbs clung to his cupid bow lips and there was a grape juice stain on his light blue T-shirt.

Genetic non-syndromic autosomal recessive progressive hearing loss.

The words were a mouthful that boiled down to one gut-wrenching truth. Kyle was slowly going deaf. Medical science could not cure him, and it was all her fault.

Turns out both she and her late husband, Jake, unwittingly carried a recessive connexin 26 mutation and poor Kyle had lost the genetic lottery. So said the audiologist, geneticist and pediatric otolaryngologist whose Fort Worth office she'd just left with the astringent smell of cold antiseptic in her nose and a handful of damning paperwork and referrals clutched in her fist.

Deaf.

Such a frightening word. It sounded too much like dead.

Deaf.

Her poor fatherless baby.

Foggy as a sleepwalker, Lissette pushed her grocery cart down the baking products aisle of Searcy's Grocery, past an array of orange and black cupcake sprinkles, candy molds in the shapes of ghosts and pumpkins, and haunted gingerbread house kits.

Her lips pressed into a hard line, resisting any stiff attempts she made to lift them into a smile for fellow shoppers. Misery bulged at the seams of her heart until it felt too swollen to fit inside her chest. It beat, as if barely stitched together, in halting ragtag jolts. A sense of impending doom pressed in on her, hot and smothering.

It couldn't be true that her child was losing his hearing in slow, agonizing increments, never to be reclaimed. She had to seek a second opinion.

A third.

And a fourth if necessary.

But with what? Consultations did not come cheaply.

Swallowing back her pain, Lissette refocused on her goal. Shopping for baking supplies. That was the answer to her money troubles.

Searcy's was the only locally owned supermarket in Jubilee, the cowboy-infused town that Jake had settled her in four years ago before he first shipped off to the Middle East. In the beginning, she'd embraced the place, the community, the culture, the cowboys, but then, bit-by-bit, her eyes had been opened to the truth. Cowboys were like everyone else. Some good. Some bad. All fallible. It had been a mistake to romanticize a myth. No man could give her a fairytale. She understood that now and she was determined to provide for herself. No more depending on a man for anything.

The store, with its narrow aisles, sometimes felt like a womb—comforting, cozy, communal—but today, it felt like a straitjacket with the straps cinched tight. Maybe it was the candy pumpkin molds, but an unexpected nursery rhyme popped into her head.

Peter, Peter, Pumpkin Eater had a wife and couldn't keep her. Put her in a pumpkin shell and there he kept her very well.

"Da . . ." Kyle gurgled with the limited vocabulary of a child half his age. "Da."

Shoppers crowded her. She needed to get to the flour, but Jubilee's version of two soccer moms— i.e., Little Britches rodeo moms—stood leaning against the shelves gossiping, oblivious to those around them.

Lissette cleared her throat, but the moms either ignored her or didn't hear her. Something she'd grown accustomed to as the middle child, bookended by more attractive, gregarious sisters.

"Um," she ventured, surrendering a smile. "Could one of you ladies please hand me a ten-pound sack of cake flour?"

"Did you hear about Denise?" the shorter of the two women asked the other as if Lissette hadn't uttered a word. "She up and left Jiff for a man eight years younger than she is."

"Get out! Denise? No way."

"I tell you, losing all that weight went straight to her head. She thinks she's God's gift to men now that she can squeeze into a size four."

"My cousin, Callie, is single and searching," the taller one mused. "I wonder if Jiff's ready to start dating."

Feeling invisible, Lissette sighed and bent over, trying to reach around them to get to the flour, but the ten-pound bags were on the bottom shelf. The woman with the single cousin had her fashionable Old Gringo cowboy boots cocked in such a way that Lissette couldn't reach it.

Normally, she would have stopped at Costco for a fifty-pound bag when she'd been in Fort Worth, but those big bags were so hard for her to lift and besides she'd driven the twenty-six miles back to Jubilee in a such a fog she didn't even remember leaving the medical complex.

She straightened. It was on the tip of her tongue to ask the women to kindly step aside when a ten-year-old boy on wheeled skate-shoes darted past, almost crashing into Lissette's elbow. She jumped back and gritted her teeth, anxiety climbing high in her throat.

Kyle was staring at her, studying her face.

Calm down.

She was on edge. Kyle would pick up on her negative energy and that was the last thing he needed. If she thought her morning had been lousy, all she had to do was imagine what it felt like to her son—poked and prodded and unable to understand why.

It hit her then, how confusing life must be when you couldn't hear. How much communication you missed. Then again, in some regards, that might be a blessing. Did she really need to hear about Denise and Jiff's crumbling marriage? Her own marriage had been filled with so many thorns that the occasional sweet bloom couldn't make up for all the painful sticks.

"Da." Kyle raised his small head, his usual somber expression searching her face through impossibly long eyelashes—Jake's eyelashes—as if seeking an answer to the silent question. *Why can't I hear you, Mommy?*

Why hadn't she suspected something was wrong? Why hadn't she realized that her baby could not hear? Why had it taken a nudge from her best friend, Mariah Daniels, for her to make a doctor's appointment?

She'd been angry at first when Mariah said, "It's funny that Kyle doesn't respond when you ask him to do something."

Lissette told herself Mariah was jealous. Kyle was so much quieter than her son, Jonah, who was six months younger. But then she started noticing how Kyle watched her hands more than he watched her face. How he never cared for toys that made noise. How his language skills lagged behind Jonah's. How he often seemed so willful, never listening when she cautioned.

Her chest tightened. Her son hadn't been ignoring her. He wasn't willful. He simply had not heard her warnings. At times, she'd been so impatient with him. She pressed her lips together, her throat clogged with shame and regret. How could she have been so clueless?

"Sweetie," said a tiny elderly woman with a severe, blue-tinged bun piled high on her head and tortoiseshell glasses perched on the end of her nose. She wore a lumpy floral print dress that scalloped around saggy calves and didn't quite hide the tops of her coffee-colored, knee-high stockings.

"Yes ma'am?"

"Would you mind reaching that box of powdered milk on the top shelf for me?"

Lissette forced a smile. She wouldn't be rude like the rodeo moms. Mariah Daniels was five foot one, so even though she wasn't particularly tall herself at five-foot-five, Lissette was accustomed to retrieving things off top shelves. "The blue box or the red?"

"The blue, please."

Lissette had to stand on tiptoes to reach it, but she got the box down.

"Bless you, my dear. Be proud of your height."

"I'm not that tall."

"To me, you're a tower." Her blue eyes twinkled. "And who is this little man? How old are you?" she asked Kyle.

Busily eyeing the baking chocolate, Kyle crunched a goldfish and did not respond.

The elderly lady bustled closer. "Are you two years old? You're about the same size as my great-grandson. You look like you're two years old."

Kyle did not react.

The woman cocked her head like a curious squirrel. "Is something wrong with him, sweetie? He's not answering me."

A dozen impulses pushed through Lissette. The defensive part of her wanted to tell the woman to mind her own business. The "nice girl" started thinking of a delicate way to explain. Her shell-shocked psyche curled the words, "He's deaf," around her tongue, but she couldn't bring herself to say it out loud.

Not yet. Not when she hadn't even practiced saying it in private.

Instead, she completely surprised herself by blurting out, "His father got blown up by an IED in Afghanistan on the Fourth of July."

The gnomish woman stepped back as if Lissette had slapped her. She gasped and put her hands to her mouth. "Oh, my Lord, you're that poor young widow that I read all about in the *Jubilee Journal*.

Oh, sweetie, I'm so sorry. I know exactly what you're going through."

You have no idea what I'm going through, Lissette wanted to scream, but she kept her taut smile pinned in place. "Thank you."

"I'm so sorry," the woman repeated and patted Lissette's forearm, and then a tear trickled down her wrinkled cheek. "I lost my boy in 'Nam."

"I . . . I . . ." Lissette stammered. She could not imagine—never wanted to imagine—losing her child. She clenched her jaw, unable to find the right words.

The elderly woman dug into a purse the size of Vermont and came up with a crumbled tissue clutched in arthritis-gnarled fingers. "They never did find his remains." She pressed a knobby knuckle against her nose, blinked through the tears. "Johnny Lee's been gone forty-four years, but I think of him every single day. He was only eighteen when the Lord called him away. Just a baby. My boy."

Their gazes locked. Two mothers united in loss.

Lissette squeezed the woman's shoulder. "Is there anything else I can get you from the top shelf?"

The great-grandmother dried her eyes. "Why, thank you for the offer, sweetie. I am running low on baking soda."

"Big box or small."

"Small. There's nothing big about me." Her congenial chuckle was back, but her faded gaze stayed caught in the past.

Lissette handed her the box of soda.

The woman raised her chin. "I'm going to tell you what I wish someone had told me. Don't try to be brave. Don't hold it all in. I know the grief is immense, but don't fight it. Cry hard when you receive bad news because that's how you will make way for tears of joy. When you can accept your losses and forgive your mistakes, then you can embrace a happy future."

The woman turned and vanished so quickly, that for one startling second, Lissette wondered if she imagined the whole exchange.

Accept your losses.

It was a strange thing to say. It felt like surrender. Lissette was familiar with surrender. She was, by nature, accepting of the circumstances she found herself in. It was far easier to give in than to put up a fuss.

When Jake had told her that instead of quitting the Army as he'd promised, he reenlisted and was going back to the Middle East, she had not only accepted it, she'd been secretly relieved. It was something she would never admit to another living soul. But when he was home on leave Jake was restless, moody. He had frequent nightmares and he would get up in the middle of the night and disappear without a word.

Sometimes he wouldn't come home for days at a stretch. He never told her where he went and if she pressed for an explanation, he'd grow surly and curt. It had been easier to tiptoe around him. She suspected he might be having an affair, although she tried not to think about it too much.

Fearing he was suffering from post-traumatic stress, she'd suggested counseling, but Jake yelled at her and even put his fist through the wall, proving to her that he did need therapy. She'd been afraid of his rage and she'd backed down, never knowing what was going to set him off or what he was capable of. He was no longer the charming cowboy who'd swept her off her feet, but she was loyal to the bone and she kept hoping that once he was back home for good that eventually he'd heal and they could become a real family.

The gossipers were still hogging the flour shelf. She took a step forward, cleared her throat, and opened her mouth, determined to ask them to please move, when the store's public address system crackled.

"Attention shoppers!" announced the store manager. "It's Searcy's five for five. For the next five minutes, any five items on the baking products aisle will sell for five cents. You have from three p.m. until three-o-five to get your purchases and check out. On your mark, get set, go!"

Before the announcement finished, the baking goods aisle flooded with customers. A sea of shoppers pushed against her, tossing her farther from the flour as they snatched and grabbed at everything in sight.

Okay, she'd go for the vanilla. It was right behind her. She spun her cart around, but a hand-holding young couple with matching facial piercings and tattoos halted right in front of her.

Hands locked, they stared her down. The young man had a Mohawk. The girl's hair was Barney the Dinosaur purple with glow-in-the-dark neon green streaks. Neither said a word, just glowered in simpatico, their gazes drilling a hole through Lissette.

Apparently, they wanted her to move rather than force them to let go of each other's hands so they could continue on their way undivided.

Fine, Sid and Nancy. Let it never be said I stood in the way of punk love.

Lissette tried to maneuver her cart off to one side, but people jostled each elbow and the cart wouldn't roll. Some sticky crap stuck to the wheels. Flustered, she picked the cart up and tried to eek out a couple of inches.

"Hey!" complained a woman she bumped against who was tossing a handful of garlic salt into her cart. "Watch where you're going."

"I'm so sorry," Lissette apologized.

The amorous duo wrinkled their noses at her, turned and stalked back the way they'd come, never letting go of each other in the about-face, even though they had to raise their coupled hands over the heads of other shoppers.

Ah, true love. Once upon a time she'd been that young and dumb.

Someone stumbled against her. Someone else smelled as if they'd taken a bath in L'air du Temps. Simon and Garfunkel's "The Sound of Silence" trickled through the music system. The irony was not lost on Lissette.

Claustrophobia wrapped around her throat, choked her. She broke out in a cold sweat. She stood frozen, wishing the floor would open up and swallow her whole so she didn't have to deal with any of this. She would have unzipped her skin and stripped it off if she could have. Her hands shook. Panic clawed her chest.

It took everything she had to curb the urge to abandon the grocery cart and sprint like a mad-woman to her quaint Victorian home in the middle of town. Grab Kyle up, clutch him to her chest, tumble into the big empty four-poster bed, and burrow underneath the double-wedding ring quilt that her mother-in-law, Claudia, had made.

She ached to go to sleep and wake up to find this whole thing was just a wickedly bad dream—Jake's death, the fact that he left his four-hundred-thou-sand-dollar life insurance policy to a half-brother she never knew existed, and now today's striking blow of learning that Kyle was going deaf.

Her son would never be a concert musician. Never speak three languages. Never hear the sound of *his* children's voices.

She'd been utterly shocked when she'd learned her husband had not named her his beneficiary. Then bone-deep anger. Followed by marrow-chilling dread when the government informed her that be-cause she was not his beneficiary she and Kyle were no longer eligible for Jake's VA health benefits.

After that blow, she'd taken out the only health insurance she could afford—a catastrophic policy with a massive deductible. None of today's medical expenses would be covered or any further expenses until she hit the ten-thousand-dollar annual thresh-old.

The only thing she knew for certain was that the money she'd been anticipating to provide for her and Kyle would not be forthcoming. Beyond a tiny nest egg in an untouchable retirement account, Jake's cutting horse and her Queen Anne Victorian, she had only five thousand dollars left from the money the Army had given her to bury Jake. If he hadn't told her numerous times that he preferred cremation to burial, she wouldn't have had even that small sum.

In this real estate market her house was more liability than asset. The only thing she had of any worth to sell was Jake's cutting horse and the accompanying horse trailer, but she just hadn't made herself go through the motions yet. She had to do something and soon. Today, she'd worked out a payment plan for the medical services Kyle had undergone, but this was only the beginning.

"Damn you, Jake," she whispered. "For treating us this way. Damn you for refusing to get help and killing what little love we had left."

It struck her then, that she couldn't really remember what Jake had looked like. Big guy. Strong. Muscled. Smelled like protein. John Wayne swagger. But that was it.

They'd been married for four years, but he'd been in the Middle East for a big chunk of that time. If she broke it down into consecutive days, they probably hadn't been together more than six months total. She'd had his child, but she'd known nothing about the secrets he kept tucked away under that Stetson. She never asked about the war. She believed in letting slumbering dogs alone. Besides, she hadn't really wanted to know what horrors he'd seen. The things he'd done.

Ostrich. Sticking her head in the sand.

But now? She had to do something to stretch her budget.

What bothered her most about losing the money was that the mysterious half-brother had never shown up. He didn't call nor had he even written to express his condolences. You would think four hundred thousand dollars would at least earn a sorry-your-husband-got-blown-up-in-Afghanistan-thanks-for-the-money card.

"I'll help you as much as I can, Lissy," Claudia said, but her mother-in-law was little better off than she was.

Lissette's own family was upper middle class, but their investments had gotten caught in the real estate crash and they were cash strapped as well. Besides, whenever her parents gave her money, there were always strings attached. So far, she'd been too proud to ask them to help, but she was going to have to get over her pride, accept the strings. She had a part-time job making wedding cakes for Mariah's wedding planning business, The Bride Wore Cowboy Boots, but her salary barely covered her mortgage.

Which was why she was at the grocery store.

Survival.

On the way home from Fort Worth, an idea had occurred to her. Cowboys had been her downfall, but clearly she wasn't the only one mesmerized by the fantasy. Why not take advantage of her infatuation? Do what you know, right? Add cowboy-themed baked goods to her repertoire to supplement her wedding cake business.

Her mind had picked up the idea and ran with it. Pastries straight from the heart of Texas made with indigenous ingredients. Velvet Mesquite Bean Napoleons. Giddy-up Pecan Pie. Lone Star Strudel.

Bluebonnet Bread. Mockingbird Cake. Chocolate Jalapeño Cupcakes. Prickly Pear Jellyrolls. Frosted sugar cookie cutouts of cowboy boots and hats, cacti, longhorn cattle, spurs, and galloping horses.

Even though it meant going out on a limb with her remaining five thousand dollars, she'd grasped at the idea. It gave her something to think about besides Kyle's diagnosis. But now that she was here amidst the five-minute sale madness, the idea seemed stupid. Throwing away good money.

What else was she going to do? Baking was all she knew. It wasn't as if she possessed the skill set for anything else.

Bake.

It was an edict. She fixed on the word.

Bake.

Something comforting. Something sweet. Something life saving. Cookies and cakes, doughnuts and cream puffs, strudels and pies. Salvation in pastries.

Bake.

Kyle dropped his sippy cup, arched his back, let out a screech of frustration. One high bounce off the cement floor sent goldfish splashing up and down the aisle.

A woman behind Lissette let out an exasperated huff and pushed past her, crunching goldfish underneath the wheels of her cart.

Kyle wailed, made a grasping motion toward the scattered crackers.

The gossiping women still hogging the flour shelf glared at her.

Yes, I'm the villain.

Finally, they turned and stalked away.

About time.

Kyle howled, tears dripping down his cheeks. Lissette snatched the sippy cup from the floor, and then thumbed through her purse for more goldfish crackers, but the bag was empty.

Get the ingredients and get out of here. He'll calm down in a minute.

Ignoring everyone else, she started grabbing what she needed. Let's see. Cake flour, check. Pure cane sugar, check. Vanilla, vanilla. Real vanilla. Not that fake stuff. Where was the real vanilla?

She searched the shelves, going up on tiptoes and then squatting down low, pawing through extracts and flavorings. Almond, banana, butter, coconut. No real vanilla. Dammit. The locus of budget-conscious shoppers had wiped it out. Now, she'd have to drive to Albertson's on the other side of town.

Couldn't one simple thing go right today?

C'mon, c'mon, there had to be one bottle left.

Without real vanilla she couldn't start her new baking project. Without her new baking project she couldn't afford to get Kyle the best deaf education. Without getting him the best education, her son's future was indeed bleak.

Oh, there was so much to think about! She had no idea where to start. The medical brochures and jargon only confused her more. She knew nothing about deafness. She'd never even met a deaf person. How could she help her child? The pressure of tears pushed against her sinuses and an instant headache bloomed, throbbing insistently at her temples.

She couldn't let her son's life be destroyed. She *had* to get that damned real vanilla.

But the cupboards were bare and Kyle was shrieking.

"Ma'am, ma'am," a pimple-face stock boy in a Black Keys T-shirt came over. "Your baby is disturbing the other customers. Can you please take him outside?"

Harried, Lissette looked up from where she crouched, the floor strewn with baking products and crushed goldfish crackers. It was all she could do not to let loose with a string of well-chosen curse words. The mother inside her managed to restrain her tongue. She stood, wrapped her arms around her sobbing child and tugged him from the cart.

Head down, she rushed toward the front door.

"Would you like a sample of Dixieland cinnamon rolls?" called a woman at the end of the row dishing out samples.

Lissette spun to face her, Kyle clutched on her hip, his face buried against her bosom. "I bet it's made with fake vanilla, isn't it?"

The woman looked taken aback. "I . . . I . . . don't know."

"That's what's wrong with the world," Lissette said. "Fake food. Nobody knows what they're eating. We're all getting artificial, prepackaged garbage dished out by corporate marketing departments—"

Stop the rant, Lissette. This woman is not the enemy. Canned cinnamon rolls are not the enemy. Fake vanilla is not the enemy.

Three months of anger and shock surged to a

head. For three months she'd been at loose ends, not knowing where her future was headed, but there in Searcy's Grocery, just weeks from Halloween, everything she'd ignored, tamped down and shut off, erupted. She stormed from the store, leaving slack jaws hanging open in her wake.

Her heart slammed against her chest with jackhammer force. Her negative energy flowed into Kyle. He fisted his little hand in her hair, yanked on it, his hopeless shrieks piercing her eardrums.

Calm down, calm down.

But she'd lost all ability to soothe herself.

Bake. The no-fail solution to runaway emotions. Bake. How could she bake without real vanilla?

Get real vanilla.

It was a nonsensical edict. Of course it was, but the command stuck in her brain. She made it to Jake's extended-cab pickup truck. She'd wanted a Prius and this was what she ended up with. The key fumbled at the lock, but she finally wrenched the door open and got Kyle buckled into his backward-facing car seat.

By the time she slid behind the wheel she was only breathing from the top part of her lungs. Her diaphragm had shut down, paralyzed, seized. Puff, puff, puff. Short, fast pants swirled through her parted lips.

Hyperventilating.

Real vanilla, whispered her mammalian brain.

Go home, commanded her last shred of logic.

She started the engine, put the truck into reverse and stamped her foot to the accelerator. Her worn leather purse rocketed to the floorboard, sending the contents scattering—makeup, hairbrush, wallet, plastic Happy Meal toys.

Dammit! She reached down for her purse.

Instantly, she felt a jolt. Heard the jarring crunch of bending metal. Tasted the wiry flavor of alarm. She lifted her head, saw a big red pickup truck filling her rearview mirror and realized she'd just hit someone.

Give yourself a Christmas present
any time of year with these delicious stories b
New York Times bestselling author

LORI WILDE

CHECK OUT HER E-BOOK STORIES FROM AVON IMPULS

The Christmas Cookie Chronicles: Carrie
The Christmas Cookie Chronicles: Raylen
The Christmas Cookie Chronicles: Christin

AND DON'T MISS HER OTHER JUBILEE, TEXAS, NOVEL

The Sweethearts' Knitting Club
The True Love Quilting Club
The First Love Cookie Club
The Welcome Home Garden Club

Available in print and as e-books from Avon Boo